TIM MILLER

WHEN THE SUN IS IN TUNE

GP
GNATCATCHER PRESS

ALSO BY TIM MILLER:

Fiction:
Spooves
Phickshun
Nine Under Par
Nine Over Par

Nonfiction:
Reading Ketchup
My Year as a Journalist (forthcoming on Substack)

"Rock music was never written or performed for conservative tastes."
Frank Zappa

(Sung to the tune of Bob Dylan's "Tangled Up in Blue")

Late one night the moon was shining

I was laying in bed,

wondering about a solar eclipse

when an idea popped in my head.

What if there was a town

that banned rock and roll?

That tried to keep the music

from getting inside its soul.

And the people in the town

came right out of rock history.

And music, just like light,

would have vitality

behind the moon

When The Sun Is In Tune,

When The Sun Is In Tune.

PROLOGUE
SATURDAY, JUNE 9, 1951

Fresh from choir practice, Matt Welsh stepped from the sanctuary into the overcast afternoon. He peered out over Riverview Park, packed for the town's first ever outdoor music festival. Classical music from the high school orchestra floated up—a slow, plodding march. His nostrils flared as he exhaled a short, peevish gust.

For Matt's money, there was no town in all the world like Riverview, which did not have a single hotel or burger joint. As a member of the town council, he was proud that he had preserved the local character, upper-class with a sense of community and place. A nice quiet town, like it said on the WELCOME TO RIVERVIEW sign. And Matt intended to keep it that way. He wasn't about to let some new council member with loose morals swoop in with music festivals and the good Lord knows what else.

He turned on his heel and felt a stabbing pain in his hip, a holdover from a car accident suffered almost a decade ago that had also left him with a slight limp. With a summer storm in the forecast due to arrive by evening, he could feel the change in atmospheric pressure deep within his joints. He used his umbrella for extra support, stopping outside the newly renovated library and glancing at his watch. One o'clock. The orchestra's march ended to a smattering of applause. He had opposed the festival, formally citing cost, potential damage to the field, and lack of parking. He kept his real reasons private. On one hand, he didn't want to attract people from neighboring towns. He didn't exactly agree with the secular character and hazy ethics of their town councils. And on the other hand—more of a tightly clenched fist—there was the matter of a certain group performing a new style of gospel music, led by a youthful, blond singer. Matt had heard some unsavory rumors.

He sat down on a bench to wait. Even on a park bench on a summer Saturday, he appeared stiff, unable to relax. He was scheduled to meet the town council's newest member, Henry John Deutschendorf Jr., who had proposed and organized the festival. Matt was wary of his name, among other things. He recalled their first meeting that spring. "Call me John!" Matt preferred Henry. It was now 1:02. Two minutes late. The orchestra started up a waltz, a bit off-key.

The wind fluttered his tie. Matt squinted at approaching storm clouds on the southern horizon behind which loomed the city of Chicago. The forecast predicted heavy rain. His hip was already starting to throb.

John was always late to council meetings, so it came as no surprise he would be late now. Maybe he won't show, Matt thought, and I can go home. He sighed, reconciling his impatience with a view of the town that always gave him pleasure.

From here Matt could see all of Riverview, which owed a great deal of its private character to geography. It was fenced in on all sides. A forest preserve bordered the north; the south had a massive rock quarry; the west had the sprawling Sara Sweet dessert factory (good for local jobs) bordered by a wide, dried-up riverbed; and the east had only one town, the even-more-exclusive Lowland Park, before Lake Michigan.

"There he is," John called, walking from his bright cherry-red Chevy convertible. Sure, that car is nice now, but wait until winter, Matt thought, taking in his fellow council member from head to toe and extending a firm handshake. He noticed, too, that John had left his top down. Matt didn't say anything.

John had floppy, sandy hair, long by men's standards, and narrow eyes that always seemed to be smiling behind his thick glasses. (They looked to Matt like women's glasses.) John was dressed, in Matt's opinion, to go bowling. He wore a loose collared shirt, brightly colored with a sunset on the back, blue pants, and tan suede shoes with tassels that Matt might expect to find in the women's department. The last detail, new to Matt, was the stubble on John's chin, reminding Matt of a rabbit's foot.

Matt, in contrast, wore a tie, shirt sleeves, and suit pants, crisp and pressed as usual. He wore his black hair short and parted to the side, his face clean-shaven, and his shoes with a gleaming polish. He had wide, dark eyes perpetually scanning his environment.

"This is really going to be something," John said. John was referring to Levi King, the singer newly arrived from Mississippi. He was scheduled to perform after the orchestra, which had finished the waltz and was now attempting Gershwin. It was clear many of its members had not practiced enough.

An appreciation for gospel was about the only thing Matt and John had in common. While Matt grew up in Mississippi, John hailed from Roswell, New Mexico, a town of alleged UFO crashes and rocket tests. Which sounded about right to Matt. He trusted John about as far as he could throw him, and now he carried that skepticism down the stairs to the crowded park grounds. They approached a hot dog vendor that Matt speculated was selling without a permit; he was dismayed when John grabbed a dog because he was "fit to eat a horse."

The two men skirted the playground full of rambunctious toddlers whose shouts mingled with the orchestra mercifully winding down. They crossed a baseball field and stood in the crowd. Matt noticed there were far more young people at the top of the hill than he had realized. Young girls, that is.

They stood in the crowd as the stage crew set up. All the young ladies were there for one reason: Levi King's good looks might as well have been classified as official Riverview Summer Scuttlebutt. Matt snorted and shook his head. John, between each inhaled bite of hot dog, went on about the singer's merits, how he had become a gospel sensation in Matt's own Mississippi and had recently arrived with his fellow Kingsmen, trying to hit the big time, making records in Chicago. But Matt wasn't listening. There were so many girls. And so young. They couldn't all be from Riverview. Where were their parents?

The wind was picking up, shaking the high branches in the elms around the stage. There was a buzz in the crowd, a nervous feeling of anticipation that made the short hairs on Matt's neck stand up. His hip ached. John was going on and on, something about Black R&B music on Beale Street.

Finally, Levi King and the Kingsmen took the stage. The band leader was a young man with slick, blond hair and long, ridiculous sideburns. The band didn't look like much—more like greasers that should be getting back for their afternoon shift in a garage. The drummer counted off four beats and the music started.

And it was … sweet as sugar. A delight. The singer did indeed have talent, a deep melodious voice with range and that elusive trait that often separated gospel singers from the rest: *feeling*.

They opened with a medley. If all this had been taking place behind them, in the sanctuary on the top of the hill, Matt would've been in a state of bliss. There, gospel music transported him from the evils of the world, the realm of man, the ugliness of greed, death, and sin. It transported him to the eternal, the beautiful. He could close his eyes and rest in God's loving embrace.

But out here, surrounded by adolescent girls under an ominous sky with branches that seemed to be waving a warning, it felt off, out of place. John, with a glob of mustard on his face, was babbling on. Would the man ever stop talking?

There was something else Matt noticed. The teenagers, the girls. They were whispering. Something in their eyes. Their bodies seemed to be collecting an electric, nervous energy from the music, one that was growing. The medley ended with a crescendo, Levi King reaching an octave higher and holding the note, raising his arms, his eyes closed. Like he was squeezing the sound, wringing it out until it was completely dry. The crowd applauded politely. But one of the teenage girls near Matt let out a high-pitched squeal. The energy wasn't released. It was still there. Their smiling faces were eager for more. John elbowed him as if to say, "Told ya so."

"You have mustard on your face," Matt said. John wiped it off with his bare forearm.

Then, a moment Matt would long remember, as if the shadow of evil itself had arrived in Riverview: a low, dark storm cloud descended like the spirit of the devil. An unwholesome energy seemed to charge the very arms of the drummer, to control the fingers of the piano player and the bass player as they pounded out a rhythm that had no business whatsoever accompanying a gospel song. Matt's eyes grew wide as the sounds assaulted his eardrums. This wasn't gospel. This was blasphemy. He watched as the young girls of Riverview started moving, shaking their bodies … it was … unwholesome. The sky rumbled. A few large, warm drops of rain fell. The storm was upon them.

John elbowed him again, his bone like the tip of a pitchfork. Matt wanted to open his umbrella, but he couldn't move, as if a snake had encircled his calves. Levi started singing and the girls started … they couldn't be … they were. They were screaming. For the singer. It was deplorable, unconscionable, immoral. Where on earth were the parents? And what of the other board members that had promised to attend? Was nobody going to stop this? Matt grunted with anger as Levi King cavorted around the stage, shaking his body to the pounding drums. This wasn't *music*, let alone gospel. He was no gospel singer. He was a floozy that belonged in a saloon. Not Riverview Park on a Saturday.

The screams were getting louder. The snake was tightening around his legs. John let out a country-boy shout. Matt looked over, half expecting Lucifer himself to be laughing in his face. That's when it happened.

Levi King thrust his hips.

The teenage girls swarming the stage absorbed it like a powerful wave crashing off the lake. For a few of them, it was too powerful; they fainted as if they had been knocked over.

The song reached a climax, and Levi King emphasized it with one more pelvic thrust. The rain began to fall in earnest, but the stage, sheltered by the tall elm trees, remained dry.

Levi's pelvic thrust snapped Matt's mind free. He would be the one to put an end to this. He kicked off the snake wrapped around his legs. Pushed away the arm that had patted him on the shoulder. He held up his hand to this devil standing beside him and repeated words that had helped him through the years: "Not today, Satan." Then he was moving, blundering his way, going as fast as his ailing hip would allow. He escaped the crowd. Up the stairs, his hip protesting with flashes of pain that seemed connected to the storm. He approached the library. It was raining harder. The crowd was exposed, vulnerable. But the band, sheltered by the trees, played on.

He hobbled into the library, waved off Peggy behind the desk, and made call after call. The mayor. Allies. Friends. Political connections. The chief of police. The fire department. A riot needed to be quelled. Noise and fire code violations.

Matt let the phone go with a clatter. He moved unsteadily back outside, standing beneath his umbrella near the same bench he had sat on in what felt like the distant past, though it was only fifteen minutes ago. It was raining buckets. John's convertible was getting drenched. To Matt's astonishment, the park remained full, the music loud as ever. A flash of lightning lit up the sky, followed moments later by a rumble of thunder. Still the crowd remained, the band played. Police arrived. The fire department. The crowd didn't want to leave. They were protesting. More police. Incredibly, the Kingsmen kept playing. Police lined the stage. More lightning, more thunder, the storm getting louder, closer. There was pushing, yelling. Matt was getting dizzy, the pain in his hip excruciating. He squinted through the storm.

The police had Levi King. They escorted him off the stage. Like a sea during a squall, the crowd was getting more agitated. Matt followed with his eyes as Levi King was taken back to a trailer behind the stage. Something was thrown at a police officer. Matt watched as a riot erupted in Riverview, his quiet little town. It raged on for another ten minutes before the state police arrived. Matt made his way back inside to the library. Not now, Peggy. He had another call to make.

"Captain?" Matt said. "You need to get to Riverview. And you need to get this so-called gospel singer Levi King as far away from Riverview as you can. What? You've heard of him. Huh? No. He's not Black. But he's as dark as sin. Come right away."

Thirty minutes later, Matt saw a man that had started as a carnival worker, made political connections across the Midwest, and began—of all things— managing music acts. Despite not being a member of the state police, he had earned a ranking nickname, the Captain. The man arrived and stepped out of a state cruiser, tightened his bolo, and doffed a ten-gallon hat. He made his way over to Levi King's trailer.

That evening, as the rain continued to fall, Matt received a call from his friend Greg Bird, the editor of the *Riverview Review*, about a photograph submitted by a high school student named Leslie Bangs. The photo showed the police dragging off the Kingsmen while restraining the next act, the Quarrymen. In the foreground, Levi King was being led away. In the background, perhaps equally striking, was the Quarrymen's drummer, local high school student Pete Best, being held in a half nelson, his drumsticks high above his head, useless. Matt convinced Greg not to print the image. Instead, the newspaper featured a picture of the high school orchestra and a review of their concert on page three.

It rained deep into the night. The storm cut power to many residents and caused basement sump pumps to work overtime. In the morning, the conversations around town were not about a group of teens arrested for dancing at some festival, but about the storm, the flooding, the fallen branches and powerlines and flooded basements.

The next afternoon, in an emergency session of the Riverview Town Council, Village Ordinance 8-67 Chapter 5, Article 309, approved June 10, 1951, passed with an 8–1 vote (council member Henry John Deutschendorf Jr. dissenting). The Article stated, in part, "Whereas the performance of live music harmful to youth, such as, but not limited to, songs that are overtly sexual, violent, or glorifying of substance abuse, will be banned from Riverview public settings." The *Riverview Review* ran a short blurb in its News and Notes Around Town section about the town council prohibiting "race music," which was performed during the outdoor festival.

That evening, as the sun set on puddle-lined streets and the hum of insects filled the air, Matt received a call from the Captain. He had Levi King and the Kingsmen in his tour bus. They had a signed contract and were on their way to Las Vegas. Satisfied, Matt hung up, turning his mind to the work remaining. He left Village Hall, on his way to one last meeting at a private location: the Riverview Historic Village's old red one-room schoolhouse. Several of the other members, the ones he could trust, would be there too. He waved at them as they left the parking lot. They had unfinished business. Marveling at the glory of God's splendor, reflected a thousand times in the myriad puddles, Matt vowed to protect this little town from the dangers of Satan's music.

*

Starting that night at the old schoolhouse, Matt and a group that called themselves the Devil Dashers went to work. After clamping down on outdoor music festivals, they blocked solid-body electric guitars from the Village Music Shoppe. Guitar lessons were prohibited. Music stores were tightly monitored for anything deemed inappropriate.

"Let us remain ever vigilant, ever mindful of Satan's furtive ways," Matt told his Dashers. They decided to hold secret monthly meetings to monitor the situation.

At the next meeting, parents arrived to air grievances about widespread teenage idleness and alcohol-infused transgressions in Riverview. "All they do is hang out, drink, and listen to these records," one Dasher bemoaned. Another Dasher made her way to the podium and, in a quiet but determined voice, shared her experience of coming home early from work, hearing the unmistakable beat of race music, climbing the stairs, and walking in on her fifteen-year-old daughter and some grease monkey from Lowland Park about to … about to … she faltered. Shouts echoed off the old schoolhouse walls. By the next meeting, the group had made a blacklist of records deemed inappropriate. Parents trashed them under cover of darkness, like thieves in the night.

The third meeting was standing room only. A common enemy had united the Dashers: this rebellious music responsible for perverting the lives of their children. Parents who had grown up during the Great Depression and served in World War II couldn't understand why their teenagers were so lazy, without direction, spoiled, and prone to drinking and staying out late. "We're providing everything a youngster could dream of, and they don't seem to want anything to do with it," a flummoxed Dasher complained. It had to be this strange music, like some disease drifting up from the dirty marshes and swamps of the south, with its seductive rhythms, suggestive lyrics, and primitive drums. What else could be corrupting them in a town as wholesome as Riverview?

After six months of meetings and clandestine operations, it appeared as if the Dashers had nipped the problem in the bud. Grade point averages rebounded. Curfews were honored. Sports and jobs and chores replaced loafing and hanging out. Discipline and manners returned; the back talk and disrespect faded away.

For two years, the quiet held. Riverview was Riverview again.

The faithfully vigilant Dashers anticipated the next threat: FM radio. To prepare, they installed transmitters (paid for with tax dollars) that gave them the power to scramble the signals of their choosing. In 1953, when a rock and roll song by Bill Haley and the Comets hit the pop charts for the first time, the Dashers were ready. The shield held. Next came Fats Domino, the Platters, and the Crew Cuts. The shield held firm. In 1955, Bill Haley and the Comets came back around with "Rock Around the Clock," the first rock song to reach number one nationwide. It was tense, but again the shield held.

"We must strengthen our defenses to match the strength of our resolve," Matt told the Dashers. He started holding two meetings a month.

Next came TV, and the Dashers were ready. A power outage on September 9, 1956, kept Riverview from seeing Elvis on *The Ed Sullivan Show*. From then on, antennae would mysteriously lose their signals during rock performances on variety shows. The next wave came: Buddy Holly, Chuck Berry, Little Richard. The Dashers met every week. And the shield held.

In February of 1959, when a plane crash killed Buddy Holly, Richie Valens, and J.P. "The Big Bopper" Richardson, some Dashers wondered if they could relax their vigilance. Instead of cutting back, Matt established a new wing of the organization: the Cars, the eyes and ears out patrolling the streets, watching and listening for violations.

Riverview maintained a reputation on the North Shore of Chicago as a safe town with an economic engine in the Sara Sweet factory that provided many residents a steady, middle-class life. After Kennedy was shot, the rest of the country tumbled into the cultural upheaval of the civil rights movement and Vietnam. Riverview seemed immune to the chaos. Matt touted his conservative policies and was elected mayor. The Dasher's meetings in the one-room schoolhouse bulged to standing room only.

When the Cars detected a house violating community standards, strange events would transpire courtesy of the Dashers. Power outages. Problems with water lines and sewage. Randomly high utility bills. Garbage uncollected. City tree crews trimming trees with chainsaws at five in the morning. Even library fines and parking violations.

One Dasher, Easton Elliot, the town's leading real estate agent, vetted families moving in. Another, Oren Benjamin, also on the school board, created havoc for families with long-haired teenage boys enrolling in the schools. Robbie Davidson, the city tax chief, imposed untenable property taxes. A local dentist never seemed to have openings. And on and on.

One particularly difficult case involving a teenage saxophone player led to a roach problem at the family's home. They finally decided to move when a third round of treatment failed to cleanse the house. Behind it all, Matt and his Dashers pulled the strings in the name of preserving property values and the town's reputation.

The next surge brought the shield its greatest test yet: the British Invasion. It withstood the initial wave, but, finally, a band pierced the shield. The Beatles. Matt called an urgent secret daytime meeting—something he had never done. Vinyl records were being smuggled into town. Beatle mop-tops and Beatle boots were popping up. "Satan's seeds are on the wind," Matt told the Dashers.

Operation Pesticide, a daring plan to eradicate the Beatles and confiscate all their records, involved a ruse of inspecting neighborhoods house by house for violating building codes. Doubt ran high amongst the Dashers.

"Isn't this burglary?" asked Lars Ludwig, the dentist.

"Can't we go to jail for this?" wondered Oren Benjamin.

Matt raised his hand to quiet the crowd, and the new chief of police, Gordon Sumner, walked in. The chief nodded, tipped his cap, and took a seat. Everyone could see. He was on their side.

One warm Sunday in March of 1966, the day before the plan was to go into effect, Matt left church and went to the Riverview Library to do his weekly research on the Beatles. It was beautiful outside, the first warm day of spring.

"Won't you come to a picnic with my sister?" his wife Bobby Jean asked.

"I must work as constantly as Satan if I am to defeat him," he responded.

He was scanning his third periodical of the day, *Newsweek*, when he came across a reprinted article by Maureen Cleave entitled, "How Does A Beatle Live?" He read one sentence and smiled. He cut the article out and went to the phone behind the desk. He smiled at Peggy while dialing Chief Sumner's private line.

"Operation Pesticide is on hold. Alert all Dashers. Do not enter any home." Then he went to meet his wife at the picnic.

"It's been so nice spending time with you," his sister-in-law offered after lunch. "Won't you come back to our house for some coffee?"

"Thank you, but I need to be alone with the Lord now," he said.

He went for a long barefoot walk along the lake, despite the soreness in his hip, praying and giving thanks. At sunset he let the cool waves wash over his feet, cleaning them, and shook his head at his fortune.

"More popular than Jesus," he repeated, sneering.

Over the next two months, Beatlemania surrounded Riverview, testing the shield and stretching it to new limits. The Dashers grew more and more anxious. Yet Matt changed the meeting schedule back to once a month.

In July, the atmosphere in the jammed schoolhouse was tense. Sumner called in extra police to ensure members didn't become unruly. Many of the Dashers started to doubt Matt himself, suspecting that he had lost his way.

"This is as bad as I've seen it," said the *Riverview Review*'s editor, Greg Bird.

Matt walked into the charged room and raised his hand in benediction. "The Lord will provide." He walked right past the murmuring crowd.

Three weeks later, a tremor started in Birmingham, Alabama. A disc jockey refused to play the Beatles. As the story spread like a ripple, Matt thought back to his afternoon by the lakeshore skipping stones. A week later Lennon's "more popular than Jesus" line was a major story in the *New York Times*. Before long over thirty stations across the USA joined the boycott. Then on August 6, 1966, Riverview, like other US cities, held a Beatles bonfire. Chief Sumner and a few other Dashers watched from a distance. They smiled as Matt himself arrived with a tree grinder hitched to Greg Bird's truck. Soon a line of people—adults *and* teenagers— waiting to shred and burn their Beatles paraphernalia stretched around the block. The shield was intact.

The decade turned. The Beatles broke up. Jimi Hendrix, Jim Morrison, and Janis Joplin died, but Matt never relented in his vigilance. True, the attending members of the Dashers dwindled, but Matt preferred it that way. He had a reliable core. Riverview remained free of rock and roll into the '70s.

In 1976, Matt retired from city government with his twenty-five-year pension in his back pocket, but he wasn't done serving—protecting, as he saw it—the good people of Riverview. In 1977 he won a seat on the Riverview Board of Education. Five years later, he had ensconced the entire school board with Dashers. During a sparsely attended meeting on Friday, July 2, 1982, they passed School Board Act #311. The provision, which "prohibits rock and roll music, or similar music, designed to incite amoral behavior in our students," was like the last stitch in a garment. It passed without fanfare. The next night, as fireworks filled the sky above the old schoolhouse, Matt and his Dashers watched what felt like a celebration of their ability to protect their town.

After the grand finale, each member stood to share updates on their respective beats: musical groups to be wary of, concerts in neighboring towns, cassette tapes being sold in a mall in Lowland Park, etc. It was routine, even mundane. Greg Bird stood up to report that the radio wave scrambler may need a new transistor, but not for another month. Andrew Winter, a police sergeant and the newest member of the Cars, stood to report that no rock music of any kind had been heard on his patrols. Matt was about to strike his gavel and adjourn the meeting when Easton Elliot, the real estate agent in charge of monitoring home sales, stood up.

"This month I observed a sudden spike in Riverview homes up for sale," Easton said.

Matt's gavel hovered in the air. He lowered it slowly.

"Seems almost random—there's no real pattern. But eight homes were put on the market last month," Easton added. "Over the past twenty years I can remember a month with two, maybe three, but never eight."

Matt curled his lips and considered the information. He had studied the issue, anticipated that it would come. "Home turnover is natural and typically follows generational trends," he said. "Probably the start of a wave of folks retiring. Oren, join Easton in monitoring home sales, ensuring the new families meet our standards." He raised the gavel.

"Also, sir—" Robbie Davidson raised his hand.

"What is it?"

"Well, it's in education, and I know that's your territory, but I thought I saw the new assistant principal hired by the high school is one Peter Best, a teacher and volleyball coach from the Evanston township district. Isn't he—"

"Yes, a highly coveted new administrator with an impeccable record for boosting sagging test scores," Matt said.

"But if memory serves, didn't he at one time play drums for the Quarrymen—the group scheduled to take the stage after Levi King?"

"That's right, they used to call him Pete the Beat," Oren added.

Rick Ocase, a mostly mute member of the cars, jumped to his feet, mumbled and gestured.

"Should we be concerned?" Greg Bird asked.

Matt raised his hands to quell any unnecessary concern. "We must never underestimate Satan's cunning," he replied. "I've made some, shall we say, preparations. I know exactly who he is. A fool that's been hit in the head by too many volleyballs."

The Dashers all laughed. Matt lowered his hands. That's when he felt the first tremble, his arm shaking uncontrollably at his side, a small, imperceptible but steady shake that wouldn't subside until he pressed it down with his gavel.

NEW MOON

MONDAY, AUGUST 2, 1982

Pete Best grabbed the last box from his minivan, containing fragile items. Sitting on top was his Beatles *Abbey Road* album clock. He heard the voice of his wife, Sandy. *Promise me, Pete. You said yourself how it's an illegal substance in Riverview. Think of your family and leave the teenage rock and roll behind.* His promise, in his mind, had a loophole. *I'll do what's best for our family.*

He removed the clock and put it back inside the van. Beneath the clock was a framed picture of his son, Roy. He heard his wife again. *Roy needs this school.* Which was true. His twelve-year-old son had particular needs. Emotional needs. He couldn't sit still. He had outbursts and would bang his head against the wall, kick chairs, pound himself with his fists. The Riverview School District had one of the best special education departments in all of Chicagoland.

Pete glanced at the floor of the van. A final box remained, the last vestige of his once vast record collection. He couldn't resist one last look and set the fragile items down again. He pulled back the front flap with DONATE scrawled in black marker, smelled the dusty smell that took him back to Rose Records on Wabash, a magical place ... He flipped through the last holdouts of his collection: James Brown's *In the Jungle Groove*, Frank Zappa's *Joe's Garage*, The Police's *Zenyatta Mondatta*, The Who's *Live at Leeds*, Sandy Nelson, *Led Zeppelin II*, *Percussion Bitter Sweet* by Max Roach, Art Blakey and the Jazz—

A car door slammed. Pete jumped. He waved at an arriving teacher. The teacher didn't see him, or acted like she didn't, so Pete turned the wave into smoothing down his curly hair. The teacher was new—teacher turnover was one of the "afflictions," according to the board and other administrators, causing sagging test scores.

Pete smiled at his reflection in the car window. It was this kind face that had served him well as an educator, a face you could trust. He removed his glasses and wiped them clean with his tie, took a deep breath, and reached down to close the flap of cardboard. He thought back to when he sold his drum kit, when he and Sandy moved into an apartment. *It's not practical, Pete.* He grabbed the box of photographs and coffee mugs and slammed the van door.

Walking along the sidewalk toward the school, he spied two more teachers who had just arrived, a short woman towing a wagon with crates full of books and a tall man with a bulging backpack slung over his shoulder. They didn't slow down but rather seemed to increase their step, so Pete relaxed his pace and took it slow. It was a little surreal, walking back into his old high school with all his memories, but now as an adult, an administrator … He followed them into the building, half expecting them to hold the door for him, but they didn't.

Pete walked into the main office and wished the office assistants, Pam Susan and Donna Henley, good morning. He walked past Principal Merchant's office, noticing it was vacant. He had yet to meet the principal, on vacation all summer. Pete was expecting him back by now.

"Will Principal Merchant be in today?" he asked, as a phone rang.

Donna answered it and Pam, not appearing to hear his question, buried her nose in a stack of file folders.

Entering his own office, Pete set down his box and began arranging photographs on his desk. The last week—moving into a new house, a new job, Roy's outbursts worse than usual with all the change—seemed to fall on him like a ton of bricks. He pulled out his favorite volleyball mug. A cup of coffee would do the trick.

In the teachers' lounge, he saw a second-year math teacher named Joan Larkin, and extended his hand, but she turned around with two cups of tea—presumably one for a colleague—so she only flashed a cursory smile.

Pete filled his empty hand with the mug, then filled it with steaming coffee. He whistled on his way back out into the office hallway. He thought about his desk, the stack of papers and work waiting for him. He looked around, didn't see anyone, took a big gulp, and found his feet turning on a dime, heading in the opposite direction. He left the main office, cut briskly down vacant D hall, reached the end, took a sharp left, waved at two teacher's assistants in E hall, and shot past the auditorium. He realized the TAs didn't wave back. They must not have seen him, which gave him the fleeting impression that he was invisible. He slowed at the entrance to M hall, which was dark with a flickering fluorescent bulb. The coast was clear. He moved fast, pretending to have an urgent destination, though no one was watching. He looked over his shoulder to make sure of this. Then a second time he looked back down the dim hall, pulling out his administrative skeleton key that opened every door in the building. He slid it into the lock, and with a slight twist of the hand, he was in. The band room.

Pete entered the vast, dark space. It was a little stadium, with steps and rows and aisles, a place for a large orchestra to rehearse. He clicked on the lights, and it was liking turning on his own memory. He couldn't get enough music as a kid. From the early records his parents played him, to the piano and trumpet lessons, to discovering the drums in middle school. The Riverview High School Band was like heaven. Marching band, orchestra, jazz club. He did it all. It's where the Quarrymen started.

He stood in the quiet and saw himself, sitting at a drum kit in the back, drumming away. He heard the band warming up, getting in tune, the orchestra performing the old songs again. He closed his eyes and smelled the familiar musty smell. He opened them and saw his old jazz group starting practice before school. He saw Mr. Francis, the young, new, strict leader whipping the band into shape. A tingling energy bubbled up from deep inside Pete's brain, a feeling of possibility, like the first day of spring … It was a million years ago and it was yesterday.

Pete climbed the steps and stood where he had played. Sometimes, when he got tired and low, or found himself pacing in the middle of the night, worried about Roy—or out of nowhere in the middle of volleyball practice—he felt like he was missing a fundamental part of himself. And he was. He had lived his entire adult life with his central passion being shuffled around from the passenger seat to the backseat to, eventually, buried in the trunk. Never in the driver's seat. He stood with his hands in his pockets, keenly aware of the silence.

He looked over at the instrument room, saw himself getting his drums for marching band practice, remembering the time Sandy came in for her clarinet, the first time they were alone together. This was a sacred place, a place kept vivid and alive in his dreams. And now that he was seeing it again with his own eyes he felt like an intruder, like he was somehow violating a source of happiness. He saw Sandy, sitting in the third row, turning and smiling at him.

Oh, Sandy. She loved him, but she didn't love music. Not like he did. For her, it was social, something to do, be a part of. She never felt like he did. He never could tell her how he felt. It was true that he didn't fight for music when he had the chance, didn't prove it to her when they were young and wild and free. He was easygoing by nature and went with the flow.

They were high school sweethearts. Sweet and innocent, when the blows started coming like rain. The music festival ending in a riot and the resulting ban. The strange disappearance of Levi King. Pete's group, the Quarrymen, breaking up. The death of their singer Len. Pete absorbed them silently, almost secretly. Sandy was the best thing in his life, and he thought if he concealed the hurt, that somehow it would keep their relationship safe.

Pete looked to where Len played saxophone in the orchestra. Quiet and shy, but with a voice like an angel. He remembered when they first heard him sing. It was like he had been hiding a set of wings that somehow no one had ever seen. He saw goofy Joey playing the standup bass and the mysterious George on violin. They were all there. He saw them in the orchestra. And he saw them at Joey's dad's garage, when they first started jamming, learning guitar. Len had only learned three chords on the guitar, but hearing him play felt like a rocket ship taking off.

Pete sat down and closed his eyes, but he couldn't shut out the rehearsal room. He saw all the faces, heard all the tunes. But mostly, he saw Sandy. He saw their life together, a life that started right here in this room with the faded yellow carpet and soundproof walls. He felt the recent struggles, heard her voice at the marriage counseling sessions describing him as vacant, far away. Roy's hyperactivity was all they ever talked about. They were holding it together, somehow, for now.

Pete stood and stretched. His cup of coffee was cold. That was all in the past. He walked down the steps and went over to the instrument room. It was open. He clicked on the light, and again he was back in high school, going to get a bass drum or a snare for marching band practice, the faint smell of metal and dust, the rows of black cases. Pete put down the coffee cup and ran his hand along the instruments, the old drum shells of birch and maple, the smooth bronze of a cymbal. He felt it and breathed it and for a moment almost believed that he was sixteen again. He grabbed a pair of wooden drumsticks and raised his arms.

"Go ahead, play," a nasal voice commanded. "And the rule 'No drinks in the band room' still applies, even if you're admin now."

Pete froze. His heart vaulted into his throat. He swallowed, turned, and saw Director Francis standing half in light and half in shadow. For a moment Pete didn't think it was really him. Like an undertaker, or a sickly figure from a wax museum. But it was him all right, the same stern face, now older; the same slicked-back hair, now bright silver; and the same piercing blue eyes that hadn't lost the slightest glimmer.

"Aren't you going to play, Peter?" Director Francis questioned in the same voice that had barked at him for adding an unnecessary fill or for being too rough with a cymbal crash.

Pete chuckled. "Oh, no," he said. "What would be the point?"

"Yes," Director Francis sneered. "It *would* be pointless. To play noise in a room that stores the instruments that make real music. Why make noise when you can make music of real beauty?" Director Francis stepped fully into the light and Pete felt his own heart thudding in his chest.

"Yes," Pete said. "I mean no. I mean you're right. Of course." Pete felt himself blush like he was sixteen again. "It's good to see you again, Director Francis."

"Mmm, hmmm," Director Francis replied. "Are you lost? Don't you know where the admin offices are?"

Pete was taller than his old band leader, but somehow it still felt like he was looking up at him. "Oh, no, just … um … you know … strolling down memory lane."

"Well don't stroll too far. You might not find your way back." Director Francis widened his eyes and walked back off into the darkness. Pete heard the door to the rehearsal room close and felt a shiver travel down his spine. He waited for a rush of feelings, the hurt and anger and bitterness directed at the living and breathing adult that could have—*should* have—done something. When Pete was young and vulnerable, but also clearly talented and optimistic. But none of those feelings came. Instead, it was just the same old sadness at the life he could have had, at the choices he made, after all, not to follow his dreams.

He stood in what he thought was silence, but it wasn't. There was a sound. Only now was he aware of it, and he wondered when it had started. It was muffled, tinny, and very soft. For a moment, Pete thought it was in his head. He closed his eyes and concentrated. His heart quieted and returned to its normal rhythm. No. It was a real sound. It was rising and falling, speeding up and slowing down. It was music. But where was it coming from? Pete walked along the rows of instruments, the sound softer or louder based on his position, when he realized it was coming from the back hallway that led out to the football field. The door leading to the hallway was ajar.

He stepped through it, the sound now more definite, clearer. It was a river of notes. But what was it? It wasn't quite a guitar. Some kind of stringed instrument, like a person plucking on a violin.

Pete walked in the direction of the sound. He went past a few closed doors and then stopped outside the janitor's office. The door was closed, but not all the way. Part of him wanted to knock; another part told him to take off. His curiosity won out and he knocked, the door swinging open.

There, sitting crossed-legged on a bright orange pillow playing a sitar, was a familiar face from Pete's youth. He had changed quite a lot. His dark brown hair was long and tied behind his back. He also had a long, thick beard. His eyes were closed, but the face, behind all that hair, was the same. A kind face, dark with melancholy that vanished when he smiled.

The name George was on his janitor's uniform.

"George," Pete said. "George, it's you."

It was George Henry, from the Quarrymen. It seemed during those youthful, musical years like they were always right on the verge, the very edge of friendship, but there was some gap that Pete couldn't quite cross, some darkness in George that Pete never understood.

"George," Pete repeated.

But the janitor didn't respond. He was in a trance, playing a song in a minor key that began to pick up in intensity. George was shaking his head, his long hair swinging behind his back, his fingers a blur, until he grabbed and held a chord, the sound rushing past Pete like a ghost.

Pete stood with his mouth open. George started to pick low, soft notes, a melody that shifted into a major key. He played flawlessly; his body slowed down, like water that had fallen from a great height and flowed smooth in a quiet, peaceful place. George finished the song and sat with his eyes closed.

Pete stood and waited. A hundred questions popped into his mind. "George … it's me, Pete. The Beat." He hadn't said that name in years.

The janitor sat with a serene expression. He was motionless except for his lips, uttering a soft mantra.

Pete waited a moment more. Footsteps. The football team was coming in from morning practice. He stepped back and pulled the door closed.

*

Pete's mind whirled as he made his way back through M hall and into the main hallway. The Quarrymen used to think of themselves as horsemen, delivering rock and soul music. George was the dark horse, a quiet soul. And now he was a custodian in the very high school of a town that banned rock music. What did this mean? Pete needed time to think, so instead of walking back to his office, where his desk sat waiting for him, he turned down E hall. He strolled down the long hallway. The lights happened to be out and another custodian, Edward Severino, was on a ladder working on the light fixture.

"Good morning," Pete said, approaching the ladder. "I'm the new assistant principal, Pete Best."

"I know who you are," the custodian replied. "Everyone knows who you are. You're the guy that's going to fix the test scores by telling everyone what we're doing wrong."

Pete looked up with smiling eyes, but the custodian didn't look away from his work.

"And everyone knows how much they're paying you too," the custodian added. "Yet they can't give us an extra measly dollar an hour? Horse hooey."

"I hear you," Pete replied. "They don't pay you enough."

"If you hear me," Eddie said, still without stopping his work, "you'll be the first administrator to hear me in ten years. This district is deaf to our needs. No raises. Barely enough bulbs to light these hallways, and these are the cheap kind. Cutting corners so they can pay each other more."

He snapped a bulb into place, and fluorescent rays beamed down.

"Yes, well, I'm sorry to hear of this," Pete said. "I will take note."

He moved on through the dark hallway. His mind was also groping in the darkness, reaching for ideas just beyond his grasp. It was like looking down on a chessboard. Director Francis, Superintendent Jag, the school board, the PTA, they all stood across from him. Where did Principal Merchant stand? When would he be back from his vacation? And now George appeared, a dark knight by his side. But what could he do? How?

He made it through E hall, turned down Q hall, and said hello to a group of history teachers. They acknowledged him, though it did seem to Pete, as he stepped out into the bright sunlight of the courtyard, that there was a reluctance behind the waves and tight smiles. It was almost as if someone had already cast him as some kind of villain. Ah, well, it was a beautiful day.

"Mr. Best," a voice called.

Pete turned and saw a woman with short brown hair, wearing tennis shoes and a bright-red-and-gray Riverview High School jogging suit, trotting toward him.

"Hello! I'm glad I caught you," she said. "Allow me to introduce myself. I'm Gayle Leneler, the assistant athletic director."

"Pleasure to meet you. Please call me Pete." The two adults stood at the crossroads of the two walkways through the grassy square lined with trees and bushes and benches. It was a change to finally talk to someone with a friendly face.

"No, the pleasure is all mine," Gayle said. "It's nice to have an athlete and former coach in administration. Believe me, the last assistant principal wasn't exactly a sports fan."

"Oh?"

"Between you and me, I think she was still bitter about being picked last in gym class," Gayle said, leaning in as if the former assistant principal might be lurking in the trees. "I saw you were a volleyball player and coach, so I thought you might want to participate in Mudfest."

"Mudfest?"

"Sure, the annual volleyball tournament on Labor Day weekend."

"Mudfest," Pete said. Everything came into focus. He was looking into Gayle's hazel eyes, but he was seeing through them, past them, to a new possibility. "Mudfest," he said again, like it was all so simple. "Of course. Mudfest, yes," Pete said and started laughing.

"It's a great fundraiser," Gayle said.

"Yes," Pete said. "I know it well. Once upon a time I played in it myself."

Gayle regarded this new assistant principal that always seemed to have a smile on his face and an openness like he was ready to listen. He had small eyes behind his glasses, but when he genuinely smiled, his inherent brightness lit up even more.

"Glad to have you on board," she said. "I won't hit you up for new uniforms. Yet." She gave him a playful punch on the shoulder.

The light jab brought Pete back. He heard the swish of her jogging uniform as she trotted away. Pete stood and scanned the courtyard, the trees swaying in the breeze, the empty benches he had sat on as a teenager, the walkway full of ghosts, generations of kids denied rock music. Pete looked at his shadow like it, too, belonged with the ghosts. He laughed to himself. Mudfest.

*

Pete left the courtyard and walked along the student union. That's when he heard what sounded like the wobbling of a sheet of metal.

He stopped in his tracks, pondering the strange sound and wondering whether it came from the student union or the cafeteria, when he heard it again. It came from the cafeteria. As Pete walked up the slight incline leading into the cafeteria, he gained a vantage point over the large open space where students normally ate, and the silhouette of a figure came into view. Pete stopped in the entrance, hovering in the shadows, and saw a man of medium height with a wild mane of curly blond hair. The man stood in a work shirt, jeans, and boots, writing measurements on a clipboard. Pete watched as he extended the tape measure in a different direction, stretching it out to a nearby wall before releasing it and again causing the sound Pete had been hearing. There was something familiar about him, something that felt like a coincidence. Pete's mind grappled with his memory and came up empty.

Pete mentally scanned the various memos and work orders he had read through until he recalled that Craftwood Lumber had been hired to build new tables for the cafeteria.

The figure turned, exposing a profile in the fluorescent cafeteria lighting. Stretching out his arms, he extended the tape measure toward the ceiling. Suddenly Pete wasn't seeing an employee of Craftwood Lumber with an arm extending a tape measure. He was seeing Jim Plant, once the best guitar player in Riverview. And instead of extending a tape measure, Jim's arm was hovering over a Les Paul electric guitar at the Riverview quarry on a Friday night. Long ago, after the state militia had shut down the festival, bands would meet at the quarry, improvise a stage, usurp the town's electrical system, plug in amps, and let it rip. This went on for several months. For one fleeting moment, he saw Jim Plant's arm swing up and down the guitar neck in a frantic rush of wailing notes, his face locked in a spasm of joy and pleasure. Instead of the white, fluorescent cafeteria lighting and nondescript walls and windows, Pete stood surrounded by rocks and mud, the earth providing warm and resonant acoustics, with nothing above but sky and the lights of the nearby factory.

"Jimmy Plant," Pete said, stepping into the vast open space.

The man looked across the empty tile floor, the tape measure hanging limp and bent at odd angles.

Pete came closer.

"Pete the Beat," Jim said as Pete approached.

The two men shook hands and regarded each other. Pete took in how time had changed Jim Plant. His wild mane of blond hair was now shoulder-length dishwater waves. His face, once angelic and androgynous, now had lines and a goatee. Small crow's feet appeared on the edges of his dark eyes, eyes that always seemed to have a glint of mysticism.

"Do you teach here?" Jim asked.

"Yes … well, not teach," Pete said. He found he was so excited he couldn't keep from smiling. "I'm the new assistant principal. This is my first day. And you must work for Craftwood, the company we've hired for new cafeteria tables."

"Bingo," Jim said. "This is my first day too, on this job. I'm the owner of Craftwood now."

The two men nodded at each other, Pete still smiling broadly.

"It's been a long time," Jim said at last.

"Yes it has," Pete replied. "Do you still … play? Guitar?"

"Oh, no," Jim said. "That all ended years ago."

"Yes, yes it did."

"Why, do you still beat the skins?"

"No," Pete said. "Not for a long time."

The men lapsed into silence again. Jim wrangled with the tape measure that remained obstinate. In Pete's mind flashed an image of the night a green car pulled up and shined its headlights over the chasm. He heard the voice calling, a voice he sometimes heard in dreams. "Kids, you can't be doing that." Minutes later the cops arrived. His parents picked him up at the station—arrested for trespassing, the final blow. The moment ended and Pete wasn't looking at a teenager shredding a guitar solo, he was seeing a middle-aged man wrestling with a stubborn tape measure that wouldn't recoil, telling him how he had never left Riverview, had worked for Craftwood since graduation, was married, and a had a son in middle school that, as Jim said, "was giving me everything and more that I had given my old man."

Pete filled Jim in on his teaching career in Evanston, his marriage, and his son that also—Pete chose his words carefully—had his own adolescent challenges.

"Yes, well, I hear the tables are really a big need," Pete said. "From what I heard, they didn't have enough seats for everyone."

"We design tables for all kinds of companies—different designs that can maximize seating," Jim said.

"What about stages?" Pete heard himself ask. The words escaped his mouth before he realized what he was saying.

"Stages? For, like, the auditorium?"

"Not exactly."

Pete's fingers fluttered on the side of his leg; he slipped them into his pocket to contain them.

He heard voices approaching. It was a tour of incoming freshmen. They stopped in the entrance to the cafeteria. Pete waved. After an introduction by the tour guide, the group moved on.

"You were saying," Jim said. "Stages?"

"I want to bring rock and roll back to Riverview," Pete declared.

Jim laughed but stopped when he saw that Pete was serious. "There hasn't been rock and roll at Riverview High since we were in school," he said. "And you know how that turned out."

"Exactly," Pete said. His hands came up, but he crossed them under his elbows.

"Pete, did you get thumped on the head too hard that day?"

Pete's face was half grimace, half smile.

"Tear gas. Batons. The state militia. Ring any bells?"

"I know, I know …"

"The hip swivel felt 'round the suburbs …"

Pete heard Jim speaking, but he wasn't listening. He was reliving that day, June 9, 1951. The day the music died in Riverview, Illinois.

"No, I remember," Pete maintained, coming back. "I was there."

"Nothing's changed," Jim said. "All the same goons are still on the town council and the school board; they're not going to look the other way. You could get canned."

"I have a plan," Pete said. Again, he had the feeling that words were escaping, rushing out of him, rather than him consciously selecting words to speak. He squeezed his fists, that they might hold a pair of drumsticks. "Have you heard of Mudfest?"

"The volleyball tournament?"

"Stages, Jimmy," Pete said. "Maybe two. Can you have them by Labor Day?"

"Even if I could, who's going to play?" Jim asked. "There aren't any—"

"Just get me the stages," Pete said. "I'll take care of the rest."

The tape measure snapped, the yellow metal slithering like a snake rushing back into hiding.

*

Back in his office, Pete sat down behind his desk. It was two o'clock. The afternoon sun streamed through his window, casting bright squares of sunlight on the floor. Three hours of work had cut his tall stack of paperwork in half. His phone was blinking, telling him he had five messages from the thirty minutes he had been at a meeting. Plus, there was a pile of notes from his assistant, Pam Susan, that required his attention. He adjusted his glasses and surveyed the various tasks, wondering where to begin. His fingers went to work on his desk with a moderato tempo.

There was a knock on the door. It was the other office assistant, Donna Henley. "Mr. Best," she said. "Don't forget the math department wants to meet at two thirty."

"Yep, got it," Pete said. For some reason he stood up. She left and he sat back down and resumed the drum rolls with his fingertips, bumping up the tempo to allegretto. In rhythm, he rolled a paper off the top of the stack, a memo about the first staff meeting of the year. His fingertip beats reached a crescendo as he scanned the document, scooped up a pen, added his signature, and finished it with a smack from his thumb. He took up the next paper, about AP history curriculum, and spotted George, across the parking lot, trimming hedges along the outside wall of the auditorium.

Pete resumed drumming, accelerating into allegro. His mind drifted to an image of his father. A World War II veteran that worked his entire career as a plumber for a heating and cooling company. Instead of the paper in his hands, Pete saw the sternness of his dad's face when he had been arrested for trespassing at the quarry.

His wrist was tapping triplets in a vivace tempo on the edge of his desk.

Pete stopped drumming, took a deep breath, and remembered his father charging down the stairs when Pete was working on a drum fill from a Cannonball Adderley tune. *What the hell is that?* his father demanded. *No race music in this house.* So Pete resumed the rigid and predictable beats of the marching band regiment.

"Focus, Pete," he told himself, scanning for the main points of the curriculum about the Age of Imperialism. He signed the document, slid it over, and began tapping a steady largo with his index finger.

Concentration was impossible. Pete thought of the college years that floated by with opportunities to join bands that he let slide. His twenties. One clandestine night at a rehearsal place in Chicago, feeling like a criminal, like he was doing something illegal, fleeing the session ... Pete picked up a pencil and alternated tapping his notepad (eighth notes) and desk (quarter notes) with the eraser. He recalled buying a drum set for the basement when they moved out of the city to their first home, a duplex in Evanston. Starting to play but discovering that trying to find both the time and other like-minded musicians proved a challenge—and then Roy came along. And that was that. His drum set collected actual dust.

Pete's tapping now included the base of his lamp with the aluminum ferrule on every fourth beat. He worked on the stapler, speeding ahead in his mind, a well-traveled trail of thoughts, to his son being born. A colicky child, terrible twos that never seemed to end. Roy banging his head so hard that they had to buy him a helmet. Pete's office was a flurry of beats and sound as he recalled having to switch to a different preschool, then struggling in the Evanston school district, again switching schools three more times after that.

Pete worked the edge of his lampshade like a cymbal, thinking how the special education program in Riverview and his new job all fell into place, on one condition. He had to sell the drums, give up the records, give up what little of rock and roll he had left. Which he did. Willingly. Mostly. Until now. He saw George, working the clippers slowly, almost tenderly shearing around the top edges of the hedge. He saw Jim Plant carrying his tools across the parking lot and placing them in his truck. Stages. Mudfest. There was a way. He may have lost out on his dream, and he thought of all the other young people that came through these hallways deprived of the same simple joy. But no longer. He was bringing rock and roll back. He hit his desk like the final beat on a snare drum. Then he set the pencil down and began rolling it back and forth, so that he didn't hear the clicking of heels in the hallway approaching his office.

*

"It's official," Superintendent Jag announced. "Nancy Brandt is the new president of the Riverview Board of Education." Superintendent Jag took two steps into his office. Pete smiled. She took two more steps and closed the door. She was tall with short, dark, spiky hair. Her appearance always had the smooth polish of someone that enjoyed looking good in the public eye. Today she wore heels and a gray business suit.

Pete glanced over at the next sheet on top of his stack. "Yes, I was just reading about that," he said, holding up the page. "Nice to see you, Brenda. Or should I say Superintendent Jag?"

"Brenda is fine," she said, sitting down in one of Pete's two chairs. "We were, after all, classmates and members of the same marching band."

"Who could forget your legendary baton twirls?" Pete asked with a smile.

"Hmm, yes, those were the days."

Pete opened his mouth to agree, but before he could she said, "Nancy holds dear the Riverview core educational values."

"Yes," Pete said, clearing his throat. "An impressive record."

Superintendent Jag raised an eyebrow, for a moment only, then her eyes searched her surroundings, the boxes and shelves. "You know," she began, "she's voted to fund both the orchestra and jazz band in the past."

"Oh?"

"Yes," she said. She played with the button of her suit jacket. "She is a huge supporter of the arts."

"Fantastic," Pete said.

A frown settled on her face. She tilted her head and scrunched her eyebrows down tight. "Peter," she began, "I hope we can speak plainly, seeing that you're now part of our administrative team. Your record of improving test scores speaks for itself." She released her eyebrows and pursed her lips.

"Something this school desperately needs after consecutive, shall we say, underperforming years." She opened her mouth, but nothing came out. She pressed her lips and looked away.

Pete nodded, looking past Superintendent Jag to George. He was on his knees, weaving his shears across some of the lower hedges. Jim Plant drove away in his pickup truck.

"The students at this school need a boost," she said. "And maybe it was just my imagination, but it seemed like there was something you were holding back during your interview. Something you were uncomfortable talking about. A method, perhaps, that helped push students over the top in Evanston."

Pete's fingers worked the edge of his desk, double time. "Holding back? Nothing comes to mind."

Superintendent Jag studied Pete, her blue eyes betraying a moment's skepticism before returning to neutral. Pete shifted his tapping from his fingertips to his knuckles, transitioning to syncopation.

"Perhaps I imagined it then," she said. "We did interview many qualified candidates that day, and you were the last. Just know that it's going to take everything you've got to make the improvements the board expects. Everything." She stood, buttoned her suit, and turned to leave.

Pete executed a roll with his knuckles, then rattled the edge of the drawer with his pinkies and thumb.

She stopped in the doorway. "I hear your son thrived at the middle school during summer enrichment," she said.

"Yes, he did quite well."

"Delightful, let's hope his progress continues." She smiled and walked out of his office.

Pete looked out the window, but George was gone.

"Superintendent Jag," Pete called, "I mean Brenda. Do you know when Principal Merchant will be returning from his vacation?"

The only answer he got was the sound of her heels down the hallway.

*

His workday over, leaving the rest for tomorrow, Pete walked to his car in the empty high school parking lot and drove the six blocks to the Riverview

District Office of Education. He made it into the multipurpose room just as the board meeting began.

"We have a chock-full jam-packed agenda for the first meeting of the new year," began President Nancy Brandt. "So, without further ado, I would like to call these official proceedings officially to order." Everyone settled in. All eyes turned to the speaker at the head table in front of the rows of seats. Hands shuffled papers. Sitting in his usual seat, Matt Welsh poured a glass of water. A throat cleared. Nancy continued, "I would first like to call Assistant Athletic Director Gayle Leneler to the podium to address the first order of business: Should Riverview High School continue to permit the Chicago Bears to practice on the high school grounds known as the back forty during the off-season as the NFL players strike continues?" She smiled at the community members in attendance. Again, a throat in the audience cleared. "I thought Gayle's little story might be a nice way to ease into the year. Gayle, the floor is yours."

Gayle Leneler, in tennis shoes and her perennial bright-red-and-gray Riverview High School jogging suit, dashed up from the front row of the gallery to the podium. She waved to the rows of people like she was running out onto the track for a meet. Her suit went *whish-whish-whish*.

"Thank you, President Brandt," Gayle began. "It's wonderful to be here. I just thought I would share this little story because I know some members of the community feel that the Bears are a distraction on the high school grounds. Some people are even claiming the Bears are responsible for our sagging test scores. But I can assure you, the only sagging scores they are responsible for are on the scoreboard at Soldier Field!"

Gayle guffawed but stopped when no one else did. In the back, someone coughed.

"No, seriously," she resumed. "I think it's a wonderful distraction that is benefiting students more than harming them. Greedy NFL owners are banning these players from expressing their athleticism. Why? Because of money. The greed of millionaires shouldn't be stopping these players from practicing the sport they love. This is a free country, and that includes the freedom to high step into an endzone. Which is, after all, an art form in itself."

She winked at Nancy Brandt.

"I won't take too much more time. I know there are many pressing issues at the start of a school year, but since this must be decided upon, I just wanted to share a little story about how one day my field hockey team asked if we could go over and watch the Bears practice. I said, 'Sure, just for a minute.' Well, all the girls put down the jerseys they were carrying, so I had to pick them up. With all these jerseys and a handful of sticks, I see these two people walking toward the back forty. I come up alongside them and who do I find myself walking next to?"

There was a moment of polite silence.

"Walter Payton."

The throat, not quite clear, made another loud attempt.

"Sweetness himself. Anyway, he started talking to me and all the girls, and he is just *so* funny. I mean he's really funny. A real jokester. The girls came up and soon he had us all laughing. The nicest man. And he says thanks for letting them use the field and makes more jokes."

Gayle paused. For a moment she appeared to lose her train of thought.

"He gave me the biggest hug. I mean the *size* of his biceps. Unbelievable. Then he says, for everyone to hear, how he's going to call me. Just a really funny, really nice man. And seriously, those biceps."

Gayle demonstrated with her hands for the board, as well as the packed conference room, the size of Walter Payton's biceps.

"Thanks, Nancy. Thanks, everyone. Let's keep the Bears and do our part to end the ban on high stepping!"

Gayle put her attire to good use and jogged quickly out of the room. *Whish-whish-whish.*

"Thank you, Gayle," Nancy said, catching her at the door, where Gayle turned and, in one motion, gave a thumbs-up and a full spin before exiting.

"Very well," Nancy said. "Now, to put the issue to a vote, should the board permit the Chicago Bears to practice at Riverview High School during the strike? All in favor, please raise your hand and vote 'Aye.'"

"AYE!"

"Opposed?"

"Nay!"

"It passes on a 6–1 vote with member Matt Welsh dissenting," Nancy said. "Next the board will hear from Roxanne Gradenko. Mrs. Gradenko is the founding member of the new organization Riverview Citizens for Drug Awareness. Her group recently traveled to Washington, DC, for a roundtable with First Lady Nancy Reagan about the Just Say No! program and its possible role in our community. Mrs. Gradenko."

Roxanne, fixing her hair, recently styled in the manner of Princess Diana, rose from the gallery and walked toward the podium.

As she walked, a middle-aged man in overalls with curly, shoulder-length, dishwater blond hair stood, dashed toward the podium, and beat her to the microphone. He issued a final, throat-clearing cough.

"Hello. I realize I'm going out of order, but I don't have all night."

"The speaker is not recognized. Deputy Copeland, please remove this person from the podium."

"Just a second there, John Wayne. I have a name. My name is Jim Plant and I'm the owner of Craftwood Lumber. I want to speak about Craftwood's proposal to build hexagonal tables for the student cafeteria. I spent all day taking measurements only to get back to my office to find out that our contract has been nullified."

"That's enough! You do not have the authority to speak. Besides, the contract had a thirty-day review process that did not meet the board's qualifications. Please remove the speaker."

"What? I've already ordered the wood. Someone needs to pay for that."

Deputy Copeland escorted Jim Plant toward the exit of the Village Hall meeting center. Jim didn't go quietly.

"Get your hands off me. I have a right to speak. I'm a citizen and a taxpayer!" he shouted as Deputy Copeland guided him out. He exchanged a bewildered look with Pete at the door.

"Mrs. Gradenko, sorry for the interruption of this intrusion," Nancy said. "The floor is yours."

Roxanne opened a manila envelope and pulled out her papers. Looking down, she began with the tone of someone who is not used to speaking in public but has rehearsed in front of a bathroom mirror with a hairbrush as a microphone. "According to recent statistics, one in five suburban high school students has smoked marijuana. In the last month, one in three has consumed alcohol. Before students even enter Riverview High School, more than 60 percent will have experimented with drugs and alcohol."

Roxanne looked up to a room of blinking eyes.

"I'm here, on behalf of Nancy Reagan, to give our students the skills and language necessary to resist the peer pressure of harmful substances that are invading our school and community."

She paused again.

"In short, to help our students Just Say No!"

A burst of cheers shot forth from the back row.

"Go, Roxanne!"

"You do it!"

"We urge the school board," Roxanne resumed, shaking a little, "to consider adopting Mrs. Reagan's programs in all schools K through twelve, but also to consider adopting a policy to enforce stricter punishments for students that are found under the influence or in possession of illegal drugs and alcohol. Thank you."

The back row erupted in cheers as Roxanne left the podium.

WAXING CRESCENT

"So that's our older brother, Dave, over on the couch," Brandon said.

"What's up?" Curtis said. He was tall and skinny with a giant head of thick, black, curly hair. He wore sunglasses and carried his instrument in its case.

Dave waved. He sat with a bowl of popcorn watching *Jeopardy!* The volume was up high.

"Comedians for one hundred, Alex."

"Comic whose trial by fire fueled his comedy routines."

"Who is Richard Pryor?" Dave shouted.

Brandon and Curtis walked down the hallway leading to the kitchen.

"Is he mad that I'm taking his spot?" Curtis asked in a low voice.

"No. Not at all," Brandon replied. "See, he's partially deaf. He was having fun on the sax, but it was frustrating for him. He's happier as the roadie. Plus, he's an older brother. And there's the whole 'Shannon and the *Little Brothers*' thing."

They entered the kitchen.

"Hello," Liz Golding said. She was making muffins.

"Hi, mom," Brandon said. "This is Curtis Ousley. I met him at science camp. He plays the saxophone. I mentioned that we needed one, so here he is. He's also new to Riverview. He moved here from Texas."

"Texas, lovely. Did you enjoy the Riverview High School science camp as much as Brandon?" Liz asked, stirring a bowl.

"Sure did," Curtis said. He took off his sunglasses. His eyes were wide and had a little glint of crazy. "I invented the forktar. I attached a pickup to a fork and rubber bands, ran it through a compressor, and came up with some crazy sounds. My initial goal was to have it talk. But the sounds were way cooler."

"Fun!" Liz said. "Welcome. The gang is downstairs. It's funny. We've only lived in the house a couple of weeks, but I feel like we've been here for years."

"C'mon, I'll introduce you to the rest of the band," Brandon said.

"Nice meeting you," Curtis called back as they headed downstairs. Going down, they heard Dave shout, "Who is Woody Allen?"

At the computer, Michael (with freshly dyed green hair) and Tibbs were playing *Oregon Trail*.

"I got typhoid," Tibbs said. "That can't be good."

Ray and Ryan were playing ping-pong. Shannon and Danny were having an argument, something to do with blowing bubbles and chewing gum. A loud bubble smacked in Shannon's face. "That doesn't prove anything," Danny said.

"It proves everything," Shannon countered.

Brandon cleared his throat with exaggerated emphasis.

"Ahem. Attention, everyone," Brandon announced. "This is Curtis Ousley, here to try out for our vacant saxophone position. As discussed, Dave will remain with the band as roadie and will still play the sax on the tune 'Mr. Mayo.' Curtis is aware the song is off-limits."

Everyone nodded.

"You should know that like me, he's a man of science, an innovator of sound, and he always wears sunglasses because he's a total badass," Brandon said, stepping into the middle of the room. "Without further ado, I present to you the members of Shannon and the Little Brothers.

"Our lead guitarist, Andrew Tibbets. Originally from Gainesville, Florida. Everyone calls him Tibbs. He's lived here on Sullivan Street a grand total of four days and can really shred. He's on the quiet side and we're pretty sure he's not a serial killer. Pretty sure, but not totally.

"Next to him at the computer is Michael Blazary. He was born in Australia, moved to New York when he was four, and, as of one week ago today, lives here in Riverview with his aunt because, as he puts it, neither parent can stand him. He plays bass and likes poking things."

"I'm a sabreur," Michael said. "Or, as they say in America, a fencer." He whipped out his sabre and carved a Z in midair.

"Over at the ping-pong table is our rhythm guitarist, Ray Flowers. His pinky extensions are off the charts. No one extends a pinky on a sus chord like Ray. He can't play on Sundays, won't say why, and doesn't go to church, so we think he's in a cult. Ray is the only native of Riverview. And it shows. Kidding!

"Over by the piano is Shannon, our lead singer and a state high school diving champion, in consideration for the United States Olympic diving team, thanks to a flawlessly executed, splash-less, backward, two and a half somersault, two and a half twist pike dive this past March, the dive heard 'round the world, or at least 'round Illinois, even though it didn't make any sound!" Brandon covered his mouth and made mock crowd-cheering noises. The rest of the Little Brothers followed suit.

"Former diver," Shannon corrected. "I'm retired."

Brandon cleared his throat. "Yes, (ahem) apparently some girls on the Riverview diving team made some (ahem) unfortunate (ahem), disparaging comments regarding thigh (ahem) width at a summer diving session."

"Bunch of anorexic bitches," Shannon carped.

"While her diving future is uncertain," Brandon resumed, in the announcer voice he was using, "what's clear is she's the boss, so be sure to do what she says and try to avoid her when it's that time of the month."

Shannon waved hello to Curtis and gave Brandon the bird.

"She was irritable for the entire move from the city, so we should be good for a couple of weeks. On the drums is little brother Ryan Golding. He's as precise as a metronome. Freakishly precise. Also, be careful. He believes everything, and I mean *everything*, you say. His reputation as a drummer and an astonishingly gullible person has spread all over the North Shore. It's a long story. We'll tell it to you some time. It all started with a horrible car accident. A horrible bumper car accident, that is."

"I *knew* he was talking about the bumper cars," Ryan said.

"And finally, on keys, Danny Kauffman, the Piano Prodigy. That's Kauffman with two f's because he doesn't give two you-know-what's. Plays in his sleep. Legend has it that he was abducted by aliens that experimented

on him. The result is that he is out-of-this-world good at piano and, just …
um … well, strange. He says before moving to Riverview two weeks ago, he
grew up in Massachusetts. But no one believes him."

Danny extended a Vulcan salutation. "Greetings, earthling."

"And I play harmonica and organ, and write songs that raise environ-
mental awareness—"

"Don't start," Shannon said, blowing a huge bubble that popped on her
face. "As you probably know already, Brandon is a science geek. And Danny,
you owe me a pack of Bubblicious. Michael and Tibbs, turn off that dorky
game and let's jam."

"*Oregon Trail* is the antithesis of dorky," Michael said.

"Fine with me," Tibbs said. "I just died of typhoid fever."

"Do you know 'Quarter to Three'?" Shannon asked Curtis. "Well, you'll
figure it out."

Everyone made their way to their place, clicked on amps, plugged in, and
tuned up. Ryan counted it off. Within five minutes, Curtis was the newest
member of Shannon and the Little Brothers.

An hour later, the jam session was over, and everyone was heading home.
The young musicians huddled in the front yard, scarfing down Mrs. Golding's blueberry muffins, goofing around and enjoying the moment. No one
noticed the vomit-green boat of a Buick that had been parked down the
street as it pulled away, sped down Sullivan Street, and peeled around the
corner.

*

Friday afternoon, the end of the first week of school. Shannon came home
and showed them the flyer. They had been playing "Superstition" when she
walked down the stairs. She held up the paper with one hand and smacked
it with the other to get their attention.

"Mudfest? What's that?" Tibbs asked.

"A big volleyball tournament on Labor Day," Shannon said. "It's kind of
a rite of passage. They do it every year. It's like the unofficial start of the
school year or something. Basically, all the popular jocks and cheerleaders
get to exclude people. Oh, and the losing teams have to eat mud pies."

"Really?" Ryan inquired. "They actually eat mud?"

"Ryan don't be so gullible," Shannon said, giving him a noogie. "The strange thing is, according to this nosebleed Florence Ballard in my biology class, this is the first time they've ever had music at the festival."

"Are you sure we can play?" Michael asked. "Even though we're freshmen? I thought it was only for upper classmen."

"Also, my alien DNA might be a problem," Danny quipped.

"It says right here," Shannon pointed out. "Right at the bottom of the flyer. See the small print. All grade levels are eligible. Now let's get to work. Tibbs, hit that 'Superstition' riff."

*

A week later, a light afternoon rain fell on the students making their way to the buses and cars in the school parking lot. Shannon and the Little Brothers piled into Dave's van. He drove them to the Craftwood Lumberyard, where auditions for Mudfest were being held.

"Why are they having the auditions here?" Brandon asked.

"In addition to playing music," Danny answered, "each band has to prove proficiency with a crosscut saw."

"Seriously?" Ryan asked. "Like sawing boards?"

"Yessir, Mr. Albert King, I know that tune," Curtis said in his deep voice, pulling down his shades and smiling with his wild eyes. The band was learning that he didn't talk that much, so when he did speak, everyone listened.

"Guys, knock it off," Shannon shouted from the front seat. "I'm trying to write a set list here."

At a red light, she passed the list over to Dave. "You're in charge of keeping track of the set list. I don't trust these imbeciles behind me." Dave folded the list carefully and put it in the pocket of his raincoat.

When they arrived at the lumberyard, the rain lightened to a drizzle and the sun came out. A rainbow appeared over the overpass leading to Lowland Park.

"Now all we need is a sign," Danny remarked.

"The universe is trying to tell us something," Michael observed as the band stood and gawked at the arc of bright colors beaming across the sky.

"The universe will only get you so far," Shannon said, pointing.

A sign outside the store said, "Auditions in the warehouse around back."

They walked around the store, past a forklift loading beams of wood onto a truck, and spotted Assistant Principal Best, sitting behind a table with another old dude with wavy dishwater blond hair. Best waved them over to a covered storage area. Columns of different types of wood rose to the ceiling, though the center had been cleared for drums, a keyboard, some mic stands, and a few amps. The heavy scent of sawdust mingled with the smell of summer rain.

Ian Anderson, a junior on the swim team everyone called Dolphin Breath, was playing the flute. The song was getting drowned out by a forklift and buzzing saws in the background.

"Thank you, Ian," Mr. Best called out when the song ended. "We'll let you know."

"Hello," Jim Plant said to Shannon and the Little Brothers, who were standing near the entrance. "My name's Jim Plant, an old friend of your assistant principal and the owner here at Craftwood. We thought this would be a good place for auditions, because you can crank the amps as loud as you want." He gave them a wink. Shannon filled out the form on the clipboard Mr. Best handed her while everyone else pulled their instruments out and tuned up.

"David, set list please," Shannon requested.

"Shoot," Dave said, reaching for the pocket of the raincoat he had left in the van.

"Whatever," Shannon said. A new round of saws began blaring in the distance and a second forklift arrived and groaned a few aisles over, straining under the weight of a bundle of planks. "Let's just do Motown tunes."

After three songs, Shannon and the Little Brothers booked a 45-minute set at Mudfest.

*

Mudfest, a fundraiser sponsored by the Riverview Lions Club, landed on a beautiful late summer day. Seventy degrees and not a cloud in the sky. It was the Saturday of Labor Day weekend, two weeks after Danny, Tibbs, Michael, Curtis, Ryan, and Ray began their freshman year at RHS, with Brandon starting his sophomore year and Shannon her senior. Dave still lived at the Golding home on Sullivan Street, where recently two more homes had gone up for sale. After a summer of uncertainty, he had a part-time job at a hardware store and was enrolled at nearby Oakton Community College. The band still had their roadie.

With their equipment loaded, they squeezed around cases and into the back of Dave's van. Other than Danny, this would be everyone's first live performance. Anxiety was like another passenger.

"Break a leg," Don Golding called.

Liz, standing beside him, waved and shouted, "Good luck!" as the van backed out of the driveway.

"This is a big deal," Dave said, navigating around a moving truck and turning off Sullivan Street.

"What is?" Shannon said from the passenger seat. She pushed in a cassette labeled Surf'n Instrumentals in Michael's handwriting and took out some eye makeup. The van cruised through suburban streets, though with the surf tunes they might as well have been going up the coast in Southern California. Not that they were too aware of the surrounding broad lawns and tree-lined streets, or a certain vomit-green Buick LeSabre on their tail.

"We're about to perform a banned substance," Dave said, nodding at the radio.

"What are you talking about?" Shannon said, concentrating on her eyeliner.

"Last week I went to the Riverview Public Library after work. I ended up in the reading room with a bunch of old copies of the *Riverview Review*, the town newspaper," Dave said, stopping at a red light. "I figured I'd read up on our new hometown. I know we've only been here a few weeks, but while you guys have been at school, I've been hanging out, looking for a job, and trying to decide what to do with my life. And I have to say, this place gives me the willies. The downtown—no one says hello. It feels like a town of robots. Or zombies. Or robot zombies. The people I work with at the hardware store, personalities not exactly brimming with life ... plus you got the big factory and quarry, out on the edges, these stark, imposing places …"

"David, honey," Shannon said, flipping the tape over and fumbling in her makeup bag. "Please tell me you have a point." The backseat was quiet, tense. Heads down. Fingernails being chewed. Someone had a rabbit's foot and passed it around.

"I do," Dave replied as the light changed and he pulled forward. "Some articles by a local journalist caught my eye. Leslie Bangs is her name. Apparently, this town has a ban on rock and roll that's been in place since the early '50s."

Shannon puckered her lips and applied dark red lipstick.

"Did you hear me?" Dave said. "A ban on rock and roll." He took a left turn, cutting to a side street, deciding the main street had too much traffic. He wanted to try the backstreets he had been learning. The vomit-green Buick followed.

"So what?" Shannon said, kissing the air.

"'So what?'" Dave asked. "The very thing we're about to play. At a public park."

"What are they going to do?" Shannon asked with a playful smile. "Throw us in jail? It's just music. Last I checked this is a free country. David, love, it's no big deal."

Dave shook his head and grimaced. Silence hung in the air until it was filled with a cry.

"Oh, that's awful," Brandon called out, rolling down a window.

And thus, in the backseat, the nervousness and stage fright vanished as the adolescents began debating the age-old teenage question: Who farted?

"'No big deal'? It's a huge deal," Dave said, looking both ways at a stop sign. He was a very cautious driver and used his eyes to compensate for his lack of hearing. "Riverview has an active ban on rock and roll music in its bylaws. Which the school district has adopted. It's a huge deal. Huge."

"It has a distinct Ryan smell," Danny said, adding another piece of gum to what was already a considerable wad.

"It wasn't me," Ryan said.

"It smells like old cheese," Curtis said. "And Ryan was eating cheese and crackers."

"See, Curtis would know," Danny added. "With those dark glasses, his sense of smell is superior."

"I don't see why it matters," Shannon told Dave. "If this town is ass-backwards, big whoop." She applied more mascara.

"It also had a Ryan sound," the now pink-headed Michael said, puffing out the window. "It *sounded* like a Ryan fart."

"It was a silent fart," Ryan protested.

"Exactly," Michael countered.

"'Big whoop'?" Dave continued, raising his voice over the arguing from the back seat. "You don't see why restrictions on self-expression matter?" He pulled a quick turn, not quite sure of the route, and lost the vomit-green car. But only for a moment. "Why does individual freedom anywhere matter? We might as well shred both the Bill of Rights and the Constitution."

"I admit my farts," Ryan protested. "You guys know that."

A chant started. "Ryyyyy-an faaarrrr-ted. Ryyyyyy-an faaarrrr-ted."

Shannon started powdering her cheeks. The heavy reverb of electric guitars from the stereo evoked crashing waves. "Don't be ridiculous," she said.

"Whoever smelt it dealt it," Ryan said. "Brandon smelled it first."

"Why not ban other forms of music?" Dave asked. He pulled into a dead end by mistake and had to turn around. "Maybe we can get them to ban jazz?"

"That would solve our Danny problem," Shannon said, applying more eye shadow.

Tibbs made choking sounds. "I'm gagging," he coughed, in mock pain.

"Knock it off," Shannon shouted without turning around.

"While we're at it, let's ban other art forms," Dave continued, accelerating past the vomit-green car. "Maybe we can get them to ban painting. Poetry. Sculpting. Oh, I know. Let's ban all art in Riverview. Art should be illegal. No big deal."

"David, you're being dramatic."

"Aren't you even vaguely aware of the history of banned music?"

Shannon studied her eyes in the mirror. The tempo on the tape jumped; the drums and guitars thrashed.

"The last century alone could take up a week of rides," Dave said, making a sharp turn back to the main road and landing in Mudfest traffic. The high beats per minute of the instrumental contrasted with the pace of the van, so Dave turned it down.

"Use your shirt as a mask," Ray yelled. "Protect the eyes."

"And the ears," Curtis added. "The tympanic membrane is particularly sensitive."

"Guys, I'm serious," Shannon said, turning her whole body. "Enough about Ryan's fart. Can you please act like you're in high school for at least the next ten minutes?"

"Fine," Ryan gushed. "I'm guilty. I farted. I farted a hundred times. My underwear is stained brown. Call the fart police. Put me in fart jail."

Dave rested his arms on the steering wheel. "Stravinsky's *Rite of Spring* caused a riot—or at least a sensation—in France in 1913," he said. "The Irish banned jazz in the '30s. They had jazz police. The church associated jazz with paganism. Other US cities have banned rock: Santa Cruz, San Antonio, Asbury Park in New Jersey—their bans just didn't last as long. And of course there's the Beatles vs. Jesus."

"Yeah, I know all about it," Shannon said, flipping the mirror back up. "Lennon said the Beatles were bigger than Jesus and everyone freaked out."

"I don't think you do," Dave responded. The tape ended. Shannon popped it out and put in an MC5 mix. They sat in a line of cars on a leafy, tree-lined street with nice houses, but they might as well have been in the middle of Detroit. "First of all," Dave continued, "Lennon said the Beatles were *more popular*—an important distinction. And the backlash, which, keep in mind, was *five months* after he said it, was extreme. There were Beatles bonfires. And not just the KKK. Boycotts. Radio stations. They were almost banned from playing in Philly and Boston."

"It's different," Shannon said. "This isn't the '60s, we're not the Beatles, and we're not saying we're more popular or bigger or more whatever than Jesus."

"It's more similar than you realize. Don't you remember Disco Demolition night at Comiskey Park? We were *at the game.* Have you forgotten the massive riot triggered by a ceremonious record detonation? It was all over music."

"Guys," Danny said, pulling his head in from the window. "It was me. I farted."

"I *knew* it," Ryan said.

The traffic cleared. They were almost there.

"I hear you," Shannon said. "I'll think about it the next time I wear my 'Disco Sucks' T-shirt. Now Dave, pass me the set list."

*

Dave parked the van. The vomit-green boat of a Buick eased past them, driven by *Riverview Review* editor Greg Bird.

"Here you go," Dave said, reaching into his back pocket and passing a folded piece of paper to Shannon.

Shannon turned off the radio and read it aloud. "Listen up, everyone. Here are the songs for today. Mon 10-2, Tues 2-6, Wed OFF, Thurs 10-3, Fri OFF, Sat 10-3."

"Shoot, that's my work schedule," Dave said. "I probably left the set list in my other pants."

"Screw it," Shannon said. "We're winging it, guys," she said over her shoulder. Meanwhile, across town on Sullivan Street in the laundry room of the Golding house, Liz pulled a folded sheet of paper from a pair of jeans.

She unfolded it and read:

Mudfest Set List
Ramones Medley
Alien Slurpees Are Yummy (Danny)
Got a Feeling (Mamas and Papas - PUNK version)
What You Gonna Do? (Manfred Mann)
I Know There's Not a Spider in the Bass Drum (Ryan)
En Garde (Michael)
I'm Blue - The Gong Gong Song (Ikettes)
Flying Without a License (Shannon)

*

"I think we should start with my new one," Danny said as they pulled gear from the van. "'Alone in a Cornfield.' Except we can change it to mud field."

"Danny, we are not opening with that weird song."

"What's wrong with weird songs? They're better than normal songs. Zappa played weird songs. He did OK."

"Yesterday we were listening to one of his songs that referenced a doily," Michael chimed in, pulling down an amp.

"A doily?" Shannon asked. "No. I know you're an alien, but I don't think *alienating* an audience on the opener is the way to go."

"It's *absolutely* the way to go," Danny shot back.

"Listen," Dave said, grabbing a pile of cables. He turned and looked at Danny. "Shannon is the lead singer. Ever heard of a guy named Springsteen? Bands have a boss. As the boss, she has the power. And that includes writing the set list. You can give her suggestions. But she's the boss. Got it?"

"Fine," Danny reasoned. "I *suggest* we open with 'Alone in a Cornfield.'"

"And I suggest we play my sabre song," Michael shouted.

"Both suggestions duly noted," Shannon replied.

Behind and below them, the wide-open field of Riverview Park was jammed with legions of mud-soaked adolescents. The realization seemed to dawn on the group at once. Besides Danny and his extensive experience playing in piano competitions, no one had ever played anywhere beyond the Golding basement, a handful of school recitals (mostly Curtis, before moving to Riverview), and the lumberyard audition. And now they were about to step in front of a thousand kids that looked like creatures from the black lagoon.

"Don't worry," Danny said to Ray as they pulled the last of the equipment from the van. "It's not like they'll eat you if you mess up." He leaned his head toward the sound of the muddy crowd. "Actually, wait, they sound pretty hungry."

There was no time to be nervous. They lugged their gear from the parking lot to the far stage just as Mr. Best introduced the next musical act on the near stage: the Riverview High School Chorus performing a set of songs from *Our Town*.

Thirty minutes later, they were set up and it was time to go on.

Shannon and the Little Brothers burst onto the Riverview music scene at two in the afternoon on Saturday, September 4, 1982. They started with a Ramones medley: "Blitzkrieg Bop > I Wanna Be Sedated > Shannon Is a Punk Rocker" (changed from Sheena). The first Ramones song might have been a bit patchy, like a bumpy liftoff, but by the time the medley was over, they had taken off, even if they were in their own little stratosphere.

The legion of mud-caked teenagers didn't how to react. They froze in the summer sun. They stood mired like blinking statues. It was loud. The beats and chords and melodies were … different. There was an aggressive-ness about it, an in-your-face sound. As "Blitzkrieg Bop" came around again for the second verse, they did what any teenager does in a potentially socially awkward situation: They played it cool. But by the final chorus, almost imperceptibly, sludge-covered heads started bobbing. Then there was something about "I Wanna Be Sedated" that caused the head bobs to spread to the shoulders and arms. It was catchy, fun. The silted faces looked around and realized that everyone was covered in mud. Nobody knew who anybody was. They had anonymity; they could enjoy the music and not worry what anyone thought. So when Shannon and the Little Brothers seamlessly transitioned to "Shannon Is a Punk Rocker," enjoy is what they did: The oozing mob let loose.

Ray, Michael, and Tibbs took to the air. Shannon howled out one last "Noooowww!" Danny, Brandon, and Curtis all hit a bass note, Ryan crashed the cymbals, and the Ramones medley ended.

The teenage mud mob stood in excited anticipation. They had a taste, and now they were ready for a meal. Shannon winked at Dave, who was standing with his arms crossed on the side of the stage. Then she looked out at the mud-drenched, throbbing crowd, almost like it wasn't real. The anticipation seemed to wobble in the balance, like it could fall back into inhibition and adolescent fear.

Danny filled the awkward moment with some Chopin. Then Shannon called out, "Pretenders, 'Message of Love,'" and the Little Brothers launched for good, reaching a cruising altitude, leaving in their wake a field of fren-zied, squirming grooviness. They soared through the next three covers: The

Zombies' "She's Not There," Pat Benatar's "Hit Me With Your Best Shot," Janis Joplin's "Piece of My Heart" (with all the Little Brothers finding microphones to sing backup vocals with their lowest collective teenage baritone: "Take It!"), followed by two originals: "Are You Sure that Popsicle Is Chocolate?" and "Flying Without a License."

They had managed to translate a couple weeks of stuffy basement rehearsals into a full-fledged rock and roll gig. Then it was over, much too quickly. And "Flying Without a License," took on new meaning, as if they really were flying. As if playing music live was so much fun that it shouldn't be legal.

When Dave hugged Shannon after the set, he saw a look in her eyes, like maybe now she understood a little more about their earlier conversation in the van, like maybe Dave, as always, did in fact know what he was talking about.

Despite Danny's brilliance on the keyboard and Tibbs wailing and leading the way on guitar, Shannon was the star of the show. Above average height, with long black hair, midnight eyes, and clear pale skin, she looked the part, a mixture of her heroes: Chrissie Hynde, Pat Benatar, Ann Wilson, and Joan Jett. She rarely put much effort into her clothes or looks or makeup. But today she was in full makeup, with a short black leather skirt, ripped T-shirt, and black boots. Singing was just like diving. She was able to calm her mind, focus her breath, live in the moment and mostly enjoy the thrill of each song as if it was a complicated dive, and not worry about making a mistake or falling hard on the water. The lyrics and notes were like twists and flips, something to concentrate and master, and then not think about, but just do. Once she found her footing, she pranced around the stage without a care in the world, confronting and challenging the Thin Pretty North Shore Image. She sang with confidence, emotion, and infectious exuberance, like she didn't give a rip if you didn't like it.

On the near stage, Mr. Best announced that a string quartet from the Village Music Shoppe was still waiting on their viola player. Jim Plant, standing in the wings, gave Shannon and the Little Brothers a thumbs-up and nodded toward the stage he built as if telling them it was all theirs. They went back out and closed the set in style, reaching a zenith of youth and triumph and freedom, with an encore featuring the Clash's "Should I Stay or Should I Go?"

The band raced toward the finish with the final verses in double time, before one final scream from Shannon: "SHOULD I STAY OR SHOULD I GOOOOOOOOOO?"

And then they were off the stage, high-fiving and smiling, leaving in their wake an entire field of cheering high school students drenched in mud.

Assistant Athletic Director Gayle Leneler whished onto the stage. She announced that the seedings and brackets for the single-elimination volleyball tournament were posted on the board by the softball fields. When Mr. Best took to the microphone on the near stage to introduce the string quartet, his main priority instead was to prevent people from being trampled as the mud-caked students surged off to play volleyball.

FIRST QUARTER

Matt Welsh held his hand over the typewriter and observed the involuntary tremor with curiosity. The effort at controlling the shaking while typing had fatigued him. Yet he made it. He thanked God for giving him the strength. Gazing up at a framed portrait of Jesus, he continued to pray under his breath, "As it should be, every day I'm more and more under your control. Amen." He pulled the paper from the typewriter and reread his letter.

Riverview Board of Education
Official Memo
From: Matt Welsh
To: Board President Nancy Brandt
Tuesday, September 7, 1982

Dear President Brandt,

It has come to my attention that last Saturday's annual town fundraising event known as Mudfest, a volleyball tournament that involves our students (which in my opinion violates several city sanitation codes), included live music.

Like every member of our esteemed board, I am a devoted and fervent supporter of the arts. Normally such an event would be cause for celebration. Yet we must not neglect the responsibility we have to ensure that the art presented meets certain moral standards.

Therefore, it is my duty to offer the following report:

A group of Riverview High School students performed songs that clearly violated School Board Act #311, which "prohibits rock and roll music, or similar music, designed to incite amoral behavior in our students."

I find it incumbent upon myself as the longest-standing public servant to also remind you of Village Ordinance 8-67 Chapter 5, Article 309, approved June 10, 1951. Multiple witnesses can attest that the songs performed this past weekend were "overtly sexual, violent, or glorifying of substance abuse," which the ordinance clearly bans from Riverview public settings.

I am also under obligation to share this violation may be connected to our newest administrative hire, Mr. Peter Best, whom I believe worked closely to organize the live music, including providing the stages. While I understand that Mr. Best has impressive credentials with regards to raising standardized test scores, I fear he may not have the moral character to make decisions affecting the musical curricula and performance opportunities offered to our vulnerable youth—Riverview's most precious commodity— the children we are charged with protecting.

I have spoken with Superintendent Jag, suggesting that she ensure high school music will be under the supervision of the expert, Dr. Albert Francis. Further, I suggest we all remain wary of subsequent attempts by Mr. Best to meddle in decisions he has no qualifications to make. Superintendent Jag has promised both heightened vigilance and scrutiny of Mr. Best's actions. Any violations on campus must be met with severe consequences.

I'm sure I can count on your support to demonstrate faithfulness to both the Board and the Village Ordinance.

Yours In Service,
Matt Welsh

*

On Tuesday morning, Leslie Bangs sat at her cluttered cubicle in the *Riverview Review* newsroom. Bright fluorescent light poured down in the windowless room. The hum of a local newspaper surrounded her: fingers clacking on typewriters, phones ringing, and the constant murmur of voices. She wore her long, straight, black hair in a bun held together with at least two writing instruments. It was possible that a third was hidden from view. As was her habit when nervous or concentrating, she nibbled on the stems of her stylish, black-rimmed glasses while another pair, turtle shell–rimmed, rested on top of her head. A third pair splayed diagonally on her typewriter's keyboard. Her mind was a steel trap for facts and stories, but she had a knack for losing eyewear and pens.

She flipped through the pages of her latest story. Instead of being published on Sunday or Monday, this morning it had been returned to her mailbox, unpublished, without a note or comments. She scanned and skimmed a third time.

A Tentacle in the Mud

By Leslie Bangs

Adolescents drenched in mud, looking more like creatures from a lagoon than high school students. Volleyballs bounding high in the air. Thuds, smacks, splatters. Shouts of alacrity. Packed stands cheering, oohing and ahhhing. Laughter and water fights and watermelon. Everyone winning — forging friendships and memories that last a lifetime. All of this has come to be expected from Mudfest, the annual volleyball tournament that kicks off the school year for Riverview High School students.

What happened on Saturday, however, was anything but expected.

On a stage just off the mud pit at Riverview Park, Students from the Black Lagoon were treated to a range of musical acts …

Leslie's phone rang. She ignored it and kept skimming.

> Included on the bill was a highly touted string quartet from the Village Music Shoppe, the RHS Chorus, the gospel group Sing Life. And, tucked inside all of this, almost like an afterthought, was Shannon and the Little Brothers playing rock, rhythm and blues ...

The ringing stopped, then started again.

> Masks of mud concealed the students' surprise ... songs as out of place as a bar of soap ...

Leslie glanced over at her ringing phone, sighed, and returned to her article.

> Many residents have heard about the new Riverview assistant principal, brought in to cure the high school's sagging test scores. However, few people remember him as the drummer of the Riverview rock band the Quarrymen — a relic of another era, a brief period when rock music thrived in this affluent suburb. Before the town quietly imposed a ban on rock music ...

The ringing ceased and, a moment later, her message light blinked.

> The songs played by Shannon and the Little Brothers represent modest feelers to test the Riverview Board of Education's stance on the three-decade-old ban, including new president Nancy Brandt. Will the board revoke, or at least soften, the fear-based restriction that has stifled a generation of area musicians?

> As Buffalo Springfield once sang, "There's something happening here, but what it is ain't exactly clear."

Leslie frowned. In a way, she was testing the waters too. When she first started working at the *Riverview Review*, in the early '60s after several years with the *Chicago Tribune*, she had clashed frequently with her editor, Greg Bird. He had shelved practically an entire book's worth of articles about music in Riverview, relegating them to the Notes Around Town section or not publishing them at all. She had been mistreated, passed over for raises, even suspended … yet she kept writing, covering the Beatles bonfires and bizarre television blackouts. Then the '70s arrived and there wasn't much of anything music-related to report on, so Leslie wrote about that, and her editor censored the article so heavily that she was left with next to nothing.

And then a couple of weeks ago, she wrote about a disturbance at Craftwood Lumber, when there was a report of a noise violation filed at Village Hall. That article had been slashed and buried again in the Notes Around Town. But at least it was published.

The phone rang. Again. She exhaled in deep irritation and answered.

"Leslie Bangs," she said.

"Hello, love of my life."

"Hi, Neil."

"I miss you."

"What do you want, Neil?"

"Don't you miss me too?"

"Neil, I'm busy. You know I'm working. Is there something you need at this very minute?"

"Just to hear your voice."

"Well, you've heard it. Now I need to get back to work."

"What are you working on? Did someone hit a washboard on the corner of Waukegan and Riverview Road?"

"Goodbye, Neil."

"Leslie, don't hang up. I'm just joking. I called because I really miss you. More than ever. I'm not sleeping. We need to talk about this."

"What's there to talk about? You won't move to Riverview, or even Chicago, and I won't move to DC. Seems open and shut to me."

Leslie spotted Greg Bird having a conversation with a photographer. A large, bald mountain of a man, her boss was hard to miss. Never mind that he drove a boat of a car the color of green vomit. She slid her story under some loose papers and pulled out the file she was supposed to be working on, the fiftieth anniversary of the Sara Sweet factory.

"C'mon, Leslie. You and I both know you want more. I can get you a job. At the *Star* or the *Post*. Then you can move forward, cover real news."

"'Real news.' Really? I don't know why I even answer your calls anymore."

"You don't. That's why I have to call you at work, three times before you even pick up."

"I cover real news. Thank you very much. I'm working on an important story right now."

"What's your important story? C'mon, tell me. I'm interested. I am."

"No, you're not," she said, nibbling on the arm of her glasses. She thought about telling him about Mudfest, knowing it would be an invitation for ridicule. "One of the largest dessert factories in the country, a key local economic indicator, is about to celebrate its fiftieth year."

"You're joking, right?" Neil said. "That's your big story. Leslie, I can get you covering the DC music scene. You're too good to be wasting your talent on that small town. Maybe cover international music, travel the world. We could be an amazing team."

"I have a job," Leslie said. "One that keeps me very busy. In a town I happen to care about."

"*Why?* Why do you care so damn much about Riverview?"

"I have to go."

"Why, Leslie? Why do you care about that stupid rock music ban? No one cares," Neil said. "No one cares that thirty years ago some kids couldn't play guitars."

"They still can't."

"So what? They can leave. They can play literally one town over. It's not news."

"I believe it is," Leslie said. "A freedom is being denied. A vital art form. By a small group of overzealous religious conservatives. But that might be about to change. This past Saturday—"

"Leslie, when are you going to let it go?"

She held her head in her hands, a pair of glasses tumbling down onto her desk.

"Leslie. Let it go. For us."

"This isn't something that can be let go," Leslie said, a little too loudly, drawing a glance from Jane Mott in the neighboring cubicle, who covered education, lifestyle, and homes and gardens. "I care. People *should* care about this."

Her editor and the photographer finished their discussion. Greg Bird was walking toward her.

"Well, they don't," Neil said. "No one cares. They don't. I wish they did, but they don't. It's a dead end. But I care about you. More than anything in this world. That's why I can't stand to see you sitting there, your five pairs of glasses and three pens on your head, going nowhere. And since we're talking about beliefs, I believe you still care about me. We fell in love, Leslie. I'm still in love with you. And I believe … we can be together again."

"I have to go, Neil. I care that no one cares about this ban. In fact, that's a perfect job description for a journalist. To make people care. Now if you don't mind, I have work to do."

She hung up. Her editor hovered over her like an avalanche about to fall.

"Leslie, how's that story on the factory's fiftieth coming along?" Greg asked.

"Good," Leslie said, standing and catching a pen that fell from her hair. "I'm on my way over there this afternoon. One thing has me a little curious. If you take away government subsidies, the factory has suffered negative earnings three quarters in a row, at a time when they're spending a significant amount on the celebration."

Her phone rang. She glanced down at it and then back to the relentlessly intense face of her editor.

"Now, Leslie," Greg said. "Here we go again. We don't need a negative headline about the town's leading employer. Not on a celebration. I swear, Leslie. I'll put Porter on this, and you'll be with Jane covering the retirement home's new garden before you can blink."

"No sir, I mean yes sir," Leslie stammered. "The story won't be negative. It's only something I uncovered in my research."

The ringing stopped.

"Yeah, well, make sure it stays out of the article."

"Of course." Leslie looked down at the little light blinking, telling her she had a new message, one she would delete without listening to.

*

There night sky was clear, with no moon. If there was a man looking down, he would have seen the vast, empty quarry, the looming Sara Sweet factory, the broad streets and leafy neighborhoods, and the squat buildings of downtown. Everything was peaceful, another serenely quiet Saturday night, until a siren pierced the air as an ambulance wailed past Village Hall.

Across the street, rising above the church bell tower like the eyes of a giant snail, two radio transmitters pulsed waves into the air. The first transmitter sent out a wave at the frequency needed to scramble WLS AM 890, the Rock of Chicago, the same wave it had been pulsing since the early '50s. The second transmitter, erected in the early '60s, sent out a variety of canceling signals, primarily taking out WROCK FM 95 but also disrupting a few other FM stations that had been known to broadcast the occasional rock tune.

A shadowy figure climbed down a ladder on the bell tower. The shadow crossed the roof of the sanctuary. Moments later, Greg Bird, also a deacon of the Riverview Presbyterian Church—an individual whose presence at such a late hour no one would question—exited the church from a side door. He took a moment to appreciate the early autumn constellations dangling in the sky, then he got into his vomit-green Buick and drove off.

Greg waited at the red light as a second ambulance zoomed by. The light changed, and he pulled out onto Waukegan Road. He drove through the sleepy downtown, turned left, and cruised another three blocks. He turned past the Riverview Historical Village, consisting of five buildings dating from 1837 to 1905, that offered visitors a glimpse of a "typical prairie community." He parked at the nearby Kipling Elementary School three spaces down from the Buick belonging to Matt Welsh, another member of the school board that no one would question for visiting a local school. At the far end of the lot, Oren's Buick sat under a tree. They spaced their cars out so as not to arouse suspicion.

Usually Easton picked up Robbie, while Rick and Oren drove separately. Greg didn't see Easton's or Rick's cars and assumed they would be along shortly. Together, the five of them— Greg, Easton, Robbie, Rick, and Oren—made up the Cars. Greg, an amateur astronomer and lifelong stargazer, tended to think of them as five points of a star, with Matt at the center.

Greg thought of the old days, when they had an array of meeting points and rode together to the meetings in full cars. But the group had dwindled. Which was fine. The remaining members were hardened and dedicated, and they knew how to do the job. There were fewer cars roaming the streets of Riverview, keeping the town safe from warping, mind-altering music, but there had been a corresponding decrease in the perceived threat level.

Greg walked over toward a one-room log cabin. The late summer evening was warm and windy, the sky full of all the familiar September stars a light-polluted Chicago suburb was entitled to. He went around a larger three-room log cabin that served as the Visitor's Center. The branches of the tall elms swayed in a light breeze.

He was about to enter the Little Red Schoolhouse, a nineteenth-century one-room school furnished with period items like old desks and an old blackboard, when he heard a sound, like a branch being stepped on. He walked over past the farmhouse and looked out over the old Riverview Cemetery. He still had his flashlight on him from his work at the church. He pulled it out and shined a light across the old graveyard, with some graves dating back to the 1840s. The wind blew the old ornamental iron gate, causing it to make a loud creak.

Greg was tall and had excellent vision, a man the Cars dubbed the Eye in the Sky because of his stellar eyesight and love of astronomy. Besides editing the local paper, he also had his pilot's license and sometimes took a single-engine plane out over the town. He knew every inch of this community. He scanned the graveyard. Another scuffling noise. He shined his light in its direction and saw a pack of raccoons hopping among the gravestones. The light reflected in the largest animal's eyes. The pack skittered along a row of graves, slinked through the fence, and clambered off into the nearby woods. The only sound was the wind. Greg stood like a lone wolf out stalking prey in the prairie.

Another Buick pulled up. It was Easton. Greg walked over to meet him.

"Greg," Easton called. "When I went to pick up Robbie, there was an ambulance in his driveway. He's had a heart attack."

Greg took a moment to gaze at the heavens and pray. And in his mind, the five points of the star became a square. For now, there would only be four men to act as invisible guardians. Greg and Easton walked into the red schoolhouse, unaware that behind the carriage house crouched Leslie Bangs.

*

Leslie Bangs had been at the only Riverview eatery open past nine o'clock, the diner known as Eats. She liked to go there after her Saturday shift. Her goal was to organize her notes for the Sara Sweet factory fiftieth anniversary. She had spent a half hour doodling. She felt stuck. Rock and roll had recently been played in a Riverview park, and here she was covering an anniversary of a factory that changed the world with fresh-frozen desserts in ready-to-use foil pans. Pound cakes, Leslie thought to herself, feeling the futility of it all. Maybe Neil is right?

Leaving Eats, she had seen Matt Welsh at a red light. The rest of Riverview knew him as the leader of the Riverview Presbyterian Gospel Choir, the former mayor, and a current school board member. But Leslie Bangs knew him as something else: the mastermind behind the ban on rock music. She knew this as a high school reporter for the *Riverview High School Sword*. She knew it as an intern for the *Riverview Review*. She knew it for the years she had gone to work at the *Chicago Tribune*. And she also knew she didn't have any hard evidence. That's part of why she wanted to come back, to tell this story about how a small group of religious conservatives prevented an entire town from experiencing a vital art form. It was a crime, one that tore at her heart, a heart already filled with wounds, guarded with instructions not to let anyone in—until she met and fell in love with Neil Cott, a rising reporter. She knew she would go back to Riverview and that he would never follow her.

As a teenager reeling from the swift pancreatic cancer that took her father, which sent her mother deeper into the throes of alcoholism, Leslie discovered songwriting. She would hide in the basement while her mother drank herself into oblivion with a random stranger. It was there that Leslie discovered her father's record collection. There was classical, but also folk, blues, swing, jazz, and Irish ballads. The songs that captivated her, that took her away from the sounds and the sadness, were songs that told stories. Woodie Guthrie singing about the dust bowl. Songs about the gold rush, whaling in Alaska, lonesome traveling songs, the Civil War, songs full of truth and beauty. Songs with the integrity that she wished her mother had. At night, instead of her mother, the Weavers wished her goodnight in the song "Goodnight Irene."

She came back to her hometown in 1962 as a beat reporter for the *Riverview Review*. As rock and roll surged into higher and higher stratospheres across the United States, so too did her own incredulity that Riverview could be an impenetrable island walled off from rhythm and blues—and that no one seemed to care. Her plan was to expose these narrow-minded hypocrites, open the door for the next generation of kids in Riverview to discover the strength and beauty she had found in music, and move on with her career and her life with Neil. That was twenty years ago. Twenty years of every article that came anywhere remotely close to rock and roll getting censored and buried in Notes Around Town, or not even printed at all.

The light changed. She decided to follow Matt Welsh for no other reason than that it was strange for a man who presumably would be up early for church to be driving around alone at this hour. Where was he going? In her VW Bug, she trailed him from a safe distance as he turned off Riverview Road and parked at Kipling Elementary. Leslie turned into a nearby neighborhood and cut the lights. She pretended to be going into a nearby house with all its lights out, but instead she ducked behind some bushes. She watched him step from his car. He was barely visible in his dark clothes as he went behind the school and disappeared. What was back there? The old graveyard? The school playground? Was this a clandestine meeting? Was he up to something nefarious? She waited ten minutes and was about to go behind the school herself, when he appeared again, moving like a ghost in the darkness. She watched him enter the Little Red Schoolhouse, which was only supposed to be open for tours on Sundays in the summer and for the annual fourth grade "Old Schoolhouse Day." Something was up. Leslie grabbed her cap, tucked her hair into it, and knocked a pen loose that clattered on the concrete. She bent down, scooped it up, and pulled on her brown sweater from her back seat to cover up her white shirt. Then she slipped into the Historical Village, the only sound the wind in the trees.

Another car pulled up. She darted off behind a tree. From the spotlight at the nearby school, she recognized the tall, lurching walk. Greg Bird. A shudder swept through Leslie's body. What was *he* doing here?

As Greg strode toward the village, she shifted from behind a tree to the back of an old-time wagon, only to step on a branch. She crouched and ran, stopping near one of the three windows alongside the single A-frame schoolhouse with the old bell tower above it. She dared one quick peek through the window and ducked back down. Matt Welsh was standing near the teacher's desk. He was praying in a somber tone. Another man was lighting the candles of a candelabra. The other men sat on the old-time student desks, heads bowed, backs to Leslie, shrouded in shadow.

"We pray to you, Lord, in your infinite wisdom and mercy," Matt said. "We pray that Robbie's heart will heal, that it will beat strong again, that he will return to us and continue our important work as shepherds of your village. We have faith, Lord, and thus we rejoice. He is in your hands, as are we. Amen."

"Amen," the other men repeated.

Leslie pulled out her notepad and scribbled. ROBBIE. HEART ATTACK?

Matt spoke again. "Therefore, despite our heavy hearts, let us carry on with our important work." He began speaking in a low monotone, and his body was still.

"It was entirely predictable. Maybe not so soon, but we expected our newest high school administrator to test the waters." Matt cleared his throat. "This *slopfest* of his. Thrusting filth into the ears of young adolescents *already* covered in filth. For someone that will purportedly help students achieve A's, so far we have one big D: disgrace."

His speech gathered speed, his volume rising and falling, with his arms getting in on the act.

"We didn't like the hire from the start. Over the summer, we adopted a strategy. We knew better than to fight the placement. Trying to block an administrator with the highest-ranking improvement of test scores in the state would seem dubious in the eyes of the community. So rather than try to portray Mr. Best as an inadequate educator with questionable morals, we decided to let him do it for himself. And that's just what he has done."

Matt paused, smiled, and nodded to the gathering. His voice deepened, his eyes widened, and his face glowed in the candlelight. He had found his stride and spoke with the conviction of a minister from the pulpit.

"I've been in contact with Superintendent Jag, and she is in accord with the plan. She's already tainted the entire staff against him, describing him as an outsider intent on attaching blame for our sagging scores to any teacher that so much as smiles at him. And now she will initiate our response to this *slopfest*. With one hand she will congratulate and pat Mr. Best on the back, while with the other she will paint him further and further into a corner. Administrative tasks. Paperwork. Superfluous curriculum research. Teacher evaluation upon evaluation, further distancing him from his staff." His voice rose to another level, taking his audience to a new height. "And soon this hack of an administrator who thinks he can come back to *our* town and corrupt *our* young with his music of rebellion, drugs, and immoral sexuality—this pied piper will soon not know his own tune. He will be uncertain of the very ground he stands on. His own missteps will be his undoing. For when he takes his next errant step, like a mouse innocently nibbling a piece of cheese, that is when our justice will snap down on him like a steel trap!"

Matt finished. His hands and arms began to shake. He gripped the edge of the podium, steadying his hands, but his arms continued to shiver. For a moment, he seemed to lose himself, curious at his own lack of self-control. Looking up, he quickly regained his composure, released the podium, and crossed his arms behind his back. Having set the course of action, he took his seat in the front row.

Outside, with the wind scattering leaves across the open field like little creatures hurrying away, Leslie finished scrawling her notes and flipped the page. She curled her lips and felt resentment festering in her core. It was like a heavy boulder sitting on a slope in her mind had suddenly rolled free and tumbled down. Of course. No wonder all her articles about Village Ordinance 8-67 Chapter 5, Article 309 faced such ruthless censorship. Greg Bird was one of *them*.

She leaned over to the open window and watched as the next man stood, emerged from the shadows, and approached the podium. She recognized Oren Benjamin as a classical pianist and elementary school music teacher. Oren droned on about how classical music—and *only* classical music—should be taught to the primary grades. She knew his work well. He had played with the Chicago Symphony and had a brief stint as a professor of classical music at Northwestern University until butting heads with administrators. When he refused to teach a course entitled "Rock and Bach" and threatened to quit, the university called his bluff. He had also written several articles, some scholarly, others for the *Chicago Tribune*, espousing the ideals and merits of classical music and the banalities, the triteness, and the dangers of popular music. What an airbag, Leslie thought. As stubborn as a mule. He refused to acknowledge that anything written after the eighteenth century had merit. She scrawled his name, drew an arrow, and wrote CLASSICAL MUSIC PURIST.

The next man to take the podium she recognized as Easton Elliot, a deacon at the Riverview Presbyterian Church and one of the top real estate agents in the area. A member of the school board. In local politics, he was an active, hard-line conservative. He had once written a letter to the editor of the *Riverview Review*, criticizing Leslie's loose morals for an article she wrote about a drama camp where girls and boys were encouraged to sing and dance together. She watched as he discussed the influx of new residents and the need for caution and vigilance. He unrolled a map and highlighted certain neighborhoods.

There was another man lurking in the shadows that Leslie strained to see but could not. She had heard him, not speaking words but making sounds during the other speeches. She added to her notes: MAN IN SHADOWS, MAKING SOUNDS.

A car arrived, the schoolhouse door opened, and in walked police sergeant Andrew Winter. He reminded Leslie of a frog with his blobby body and thick glasses. A flabby Southern gentleman. He reported that his route had been quiet. One development to keep on eye on, he croaked in his Kentucky frog drawl, was that the Village Music Shoppe had hired a guitar teacher from Spain who was teaching classical guitar. There were three classical guitars for sale in the store. Leslie listened as the group debated what to do. They arrived at the conclusion that they would monitor the situation, send a letter to Mr. Taplin, the owner of the shop, to remind him of the village ordinance against solid-body guitars, and send in "extras" (wives, neighbors, etc.) to purchase the three classical guitars and have them sold to a music shop in the city.

The next man's words caused Leslie's blood to boil. It was her editor, his long legs gigantic next to the old-time desk. He was discussing the transmitters on the church tower. She knew he dabbled in radio waves. She scanned her memory, gathering what she knew of his personal life. He had a daughter who was rumored to have battled drug addiction. She wrote his name and drew an arrow to DAUGHTER ON DRUGS?

Then she heard it.

"Articles from the suburban edition of the *Tribune* that wouldn't run, and of course the latest muck from our own musical muckraker, will be shuffled aside …"

It all made sense. Twenty years of being dismissed, "shuffled aside," all from the hands of this bear of a man. Musical muckraker? She had every mind to barge in, to demand to know what was going on, to call the police—except the police were already represented. *They* were the ones committing the infractions. But something else held her back: A breeze tickled her nostril. She flipped her notepad closed and held her breath, but it was no use; the sneeze erupted from inside her. She used the momentum from the sneeze to break away, to run. She didn't look back, weaving behind the log house and then sprinting across the open field into a small crop of trees. She cut over behind an apartment building and, rather than dash into a gated community, took the chance to cross Waukegan Road. She darted across traffic to the sound of sirens and flashing lights behind her, in the direction of the Historic Village. Her lungs strained with an exertion she hadn't felt since her high school cross-country days. In front of her was an overpass, beyond which were the factory and the quarry. The sirens were getting louder, approaching. The quarry is too far, she decided. The factory is closed off. In a moment she made up her mind. She ran back across Waukegan as a police car curled around the corner. Her lungs burning, sucking air that seemed beyond her reach, she retraced her steps, bolting back behind the apartment building, through the trees. And rather than enter the Historic Village, she crouched in the Riverview Cemetery.

The sirens wailed off into the distance. When the sound receded, Leslie waited for any disturbance from the Historic Village. One by one, the remaining men left the old school and drove off. When she was alone with the wind and the dead, she stood against a stone monument and, looking up at the stars, thought to herself, Now I know what I'm up against.

*

The next day was Sunday, Leslie's day off. She woke up, brushed her hair and tucked it into her cap, and jumped in her VW. She turned on 94.7 and listened to the static. She jammed on the accelerator, flooring it out of her condominium subdivision without bothering to wave at Mrs. Valdez, out watering her balcony garden. She needed to get out of Riverview. She gunned it through two yellows, ran a third, and stopped at the last light before the highway. The radio was still static. Her mind felt fuzzy too. This was more than one man pulling strings at Village Hall. This was a group. An organization. Maybe even a cult. They were sinister. They were underground. Did they have masks? Handshakes? Rituals? And Greg Bird. Her editor for twenty years.

The light changed. She floored it across the town border, accelerating up the overpass leading into Lowland Park. The static crackled and suddenly the radio came through clear as a bell, a soaring guitar solo.

"That was a little taste of AC/DC's album *Highway to Hell*," the DJ said. "The band's first album to crack the top 100, it's now up to thirty-three on the charts. We've got Fleetwood Mac up ahead, so stick around."

Leslie turned off the radio. She wanted to scream. How had she not realized this before? The bastards are scrambling the radio signals. Plus, they're patrolling streets, monitoring the Village Music Shoppe. What else are they up to? Are they just in Riverview? What *was* she up against?

Out of nowhere, she started to laugh. She acted like she didn't know where she was going. Like the part of her that was driving didn't know, like someone else was behind the wheel. But she knew where she was going. It was time for a drink.

*

At eleven-fifteen on Monday morning, Leslie pulled into the Sara Sweet factory. Her hangover, which she had expected to be worse since it was the first in over a year, was manageable. She walked in the main entrance, received her press credentials, and made her way to the cafeteria. The tables had all been pushed to the edges, flanked by chairs. Some of the tables had various sweets that were made in the factory: pound cakes, raspberry strudels, and cinnamon rolls.

A podium stood in the front of the cafeteria alongside three flagpoles from which hung an American flag, an Illinois state flag, and a Sara Sweet flag. Above the podium hung a banner, a little tilted, that said CELEBRATING FIFTY YEARS!!! A group of dignitaries and higher-ups in suits were shaking hands and mingling near a row of chairs in proximity to the podium. Leslie had been on the factory beat for years and recognized the CEO, the board members, and Sara "Sweet" herself. They were all members of, or otherwise connected to, the family of Sara Sweeney. There was one man she didn't recognize, standing off to the side of the group, a tall thin man with his nose buried in a folder.

In the corner opposite the podium sat an orchestra in formal clothing, playing what sounded like a 1940s swing tune. There were pink and white balloons everywhere, a few concentrated rows of them near the podium, and an empty space in the center of the room, what could be considered a dance floor.

Leslie walked toward the side of the stage to the row reserved for the press. Five chairs: one for her, one for the *Chicago Tribune* suburban reporter of the month, and the usual PR nosebleeds from the factory.

She wasn't hungry, but the factory lemonade was at least something refreshing at these things. Her headache, she noticed, was almost gone. She went to the refreshment table and filled up a plastic cup, standing a few feet away from some old pals. Pals, as in mean high school girls that hadn't changed at all besides aging twenty-five years, led by Leslie's teenage arch-nemesis, Courtney Harrison. She used to tease Leslie about everything: her hair, her clothes, her lack of boyfriends, her lack of friends, that she wrote for the school newspaper, that she sang in the drama club—basically that she existed. Like they were back at their lockers in D hall, the women didn't acknowledge her now. Leslie filled a cup of lemonade and overheard their conversation.

"I can't even imagine," Virginia Hensley mused.

"It's all over Lowland Park," Courtney replied. "Kids are smoking it in the bathrooms—in the *middle schools*. It's a real problem. Once drugs get into the community, they spread like a weed through the schools."

"I'm glad they're not in Riverview," Virginia said. "Having the factory in between probably helps. Like a buffer."

"That helps, sure," Courtney said. "But I think there's more to it. Riverview is just a better community. More wholesome. A place with values. I think about that area around the Water Tower in Lowland Park, along the lake. All those teenagers hanging out with nothing to do. No wonder they get into drugs and trouble."

Leslie coughed an expletive in their general direction and returned to her seat. The ceremony was about to begin. She got out her notepad and fumbled in her purse for a set of glasses. The first two cases were empty, but the third had an old pair. Likewise, the first two pencils she pulled up had busted tips, but then she found a pen.

She surveyed the faces of factory workers milling about, some of the people she had gone to high school with. This was a party, a celebration, but it felt to Leslie more like a life insurance convention. There was a sterility, a heaviness to it all. No one seemed to laugh or have any emotion of any kind, like there wasn't enough air in the room.

The orchestra finished playing. No one seemed to notice. The factory's CEO, Mark Stein, approached the podium. He had married one of the Sweeney daughters. The founder, William Sweeney, now deceased, had only daughters and didn't trust the business to them. He turned it over to Mark, who had managed the factory for the last fifteen years. Leslie had heard his speeches before. She jotted down a few notes for her article and then tuned him out, instead watching the tall, thin man at the end of the row of dignitaries that she didn't know. He still had his face buried in a folder, but his leg was bouncing like a jackrabbit.

Mark blathered on about the success of the factory and how it wouldn't be possible without the hard work of blah blah blah. Then came Sara Sweet, the cutie that William Sweeney originally named the factory for. Now in her fifties and—Leslie well knew from AA meetings—a recovering alcoholic, she had lost more than a little of her sweetness. She rambled on about how proud her grandfather would be. Snore. Leslie looked at her watch, then out at the audience of factory workers, thinking there really was something off. She watched them, bland and listless, seated heavily on folding chairs shoving pastries into faces devoid of any enjoyment.

More dignitaries rambled on. Leslie added some notes to her pad and covered a yawn. A scene from last night flared up in her mind, a backseat, drunken debauchery with a stranger; she quickly extinguished it and focused on the present. Each speaker spewed out the usual drivel as Leslie counted the yawns that flashed around the room like lightning bugs on a summer night. Then suddenly it was the tall man's turn. He removed his suit jacket and strode to the podium in long strides, like he left his nervousness behind with his coat.

"Greetings, my name is Vincent Furnier and I'm asking you to elect me the next president of your worker's union." Leslie perked up. He rolled up his sleeves as he looked out over the crowd. "I don't believe I'm overstating things when I say that as a country we currently stand on a large precipice, swaying in crisis after crisis, about to plunge into an economic abyss." He paused and looked at the audience with his long, thin face. "The energy crisis. The cost of gas, electricity, not to mention homeownership. High inflation. All of these have a ripple effect on what everyday Americans can afford. And we know that an apple pie from a Sara Sweet factory, made in America by Americans—is about as American as it gets. But it's not hard to imagine a world where Americans can no longer afford a sweet treat. Especially if liberals and their socialist labor policies have their way.

"I'm here today, as a representative of Ronald Reagan and the Republican Party, to stand up to the loose liberal policies that don't seem to understand basic economic principles, like supply and demand and paying a decent wage to factory workers."

There was ripple across the audience. Leslie noticed it, like a large body of water being disturbed after a long period of calm.

"And just as you have a choice this November at the ballot box, an opportunity to restore conservative values and common sense in the United States Congress, so too you have a choice for who represents your labor union. You can choose my opponent, who's not even here today because he also happens to represent a union of workers at a liberal ice cream company in Vermont, one that is rumored to be courting members of the Grateful Dead rock band about naming flavors after them. Folks, this isn't Bing Crosby's vanilla ice cream. This is drugs and rock and roll. Do you want that debris in this factory? I mean, what are they smoking over there? What might seem innocent is anything but. They are seeking to brand flavors to appeal to our vulnerable youth."

Leslie's pen worked overtime, adding question marks. It was the first she had heard about the Vermont ice cream union.

"It's not a marijuana farmer I need to warn you about," Furnier continued. "Instead, I'd like to remind you about a certain peanut farmer. It wasn't that long ago that the policies of Jimmy Carter and other Democratic officials, both across this country and right here in the state of Illinois, hamstrung businesses that should have been thriving.

"Now, with their solid, reliable labor policies, Ronald Reagan and the Republican Party have spent the past two years trying to clean up an economic disaster. Mr. Reagan has personally offered his support for my candidacy to be your labor union president and represent you faithfully, which is what I plan to do. A vote for me is a vote for conservative common sense."

Leslie noticed the fidgeting of the crowd, little shifts and creaking folding chairs.

Mr. Furnier raised his arms toward the row of dignitaries. "I want to thank the Sweeney family for inviting me to this celebration, and I ask for your vote in the upcoming union election. I urge you to listen closely to Republican local, state, and national candidates as they explain why staying the course with their policies will keep the American economy on track. Ronald Reagan himself asked me to come here to offer my representation. A vote for me will keep a burned-out radical liberal, his brain fried from too many Grateful Dead concerts, from leading this factory down the toilet. Thank you."

Furnier closed his folder and returned to his seat like a hawk gliding back to his perch. There was a light applause; the audience, briefly agitated, regained its calm exterior.

Mark Stein and Sara Sweeney made their way back to the podium. Sara seemed a little unsteady and, once near the microphone, she hiccupped, a loud piercing high note that came out of nowhere. Leslie figured perhaps she was back off the wagon too.

"And now," Mark Stein said, "all the way from Vernonshire, the Vernonshire Orchestra … hit it."

The band jumped into a swinging big band ballad. Leslie's headache surged back to life. She recognized the melody as "Stardust." She sat and listened and watched. Nobody stood up. Nobody danced or seemed to be listening to the music. One man started bobbing his head, but it was only to gobble up a crumbling slice of pound cake. Another woman with a cinnamon roll on her lap started dozing. A cymbal crash from the orchestra startled her awake, causing her cinnamon roll to hit the floor. Leslie watched the woman scrape it back onto her plate. Enough of this. She tossed her notepad and pen and glasses into her purse. Then her boot heels clicked across the floor as the band slogged on.

Out in the sunshine and fresh air, Leslie took a deep breath, hoping to clear her head. She almost had it, a moment of calm, but then thoughts started rushing in. The only thing even vaguely newsworthy was the union election, but Greg Bird would most certainly not want anything about that in her article. Besides, all this factory business only seemed like more of a hassle, a distraction from what she really wanted to write about: rock and roll.

*

Across town at Riverview High School, George the custodian sprayed the next window of the large trophy case near the front entrance.

"George?" Pete called out, approaching the case.

George whispered with his eyes closed. "Hare Krishna."

"George," Pete said, putting a hand on his shoulder.

"Yes?" George turned.

Pete looked into the custodian's deep brown eyes. They seemed full of emotion, on the brink of tears, but Pete couldn't tell if it was joy or sadness. Pete looked away, confirmed that the hallway was empty, then spoke.

"Do you ever speak with Richard Starkey, the custodian at the district office?"

"Yes," George said, smiling and resuming his work with the squeegee.

"Have you spoken with him recently?" Pete gave George's reflection a meaningful glance.

"Yes."

The two men looked at each other's reflections in the glass. Pete took a step closer. "What are they saying?" he asked in a low voice.

George opened the trophy case and ran his finger along the top shelf. He closed his eyes, rubbed his fingers together, and examined them for dust.

"What I feel, I can't say."

"You can't ... *say?*" Pete asked.

George held his hand up to his own face and scrutinized the tips of his fingers.

"You feel what?" Pete asked in a hushed tone. "Dust? Or do you have feelings about what Starkey said?"

George smiled. He rubbed his fingers on his pants and held up the blade of his squeegee. "You know my squeegee is here, any time of day." George winked and ducked his head into the case.

Pete glanced down the empty hallway and beat his knuckles together. George examined the window for streaks from the inside. "That's ... reassuring ... George ... that you're here."

George squirted a new window with glass cleaner and held up his squeegee.

Pete removed his glasses and rubbed his eyes. "An open mic," he blurted. "I was thinking of starting next week, for *all* types of performances." He replaced his glasses and glanced around the empty foyer. "De-emphasizing the rock part, if you will. I was thinking of writing a formal letter to the board, citing my research and the benefits of live music, but perhaps it seems better to proceed ... *informally*, for now."

"If that's what you need, then I'll try my best to make everything succeed." For a moment, it seemed as if George was talking to his squeegee. They both stood and watched the drops dripping.

Finally, Pete spoke. "If you see Richard again, can you ask him if he's heard anything? About Mudfest, that is."

George stared, transfixed, as the drops gathered at the bottom of the pane of glass. "Tell me, who am I?" he asked, as if to the drops. "Without you, by my side." He held up the squeegee and, with one clean, smooth swipe, the window was clear and dry.

"Thank you, George. Anything at all would be helpful."

George misted another window and began humming.

Pete watched him a moment longer, the bearded custodian lost in the drops, then turned and walked down the hall. As he walked away George called out.

"Hare Krishna. Hare Rama."

WAXING GIBBOUS

Pam Susan smiled at Roberta Anderson, the newest member of the Riverview Board of Education, having captured the seat vacated by the recently deceased Robbie Davidson. (Besides President Brandt, Roberta was the first new Riverview politician since Oren Benjamin had replaced Henry John Deutschendorf Jr. in the early '60s town council.) In the open election to replace Robbie, Roberta grabbed everyone's attention when she stepped onto the runoff election stage wearing a cherry red suit, confusing the crowd by saying she had just flown in from Canada on a seagull, and, as a successful painter, she was determined to resurrect art education in Riverview. Members of the conservative base, thinking their candidate was a shoo-in, were caught off guard when she won.

"Nice shoes; are those suede?" Pam asked, looking at Roberta's bright blue heels, popping on the off-white office floor in need of a wax.

"They sure are," Roberta said, pulling down her sunglasses to flash a wink.

"Right this way," Pam said. "I'll show you to the new computer lab."

"Aren't we going to the newly renovated student union?" President Nancy Brandt asked, a question that went unanswered as Roberta's blue heels twisted on the tile and followed Pam's clicking heels down D hall. Matt Welsh, bringing up the rear, pressed his trembling hand to his side.

Across campus, the student union was filled to capacity. Students squeezed onto the couches and sat two to a chair. The floor was a sea of cross-legged adolescents. Still more students stood crammed in shoulder to shoulder, all the way to the door, spilling out into the hallway. Freshmen lined the broad windows, straining to see and hear what they could.

A drum kit, an electronic keyboard, three amps, and two microphone stands had been set up on a small wooden stage. Mr. Best approached one of the microphones. "Good afternoon, everyone," he said. "It's great to see so many students interested in … eh, live art." He paused briefly. Exactly one student clapped, and that was followed by mock applause and jeers.

"First off," Mr. Best continued, "I would like to thank our custodian George for setting up." He indicated George standing in the corner.

The students clapped robotically.

"Next, I would like to say open mic will be once a week. The open mic is exactly that: open. To performers of all varieties. If you would like to participate, there is a weekly drawing for nine different slots. Three in each period: four, five, and six. Please see Ms. Susan in the office for sign-up forms."

Mr. Best looked down at a notecard.

The students sat as he read through a list of expectations regarding audience behavior.

"Finally, for any music performed, if you are so inclined, songs cannot contain references to sex, drugs, or alcohol." Mr. Best looked around the room with his go-to *don't test me* expression. "Without further ado, I would like to welcome Morris Jameson and the Windows, making their Riverview music debut here at open mic. On lead vocals, Morris Jameson. On drums, Denny Johnson. Keyboard, Manny Rayzereck. And on guitar, Craig Roberson."

There was a smattering of applause, but clearly the students were disappointed. They weren't exactly sure what they were hoping for, but it wasn't this: a band they had never heard of, consisting of all *freshmen*.

The Windows sat down at their instruments. Morris walked up to the stage wearing all black and turned his back to the audience. He whispered a title that was inaudible. He began, speaking quietly rather than singing, with the band seeming to improvise to his spoken words. It was hard to hear him.

Everything swirls down

The skin is sticky

The body has no parts

A flushing sound encroaches.

The Windows ad-libbed. Denny alternated between jazzy rhythms on the cymbals and clusters of crashing snare and bass. Manny closed his eyes and played a very basic bass line with his left hand and trance pulses with his right. He swayed his head, occasionally revealing closed eyes behind his bangs. Craig played only notes that slid up or down, making his guitar sound like a wounded animal.

We are ashamed

Of bedwetters whom we punish

If soaking sheets were burned tomorrow

Fire would be void of power.

Morris Jameson started howling. Behind him, the drums erupted into stuttering clatters. Craig's guitar squealed.

We cannot escape the goodnight sip

We micturate

From the body

Flowing out into our parents' sheets

Wet in the dark

Feedback through Craig's amp pierced the air of the crowded room. Students covered their ears. Craig made no effort to stop it. Manny kept up the trance while Denny pounded the skins. Then all went quiet.

Detergent is our favorite lubricant

The windows watch.

Morris fell to the ground, writhing, while the band crashed down with one last intense groan of sound that made the front row cower. Mr. Best made his way to the microphone.

"Thank you, boys," he said. "Interesting … a lot going on there. This is after all open mic, open to all artists of all stripes … um, well, let's give them a hand."

No one clapped. Some students exchanged glances of mild disgust. Morris was on the ground, sucking his thumb.

"Next up," Mr. Best announced, "Junior Walt Mixon will be performing magic and optical illusions."

*

Saturday afternoon, a week after getting his driver's license—much to Shannon's chagrin—Brandon drove with Danny to White Hen Pantry, Riverview's only convenience store. They walked in, grabbed sodas, and waited for a woman to buy a pack of cigarettes. When she was gone, they walked up to the cashier. He was a middle-aged guy with curly black hair, glasses, and a worn face. His nametag said Lou.

"Good afternoon," Danny began, a little too slowly, like he had rehearsed. "It's a perfect day outside."

"It is nice," Lou agreed. "What are your plans?"

"First the zoo, then a movie," Danny said, reciting his lines.

"That does sound perfect," Lou replied with a smile. "Will you be feeding the animals?"

Danny and Brandon shared a glance, surprised that it was working. "We plan on feeding one zoo animal," Brandon managed.

"Only one?" Lou asked with a glint in his eyes.

The two boys looked at each other and exchanged a nervous laugh. "One oughta do it," Danny said. "I believe the hungry, hungry hippo. One animal, two hungries."

Brandon shot Danny a look that said, *Don't push it.* Then he offered Lou a polite smile with the money for the sodas, plus an additional twenty-dollar bill.

"You guys make me forget myself," Lou said, ringing up the purchase and giving Brandon his change. Before Brandon could pick up the soda bottles, Lou grabbed them and put them in a white bag with a lump already in the bottom. He pushed the bag into their hands.

"Enjoy this perfect day," Lou said.

"Thank you," Brandon and Danny responded in unison, and walked out.

*

"I can't believe the White Hen dude sold you a bag of weed," Shannon said. "And what's that weird code about the zoo? Here, take a hit, try a little." She held out the joint to Ray.

They were on the Golding family's back porch. It was a warm September Thursday evening. The Golding parents were at a parent-teacher conference for their now eight-year-old second grader, Amber.

"You can wash it down with this," Shannon said, handing Ray a luke-warm can of Budweiser.

Tibbs, Danny, Michael, Curtis, and Brandon were all smoking too. It smelled like a skunk. The Jimi Hendrix portion of Andy's *Obsurd* [sic] *Guitar Tape* was blasting from a boombox. Ray turned down the joint the first time around. Then the second. But on the third, when Shannon said, "Music is way better when you're high," Ray took a big hit and coughed prodigiously.

Everyone laughed as he gulped warm beer.

"If the leaves rustle hard enough," Brandon observed, "maybe they can become rustle sprouts?"

"That's not a bad name for a band," Michael, now with orange hair, added.

Brandon walked over to a leaf scraping along the concrete. "C'mon, little buddy. Rustle with all you've got!"

"Hey, Ryan," Michael called. "Have you ever considered changing your name to Ryna?"

"No, why?"

"Because then it would rhyme with vagina. Ryna vagina."

"No one calls my brother a vagina," Shannon said to Michael. "No one but me. Now you have to eat this spoonful of peanut butter."

"With pleasure," Michael responded. Everyone watched as he chomped the glob in one fell swoop. The Hendrix portion of the tape switched to Van Halen. Michael's jaw worked overtime as he leaped up, grabbed his sabre, and danced to the beat.

The joint worked its way around. Ray took four hits and was properly stoned out of his gourd. For one precarious moment, his thoughts hovered over an edge in his mind. Down below was the dark place, the place that grew every Sunday, a pit in his mind filled with snapping crocodiles of fear, doubt, and sadness. He almost fell, down into the clenching turmoil, but a new Van Halen track started: "Love Walks In." He caught the melody like a lifeline, and it pulled him up and back to his friends. He was in a band, and there was no time for self-pity, he told himself. Everyone was laughing at Michael, still working on the glob of peanut butter.

When the joint burned to a roach, they put it out and went inside to jam. First, though, Shannon announced to the whole band the fact that a certain member, not naming names or pointing fingers (here she glanced at Tibbs), had yet to write a song. And that this had not gone unnoticed. She repeated, the whole time glaring at Tibbs, the expectation that everyone in the band writes.

Plug in. Tune up. Lights off. Blacklight on. Ryan counted off four beats and they started in on a new Danny composition, "Telepathic," but Ray couldn't play. He couldn't keep the rhythm. He was too stoned. Shannon sang harmonies to Danny's lead and danced around the room.

Every song I play is automatic

The message from the ship is telepathic

She jumped up on the couch for the chorus.

Here comes a funky groove

To make the earthlings move

Sorry to be so emphatic

It's coming to me …

It's telepathic

Before the second verse, Shannon went over to Ray.

"It's OK," she said, handing him a bag of Doritos. "I remember the first time I got high."

Right next to him was a closet full of old Halloween costumes. Shannon pulled out a giant pair of white wings and walked back into the room. Curtis finished the song with a sax solo inspired by the Stones' "Can't You Hear Me Knockin'." Ryan hit a final cymbal, and there was a little lull.

"What should we play next?" Michael asked.

Tibbs filled the silence with the opening notes to Pink Floyd's "Shine on You Crazy Diamond."

Ray closed his eyes. It was like he was floating, out into space, the music carrying him along.

Then he heard Shannon call out, "Ray's tune, 'Chain Reaction of Yawns,'" his first songwriting effort.

The black light illuminated a Led Zeppelin poster: the Swan Song logo, Led Zeppelin's record label. It portrayed Icarus, the ancient Greek youth, arms extended, reaching for the sun. Besides the black light, a single candle on a music stand allowed Shannon to read lyrics. Ray ate the Doritos and watched Shannon dance about with her wings bouncing to Tibbs's Stevie Wonder–inspired intro.

He watched her glide over to the microphone, stand in the center of the room, and belt out his words.

Yesterday stabbed daggers

Into my dawn

I shivered and staggered

All morning long

I was worn out and haggard

From all I've done wrong

In the moment that mattered

All I could do was yawn.

Ray licked his Dorito fingers as the song abruptly stopped. Shannon and all the Little Brothers executed mock yawns. He sat transfixed by the image of the winged Shannon gliding with the glowing Icarus behind her. She started the next verse.

Tomorrow pokes holes

Into my dreams

I'm sinking before

I row down life's streams

Nothing is real

As real as it seems

In the moment

that matters

All I can do is scream

Shannon let loose a piercing scream. Danny's fingers exploded into a solo while Brandon and Tibbs laid down a groove. Beneath it, Michael thumped a funky bassline, Curtis honked some low swing, and Ryan kept a steady beat. Ray closed his eyes and let the music sink in, trying to absorb it, hold it. The original riff was his. It was a simple three-note Stevie Wonder rip-off from a blues scale, but the song had grown. He tried to take in the various intertwining pieces, unraveling and coalescing like some kind of strange genetics. The music glided along. Ryan filled the spaces with staccato bursts. The band slowed down into the bridge like an elephant stepping onto a pond of ice.

Ray opened his eyes. Shannon stood over him with her wings glowing and enormous.

She leaned down and whispered the bridge lyrics, hovering inches above his face.

Now we're bound by a chain of yawns

Bound, bound by a chain of yawns

Shackle our dawns.

She was so close, he thought she was going to kiss him. Her eyes, dark in the low light, stared directly into his. Then, instead, from behind her massive white wings, she held out a glass of water.

"It's called cotton mouth," she said and signaled to the band. As a unit they found solid ground again and took off into another verse. Shannon pranced back to the music stand.

So, I started

A chain reaction of yawns

We're all the same

With the same-sized lawns

No knights or bishops

We're all just pawns

She looked at Ray from the center of the room, her wings in line with the poster's wings. He felt there was something mocking in her, teasing him.

I turn to tell you

But you've already gone

Where did you go?

Where have you gone?

Dave hit the strobe light, and the spell was broken. Ryan kicked in a new tempo, to match the lights. Danny and Brandon followed. Shannon danced off in the flashing light, her wings casting giant shadows on the wall. Ray closed his eyes, trying to follow, but it was harder now. It was like a wave pool, the energy coming at him from too many directions. As he turned to face one sound, a sound from another direction would hit him. He turned to face this new sound and another sound from another direction came crashing over him. He was spinning. He opened his eyes. No avail. The music was going faster. Curtis was wailing at the center of a merry-go-round out of control. Ray stood up. He ran. Past the waves of sound. The flashing wings. Up the stairs. Outside. To the porch, away.

He looked up at the clouds, the world spinning. He lay down and closed his eyes, nausea rising in his chest. He jumped up and made it to the bushes to puke, then staggered over to a lawn chair and lay back down, closed his eyes to the sound of his father's voice.

It was Brandon that shook him awake.

"You better go home," he said, offering him eye drops.

Ray walked to his house in drizzling rain, oblivious to Greg Bird's vomit-green Buick parked across the street. He went straight upstairs without greeting his mom. She came up and knocked on his door.

"I don't feel good," he said through the door. She came in.

"What's wrong?"

"I have a headache," he said, his head to the wall.

She came over and felt his forehead with her palm.

"I'll bring you some aspirin," she said. "You need some sleep. Your eyes are all red."

*

Once again, Pam Susan winked at Roberta Anderson. Once again, Roberta, in her blue suede shoes, followed the office assistant as she led the school board on a detour. Today's destination: the new foreign language lab in D hall. Across campus, the student union was at capacity. Bodies filled every available space.

Assistant Principal Pete Best walked to the microphone. "Welcome to our second week of open mic. It's exciting to see so many students supporting live art at Riverview High School!"

The students cheered with what Mr. Best perceived as legitimate enthusiasm.

"Reminder that the open mic is a forum for all types of artists and performers. If you are interested in performing, please see Ms. Susan in the office. She handles the weekly drawing, which is random. Also, I want to remind students of the decorum expected of all audience members."

Scott Kline, huddled on a couch with several other students, let loose a "booooo," a little too loudly. His face turned as red as his hair when he realized Pete had heard him.

Mr. Best cast his *test me again and see what happens* look.

"What happened last week, with students booing a juggler, is unacceptable," Mr. Best declared. "This is an open forum that encourages students to take risks, to gain experience performing, to grow, and to learn. Students that engage in behavior that is deemed harmful to this process will not only be prohibited from entering but will also face disciplinary consequences." He looked around the room. In the corner George gave him a *that's the ticket* nod. "Very good. Without further ado, let's get to today's art. First up we have the Windows, once again coming out on top of the drawing. Let's give them a hand."

Denny, Manny, Craig, and Morris walked onto the stage. The students in the crowd all turned toward each other as if to say, "Seriously, these guys again?" Morris wore all black, like it was some kind of uniform. He grabbed the mic on its stand and turned his back to the audience. Denny had brush sticks. Craig wore sunglasses and played a nylon-stringed classical guitar. Manny sat down and started playing long, droning chords on the organ setting of the electric keyboard.

"'The Fangled Critters,'" Morris said. Like the first performance, he started by speaking rather than singing. In between each verse, Craig played the classical guitar flamenco-style. Denny brushed a Latin beat. Manny floated a soft droning progression on his keyboard.

Snakeskin snorkel

Indian goggles

Brilliant bubbles

She swims in a disturbed river

Mississippi kiddie pool

Morris pulled up his thumb for a quick suck and started again.

You slip and slide thru the summer lawn

We are the blades of grass beneath you

Scorched by the sun

Drenched by the hose

Matted down by your eager wildness

We hear your laughter

On the verge of decay.

Another quick thumb suck, while Craig's fingers splayed across the strings.

Our lawn is a pasture

Without cows

We have no nipples to squeeze

The garage is pried open

The lawnmower sits throbbing

The gardener has a fever

Our wet dreams will receive her

Morris pulled the mic off the stand, crouched, and sang into the microphone in a soft, lilting voice. His hair covered his face.

Ignore the distress

And leave with the rest

The party is over

Punish the naked

With a four-leaf clover.

Morris collapsed into the fetal position and sucked his thumb. Manny put his head down on the keyboard, his forearms making one last forceful jarring sound. Denny eased the Latin rhythm, the brush sticks losing momentum like a pendulum slowly dying. Craig stepped to the middle of the stage and finished with a flourish of Spanish flamenco guitar.

Mr. Best came to the microphone. "Thank you. Once again … um … very interesting," he commented, clapping and motioning to the stunned audience that they should clap too. "Ladies and gentlemen, the Windows," he said, clapping a little louder. A few scattered students vaguely complied. "Up next, we have Bernie Rodgers, a ventriloquist, with his special guest, Good Company."

Twenty minutes later, Mr. Best stood with his eyes closed as another Riverview band, Gobbledegook, made their debut with a cover version of the Clash's "Train in Vain." His left hand matched the bass drum; his right hand stayed with the snare. He rolled his knuckles on his thigh for the drum roll, using both fists for a cymbal crash. Not bad, he thought. With a little guidance this drummer could be a legit percussionist.

He opened his eyes to see the students' smiling faces. Forty minutes earlier these same faces were tight, closed, eyes filled with insecurities, expressions of anxiety and doubt. Now they were relaxed and grooving to a beat. He removed his glasses, rubbed his eyes, and looked from the crowd to Gobbledegook, whose faces beamed with pride and satisfaction. He saw George in the corner, euphoric. And then Mr. Best's heart hit his stomach. He gulped, or tried to, but found he couldn't swallow. His hands, which had been loose and keeping a beat, now froze. His palms instantly slicked over with cold sweat at the image of Director Albert Francis standing in the doorway.

It wasn't the man's rigid posture that chilled Mr. Best to his core. It wasn't the curled lips or the expression on his face. It was his piercing blue eyes, livid with rage.

*

Two hours after Gobbledegook closed the second open mic, the 2:45 bell sounded, announcing the passing of another school day. Pete stood in the front foyer watching the flow of students off to fields, weight rooms, rehearsals, or myriad other extracurricular activities. It was subtle, Pete felt, but it was there. A little difference. A little less pressure to conform. Like wisps of electricity still reverberating after a big jolt.

Minutes later, once the flow lapsed into a dribble of stragglers, Pete went into his office and plopped down at the desk with a mountain range of paperwork. There were two messages on his phone. He picked up the receiver and listened. The first one was from Roy's school administrator, the other from his wife, Sandy. Roy had had another episode, headbutting a classmate. Pete picked up the phone to call his wife but put it back down. He rolled his fingers on his desk, arranging the papers into neat stacks, trying to decide where to begin, when he heard a low purring sound out in the hallway.

Moments later, George walked past his door, buffing the office hallway. George stopped and turned off the buffer. He retrieved a nearby cleaning cart and headed into Pete's office.

"George … ?" Pete began, but he didn't know how to finish off his question.

George stood in front of him, waiting, his dark brown eyes open wide.

Pete opened his mouth as two math teachers appeared outside the open door and started a conversation about a recent test.

"Ummm …" Pete managed with raised eyebrows. "How do you like the new Floor Buffer 3000?" he asked finally, arranging his papers, even though they already stood in neat, perfectly aligned stacks.

"There's something in the way it moves," George said, emptying the garbage. "It buffs the floor like no other."

"That's good," Pete said. "I'll be sure to pass that on to the board. They were reluctant to spring for it." He lowered his voice. "So, about this open mic—"

"There's something in the shine that I know," George said, replacing the liner of the wastebasket. "I don't need no other buffer."

The teachers in the hallway moved on.

"Hmm, yes, I've noticed the halls are really gleaming," Pete said. "Now, if we could cut to the chase. Director Francis—"

"Something in the machine's style that shows me," George said, dusting the shelves. "I don't want to leave it now."

"Yes, it's a fine machine," Pete conceded, throwing up his arms and accidentally knocking over one of his stacks of papers. He sighed and stood to pick them up. With the clutter of papers in his hands, he went to his doorway, scanned the hallway, and noted that the coast was clear.

"Have you heard anything, George?" he asked hastily, almost in a whisper. "Anything about the open mics?"

"You know I believe. I believe and how."

"You believe," Pete repeated. "You believe … what exactly? Did Director Francis say something? Does the school board know? Why do they keep showing up on days when we have open mic? What about Superintendent Jag? What are they saying? Have you spoken with the custodian Richard Starkey at the district office?"

George started to water the plants.

Pete closed his eyes, clenched his fists, and used his knuckles to massage his temples. His phone started ringing. He knew it was Sandy.

"I have been trying a new fertilizer," George said.

Pete opened his eyes and looked from the floor to the plants. "What? Fertilizer? Well, they *are* very healthy-looking plants," he said, at a loss. He dropped the mess of papers on his desk.

"If you're asking me how much these plants will grow," George said, "I don't know. Stick around though, and it may show. I don't know. I. Don't know."

Pete nodded and exhaled a deep breath. "I hope to stick around for a long time," he said. "An assistant principal's work, like a custodian's, is never finished." He executed a *ba-dum-tss* with his right palm on his desk. "Now George, can you at least tell me—"

Pam Susan came in with a knock, carrying a stack of envelopes.

Pete smiled, hesitated, and recovered "—if you'll be able to have the gymnasium buffed before tomorrow's home volleyball game?"

"Something in the way it buffs," George said. "And all I have to do is think about it."

Pete nodded, adjusting the perfect knot on his tie. He let the phone go to voicemail.

"Your mail," Pam said, dropping the stack of envelopes. "Also, Superintendent Jag said that your assessment of the new senior parking plan needs to be rewritten."

Pete frowned. "Did she say why?" he asked, flipping through the mail.

Pam shook her head and pointed at her watch. It was 3:01, the end of her contract hours, which she honored meticulously. She turned and walked out.

"George," Pete implored, looking into George's deep brown eyes. "Be straight with me. Do you think this whole thing is …"

Just then a crowd of teachers streamed by, heading to a meeting.

"I mean … do you think, George, that what I'm doing, what we're doing …" Pete's voice trailed off. At the bottom of the stack was a postcard from Las Vegas featuring the famous sign. It was from Henry Martin, a former Riverview High School music teacher from when Pete was in school. Director Francis, according to rumor, had edged him out for doing soul music. For the last twenty years, instead of arranging music for high school theaters, he had transitioned to arranging flowers. There was only one sentence, in all caps: THE KING IS ALIVE.

The thoughts inside Pete's head became like disconnected gears spinning. Levi King—alive? Sure, there were a few rumors back in the day amongst Riverview musicians that Levi King was alive and still performing, but Pete had never believed them. There was never any hard evidence. "Levi King is alive," Pete heard himself say out loud. And suddenly it was as if all basic facts might not be what they seem. Questions rose to his consciousness like bubbles bursting. Where has Levi been all these years? What did it mean? Did it change anything? Pete's phone rang. He answered it, his arm and voice acting more out of reflex than conscious thought.

"Hello. Yes, dear, I was just going to call you. I heard all about it."

Sandy started in, so that Pete didn't hear or notice as George wheeled his cart out of the office, saying, "You know I believe and how in the Floor Buffer 3000."

*

Brandon and Danny pulled into White Hen Pantry. They followed their routine. Drinks. Wait for the store to be empty.

"Hi," Danny said. "It's a perfect day outside."

Lou smiled. "When it gets dark, it's time to go home," he remarked, bagging their items. They paid and left.

*

Sunday afternoon. Matt Welsh lowered the needle on "All that I Need Is Jesus" from an old record called *Echoes of the Sacred Harp*. He lay down on the couch as the music floated up into the room. His body ached: fatigue from the week, as well as a low-pressure system moving in off the lake caused his hip to throb. The good Lord provides, Matt thought, and that includes time to rest.

His head hit the pillow and soon he was far away, remembering …

Growing up in the Deep South, his father was the pastor of the Second Baptist Church of Tupelo (after a split with the First over accepting members saved in another denomination). For Matt and his twin brother, Alfie, seeing their father preach from the pulpit every Sunday was a guiding light to the glory of God. Their childhood revolved around the church, singing in the choir, and learning the piano from their mother. During their teenage years, however, Alfie began to stray. He would sneak out at night with older kids, driving across Tupelo and as far as Memphis, slinking into house parties, juke joints, Elks Lodges, fairgrounds—anywhere and everywhere—with big bands playing swing, blues, and boogie-woogie. One night, not long after their sixteenth birthday, a month before Japan bombed Pearl Harbor, Matt followed Alfie on one of his adventures and witnessed it firsthand: sin. Sex and loose women, alcohol, cigarettes, suggestive lyrics about animals, and a primitive rhythm that sounded like the very drums of Hell. He grabbed Alfie by the ear and drove him home, only to be struck head-on by a drunk driver on a two-lane country road. Matt swerved too late. His brother died. Matt suffered five broken bones, including a shattered femur and hip.

Staying behind with the world at war tested Matt's faith. He felt broken and useless, lying in bed day after day, cast off into a desert of self-pity like a servant in the Old Testament. Until his mother wheeled the Victrola into his room along with the family's collection of gospel records. The music lifted his spirit, got him back to the chapel, singing in the choir with a new purpose. That's when he met his wife, Bobby Jean. The Lord healed his broken body and his wounded spirit. In six months, they were married and he started working for a pie plant, delivering frozen cream cheesecakes. When the war ended, Matt accepted a promotion to a northern suburb of Chicago. There was no Baptist church, but Matt found the leadership of the Riverview Presbyterian Ministry closely aligned with the Baptists, or close enough, and he and Bobby Jean joined the choir. It wasn't long before Matt won a seat on the local town council. The years began to flow by, like water through a broken-down dam.

"Matt?"

It was Bobby Jean.

"The telephone is for you."

Matt sat up. It was raining outside. The record was still spinning, but it was no longer playing the sweet sounds of the Lord's music. Matt rubbed his eyes and picked up the phone in his study.

"Board Member Welsh, this is Director Francis. We have a situation."

*

"Trevor, dinner is ready."

Roxanne Gradenko returned to the kitchen and finished setting the table. She placed the silverware and poured two glasses of milk: one for her older son, Trevor, and one for his little brother, Cotter. She put the plates on the table, along with a salad bowl.

"Diiiin-ner," she called, poking her head into the hallway, primping her Princess Diana–styled hair in the mirror.

She sat down while Cotter washed his hands. He plopped in the chair and shoved a roll in his mouth.

"Honey," Roxanne said. "Wait until your brother gets here and we can say the blessing. TREVOR!"

They sat together for a minute. Roxanne watched Cotter play with his fork.

"Unbelievable." Roxanne stood up and tossed her napkin down on the table. "Wait here. Don't take another bite."

She went out into the hallway and up the stairs. "Get your butt down here, mister," she called as she rounded the staircase. She knocked on his door as she opened it and found Trevor sitting at his desk, back toward the door, headphones on.

"Trevor," Roxanne said with a huff. "I've been shouting for you to come to dinner." She pulled out the headphone wire connected to the stereo. Suddenly Prince's voice filled the room.

"What on earth are you listening to?"

Trevor made a move for the stereo, but Roxanne blocked him.

"Oh, my." Roxanne's jaw dropped. Her face turned bright red.

"What?" Trevor demanded.

Roxanne hit the stop button on his tape deck. She pulled the tape from the stereo. "*Dirty Minds*? What on earth has gotten into you?"

"Mom, it's only music. I don't even know what the words mean."

*

"Hello," Courtney Harrison answered the telephone. She was slicing peppers.

"Hi, Court."

"Hey, Rox."

"How's it going, dear?"

"Oh, you know," Courtney replied.

"How's it going with Nico?" Roxanne asked. In the background, Cotter was watching *Star Wars* and making blaster sounds.

"Not so good," Courtney said. "I caught her with pot again on Saturday."

"You're kidding."

"No. I wish I was. I thought we got through to her. But apparently not." She held the knife suspended over the cutting board.

Roxanne moved into the pantry. "How did you find it?"

"A joint fell out of her jacket. Right onto the kitchen floor."

"That's terrible. Where is she getting it? Remember, the Just Say No! coordinator says to work with local law enforcement to follow the drugs to their source."

"She denies everything. She says it belongs to her boyfriend, Chris. I did finally get her to tell me that he buys it at White Hen Pantry."

"Let me write that down. White Hen, the one on Riverview Road?"

"That's the only one I know of," Courtney said. "I'm afraid I have to cancel our movie plans next weekend. We're going to have a mother-daughter weekend and try to come to an understanding. Sorry." Courtney started slicing again.

"Oh, I don't mind. We can see it another time," Roxanne said.

"How's the weekend after?"

"Not so good. I'm going to a trade show downtown. A lot of the big department stores are selling off their fine china. The industry thinks there's a big demise in china, but I see opportunity for my little store. High-quality bone china for dirt cheap."

"I don't know how you run a home goods store and the Just Say No! program while raising two boys," Courtney said. "With a husband always on the road."

"It's a balancing act for sure." Roxanne peeked out at Cotter diving over the couch and blasting.

"*Pew. Pew.*"

Courtney grabbed more peppers and sliced off their stems.

"Listen, there's another reason I called," Roxanne said, moving back into the pantry.

"I'm listening." Courtney kept the tip of the knife on the cutting board and divided each pepper into halves and then fourths.

"Is Nico listening to a lot of music, like Trevor and a lot of kids these days?"

"Sure. She always has her headphones on. It drives me crazy. I had to take her Walkman away just last week."

"*Me too.* Drives me nuts. It's like a wall between Trevor and me."

"It *is* like a wall."

"Does Nico listen to Prince?"

"Prince? I don't know. I think there's a queen. Not sure about a prince."

"The other night I was calling Trevor down to dinner. And I just kept calling and calling. Over and over again with dinner getting cold. I go upstairs to his room, and he's got his headphones on. I pull the plug and hear the most offensive, dirty filth I could imagine."

"No." Courtney held the knife aloft, like somehow the peppers where now contaminated.

"It was a song about—you'll never believe."

"What?"

"Oral sex."

"Get out!" Courtney cut her thumb. "Ouch." She hurried to the sink and ran water over the bleeding cut.

"Are you OK?"

"Fine. I just cut my thumb." She winced. "A deep one. What were you saying about the song?"

"It's about some hunk seducing a virgin on her way to her wedding. Giving her head. In the song the virgin actually *comes* on her wedding dress."

"That's terrible. It really is." The wad of paper towel Courtney held up to the cut turned bright red.

"The album is by this Prince fellow, and it's got a real doozy of a title, I can just tell you. It's called *Dirty Minds.*"

"Why would Trevor—? How would he even—?"

"I'm way ahead of you,' Roxanne said. "The songs are all like that. Complete rubbish. There's a song about incest. It's called 'Sister.' You can imagine where it goes from there."

"Goodness." Courtney kept up the pressure on her wound.

"Not only that, but the sister is twice his age. Which makes it pedophilia. It's disgusting."

"I'm speechless."

"The thing about it is, even though the title is suggestive, there really is no way for parents to *really* know what our kids are listening to."

"Like a rating for movies."

"Exactly," Roxanne said. "Music has no rating system. Nothing for language or subject matter or anything. They could be listening to literally anything."

"Hmmm. Well, I'm glad you shared that. I'll have to investigate Nico's tapes. What did you say that musician's name was, the one with the blowjob song?"

"His name is Prince. Court, we've got to do something. Drugs and music are rotting our kids' brains."

"What can we do?" Courtney asked.

"I'll think of something."

The two friends said their goodbyes and hung up. Courtney went to the bathroom for a bandage. Roxanne stepped out of the pantry. Han, Luke, Chewy, and Princess Leia were in the garbage compactor.

*

Riverview Board of Education

Riverview High School Auditorium

Workshop Meeting 7:30 p.m.

<u>*Call to Order*</u>

<u>*Document Approval*</u>

Minutes of Monday, September 13, 1982

<u>*Business*</u>

#6450 Student Drug and Alcohol Policy, providing mandatory suspension of any student who either uses, possesses, or distributes drugs or alcohol during school hours or on school property, or who attends any school activity under the influence of drugs and alcohol. PASSED 7–0

Rushed distribution of Nancy Reagan's Just Say No! anti-drug program materials in schools K-12. PASSED 7–0

Roxanne Gradenko introduced recommendations from the Parents Music Resource Center, a Washington, DC, advocacy group, to require local music vendors to label records deemed threatening. Further research required.

Booster club members Jack Haley and Alan Mayer proposed that the board and club jointly fund the construction of an all-weather outdoor track to be ready potentially for the fall 1983 season.

Pete Best submitted a vote for new octagon tables in the lunchroom. DENIED 6–1 (Roberta Anderson dissenting).

Any music used as curriculum or in extracurricular activities at Riverview High School must undergo a new approval process designed by Director Francis. APPROVED 6-1 (Roberta Anderson dissenting).

Roberta Anderson submitted a motion to remove the Ten Commandments from Riverview classrooms and restrict prayer by Riverview students. DENIED 6-1.

A restraining order has been issued for Riverview resident and Craftwood Lumber owner Jim Plant for obstructing board proceedings.

<u>Items from the Commission</u>

As Introduced

<u>Items from the Staff</u>

As Introduced

<u>Adjournment</u>

*

Brandon and Danny pulled into White Hen Pantry. They followed their routine. Drinks. Wait for the store to be empty.

"Hi," Danny said. "It's a perfect day outside."

Lou smiled. "Instead of feeding animals in the zoo," he replied, "why don't you guys go see a movie?" He bagged their items, winked, and smiled. It was a crazy smile, they agreed in the car later. The smile of a madman.

When they opened the bag they found, instead of a bag of weed, what looked like a pad of miniature stamps with little bananas on each square.

*

That night rain clouds hung low over the Golding household. The steady pitter-patter sound was like fingers tapping on the windows.

"Put it on the tip of your tongue," Shannon instructed.

Danny, Tibbs, Michael, Ray, Brandon, and Curtis each reached forward for a small white square with a little yellow banana. "La la la," Danny sang with his tongue extended.

"It should start working in about thirty minutes," Shannon said.

Ray sat on the couch in the living room and, for a moment, panic seized him. What if he fell down into his hidden fears? What if his band found out about his anxiety that snapped at him like a crocodile in his nightmares? How long could he keep the secret of his father? What if he couldn't handle this drug? But there was no time to be anxious. Michael poked him with his sabre, and it was time to play music.

After a quick nod to Dave and Amber playing checkers, they went down to the basement and started to jam. Lights off. Blacklight on. Plug in. Tune up. They played three tunes back-to-back: the Stones' "Confessin' the Blues," Joan Jett's "I Love Rock 'n Roll," and Little Richard's "Jenny, Jenny." Without stopping, at the end of the Little Richard tune, Shannon gave Danny a signal. It was up to him to pick the next song. He segued into his own original composition, "No Clocks in Space." That's when it all started.

Shannon clicked on the strobe. Tibbs watched the wings of the Zeppelin Swan Song figure start to flap on the poster. He stopped playing to rub his eyes when the figure flew off into the air. He watched as it flew higher and the wings caught fire. He wasn't really thinking—more like reacting. He set down his guitar, grabbed an empty cardboard box that was sitting on the floor, and jumped up on the sofa. He reached up, cranked the window open, and held the box out, right at the level of the ground outside. He watched as the flaming Swan Song figure fluttered close to a bookshelf filled with records and songbooks. Once some rain had collected in the box, he dashed over, tripped over Ray, and flung water at the Swan Song figure, only to have it fly off like a butterfly.

The water hit Brandon on the keyboards, startling him. "What was that?" Brandon asked. "A box of rain?"

"What?" Curtis asked, licking a new reed.

"What's with the box of rain?" Brandon shouted into his microphone.

The band shifted to the Dead tune. Tibbs staggered to his feet. Shannon was too busy dancing, so Danny started singing the first verse.

With mounting terror, Tibbs watched the burning-winged figure soar across the room. "He's burning down the house!" he shouted.

Curtis heard the call clearly and, with his sax, steered the band over to the Talking Heads song like an engineer on a runaway train. The band struggled to follow but managed to kick into gear with Shannon stepping up to the mic for a "Watch out!"

To his dismay, Tibbs saw the figure with flaming wings land, set small fires here and there, and take to the air again. Barreling over to the mini fridge, Tibbs pulled out a water bottle and set about putting out all the little fires in the room, spraying water into the strobe light. Shannon sang, "Burnin' down the house!"

Michael, feeling the splatter of water and seeing the open window, called out, "Is it raining in here?"

Danny thought he heard Michael call out the Buddy Holly tune "Raining in My Heart." As Shannon finished singing "fight fire with fire," Danny signaled Michael and Ryan. The band swerved over, like a car that's about to miss an exit on a highway, to the Buddy Holly song. They sputtered and stalled but managed somehow to navigate the tempo shift. Shannon signaled the band into the new number.

They didn't make it past the first verse. Tibbs thought the winged figure had landed on Brandon, so he rushed over and doused him with water, crying, "He's burning you!"

Brandon, still wiping off his glasses after the box of rain, heard "Burning for You." He shrugged and signaled the band. Ray managed to get Ryan to follow him into the opening riff. Tibbs gave up trying to put out all the individual fires and decided to go for the figure that was now like a butterfly changing colors from orange and yellow to a dazzling blue. To

Tibbs's horror, he saw that the flames on the wings had progressed to the figure's flesh.

"It's burning up!" he shrieked, spraying another bottle.

Ray heard "Burning Love." Before Shannon even started the first verse of "Burnin' for You," he jerked the band to the Elvis tune, and they veered musically like a spinning vehicle that had lost all semblance of control.

Michael, fed up with the shifting songs, called out, "What's Going On?" causing Danny to play the Marvin Gaye song, but the rest of the band kept going with the Elvis tune as Tibbs tried in vain to drench the fiery winged creature.

Finally, Shannon screamed at the top of her lungs into the mic. "STOOOOOOOOOOOOP!" The band screeched to a halt.

"Do you guys hear that?" Everyone was dripping wet. Tibbs watched the winged figure land on a wet blotch of carpet, stop drop and roll, and, with a fizzle, return to the poster with a trail of smoke.

"It sounds like the garage door," Ryan said.

"Mom and Dad."

"I thought they were at Ravinia."

Brandon looked out the windows that peeked over the ground. "It's raining cats and dogs. The show must have been canceled."

"What do we do?"

"I'll handle it," Shannon said. "They already think I'm crazy. I'll tell them I'm thinking of diving again. That will make them happy. Scatter. Meet at the Lyman House in an hour, by the old schoolhouse. Someone bring a guitar and keep it dry."

*

In the confusion that followed, Tibbs and Ray managed to slip out the garage door with a guitar and an umbrella. They walked the half mile to the Riverview Historic Village. (Ray knew the village from the rite of passage known as Prairie Day, a full-day field trip for fourth-grade Riverview students when everyone including the teachers did their best to dress up in clothes from the mid-1800s and travel back in time. As far as Tibbs and the rest of the Little Brothers knew—along with the growing number of other

Riverview teenagers experimenting with pot—the empty buildings made a perfect place to meet and smoke on the weekends. The lock on the gate was old and could easily be picked with a paperclip, a trick that also helped with clogged marijuana pipes.)

Tibbs and Ray arrived at the old cabin to find the door cracked open. There was candlelight and the sound of acoustic Delta blues.

Mmm-mmm-mm-mmmmmmmm

Mmm-mmm-mmm-mmMM

Tibbs peered in. There was a young man wearing a white three-piece suit, a white tie, and a white felt hat. He sat cross-legged on a stool in the corner. His suit was immaculate. He wore wire-rimmed glasses and had a short, neat, pointed goatee. The man started to sing. Tibbs and Ray recognized the tune as "Come on in My Kitchen."

You can play this song

You can play along

Just come on, in my kitchen,

cuz it's going to be raining outdoors—

Tibbs pushed on the door. It creaked, and the man stopped playing. He turned to Tibbs.

"Well, what do we have here?" he said. "A couple of insurance salesmen." The neck of his guitar slithered up his shoulder like a snake.

"Are you real?" Ray asked.

"I'm as real as anything in this world," the man responded.

The snake curled around his back to his other shoulder.

"What's your name?" Tibbs inquired.

"They used to call me the Gentleman at the Crossroads," the man said. "You can consider me a tradesman. I make trades." He coughed, and used his gleaming white handkerchief to wipe his mouth. They could see that the cough had produced a bright red splotch of blood.

The snake hissed. He smacked it on top of the head. It snapped back into the shape of a guitar neck, and he played a few reedy licks, effortlessly moving from hen-picking to a slide to a chucka-chucka rhythm. It sounded like there were at least seven guitars in the room.

"Do you like that?" the man asked, licking his lips. Tibbs and Ray could see in the candlelight that he was sweating profusely. There was a dab of blood still on his lips. "I learned it a long time ago. Long before men came along and named this land Illinois." The guitar wailed a mournful note. "Or Chicago. How do you like that? A word for a stinky onion."

The guitar made a somber, crying sound.

The man looked at the guitar case in Ray's hand. "Do you want to play or are you just carrying around luggage?" he said, moving his tongue along his front teeth. He used the handkerchief to wipe the sweat from his brow. Then he coughed, and a drop of bright red blood landed on his lapel.

"Um …" Ray mumbled, looking at Tibbs.

"Because I can help you *really* play."

A Delta blues guitar lick exploded and reverberated around the cabin. They looked for other players in the corners of the dark room. The man's fingers were a blur of ferocious picking. The tempo accelerated, faster and faster, until smoke poured out of the sound hole and floated up. His guitar burst into flames, which he extinguished with a chucka-chucka rhythm. The muted strings popped and sizzled as he smacked beats with his palm, knuckles thudding the body with hollow off-beats. A few final puffs floated up. The smoke cleared, revealing his wide smile fading into rigid anguish while he used his ring finger to slide up, bend and hold a high bluesy note. He grimaced, doubled over, and held the note. Slowly, he released the note as the torment gave way to bliss. He settled into a slow, grinding twelve bars as a siren sounded in the distance.

"Uh-oh," the man said. "Do you hear that? Riverview's favorite instrument, playing Riverview's favorite song. You boys better think twice about playing the Gentleman's music in this town. They're going to shut you down. Just like they did to that first group of white boys."

The siren was getting louder.

"They'll say, 'Quit playin' that devil music.'"

He laughed a wheezy laugh, twisting the point of his goatee. "But no one says you have to stay around here." His laugh turned into a cough. He made use of the other side of his handkerchief. Ray and Tibbs noticed his suit wasn't, in fact, clean, but dirty with frayed sleeves.

There was the siren and the rain and the rhythmic sound of the man picking and strumming the blues.

"I once made a deal with a man that hid in this very house. Right underneath these floorboards. Yes indeed. All it takes is a handshake. He made a simple agreement. A bargain."

The siren was getting louder.

"And they shut it down for him too." He cleared his throat, studying the two young men. "'Not in this town,' they said." He shrugged. "Before him, I made deals with Natives. A whole tribe used to live along that old dried-up riverbed. Used to flow something fierce. And long *long* ago, I even made deals with the animals. They had their own music. The wild horse and the buffalo and the mountain lion and the deer."

He played the first riff again, this time soft and controlled. Still there was the sound of the rain and the siren. Ray and Tibbs stood in the doorway transfixed, looking at the blur of his long, thin fingers as he launched into another picking pattern.

"But that music is gone now. Gone forever. No one will ever know what it sounded like. Gone with the prairies. Gone with the forests and rivers. Farms and dams now. Gone with the—"

There was a crash of thunder. He stuck his index finger deep inside his ear and began digging, like an insect had burrowed deep inside. "I guess I should be going now, too," he managed before another coughing fit. The fit passed and he spat blood on the floor. "Remember, if you ever want to make a trade, you know where to find me. All it takes is a handshake." He licked his lips, smiled, and played one last turn around and disappeared into the floor. "I believe I'm sinkin' down," he said with one final haunting glance.

For some reason, Ray felt an urge to tell Tibbs about everything. His dad, Sundays, the nightmares. "Tibbs," he began. "I've something I need to tell you—"

The siren was upon them. Shannon burst into the cabin. "Don't just stand there! Cops!"

They all scattered outside to the sound of the approaching sirens, thinking they were busted, dead to rights, only to hear the siren pass them on Waukegan Road, stopping a block ahead where there was a bad car accident smoldering in the rain. Two cars had T-boned. One of the cars was a vomit-green Buick.

*

It was Monday, late afternoon. Pete Best wandered the empty hallways. Another phone call from home, another incident with his son, Roy. This time headbutting and breaking a glass window. Stitches. Another argument with Sandy. Another meeting with the marriage counselor on the calendar, meetings that went nowhere.

This was a mistake, he thought. This whole thing. Stupid. That's not how the world works. You can't change the past. You can't return to the scene of a crime and think you can undo what has been done. Bring rock and roll to Riverview. What a fool!

His office was the last place he wanted to go, but there was work to be done with tomorrow's deadline. The paperwork was incessant. Walking the empty halls helped him think, get away from all of it. Footsteps and the sound of squeaky wheels interrupted his train of thought. He slowed his pace as he rounded the corner and saw Eddie Severino, the night custodian, pushing a waste cart and coming toward him.

"Evening, Eddie," Pete said as he approached.

He got nothing in response but a cold shoulder and creaking wheels echoing down the hall. What the hell? What is it with this place? It was like he had some horrible disease, and any kindness would lead to an infection. Sure, he had George, but sometimes Pete wondered if George was all there. Like maybe he was playing a few cards short of a deck. And then there's Jim Plant, having to be restrained and handcuffed at a board meeting. Not exactly a stable ally. And then, this crazy new idea he had been entertaining. Levi King.

It's too much, Pete thought. It can't be done. I'm all alone, playing the fool. Mudfest, open mic … who am I kidding? Roy's school isn't what we expected. It's only a matter of time until it all crashes down. Director Francis won't sit back. I might as well resign now before they fire me. Maybe I can get my old job back.

Pete stood in the flickering light of D hall. Ahead of him, Eddie rounded with his groaning cart. Pete turned and saw his old locker. D121. For a moment he was opening it up again, seeing all those cut-out pictures on his locker door, the bands he and the Quarrymen had discovered: the Cardinals, the Swallows, the Four Bars of Rhythm, the Five Blue Notes, the Melodaires, the Armstrong Four, and the Clovers. It was as if all the pictures were still there and had never been taken down.

In his mind, Pete slammed his locker shut. Like hell I'll quit. I've only just begun. He turned on his heel and strode from D hall, heading straight to his office. When he reached the main office, he stopped in his tracks. His door was closed. He had left it open; he was certain. It was part of his policy. To always have an open door. He reached the threshold and heard the murmuring voices. He swallowed hard, gripped the doorknob, and twisted.

There they were, like an evil horde. Superintendent Jag, Board President Brandt, Matt Welsh, and a couple of the other board members whose names he couldn't think of now but who always reminded him somehow of zombies. And in the corner, with those bright blue eyes and that wicked grin, Director Francis.

*

An hour later, the business was done, and the office was empty. Eddie pushed a vacuum through the main office, the motor filling the air with an inconsistent whir of struggle. He stopped outside Pete's office and noticed two pieces of mail in the trash can he had emptied earlier in the night. He stepped inside, picked up first a torn envelope and a crumpled letter and read the address on the envelope: the Village Music Shoppe. He uncrumpled and read the short note addressed to Pete the Beat informing him that the Village Music Shoppe had a new a guitar teacher: Rik Frets. It was signed, Tap. The second was a postcard of the Hollywood Hills. The back had one sentence written on it. It said: On The King's Trail, signed by Henry Martin.

*

At 8:58 Tuesday morning, Leslie Bangs settled into her cubicle, still waiting for the aspirin to take the edge off her headache.

"Hey Leslie," Jane whispered, swiveling her chair to look at Leslie from her cubicle. "Did you hear? Greg was in a bad car accident."

"What?"

"Saturday night," Jane said. "They took him to the hospital in Lowland Park. A drunk teenager ran a red light. It doesn't look good. Kent Davies is our acting editor. They sent him from the *Lowland Park Press*."

Leslie absorbed the news. Greg Bird, the editor that had controlled this newsroom with an iron fist for thirty years. Car accident. Kent Davies, an unknown. "That's terrible," she heard herself say.

"Isn't it?" Jane said, swiveling away. "Awful. Anyway, like the mail, the news never stops. I've got to finish this article about RHS Assistant Principal Pete Best. Apparently, they're sending him on a learning tour of area high schools. Why hire the guy if you're going to send him away? Plus, I have a source telling me Principal Merchant is still on summer break."

"Interesting," Leslie said, rubbing her chin as if calculating another clue. She turned and pulled from her typewriter the story she had been working on over the weekend. More tedium about the union at the Sara Sweet factory: a debacle of an ice cream social from the opposition union candidate. She pulled out a red pen and began to proofread. Kent Davies, she reminded herself, nodded, and again began to read. She had to read the first sentence three times before it registered in her brain.

FULL MOON

To the east of Riverview, the sun rose above the trees surrounding the water plant in Lowland Park. One block away, the plant's superintendent, Rod P. Pringle Jr., and the plant's architect, Arthur N. Coffin Jr., sat at their usual Sunday breakfast at the Sunrise Café, looking out over the lake. The main topic thus far had been possible uses for the old, empty laboratories on the ground floor. When none of the proposed ideas seemed desirable, they left that subject and moved on to their respective sons and the increasingly unlikely possibility that either would follow in the family trades of engineering and architecture, respectively.

"All mine wants to do is sit around and play guitar," Pringle Jr. said, taking a bite of bacon. "His grades are shit."

"Funny," Coffin Jr. responded, sipping his coffee. "Mine does nothing but strum all day in the garage. We make him do an hour of homework before he can play. Otherwise, he won't even *sniff* his schoolwork. Music is all these kids on our street do. It's coming out of every garage. They wouldn't know a job if it smacked them in the face."

They looked at each for a long moment.

"You don't think … ?" Pringle Jr. broached tentatively. "Maybe turn those labs into a venue?"

"I don't see why not. If you can't beat 'em, join 'em."

*

It was a drizzly late September Thursday night in Riverview. Gusts of wind yanked leaves off the trees. Rick Ocase pulled off Waukegan and parked his mustard-yellow Buick LeSabre outside the Riverview Public Library. He watched the leaves dance, bright yellows, reds, and oranges. Sometimes they formed little tornadoes, or a swath of them rushed in a bold gust, or they drifted into the street, or they got trapped in places and formed restless piles. Rick pulled out his trusty steel thermos, poured a cup of steaming coffee, and watched the leaves.

First, they lost Robbie to a heart attack. Now they'd lost Greg to a senseless and tragic accident. And in the wake of these tragedies, Easton, their real estate guru, up and moved to Florida. A deal he couldn't pass up. That left Rick, Matt, and Oren, except Oren's vision was going, claimed he couldn't drive at night. So now it was just him and Matt, with the leader's shakes getting noticeably worse at the last meeting.

They still had a strong police presence. At the last meeting, Chief Gordon Sumner provided some alarming statistics about the rising rates of alcohol and drug use amongst minors in Riverview. The drugs were getting more serious. The drinking and driving had claimed three lives in the past month, including Greg's. Deputy Copeland and Sergeant Winter testified that they were regularly finding pot in the middle schools and even found it on the playground of Wilmot Elementary. The source of the drugs remained elusive, but they had some leads.

Rick blew on his coffee and watched a family walking out of the library. The wind inverted the young mother's umbrella. She struggled with it but didn't stop moving, pulling her children along in the wind and rain. A pile of leaves trapped by the bike rack swirled free and surrounded the family. The mom attempted to hurry her children along, but they resisted. With one hand she held the busted umbrella; with the other she pulled the children, who only wanted to play in the twirling leaves.

It was like a painting, Rick thought. The bright yellow raincoats. The dark blue bag of books. The green upside-down umbrella. The blurred colors of the leaves surrounded by the gray concrete and brown bricks. The faces of the children contrasted with the face of the mother.

And then Rick wasn't seeing the young family. He was seeing the family he never had. He let himself imagine Suzie and their children, and that Suzie wouldn't be dragging and berating their children like this mother.

No. Suzie would let the children enjoy the moment, get lost inside those little leaf tornadoes, have fun and laugh—

Stop it, Rick told himself. Stop. Because of where it leads. He took a gulp of coffee.

They still had six out of seven members of the school board, but now Greg's seat was open. And on the town council, with Easton moving away and another Dasher retiring, suddenly instead of 9–0, they had two seats up for election. Young families new to Riverview wanted to get involved. Rick was smart. He knew the tide was turning.

It was five o'clock. Two minutes later, like always, Suzie came out of the library. She wore her pink raincoat and black boots. She pulled along her rolling case, and Rick imagined what her usual haul contained: poetry, history, a biography … his girl was so smart. She walked around the corner to where she usually parked, over by the park and the police station, and drove away.

Rick sipped his coffee and watched the leaves.

*

Thursday night, rehearsal night at the Golding household. Ray was playing bar chords. They sounded good. He looked around and turned his amp up.

They were waiting on Tibbs. Danny was at the keyboard blazing through scales. At the home computer, Ryan was playing his father in the Earl Weaver simulated baseball playoffs. Michael was watching and doing play-by-play with his sabre as a mic. Shannon was up in her room, listening to music. Dave was teaching his now nine-year-old sister, Amber, how to play chess. Brandon was reading the *Riverview Review*. Curtis was swabbing the tone holes in his sax. Ray sat in the middle of it all, strumming, listening to the cacophony. Lately, his nightmares had been less vivid, calmer, muted for some reason.

"Hey, check this out," Brandon said, passing the paper over to Ray.

Ray glanced and read the headline out loud. "'New Assistant Principal of Riverview High to Go on an Extended Tour of Local Schools.'"

"No," Brandon said. "Below that."

"'Sara Sweet Factory Labor Boss Touts Reaganomics.'"

"No, not that either. Down at the bottom, in the Notes Around Town."

"'Lowland Park Water Tower to Serve as Venue for Local Youth Music Acts. Auditions This Weekend.'"

"Alan Freed hits a three-run shot to left," Michael called out. "The Bluebirds take a commanding three-run lead in the seventh."

"We should check it out," Brandon suggested.

Danny came over. "I'll check with my spaceship," he said.

"Deep drive down the line," Michael cried. "Gone! Back-to-back bombs for Charles Berry and the Bluebirds. Unbelievable."

Two innings later, Tibbs showed up and Shannon came down the stairs. Curtis had reassembled his sax and started blowing, adding to the din.

"Hello, Tibbs," Shannon said, plugging in her mic. "Do you have a song?"

Tibbs smiled. "Still working on it," he said.

"Figured. Let's open with 'See See Rider,'" she called out. "Hey, who tampered with my microphone?"

Dave and the Little Brothers all exchanged glances.

"It smells like ass."

Danny and Brandon burst into laughter.

Shannon glared at them. "What did you do?"

"Nothing," they parroted simultaneously. Danny coughed to stifle his mirth.

"You know, I did hear something rattling around Ryan's bass drum," Brandon suggested.

"What? What are you talking about?" Ryan asked.

Shannon walked over and inspected the drum.

"What the … ?" She held up a spray can. "Liquid Butt. Fart spray? Are you guys serious?"

"I didn't do it," Ryan pleaded. "It wasn't me."

She turned and started spraying. The air filled with odor, mock protest, and laughter.

*

On the Saturday of the last weekend in September, Shannon and the Little Brothers drove east to the water tower in nearby Lowland Park. Another rainy day. They arrived at two fifteen, and there was already a line out the door. A girl at the end of the line wearing a raincoat turned around and regarded Shannon and the Little Brothers while blowing a huge pink bubble. When the bubble popped, she informed them that the wait to audition was over two hours. She introduced herself as a singer named Beth from a band called Wawhoo Wang-Wang.

"Three songs or fifteen minutes," she said. "And you gotta wait in line."

They stood in line. Only Dave had thought to bring an umbrella. They crowded under it and all got a little wet. Moments later, an all-girl punk group arrived behind them. They all wore leather jackets. A girl with bright orange hair introduced herself, speaking only to Shannon as if she lived by a rule to ignore all men. Her name was Joan, and her band was called Whack-A-Whack. She liked Shannon's leather jacket. Moments later, Joan invited Shannon—and *only* Shannon—to hang out in their car. In full ignore-men mode, she ensured that the mannequins Shannon was with would hold her place in line.

Michael announced that he was going back to the van, claiming he forgot his sabre, and held his hand out toward Dave for the keys. Dave raised his eyebrows, pulled the keys from his pocket, and held them in the air. "No driving or smoking," he said, and tossed Michael the keys.

"Why do you need your sabre?" Curtis called after him, leaning on his saxophone case and wearing sunglasses even in the rain. Michael dismissed the question as superfluous, not even turning around. No one else said anything and Curtis nodded, like he had just gleaned another necessary tidbit of information for playing with this band.

"Wait, we'll go with you," Danny called out, grabbing Brandon by the sleeve.

"What? Why?" Brandon asked. "I'm not gonna be his fencing dummy anymore. We've gone over this."

"Just come on," Danny said, pulling him out into the rain and leaving Ray and Curtis standing with Dave under his umbrella. At least now they were dry.

*

Freshly stoned, Brandon, Michael, and Danny rolled up the windows, sprayed air freshener, and emerged from the van. Brandon and Danny left Michael practicing his wrist parry under a tree, singing along on his Walkman to another obscure album sent to him from a mate of his in Australia. This one was called "Pornography," by a band called The Cure. Rather than stand in the creeping line, Brandon and Danny decided to explore the Water Tower. They walked past the other Little Brothers with a quick "gonna hit the john." Inside, a line of musicians curled around and descended the stairs. From below, heavy metal blasted off the bricks and stone, filling the damp air with the drone of guitars and growling lyrics.

They dipped into the bathroom, came out, and made their way into the lobby on the first floor. They encountered a display dedicated to the history of the Water Tower. There was one other person in the room, an older kid with a jean jacket and red mohawk.

Brandon started reading; the last sentence he read out loud.

"*In time, however, Lowland Park citizens became tired of drinking 'liquid mud,' so in 1899 the town council directed the water works superintendent to design a water filtration system.* Liquid Mud could be a great song," Brandon said. He pulled out a notebook and began writing.

Danny used his eyebrows to express his skepticism.

"You've got your whole alien abduction theme," Brandon said, still reading. "This could be mine. It took them thirty years to commission the plant!" Brandon exclaimed. "Let's see … that could be like a bridge." He chewed on his pen.

Danny's attention was on the dude with the red mohawk wiping a booger on the wall.

"I could see the filtration terms building up to a crescendo," Brandon said, whispering the words and searching for a melody.

"Coagulation?" Danny asked, turning away as red mohawk now filled the space with the sound of deep-chested loogie hocking.

"Ah, yes, Mr. Coffin, the famous architect of claustrophobic buildings," Danny said, looking at a black-and-white portrait.

They moved to the next display, Brandon scribbling away in his notebook. "This is great stuff," he said. "This could be a chorus." He started singing off-key, "From the tank we store, into the glass we pour ..."

Danny rolled his eyes. "You need to get out more," he said, moving to the next display. "Who cares about this shit?"

"Water is fundamental to life," Brandon countered, as if this was obvious. He began reading out loud again, *"Another thirty years passed before the city acted to meet the growing needs."* The splat of another loogie echoed off the red brick walls.

"Another thirty years," Brandon whistled. "Maybe we could do something like that Zeppelin tune 'Ten Years Gone.'" He sang the verse and then wrote in his notebook.

Holdin' on, thirty years gone, holdin' on ...

"It could be like a rock opera, or at least a song trilogy," Brandon said.

"Or it could be the Strangest Music in the History of the World," Danny said. "Weirder than Michael's fencing songs."

They skipped over a part about the '60s, as red mohawk was using the reflective glass to comb his mohawk, which didn't need it. At the next display, about the '70s, Brandon started reading in a hushed voice.

"... an updated laboratory with 440-volt pumps ... That's some serious voltage."

"Stu, we're up next," someone called from the foyer. "It's time to gobble some lighting."

Red mohawk, apparently named Stu, glanced at Danny and Brandon like they were another artifact of dubious interest and walked out.

Brandon read the last display. "'Some prominent features of the renovation project include a zebra mussel control system which protects the intake pipeline from clogging by mollusks ...' A zebra mussel control system? This is pure gold."

He flipped over a full page of scribbled notes and wrote at the top: ZEBRA MUSSELS OUT OF CONTROL, a song which next week Shannon would flatly refuse to rehearse, saying, "Should we change our name to the Water Tower Historians? I don't want to put our audience to sleep."

"Fine," Brandon would reply. "It will be the first song on my solo album." The argument would lead to the red notebook in Brandon's hands being labeled with the following words written in black Sharpie: BRANDON'S SOLO SONGS (SHANNON KEEP OUT).

Two hours later, after a medley of Motown songs, Shannon and the Little Brothers had booked a regular Saturday night gig.

*

And so, the first weekend in October 1982, a five-minute drive from the border of a town with a ban on rock and roll music, an old laboratory in the basement of the Lowland Park Water Tower became a music venue for local teens and aspiring musicians from across the North Shore. (It also became the rehearsal space for an acoustic songwriting duo known as the Pringle Coffins.)

They relocated all the water filtration equipment and repurposed old lab tables to build a stage standing before a spacious rectangular room with nothing but an old 1930s water pump in the corner. The solid brick walls provided excellent acoustics. As the fall progressed, the hall would provide welcome warmth in the chilly evenings, thanks to abundant body heat from the crammed teenage audiences. In the beginning, though, it was sparse and dank with the smell of mud and old chemical spills.

But the rank odor didn't faze the adolescents that drove out every weekend in vans and station wagons. The 125-foot tower seemed like a structure erected not for water, the substance upon which all life depended, but for an equally vital and life affirming material on which *their* lives depended: music. And with the experienced guidance of a new guitar teacher named Rik Frets at the Village Music Shoppe, the quality of the songs played steadily improved.

Due to ample coverage in the *Riverview Review* by one Leslie Bangs, more and more people became curious about these developments, including Matt Welsh and his Devil Dashers, whose cause at the start of October suffered the loss of another seat on the town council when Cecilia Simon was elected mayor of nearby Naperville and left Riverview.

*

A routine developed. Tuesday, Shannon and the Little Brothers messed around in the basement, experimenting with songs. Thursday, they polished them up and finalized the set list. Saturday, they piled into the van and Dave would drive them to the Lowland Park Water Tower to play an hour-long set. Incrementally, their catalog of songs grew, mostly rock, rhythm and blues covers straight from Don Golding's record collection.

It was a Tuesday night. They had just finished working through Michael's "The Grip and the Blade."

"Shannon, can I see you a minute?" Liz Golding called from the top of the stairs. Tibbs put on a record. It was Lightnin' Hopkins's "Baby, Please Don't Go."

"Every single one of my friends has a driver's license," Shannon cried. The rest of the band could hear her through the ceiling above them. "Every. Single. One."

"And you can too. Once you pay your insurance premiums. Which are higher because someone decided to drive before they had a license and got into an accident."

"It was a minor fender bender," Shannon countered. "The rates are ridiculous."

"We don't set the rates."

"No one was even hurt. It's almost like you wish someone had been hurt. What if—"

"Shannon, don't be ridiculous," Liz said. "I'm not going to listen to this."

"Dad."

"Listen to your mother."

"Ugggghhhhhhhhh!"

"We might be willing to discuss your driving," Don Golding began, with a glance toward Liz "if you are willing to discuss your *diving*, as in joining the Riverview High Diving team."

"No!" Shannon shouted. "Absolutely not. I'm done."

"But you've worked so hard—"

"The Olympic coaches are still calling. We thought you were reconsidering—"

Shannon came barreling down the steps as they reset the needle to hear the chords one more time. Then they played "Baby, Please Don't Go" one time through, right along with the record, Shannon howling into the mic. "Dave, add it to the set list for next week," she said when the song was over. "Put it as the opener. And I'm sick of playing so many covers. If we're going to stand out at the Water Tower, we need to be playing more of our songs. Dave, read me our list of originals."

Dave picked up a folder on the coffee table and began reading.

No Brandon, We're Not Playing That (Shannon)
Flying Without a License (Shannon)
What's The Point? (Michael)
The Grip and the Blade (Michael)
Chain Reaction of Yawns (Ray)
But Liquid Butt (Ryan/Brandon)
Bright Light in the Field (Danny)
Tractor Beam (Danny)
Can You Feel the Probes Tonight? (Danny)

"That's enough," Shannon barked. "We need more songs that aren't weird as shit," she added, glaring over at the keyboard.

"What?" Danny whined. "My alien abduction stuff is better than a song about Liquid Butt. And at least I'm writing songs." He shot a glance over at Tibbs.

Shannon considered his statement, looking over at a Miles Davis *Kind of Blue* poster, like Miles might shed some light on the issue. "This is true," Shannon said. "In great bands everyone contributes. Everyone in this band needs to write. *And* sing. Lead vocals. For at least one song."

"Sing? Oh, come on," Ryan said with a rattle on the snare drum.

"If Keith Moon can sing 'Bell Boy,' you can sing something," Shannon said, looking from member to member. "We'll start a rotation. Each week is someone else's turn for a new song." She walked over and glanced at the song list. "Ray, you're up next week. Curtis, you're up after that. Tibbs, you have three weeks."

*

To the complete surprise and delight of Pringle Jr. and Coffin Jr., respectively, the Water Tower became a burgeoning music scene for the north suburbs of Chicago, with live music on Saturday night from seven until eleven p.m. Tickets started at one dollar, but quickly rose to three and then five. Proceeds were used to pay security and purchase snacks and soda for a stand in the back.

Since Chicago was too far and the suburbs—beyond the banality of Riverbrook Mall—offered essentially zero in the way of entertainment for a teenager, suddenly the Water Tower became The Place To Be. To be seen, to meet up, to make out, to experiment with drugs and alcohol, to explore their bodies, and to just plain get away from the adult world. For Ray, Ryan, Tibbs, Danny, and Michael, navigating the waters of their freshman year, it was an immediate education on high school life, social norms, and rebellion. The water district flag, flying high over the Water Tower, became a secret symbol of rock and roll.

Like the demand for water in the decades before, the demand for music continued to steadily increase and expand to further reaches of the North Shore. Lincolnshire kids descended on the Water Tower to see their local heroes, the Butter People. Mundelein teens flocked to see the pop group Hip to Be Circles. Naperville kids showed up to see the punk band the Shivers and a KISS-inspired band with a snake theme, HISS. And rising demand also emerged from Riverview, which was experiencing both a change in homeowners of a few concentrated neighborhoods and a new condo development full of young families with music-loving adolescents.

"Should we add Friday nights?" Pringle Jr. asked Coffin Jr. over their usual Sunday breakfast.

Coffin Jr. punched away at his calculator. "Let's wait," he replied. "I want to see that space like a tin of sardines first."

"Things are getting testy," Pringle Jr. said, shoveling eggs into his mouth. "There was almost a fight last weekend. I think more than a few kids are sneaking in booze. And I definitely smelled marijuana last night. We may need more security."

Coffin Jr. nodded and sipped his coffee. "Let's open up Friday nights," he said. "It's too crowded. They just need a little space."

*

October 26, 1982

Rock Music Keeps on Creeping On
By Leslie Bangs

No news is good news from Village Hall. Two months after a local band splattered Mudfest with gobs of pure rock and roll, the town council has made no mention of any violations of the rock music ban.

And nowhere is the vitality of the North Shore music scene more evident than the Water Tower in nearby Lowland Park. Adolescent bands from across north Chicago are performing every Saturday night. The groups first started a few weeks ago to sparse crowds. But the crowds are growing.

Yet many of the bands are ignorant of the turbulent history of rock and roll in the area. Last Saturday night I sat down with members of three bands from right here in Riverview that claimed to have no knowledge of the ban: Gobblers of Lightning, Gobbledegook, and the Polyps. In fact, both the Gobblers and Gobbledegook showed more concern over the similarity in their band names than any playing restrictions from Village Hall.

When I pressed Joey Brown, the singer for the Polyps, about the city potentially censoring rock music again, he responded with a defiant tone. "We're just kids having fun. What's wrong with that?"

Ignorance is bliss for a new generation of rock music lovers. The lack of knowledge of the town's contentious history with the art form might be a blessing in disguise as they write a new chapter, which also happens to be a love story.

*

It was a cool, clear November night. Rick Ocase sat in his mustard-yellow LeSabre and watched the cars in the Water Tower parking lot come and go, full of teenagers. He noticed clouds of smoke float out of windows and mingle in the air. He heard the crunch of beer cans being stepped on. He saw bottles and joints being passed around under the yellow streetlamps.

Where are the police? He thought of calling Chief Sumner but remembered the last Dasher meeting. "It's Lowland Park," Sumner had said. "We've told them about what we know, but ultimately, it's their jurisdiction."

Then Rick saw what he was waiting for: A group of musicians came out from the side of the tower. They loaded their instruments into a van, piled in, and pulled out of the parking lot heading west, toward Riverview.

Rick followed them. He tailed them across the town border, past the factory. He trailed behind as the van drove along the first neighborhoods, the Historic Village, Village Hall, and downtown, then under the bridge and past more neighborhoods. Rick turned with them into a neighborhood on the southwest side of town. At a prudent distance, he followed them through the suburban streets, winding among the sleeping houses. He saw where they turned in, but he did not follow. They lived on Sullivan Street.

He thought of going back to the Water Tower, of following more Riverview teenagers violating the town's rule. But he didn't. Instead, he sat right on the edge of Sullivan Street until sunrise, thinking of Suzie.

*

"Enjoy your lunch," Matt Welsh said, leaning in and kissing Bobby Jean where he always did, smack dab in the center of her cheek. He watched his wife join her friend and waved as they drove off for lunch. Then he walked across the church parking lot to his favorite shady spot. The two choir robes he carried swayed in the breeze. It was a warm November Sunday with bright clouds marching across the sky.

He unlocked his boat of a car, a shit-brown Buick LeSabre (a retired Dasher was a Buick salesman and years ago offered a significant group discount on LeSabres), and hung the robes in the backseat, thinking about how he would be hanging them up for the last time. He eased his portly frame into the driver's seat. Sylvester Stone, a new member of the choir who moved from Texas only three weeks ago, wanted to introduce a new gospel sound.

Well, he can have it, Matt fumed. Take the whole thing, the whole choir. You can have it with that organ sound. It's not the Lord's music. It's perverse, is what it is.

Matt pulled his car door shut, harder than he realized. As if that wasn't enough, this Stone's wife is running for the vacant seat on the town council. Rose Stone? What kind of name is that anyway? It felt like the town he had dedicated his life to protecting was being invaded on all sides and nowhere was safe, not even his own church choir.

He was moving his keys toward the ignition when the tremors started. They were getting worse. He jabbed but missed the slot. Once. Twice. A third time. He closed his eyes, steadied his breath, and prayed. The shakes did not abate. He opened his eyes and watched God working His wonder through his own vulnerable human hand. "God is good," he whispered, and with his unsteady left hand he grabbed his right wrist and slid the key into the ignition.

He reached to turn on the radio, then he remembered this weekend his gospel station was having a pledge drive. His hand hovered over the tuning knob. He regarded the slight tremble, and then God gently eased the involuntary shake so Matt was able to steady his wrist. He decided to perform an experiment. He switched to FM, turned the dial. The first station, fuzz. The second, fuzz. But the third, there it was, clear as a bell. Like a dam, the shield was cracking, and the flood was coming. The devil's music, flowing into Riverview, into virgin ears, and corrupting young minds, innocent as lambs. Musicians, wolves in sheep's clothing. Matt prayed, turned off the radio, and backed out of the parking space.

In silence he turned right, away from downtown and the traffic, but had to wait for a freight train at a railroad crossing. He closed his eyes to the stream of rail cars and prayed for patience. Once the tracks were clear, he followed a gently curving road along broad lawns, easing past kids on bikes and people walking their dogs, to his driveway. Upstairs, he hung up the robes and changed. Back down in the kitchen, without Bobby Jean home, he had to make his own ham sandwich. He said grace and opened the *Riverview Review.*

There it was on the front page. The town council runoff election. The Dasher candidate was a long shot. Results would be final today, likely out tomorrow, but Matt had a source on the local election board. He turned the page only to find another article by Leslie Bangs about Satan's cunning, erecting a temple beneath a tower of water. He couldn't finish either the article or the sandwich.

He put his plate by the sink and went into his study. From his stack of vinyl gospel records, he selected the Dixie Echoes. Noticing the tremor in his hand was absent, he lowered the needle down on "Now I Have Everything." He flopped onto the couch, feeling the fatigue of the week recede as the bliss of the Lord's music entered his soul. Matt knew that if God had an eleventh commandment, it was that the Sunday Afternoon Gospel Hour Shall Not Be Disturbed. He closed his eyes, adjusted the pillow beneath his head, and hummed as the music carried him away …

But not very far. The phone rang as the second chorus resolved. The results. He lifted the needle and picked up the phone.

"Hello?"

"Matt? Hi, I hope you don't mind me calling on a Sunday."

"I don't mind, Angela. I never mind a call from an angel, especially one on the election board."

"Stop. OK, keep going." Angela laughed. "I thought you would want to hear the results today, before they are released tomorrow."

Matt glanced at a framed portrait of Jesus on his desk. "And?" he asked.

"Not the result you were hoping for. Rose Stone is the newest member of the town council."

Matt let out a long, slow breath.

"At least the board has some diversity," Angela offered.

Matt stared at a patch of afternoon sunlight streaming through his window. "Was it close?"

"No. Not enough for a recount. The results will be released in a special announcement tomorrow. She'll be sworn in at the next meeting. Are you worried she will meddle with our school system?"

"Only the good Lord truly knows," Matt said, feeling the short, trimmed hair on the back of his neck. "But I guess we'll find out soon enough. We still have a comfortable majority on the school board, and Superintendent Jag. And our president, Nancy Brandt, has been quite … pliable. Thank you, as always, Angela, for your steady faithfulness to our mission. You are a true Dasher."

"Matt, I wanted to tell you, my son went to that tower last night. The one with the music. He's still asleep. I went into his room, and it smelled like … like alcohol. I'm worried. This is not like him. Isn't there something more we can do?"

"Pray. That is where we must always begin. Then get out of His way. Amen."

"Amen."

Matt hung up the phone and cast a supplicating look at Jesus, with his deep brown eyes and sorrowful expression, carrying a lamb on a hillside.

"I have kept the devil's music out of this town for thirty years," he said, "according to Your wishes. It will be a cold day in hell if these wolves think they can breeze in here and change that. Over my dead body." He crossed himself. A shiver traveled along his spine, escaping out his elbow as a little boogaloo shake. Matt thought of all the gaps and openings that Satan had pierced in the shield Matt had spent his life maintaining, and his whole body began to convulse. He dropped to his knees and prayed, asking the Lord to send him a new shepherd, someone to ease his burden. When he felt steady, he rose and with the hand of Jesus holding his, he put the needle on the next song of the record, "Lord, Lead Me On."

*

A full moon rose over Sullivan Street on an unseasonably warm Sunday evening in early November. Most of the leaves had fallen, and the wind carried the last gasp of autumn warmth. A worker guided a dolly loaded with boxes down the ramp of an open moving truck. The semi sat at the end of the street in front of yet another FOR SALE sign, with a SOLD sticker attached. Skateboards and bikes flew past, cruising to the dead end, where a game of stickball had reached the tense late innings. Stevie Wonder blared out of an open window.

It was getting dark. The workers set down the last of the boxes in the garage, and the moving truck pulled away. The stickball game ended with a dramatic strikeout. The music stopped. Doors opened and parents called kids home to dinner. Outside the house with the SOLD sign out front, a glow-in-the-dark frisbee clanged into the trunk of a tree. Up in the branches, in an opening in the leaves, two eyes peered down through thick glasses at the iridescent disc being retrieved.

The front door opened. "Brian, are you out there? Brian?"

*

Young, skinny Brian Jones Wyman slouched on the couch in front of the TV. Flashing images bounced off his glasses. With his tongue he flicked the rubber bands on his braces. Every few moments, the sitcom audience laughed, but his face was like stone.

The phone rang.

"Brian, can you get that? I'm making dinner."

Brian didn't budge. Two more rings.

"Brian, for Pete's sake." Aunt Bertha put the pots on simmer and picked up the phone.

"Hello."

"Hey, sis."

"Hey, Casey. Brian, your father is on the phone."

The sitcom audience laughed. Brian sat like a statue.

"How's everything going, Bertie?" Casey asked.

"We're fine, settling in. Barbara is up in her room studying and Brian is watching television. How have your flights been?"

"Fine. A little turbulence in Texas midweek, but overall, just fine."

Bertha poked her head into the family room. "Brian, come say hello to your father."

"Hello," Brian said to the television.

Bertha regarded him for a moment, then let it go and returned to the kitchen. "Listen," she said. "I've been thinking about Brian. I know you're against him seeing a therapist, but I was thinking about a different kind of therapy."

"I'm listening."

"I was thinking about giving him his mother's guitar."

Silence on the other end of the line.

"Hello? Are you there?"

"He doesn't need a guitar, he needs chores and a sport to play," Casey said.

"Look, I know I'm his aunt and not his parent," Bertha said. "And I'm no child psychologist. But I know when a kid is hurting. He needs a way to deal with his feelings. He needs something that can help him process what happened. I looked out today and this street is loaded with kids. I saw a group about his age all carrying guitars. This street has music playing nonstop. He needs friends."

"I don't think it's a good idea."

"Well, you're not here during the week. You're flying planes around the country. I'm his parent during the week. His mom's old guitar is just sitting up in the attic. I'm giving it to Brian tomorrow. And I'm looking to see if Riverview has a good guitar teacher."

"Music has done enough harm to our family," Casey snapped. "That's the whole reason we moved here."

"That's in the past," Bertha said, speaking to a dial tone.

*

A week later, the first snow of winter frosted the ground. Ray Flowers made the fifteen-minute trek to his first guitar lesson at the Riverview Village Music Shoppe, a former farmhouse from the 1800s that had been renovated. Whenever he was alone, like now, his mind dwelled on his father, the memory of the feds bursting in on Father's Day. The arrest and charges of tax evasion. The trial over the summer. The beginning of his nightmares. The guilty verdict in August and the weekly family outings to Joliet on Sunday to visit his dad in prison. A police car slowed as it passed him, interrupting his thoughts. That was strange, he mused, like he was some kind of criminal too. He crossed the railroad tracks and saw the Music Shoppe through the trees ahead. It felt like he was approaching some kind of oasis.

As he stepped in, the door sounded Beethoven's Fifth. He set down his Seagull and blew on his hands.

"Hello!" called a man in a tie-dye shirt and yellow, wire-rimmed glasses. "My name is Mr. Taplin, but you can call me Tap. You must be Ray Flowers."

Ray nodded.

"You're all set up for your first lesson with our newest guitar teacher, upstairs and down the hall on the right." Tap indicated the staircase. "Have fun!"

"Thanks," Ray said, grabbing his instrument and heading up the stairs. He went down the hall, past the sound of violins and trumpets behind closed doors. At the end of the hall a door stood slightly ajar. Ray knocked as he entered.

"Hello there, Ray." A short, older man in a sweater and corduroys reached out and shook his hand vigorously. "Wow, we need to warm you up. Come on in. Name's Rik Fretterman, but everyone calls me Frets." Frets had no hair on the top of his head but managed a ponytail with what he had left. Ray had noticed one of the cars parked outside had a New York license plate that said GO FRETS.

"Have a seat. What do you like to play?"

There was just enough space in the cluttered room for the two seats and a music stand.

"Ummm ..."

"Maybe we should start with some hot chocolate? Looks like you could use some—your face is still red. Back in a jiff."

Ray took in the walls, plastered with unfamiliar album covers: Woody Guthrie, Pete Seeger, Lead Belly, Peter, Paul and Mary. There were also pictures of people Ray didn't know. They were poets: Walt Whitman, Dylan Thomas, William Blake, others from ancient times ... the only photograph on the wall that Ray recognized was Elvis Presley.

Nestled between the faces were four different guitars hung on the wall, two acoustics (one a twelve-string), an electric, and a bass. The rest of the room was messy: shelves stuffed with books and sheet music, the desk a wasteland of paper and song books, a harmonica and some contraption for holding it, an amp with wires strewn about. There was a half-eaten tuna fish sandwich and an apple with one bite that was browning. In the corner was a tall, serious-looking instrument that Ray would soon discover to be a bassoon. The floor had picks, crumpled sheets of paper, and what Ray would soon learn was a capo.

Ray recognized an album near the record player on the floor and regarded a picture of the four Beatles, looking down, leaning over a ledge with floors ascending above them. He was thinking that this couldn't have been more different from his first music teacher, Ming and her sterile room with the immaculate piano.

After a minute Frets burst back in with a steaming Styrofoam cup. "Here ya go," he said. "That ought to do the trick. It's cold out there. Brrrrrrrrr."

Ray blew on the cup and took a small sip. It was still too hot.

"Let's see what you got in here," Frets began, opening Ray's case. "Yep. It's a guitar."

Frets winked, and for a moment Ray thought he might be a little crazy. "Mmmm, a Seagull. These have a great sound. Your first guitar?"

"Yes," Ray confirmed, blowing into the cup. "My dad gave it to me."

"Wonderful. You keep blowing on the cup, you'll be ready for the harmonica. What grade are you in?"

"I'm a freshman at Riverview High," Ray said, sipping a melted marshmallow.

"Ah yes, I know those halls of conformity well. How long have you been playing guitar?"

"Just like six months. I took piano lessons for a couple years. But I'm in a band where everyone else is pretty good, so I've been learning a lot."

"That's the best way to learn. Here, let me clear some space for your drink."

Frets moved a pile of papers, and Ray put his cup down.

"So, anything you'd like to play?"

Ray looked at the four smiling faces, the haircuts and the suits.

"The Beatles?"

"The Who?"

"The Beatles."

"Ohhhhh, right. I think I've heard of them. Let's see here …"

Frets stood, pulled open a file cabinet, and grabbed a couple of sheets of paper. "This one's called 'A Hard Day's Night.' You're gonna love it."

*

"See you next week," Frets called to Ray as his next student walked in.

"*The Modern Method*," Frets said, picking up the book Brian had brought. "What makes it so modern?"

"I don't know," Brian said. "My aunt gave it to me."

Frets thumbed through the pages and set it back on the stand. "Want some hot chocolate? The wind's really blowin' out there."

"No thanks," Brian said.

Frets smiled, and they sat together for a moment. Then Frets suggested, "Go ahead and pull your guitar out; it won't bite."

Brian complied.

"Give it a strum," Frets said. "Make some noise. Let it loose."

Brian gave the strings a tentative swipe. The guitar was horribly out of tune.

"Whoa, we've got to tune that baby up."

Frets took the guitar and tuned it while Brian plucked at the rubber bands on his braces with his tongue.

"First time playing a guitar?"

"Yes," Brian conceded. "My aunt's making me. I don't really like music. My family doesn't. Like it, I mean."

"Nonsense," Frets said. He finished tuning the strings and handed the guitar back to Brian. "Unless your family consists of robots. Everyone likes music. Sing me a song you know, something easy."

"That's just it," Brian said. "There isn't any song that is easy for me. I can't even sing 'Happy Birthday.' I'm not musical. My sister is like this flute prodigy."

"No, no," Frets waved his hand. "Music isn't like that. Sure, some people have more talent than others … maybe? Maybe not. Music is inside everyone. It just is. If there's been people on this planet, they've sung songs. Spiders spin webs. Frogs ribbit ribbits. We have language and songs and … and … eyebrows. It's part of the human genome. A human without music is like a face without eyebrows. Talent isn't like some floating rib. Or a floating eyebrow … hmm … maybe that's my next tune? Let me write that down."

He grabbed a pencil and scribbled on a wrinkled sheet of paper with coffee stains. "Here, sing me 'Twinkle, Twinkle Little Star.'"

"I told you. I can't sing."

"How about hum? Can you hum it for me?"

"I don't know how to hum."

"Give it a shot. Close your eyes and hum."

Brian closed his eyes and started to hum. "Hmm hmm, hmm hmm, hmm hmm, hmmm—see? I'm terrible."

"That wasn't terrible. That was good. You hummed it note for note. Now, let's see if we can find those notes on the guitar."

Ten minutes later, erratically and with a few muffled notes, Brian Jones Wyman finished playing his first song on the guitar.

"Let's play it one more time, together. Good. That's it! 'How I wonder where you are?' Now that's a lyric. For practice this week, I'm going to give you a list of one-octave songs. I want you to hum them first, then try to find them on the guitar—pick any string. 'Song of Joy.' 'Yankee Doodle.' Let me think, a few more. Let's learn the music already inside your head." Frets dug through the mess of papers on his desk.

Brian put his guitar back in its case. He turned his head so Frets wouldn't see that he was crying.

*

At 11:15 a.m. on the Monday before Thanksgiving, Leslie Bangs pulled into the Sara Sweet factory and parked in the usual row reserved for visitors. Like always, she walked in the main entrance, received her press credentials, and made her way to the cafeteria. The tables once again pushed to the edges, flanked by chairs, and this time loaded with lemon-glazed pound cake.

Leslie skipped the sweets, grabbed some black coffee in a Styrofoam cup, and sat in her usual seat along the side of the stage, reserved for press. Her headache this morning pounded on the front of her skull like a jackhammer. As the workers from the factory slowly filled in, Leslie pulled out her notepad, and—after a bit of scrounging—found a pencil in the bottom of her purse. She next took out the manila envelope Neil had mailed her.

Without her asking, he had sent a full report on Vincent Furnier's background and affiliation with the Reagan administration. She skimmed through his education, studying political science and economics at Princeton. His work experience in local government, implementing fiscally conservative policies. She made her way to the next page and read up on how he had become involved with the Republican Party, Ronald Reagan, and a right-wing political action group called American Families First that ran into some legal trouble by crossing the boundaries between church and state in public schools. She flipped the page, when Neil's letter fell at her feet.

She had stopped reading his letters, even though he sent them weekly. She kept them in a drawer, and they had remained sealed until her recent fall from the wagon. This morning, she woke up with the letters scattered across her bed. Deep down, she loved him. But it wouldn't work. They had made their choices. Careers must come first. He had chosen Washington, DC and national politics. She had chosen Riverview and exposing a ban on rock and roll. What was done was done. She picked up the letter and returned it to the envelope, along with the other research materials. She glanced at her watch, gulped her black coffee, and sighed. You'd think a dessert factory would have better coffee. The press conference was supposed to have started five minutes ago. She pulled out yesterday's *Riverview Review*, which also sent flying a tampon, lipstick, and a pair of glasses. She scooped up the stray items and put the glasses on her face. She started reading Jane Mott's article about the last board meeting, how Jim Plant, the owner of Craftwood Lumber—already under a restraining order not to appear in person at board meetings—showed up in a disguise to dispute his canceled contract for cafeteria seating at the high school. He was physically restrained and arrested. He declined his right to remain silent as they took him away, and instead he howled that "every kid deserves a place to eat lunch." The article closed with the hiring of a new dean at the high school and speculation about when, if ever, Principal Merchant would return from a leave. Then Leslie moved on to a blurb in the Notes Around Town section about how the police believed drugs infiltrating Riverview were coming through one main channel fronted by a legitimate business. Drug enforcement believed they were homing in on this source, but they asked community members to be vigilant at local stores and places of business. Kent Davies had proved to be a fair and impartial editor. These are stories worth covering, Leslie thought. As opposed to this factory nonsense. What's the point of these meetings? Even the factory workers don't seem to care … Leslie folded and put away the newspaper as Furnier took the stage, fifteen minutes late.

He greeted the workers and thanked them for their support in electing him president of their union. After disparaging the alternate candidate, the ice cream union boss, as a pothead, he began talking about Reagan's national economic policies and how they would benefit communities like Riverview and American jobs like the ones at this very factory. Leslie watched as the workers set down their cake to applaud.

Furnier, now with a short, trimmed beard on his long, thin face, then transitioned into Reagan's social policies. How Reagan and his administration would support families and neighborhoods in the fight against crime, violence, poverty, and drugs. He recognized Roxanne Gradenko for representing Nancy's Just Say No! program.

Leslie watched Roxanne stand and take a bow. Roxanne acknowledged the brief applause and sat back down, the same girl who had put her bloody tampon in Leslie's locker in high school (Leslie was sure it was her), who had bullied her about being different and not pretty and dressing like a boy and a hundred other bitch reasons. This same high school prom queen was now sitting in a folding chair at a dessert factory, shoving lemon-glazed pound cake in her stupid face.

Leslie scanned the room, the faces stuffing their mouths with little cakes. They were like humans that had been given some strange potion to make them act like cows, munching on pound cake like it was grass. Their eyes were almost not human, veering toward bovine.

This isn't sweetness, Leslie thought. This isn't how life should taste, scarfing some mass-produced treat, licking your fingers for the crumbs of some corporation in exchange for a salary with a pension and health benefits. There had to be more to life. These people have dreams, desires, hopes, passions. And what do they get in exchange for their labor? Safety and a slice of pound cake?

The speech ended. Everyone set their plates down and stood up applauding. Leslie looked down at her blank notepad, wondering how she would fill out her article for tomorrow's paper. Maybe this could be her last time covering this place. Kent had published her recent story about the Water Tower, even if it was on page twelve. Maybe that could be her new beat … maybe she could finally be the rock and roll journalist of HER dreams. The town was changing. The previous weekend the Water Tower had sold out both nights … Feedback on the microphone, like a needle jabbed in her ear, brought her back to the present, which seemed hopeless. Mark Stein, the CEO, was rambling on about Reagan, about how the president was welcome to come and visit Riverview anytime he liked. Yawn. Then she remembered she had Neil's reports. She could do a profile of this Furnier character and his connection to the Reagan administration. Not exactly rock and roll, but at least she had an article. Neil, bailing her out again. She grabbed her purse and headed for the exit. A little hair of the dog would do nicely.

*

Scratch scratch scratch, scratch scratch scratch.

Brian reached over, put on his glasses, and tried to locate the source. He concluded that it was coming from the corner, inside his guitar case. He watched as the ends of the guitar strings slipped out of the case and undid the clasps. He yanked the covers up to his chin as the last clasp rattled loose and the case flung open. Light from the sound hole projected an image onto the ceiling.

The image was blurry. Sound came in and out. He could hear a flute mingling with television noise. He heard a sitcom audience laugh. Gradually, the image on the ceiling sharpened into focus: It was him, sitting on a couch with the light of the TV flickering on his glasses. Barbara, his older sister, hovered in the background, practicing her flute.

A voice began speaking, the words muffled in a drone. It was his father's voice, outlining the conditions Barbara had to meet to play the flute, something his father disapproved of.

The flickering light went away. His sister joined him on the couch. One of the guitar strings reached up and twisted the knobs on its neck, causing the channel on the TV to change. Now his father was on television. His voice continued in a faint drone.

Brian pulled the covers to his nose and peered up at the image on the ceiling. He watched himself plucking the rubber bands of his braces with his tongue. Barbara held her flute and worked at the fingering, as if practicing a difficult part over and over. His father's voice came through.

"I'll be home most weekends."

The images on the ceiling sped up, fast-forwarded, then stretched out into slow-motion. Brian noticed that now three strings were fumbling with the knobs on the neck of his guitar. Barbara was talking. Then his father. Then Barbara again—their voices alternated between that high-pitched, chipmunk quality and low and slow. The strings of the guitar kept twisting knobs and eventually found the right speed again.

"I've arranged for you to live in Riverview with your Aunt Bertha and Uncle John," his dad said, his face in focus on the TV. "For the time being. During the week they will act as your parents."

The framing of the image on the ceiling slowly crept up and focused in on Brian. A close-up on his face. Closer. His mouth. The discussion continued, but the main sound was the amplified vibrations of Brian's tongue plucking the rubber bands in his mouth. Suddenly his dad's televised face was on the ceiling with curled lips.

"We have to forget about the past."

Everything went dark, and the guitar case snapped shut. Brian stared out at his empty room, bright with moonlight.

*

Ray played through the chorus one more time, punching the last chord for emphasis.

"That's it!" Frets exclaimed. "You're getting it. That gives you two new songs to work on this week. You got 'Catfish Blues' and a little rock and roll with Petty's 'Even the Losers.'"

Outside the door, Brian stood with his guitar in hand. Frets held up his index finger to give him the *just a minute* signal.

"Remember, take the blues nice and slow, then turn up the amp on the Petty tune. Really rock it out," Frets encouraged.

Ray nodded. "Thanks. I really like both songs."

"Yeah, you bet. You'll really dig this Petty guy. No surprise his songs are on the charts. But like I told you, don't just listen to the hits."

Brian glanced at his watch in the window.

"Listen to the whole album. That's where the treasure lies. The diamonds in the rough. Plus, it will help you develop your ear. When you like a song, think about what it is you like. Try to define it. Same thing if you don't like a song. Keep a little notebook."

Ray nodded and smiled. Frets kept going about the notebook, but Ray wasn't listening. An idea had popped into his head for a song called "Taming the Crocs." He wasn't having nightmares anymore, or panic attacks, and whenever he felt down, he started playing a Beatles song Danny had taught him, "Let It Be."

"You could call it the 'The Journey to the Center of Your Ear,'" Frets suggested to Ray.

"Thanks, Frets," Ray said. "See you next week."

Brian knocked again.

"Well, I guess we're out of time," Frets shrugged. "Have fun. Lots of different versions of 'Catfish Blues' out there. Not just Hendrix. You can find one by B.B. King. Not in this town, but any record store worth its salt has a blues collection. Originally that tune comes from the Deep South, the 1940s, but it probably goes back further than that."

Brian opened the door.

"It's 4:03," Brian said. "My lesson is supposed to start at four o'clock."

"Right," Frets agreed. "Just finishing up here with Ray. You guys are classmates, right? You should jam!"

Ray's body language said *why not?* Brian stood in the doorway, stiff as a board. He shifted his feet, and his lips tightened. Frets stood up and put his guitar on the wall. "We can go over by a few minutes if you're worried about the time." The three bodies and guitars made for a tight squeeze. "Catfish Blues,'" Frets continued, helping Ray with his case. "Muddy Waters has a version too. But he calls it 'Rolling Stone.' If you listen closely, that's where

Hendrix's 'Voodoo Chile' comes from. Far out. Ray Flowers of Riverview, playing a song from the Delta. Plaintive longings that live on." He ran his hand over the top of his bald head and down to the gray ponytail in back. "That's the power of music."

Brian sat down. Ray walked into the hallway and down the stairs.

"OK, Brian, let's hear one of those one-octave tunes. How about 'Yankee Doodle'?" Frets asked.

Brian took a deep breath.

"I didn't practice," he admitted. His tongue plucked the rubber bands on his braces. "Also, I go by B.J. now."

"All right, B.J.," Frets said. "It's a new week. How about we go over the strings? Do you have any friends named Eddie?"

"I don't have any friends."

"What? Well, the guitar can be a friend."

B.J. lifted his glasses and rubbed his nose.

"The reason I bring up Eddie," Frets maintained, "is that you can remember the strings with this line: Eddie Ate Dynamite. Goodbye Eddie. E-A-D-G-B-E. That's standard tuning."

B.J. twanged his rubber bands.

"Because you definitely need friends," Frets remarked. "Though preferably not ones that eat dynamite."

*

Over the Thanksgiving break, Ray's and Tibbs's moms had arranged for Tibbs to start lessons on Mondays so they could carpool and accommodate Bonnie Flowers's shifting work schedule. In addition to working as a legal secretary (which came in handy during her husband's trial), she had taken on a second job three days a week waiting tables. Ray and Tibbs were to ride the bus together from Riverview High School over to the Shoppe and have their lessons at three thirty.

Frets didn't have the four o'clock slot open, but he did have the four thirty. So now Frets's Monday schedule was: 3:30 Ray Flowers, 4:00 Brian Jones Wyman, 4:30 Andrew Tibbets, a.k.a. Tibbs. This schedule also meant B.J. spent usually fifteen minutes on the couch in the lobby with Tibbs before his lesson, and sometimes fifteen after with Ray Flowers while waiting for Aunt Bertha. Ray and Tibbs also got thirty minutes of jam time in between their lessons. Occasionally Tap came over and joined them on the bongos.

*

Down on the first floor, Tibbs, the Village Music Shoppe's newest student, called from the couch: "Yo." Ray, fresh from learning some Johnny Cash tunes, walked over and sat down.

"You gotta help me," Tibbs said with his hands together as if in prayer.

"With what?"

"I need a song. Tomorrow I'm up. And I got nothing. Nada. Zip."

"Maybe you could write a song called, 'Nothing, Nada, Zip'? Like that Who song we were listening to?"

"Haha, funny. Seriously, have you got any other songs? You're not up again for like six weeks. You gotta help me. I think Shannon is serious about this No Write No Play rule."

"We'll come up with something," Ray offered. "Hey listen, you know the reason I can never play on Sunday?"

"No," Tibbs replied.

"It's my dad," Ray said. "He got in trouble for tax evasion, last summer, before everyone moved onto our street. He's in prison, in Joliet, and we go and visit him. I've been wanting to tell everyone, but I didn't know how."

Tibbs scratched the peach fuzz on his chin and considered this information. "Well," he said. "It's better than being in a cult. I think everyone is going to be relieved."

Ray laughed. Beethoven's Fifth sounded, and a crowd of RHS students poured in, along with a strong stench of skunk.

"Can I help you?" Tap said from the office.

"Where can we sign up for guitar lessons?" the leader of the surfeit asked.

*

Scratch scratch scratch.

He didn't want to open his eyes. But he did, to the sound of rattling clasps. Lit up by the full moon, B.J. watched the strings push open the case.

He dove under the covers, but he still heard the guitar string legs as they moved to the bare wood floor right by his bed.

It reached the rug and made muffled sounds. It bumped into a music stand and knocked it over. The stand hit the guitar insect on the way down. When B.J. looked over, part of a guitar string leg had been detached and was twitching under the stand. Now with five and a half legs, it moved into B.J.'s closet, making a racket as it bumped around and stumbled over his shoes. He thought briefly of jumping out of bed and closing his closet door to trap the guitar insect inside, but he was too afraid.

From deep under the covers, he could hear it scratching the wall. The severed leg was still twitching under the stand. He could hear his clothes being pulled off hangers inside the closet, the metal wires clattering to the floor. The guitar insect crawled out of the closet with a black sweatshirt draped over its neck and body. It crawled slowly, impeded by the sweatshirt, trying with futile wiggles to break free. Then it smacked up against a wall. Feeling its way, the guitar insect managed to climb the wall, the sweatshirt slipping off, but something happened to its center of gravity—perhaps the sweatshirt coming loose gave it an unexpected jolt. Either way, the insect fell onto its back. The five and a half legs moved uselessly in the air. One of the legs managed to reach the edge of B.J.'s dresser. With infinitesimal pushes its body moved, turning until it was able to use two legs; another few pushes, then three legs were on the dresser and the guitar insect flipped itself over. The fretted neck turned. The knobs peered at B.J., who was peeking over his covers.

The sound hole shined a light. It projected a blurry image that the knobs twisted into focus. B.J. watched the ceiling with frightened awe. He saw himself five years ago, as an eight-year-old, with his parents in Lucy's old room.

"Can we go swimming now?"

"Just a second, B.J." his mom said. "Daddy and I are having a discussion." She threw a soiled diaper into the diaper pail.

"Are you guys fighting? It sounds like you are fighting," Barbara said.

"It's a discussion. Daddy and I are discussing something that we don't agree on."

"We're not fighting," his father said. "Because your mother is not going to be singing in some traveling band. End of discussion."

"Who said anything about travel? We would be playing Saturday nights in the city. That and the recording deal. That's all there is right now. No one has said anything about touring."

"Can we pleeeeeeeeaaaaaaaasee go swimming now?"

"Just a minute, B.J." his mom said. "Stop asking."

Lucy started crying.

"Can I get a two-piece swimsuit?" Barbara asked. "When can I get a two-piece?"

"When you're grown," his father said. "Or when you move out. Whichever happens first." He walked out of the room. "I have to leave for work in ten minutes," he said from the hallway.

"When can we go swimming?"

Lucy's cries grew louder.

"Enough!" his mom said, throwing her hands in the air. "Barbara, get the hose and go fill up the pool. You have to practice piano before you can swim. B.J., love, go with her and help."

The two older children left the baby's room.

The image closed in on his mom. "For goodness' sake, give me a moment of peace."

The ceiling went blank. The guitar insect crawled over and ate the half leg trapped under the stand, the end of the neck opening like the mouth of a snake. Then it went back inside the case, which snapped shut. B.J. lay in his bed, trying to figure out if he was dreaming.

*

"Ray." It was Tibbs, with Danny.

"Quick, follow us," Danny said.

Ray did a one-eighty and headed back down the hallway. He was carrying his guitar, which he had spent his lunch period strumming in the courtyard. "Where are we going?" he asked.

"Come on," Danny beckoned.

The bell announcing the start of seventh period rang. The three walked quickly along, turned the corner, and found themselves in the front foyer. They sped along and took a quick right down a hallway toward the music room.

"Where are we going?" Ray asked again.

"Just come *on*," Danny insisted.

They went past the music room and ducked into the instrument storage room. Ray followed them to the back, behind a stack of tubas, where Michael and Ryan were waiting.

Danny pulled out the bowl. It went around twice, quickly. Michael cashed it out into a nearby baritone. Then they were running, Ray struggling to run as fast as he could while carrying his axe. Out of the music room, down the foyer, and back into the hallway. Danny was pretending to be their math teacher, Mr. Keen.

"Young man, your shoelaces are untied," he was saying in a perfect imitation.

They split up. Ray walked into Mr. Fair's history class. Mr. Fair looked up from his desk with a frown. Ray set down his axe in the aisle and sat down. On the blackboard was the following quote:

Thomas Mann once wrote: *"A man lives not only his personal life as an individual, but also consciously or unconsciously the life of his epoch."*

Under the quote, Mr. Fair had written:

- *Paraphrase (put into your own words) this quote. (Two sentences min.)*

- **How does this quote relate to JFK's remarks?** *"All free men, wherever they may live, are citizens of Berlin, and, therefore, as a free man, I take pride in the words 'Ich bin ein Berliner.'"*

Mr. Fair stood and began walking around the room. Students were writing in their notebooks. The only sounds in the room were the buzzing of fluorescent lights and the scratching of pens on paper.

Ray pulled out his notebook and a pen.

Dean Early, newly hired by the district, walked into the room. He stood in the doorway, crossed his arms, and regarded the students writing with their heads down.

"Please finish your thoughts," Mr. Fair said. "Our discussion begins in two minutes."

Ray's pen hovered over his notebook, his mind whirling like a spinning top, wondering: Was it just him, or was this new dean staring suspiciously with stern eyes right at him?

"Mr. Flowers," Dean Early said. "Please come with me. And bring that *case* of yours."

Ten agonizing minutes later—which to Ray felt like an eternity—he returned to class with a warning not to bring his guitar to school. A "learning distraction," Dean Early had called it. He could pick it up at the end of the day. For a tense moment Ray thought Dean Early knew he was high, that he was in huge trouble as the tall man with the short, neat mustache scrutinized him, that he would end up in some kind of juvenile detention center like his father. But luckily a fight broke out in PE, and Ms. Susan summoned Dean Early to the gymnasium.

*

The full moon cast soft, bright moonlight into B.J.'s room. The guitar insect wasn't crawling so much as it was pushing itself along the floor. There was a high-pitched pulse, almost inaudible. It sounded like the insect was either crying or screaming. B.J. peeked out from under the covers. Faint wisps of some material dangled from the neck, along the frets, clinging to the body. The insect pushed itself closer to the low blue light of his alarm clock. He saw what it was: spider webs. The next thing he saw made him gag. There were hundreds, maybe thousands, of tiny ants crawling on the guitar insect. They were fighting each other for access to a wound, right near the sound hole. The long, steel-stringed legs pushed the guitar insect along weakly. It made it halfway to its former position in the center of the floor. The sound hole came alive with light, causing the ants to scatter in a frenzy. The message sent by antenna was: RUN LIKE HELL!

The film resumed. The light flickered unsteadily. The sound quality was poor. B.J. watched, rapt.

Barbara came running in and sat down at the piano.

"Major scales and arpeggios for warm-up. Key of C, G, and A minor," his mother called out. Barbara started. B.J. could be heard splashing, playing some game by himself outside. Lucy was making happy baby noises in her high chair.

His mom said, "Well, it's a sweet life with your little face. Mommy's not going to leave you. How could Mommy choose anything over your sweet little face? I could eat you!" She made chomping noises as she nibbled on Lucy's neck. "Chomp. Chomp. I could eat your face!"

The baby giggled.

Barbara moved on to the key of G.

His mom cleaned Lucy's face with a wet rag. She removed the bib and pulled the baby free of the chair. She carried her outside and walked over to the kiddie pool in the yard.

"Man the torpedoes," eight-year-old B.J. called. "The submarine is ready, sir. PSCHSUWSHHH!"

"B.J., honey, watch your sister while I get Barbara started on her lesson," his mom said, putting Lucy down in the water. "How does that water feel? Splash, splash."

Lucy started to whimper.

"Don't worry, baby. Big brother is here," his mother said soothingly. "He's watching you." Then, to B.J., "Watch her. Don't take your eyes off her."

His mom went back inside as Barbara finished the A minor arpeggios. They worked together on a Beethoven piece. Barbara was having some difficulty with a measure. The insect fast-forwarded.

"That's it, you've almost got it," his mother said. The movie on the ceiling flashed erratically.

"We have to protect the baby at all costs," young B.J. called. "All ships to starboard! All guns on the enemy! Fire away!"

Lucy laughed and splashed.

"That's it, now you've got it," his mom said, back at the piano. "My talented daughter. Is there anything she can't do?"

Barbara smiled and leaned on her mom's shoulder.

"Here, I want to teach a song to you," she said. "See if you recognize it. I used to sing it to you when you were a baby. I sang it for B.J. And now I sing it for little Lucy."

Golden slumbers kiss your eyes

Smiles awake you when you rise

Sleep, pretty wantons, do not cry

And I will sing a lullaby.

"And now you repeat the beginning," his mom said, playing slowly and evenly.

Rock them, rock them, lullaby.

Care is heavy, therefore sleep you

You are care, and care must keep you;

Sleep pretty wantons, do not cry

And I will sing a lullaby

Rock them, rock them, lullaby.

"Isn't that a sweet song?"

"It is," Barbara said. "I remember it."

"Oh, I bet you do. I used to sing it all the time. To B.J. especially. Like clockwork, that song would stop his crying, and he'd go right to sleep."

"I remember it too," young B.J. said. "Can you play it again? I want to hear it again."

"Brian Jones. You're supposed to be watching—"

The film ended abruptly. White light flickered. Fuzz. Darkness. B.J. looked down as the insect coughed up bright green liquid. Ants covered its body. He watched them lift the guitar, the neck drooping. All the frets were being stripped off and carried individually, as were the string legs, bridge, tuning knobs, and pick shield. They carried the body and its parts out the door. B.J. woke up to his Uncle John hovering over him.

"B.J. Do you feel OK? You're warm. It feels like you might have a fever."

*

B.J. walked around the corner from E hall into D hall. Jackson Irons of the Wobble Dobbles came running by and, with a swift slap, knocked B.J.'s books from his hands.

"Blow Job," he called as he ran past.

B.J. bent down to pick up the books, but Clare Danko kicked them away.

"Big Jerk," she said.

B.J. shook his head and again bent down to pick them up. Then Joey, the lead singer of the Polyps, gave his rear end a shove. "Blow Job blows!" he said, to the laughter and amusement of those standing nearby. When B.J. went forward, his glasses slipped off his face and Brad of the Laughing Tadpoles stepped on them. Dean Early came around the corner as the crowd began chanting: "Blooooooow Job. Blooooow Job. Blooooooow Job."

"It was an accident," Brad claimed later, in Dean Early's office.

*

"Can I ask you a question, Frets?"

"Shoot."

Tibbs strummed a little walk-down ditty, C to A minor. "It's just, um, I don't know. It's kind of stupid."

"There are no stupid questions. Just stupid guitar teachers. Kidding! What's the trouble?"

"Well, I don't know ..." Tibbs faltered, hanging on the A minor chord, adding a high G as a hammer-on.

Frets took a sip from his coffee mug. "Just spit it out."

Tibbs muted his strings. "Have you ever heard of writer's block? I mean do musicians get that too? Like a creative block?"

"It happens to everyone. Creativity is a mystery. It ebbs and flows. There are ways to get more flow, though, if you've got some ebb going on. Ah, the dreaded ebb. That sounds like a song right there." Frets played an E minor and sang, "The dreaded ebb ... like a spider's web ... what else rhymes with ebb?"

"Yeah, well … I guess I've got it. Been stuck lately." Tibbs started strumming again, an F suspended chord.

"Bummer. It's part of it. Getting through the blocks. Or around them."

"My band, see, we've got a rule where each practice someone has to bring in a song. A while back, it was my turn. I couldn't come up with anything. Ray Flowers helped me out."

"Ah yes, the Flower Man," Frets said.

"The next time it was my turn, I got stuck again. A total freeze job. Now each week, when we get together to rehearse, the singer, Shannon, busts my balls. She even came up with a song called '2025—When Tibbs Writes His First Song.' She's totally in my head."

Frets scratched his beard. "One trick is to be someone else. Reinvent yourself. The Beatles did it. Don't be Tibbs. Be Sergeant Pepper. Except that's been done. Maybe Lieutenant Pepper? General Salt? Anyway, the point is, if you pretend you're someone else, it can free you up, help you write from a different perspective."

"Huh," Tibbs said. "Never thought of that." He moved from the F chord to running through F pentatonic scales.

"The other thing is to start small," Frets said, picking up his guitar. "Sometimes the way to write about *big* things is to write about *small* things. It's a good way to get practice and develop as a songwriter. If you listen to the lyrics on *Dark Side of the Moon*, it's mostly about mundane, everyday details. Like breathing." Frets strummed the intro to "Breathe in the Air."

"'Don't be afraid to care,'" he continued. "It doesn't get much simpler than that. Oh, wait. It does. The next verse is about a rabbit digging a hole. But when you combine it all, you've got the *Dark Side of the Moon*. Big ideas. Time. Money. Us and Them. A new way of looking at the world, from a single ray to the spectrum of colors. But it starts with the mundane. Add it up. And if you pick the right pieces, you've got a great song."

Tibbs nodded. "Everyday things. Got it." He stared at the neck of his guitar, closed his eyes, and sang.

"Sitting with Frets." He played a C chord. "Um … Uh …"

He stopped playing.

"Shit! Shit! Shit!" He punched a G power chord. "It's like I've got a wall in my brain I can't get around."

"That's a start right there," Frets said.

"I've got a wall in my brain," Tibbs sang. He was strumming the C chord with increasing volume and frustration. "I can't do it …"

"Nice."

"My head is empty, it's so …" He dragged his pick along a D chord, then opened his eyes, looking at the ceiling. "So …" He muted the strings with a slap, then said tunelessly, "Empty."

"I've got a wall in my brain," Frets offered. "My head is empty as a … glass?"

Frets smiled at Tibbs, but Tibbs's hanging head missed it.

"Remember, songwriting takes time," Frets said. "Practice, like an instrument. Usually when you try to force it, it doesn't happen. But if you keep your ears and mind open, ideas come your way. Keep listening. Be curious and observant of people and the world around you. Keep a notebook. Here, let me play something for you." He hung up his guitar and rifled through a stack of records. "Here, listen to this," he said, adjusting the needle. It was Stevie Ray Vaughan singing "Give Me Back My Wig."

"That's great American rock and roll right there. And what's it about? Two bald people falling in love. Rock and roll songwriting at its finest." He was rifling through his records again. The song ended. "Ah, here. Another great example. 'Little Red Rooster.' It's about a chicken."

There was a knock on the window.

"Welp, my next student is here," Frets said as the Stones wailed away. "My schedule is packed to the gills. I guess my point is: have fun."

*

On Friday afternoon, following a note from Dean Early, Brian Jones, a.k.a. B.J., used the Q hall exit in the back of Riverview High School. He walked around the police cars of Deputy Copeland and Chief Sumner, called in two hours prior on a report of students smoking weed in the locker room. He walked along the student-driving course, past the sophomore parking lot and the wooden stumps that kept cars from driving onto Summit Drive. He walked another block to Overland Trail and, looking down at Dean Early's note, stopped at a brown van idling with the words GRADENKO HOME GOODS on the side.

"Hello, Mrs. Gradenko," he said.

"Hi, Brian."

"Please, call me B.J. It's my name now."

"B.J.? OK, sure. What happened to your glasses? Can you see with those cracks?"

"They broke. I stepped on them by accident."

"Don't you have a backup pair?"

"They hurt my nose. I taped these until I can get new ones. My aunt's supposed to take me today after school."

B.J. looked down the street as he lied.

"These kids," Roxanne tsk-tsked, shaking her head. "Here's your letter of recommendation from the Parents Music Resource Center." She handed him a manila envelope. "There are ten copies. I'm not sure how many colleges you plan on applying to. If you need more just tell me. Only a freshman but already preparing for college. You're way ahead of the game. It's admirable."

"I'm planning on skipping high school," B.J. said, taking the envelope and putting it in his bag. He glanced in both directions down the street. He pulled out his notebook, ripped two pages from it, and handed them to Roxanne. He stood there watching the road while she looked them over.

"Brian, are you sure this is right?"

"Please, B.J."

"B.J., sorry."

"Yes."

"You actually saw them smoking?" Roxanne asked.

"Yes."

"And you think you can find out where they got it?"

"Yes," B.J. said.

"Don't feel like you have to put yourself in a situation you're not comfortable with," Roxanne said. "I know you're a new student and it takes time to adjust. Are you sure you want to help the Just Say No! campaign?"

"I'm sure," B.J. said. "I don't want to be at a school with a lot of drugs. My mom did drugs. And all the bullies are a bunch of boozers."

"Very good," Roxanne said. "You're a very brave young man. We'll be in touch."

She drove away. With his tongue, B.J. plucked the rubber band on his braces, a habit he had picked up whenever he was nervous, which was basically all the time.

*

Leslie Bangs sat staring at the blinking lights. It was a pattern. Three messages. The flashes were in time with the sledgehammer pounding on her brain. Her desk was chaos. On top of the pile sat a cold cup of coffee, and yesterday's article about the latest drug bust and the lack of leads. These police, Leslie thought, like the Keystone cops.

She had kept it hidden, her alcoholism, from everyone. It was a challenge two years ago, when she got her second DUI and lost her license for six months. She rode her bike to work or got a ride from her retired neighbor during inclement weather. But with Neil out of the picture, her family long since splintered and an afterthought, it wasn't all that hard.

And for a period, she had been good. She liked her parole officer. Frankie. With curly hair, a mustache, an earring, and a twinkle in his eyes. He always treated her with kindness and boundaries, almost like a father.

Her drinking had started in high school. It was a good way to deal with all the chaos in her life: her parents splitting up, her sister turning psychotic, the bullying at school. Even her cat died. She had drinking and music and writing. Then, after the ban, she had only drinking and writing, which meant she couldn't write about the one thing she wanted to write about. Not really, anyway. So finally, she just had drinking.

But then for a short, magical time, she had Neil. And she didn't need to drink that much, though she still did. Then he went away, and again all she had was drinking. She was a functional alcoholic, keeping her little secret, writing local journalism despite the little shakes and headaches. She was such a talented writer she could write articles in her sleep.

Then the DUIs started. The second time, she wrecked her car, and she cleaned herself up. Joined AA. Stayed sober. Until now. Music was back. And there was no editor to censor her and suppress her stories. She knew not to go back down, to mix alcohol with depression. But the other way, hope and wellness, was unknown. Was she running toward a light or an oncoming train, another crushing disappointment? The uncertainty was too much. So she was back on the sauce, staring at blinking lights with a pounding head when a wave of nausea hit her.

She just made it to the ladies' room, splattering the toilet as she ran in. But she was close enough, so the cleanup wasn't too bad. She made it back to her desk, pulled out two pairs of glasses from her purse (putting one pair on), three pens, and two hairclips before finding her little bottle. She took a quick gulp, dug around in her purse for some gum, and had just crammed in two slices of Juicy Fruit when Jane tapped on the wall of her cubicle.

"Did you hear the latest from Riverview High?" Jane asked.

"No, what happened now?" Leslie asked.

"Principal Merchant announced his retirement," Jane said, her eyes behind her glasses making her look like an owl peering over the cubicle wall. "He's not coming back after the winter break. I guess he finally bought that sailboat and is moving to the Caribbean."

"No kidding," Leslie said, swallowing another wave of nausea. "Who's going to replace him?"

"Well, that's the frustrating part," Jane remarked. "I swear, sometimes that school district is like Fort Knox with their information. Last night at the board meeting, the assistant athletic director, Gayle Leneler, went on and on about letting the Chicago Bulls shoot a commercial in the gym. Apparently, some board members had concerns about if Orlando Wool- ridge shows up and draws a crowd."

"That's absurd," Leslie said.

"Completely," Jane agreed. "Gayle told this whole story about how they already tried to shoot the commercial once, on the sly, but the Big O didn't have sneakers. Dean Early was going to let him borrow his, since blah blah blah, and the whole time I'm thinking, You just announced the principal is leaving and this is what we're talking about? Never mind that they've hired a second dean, a Ms. Grunderson, and two new security guards."

"Do they have any candidates at least?" Leslie inquired.

"We can only speculate," Jane replied. "The new assistant principal, Pete Best, is like a ghost. He vanished on some assignment to tour local schools, but he might as well be in Timbuktu. So I guess it could be Best, but they seem to really like this other new dean, Early, and then of course they could always do a search and bring in someone. The interesting thing is, with another new school board member, there are now two out of seven that are relatively unknown. I guess we'll have to wait until the next meeting to find out."

Leslie nodded, smiled, and excused herself to the bathroom.

*

Bright sunlight streamed into the Golding kitchen on a Sunday afternoon. Ray walked in the always-open backdoor. He sat down next to Ryan, who was pouring milk into a bowl of Frosted Flakes. Ryan was surprised to see him, but lately he was afraid to ask questions and get teased. Besides, there was something bigger going on now.

"Baby? You think *I'm* being a baby?" Shannon shouted at Michael. "Screw you. You're out of the band."

"You can't do that," Michael said, twirling his sabre, his orange-mohawked head in the always-open pantry.

"You don't think I can?"

"No. That requires a band vote."

"Well, I just did. As of right now, this very second, you're out of the band," she screamed and stormed out.

"Fine. Good luck finding a replacement," Michael shouted after her. He stabbed a Fruit Roll-Up with his sabre and walked out.

"What did I miss?" Ray asked Ryan, munching.

"Shannon passed her driver's test on Friday afternoon," Ryan informed him. "She drove the van last night, since we didn't have a gig. This morning my parents found Michael's bowl under the seat. It blew up into a big argument. My parents took away Shannon's license and, well, you saw the result. I thought you were visiting your dad today."

"I was," Ray said, heading to the cupboard for a bowl. "There was a lockdown, so they canceled visiting hours."

The next Saturday at the Water Tower, Stevland Morris, one of only a handful of Black students at Riverview, a starting linebacker and power forward on the basketball team, a real jock, filled in on bass for a set of standard blues and soul covers.

"That's what friends are for," said Stevland, after the set.

The next Sunday at ten o'clock, a freshly blue-mohawked Michael, along with the smell of bacon, greeted Ray as he walked into the Golding kitchen. He had overslept, and his mom had given him another week off from driving to Joliet. Tibbs and Ryan were eating French toast at the table. Brandon was washing the dishes. In the living room, Danny was teaching Amber to play the song "What'd I Say."

Michael turned back to Shannon. "I accept both your non-apology and your offer."

"It has to be a real diaper," Shannon warned.

"Oh, it will be," Michael said. "It will be."

*

Monday, December 6, Ray arrived at Riverview High School. It was the second day of his punishment for coming home past curfew with beer on his breath. He went to the cafeteria, but didn't see any of his friends, so he left. He walked down D hall, rounded the corner to E hall, and spotted Tibbs, strumming a guitar near his locker.

"How long you grounded?" Tibbs asked.

"Undetermined," Ray said. "All she said was, 'We'll see.'"

"That's at least two weekends in parent speak," Tibbs said.

Ray sat down, about to say something about Dean Early's warning, when Stephanie Nix, Tibbs's recent girlfriend, arrived. She leaned over, kissed Tibbs on the lips, and plopped down. They were playful about where she would sit. She wanted to be right next to him, but he needed space for the neck of his guitar.

"Stop," Tibbs said.

"No, you stop."

"Scoochie."

"I *am* scooching."

"No, the other way. I'm trying to tune up here."

"Oh, is this bothering you? Is my being close annoying?"

"Yes. I can't stand having your boobs in my face. It's really annoying."

Stephanie settled in next to Tibbs. The young musician started picking at chords and notes. A tune emerged. It was Otis Redding's "Dock of the Bay."

Tibbs started singing. Midway through the second verse he started to ad-lib.

I left my home in R-view

And headed for my local High

Cause I got something to live for

Looks like Steph's gonna come my way, so

I'm just sitting on the floor in E hall,

Watching the students walk away

Just sittin' on the floor in E hall

Wastin' tiiiiiiiiiiiiiiiiiii-AYEE-Ayyemmmmmmmeee

Tibbs played the melody as a solo while Ray sang the bass line over it, slightly off-key. Stephanie used her pencil and a binder for the beat, a tad erratic.

"Hey, you kids can't be doing that."

It was Bob, Riverview High School security guard, over six feet tall, in white shirt, black tie, gold badge, blue pants, and black shoes. He, along with Josephine, were the new faces of authority at RHS, brought in along with Dean Early.

"There's no guitar in the hallways," he said, hustling over. "There are early bird classes in session." Tibbs encased his guitar, and the three students followed Bob to the office.

"To be clear," Dean Early decreed from behind his desk. His big coif of brown hair was combed perfect, as always. "There is to be no guitar playing at Riverview High School, period."

"Sir," Tibbs tendered, "shouldn't we be encouraged, rather than discouraged, to pursue musical training?"

"There is marching band, orchestra, and jazz band," Dean Early responded. "I believe you are a marching band dropout, if I'm not mistaken, Mr. Tibbets."

"You are not mistaken," Tibbs said. Stephanie laughed. Dean Early glanced at her and she straightened up. He typed on his computer and glanced from the students to his screen.

"Looking over your grades, Mr. Tibbets, I see you are not passing freshman English. Perhaps you should be pursuing your *academic* training?"

"Yes, sir," Tibbs replied.

"Good. No guitars at school. Raymond Flowers, you've already been warned." He tapped away at his keyboard. "Another violation will result in an in-school suspension. And Ms. Nix, Dean Grunderson would like to see you regarding your wardrobe."

"My what?"

"You heard me."

*

That Friday at the Water Tower, since conversation was the norm during the Pringle Coffins' acoustic set, word of the guitar ban spread quickly to all corners of the musical landscape.

"He can't do that," Diamond Roth of Cool Pressure said as the singer-songwriter duo lurched into a painfully erratic and off-key cover of Dylan's "A Hard Rain's Gonna Fall."

"That's bullshit," Anne, the bassist of Whack-A-Whack, said.

"Yeah," Debbie, Whack-A-Whack's keyboard player, agreed.

"We gotta do something," Derrick, the drummer of Glass Eye, bellowed.

"Right on," Brad, the guitarist of the Laughing Tadpoles, chimed in.

Art Coffin III's voice cracked on the word "rain," and not in a good, Dylanesque way.

"We'll stage a protest," proclaimed Stu, the lead singer of the goth metal group Gobbler of Lightning.

"Let's do it!"

"They can't control us," Beth, the singer for Wawhoo Wang-Wang, cried. "We have rights."

It was Rod Pringle III's turn for a verse. To go along with his monotone voice and arrhythmic strumming, he mumbled through the lyrics—again, not in a good Dylan way. In addition to pitch, he struggled with volume; he was all over the place.

"This Monday," Stu said, his black-nail-polished index finger in the air, "we all bring guitars."

"Right on, man," Derrick from Glass Eye said.

"Fuck yeah!" Bryce, guitar player for Glass Eye, shouted, grabbing Derrick's shoulder.

"We'll play protest songs, right in the front foyer," Patrick from Whack-A-Whack said.

Art Coffin III took the next verse. The mumbling had spread like a virus in the air. There were too many lines they didn't know.

"First song will be 'Get Up, Stand Up,'" Stu determined. "If you don't know it, learn it by Monday."

"We gotta get some Clash in there," suggested Brad from the Laughing Tadpoles. "What about 'I Fought the Law'?"

"Yeah, but the law won," Debbie pointed out. "We don't want the school to win. We wanna win."

"What are you, a cheerleader?" Brad retorted. He followed with an imitation of a cheer.

"Screw you," Anne shouted, defending her Whack-A-Whack bandmate.

"You're an asshole," Debbie added.

"Stop it," Stu commanded. "Save it for the admin. 'I Fought the Law' is fine."

"We can't do a protest without 'Give Peace a Chance,'" Derrick reasoned.

"We can do whatever the fuck we want," claimed Beth from Wawhoo Wang-Wang.

"Yeah!"

"How about some CSNY, 'Ohio'?" Paul, a guitar player for the Wobble Dobbles, suggested.

"Jesus," Brad said. "No one got shot."

"I'm just saying—" Paul shrugged.

"Well don't."

"Dick," Debbie said.

"Enough," Stu commanded. "We've got three songs: 'Get Up, Stand Up,' 'I Fought the Law,' and 'Give Peace a Chance.' We'll play those three songs over and over until they drag us out."

"What about 'The Times They Are A-Changin'"?" Paul offered.

Brad was quick to imitate his voice, an octave higher, "What about 'Lil' Bo Pete Has Lost His Sheep'?"

"Asswipe," Debbie chimed in.

"Drop it," Stu barked, arms extended. "No Dylan. We wouldn't want Pringle Coffin over there to sing."

Art Coffin III, his voice hoarse, his guitar completely out of tune, muttered his way through the final verse. He reached the last line of the last chorus with a final, exhausted strain of words.

A hard raaaaaaaaaain's a-gonna fall

*

To the amazement of a still-grounded Ray Flowers, the following Monday he arrived at school to find a herd of guitarists strumming protest songs outside the front foyer. There were students tapping on bongo drums and shaking tambourines. Some didn't have instruments and just sang.

Security guards Bob and Josephine and both deans, with bullhorns, were out in front of them, warning arriving students that anyone who stopped to listen would face consequences. A few students dared to linger, but the security guards quickly dispersed them.

The strategy worked until Jenny Glass, photographer for the *Riverview Review*, dropped off her daughter.

"No cameras, ma'am," Dean Early called out.

"You're kidding, right?" Mrs. Glass responded, snapping a picture of the cross-legged guitarists as Stu led the group in belting out "Get Up, Stand Up."

"Ma'am, we would appreciate some discretion," Dean Grunderson said, covering her bullhorn's mouthpiece. Then into the bullhorn: "Keep moving. Do not stop. Anyone that congregates will be taken to in-school suspension."

"Don't ma'am me. I'm a journalist," Jenny retorted, snapping another picture. "It's literally my job to document this."

"Yes," Dean Early said. "We are all for a strong local press, but in the interest of maintaining order, we ask—" Both deans turned.

Anne, from Whack-A-Whack, recognizing the photographic opportunity, jumped on her guitar and rode it around like a broomstick.

"Young lady," Dead Grunderson warned. "Think of the consequences of your actions!"

A crowd was gathering—students and parents. Bob and Josephine, resembling mall cops in their uniforms, stood helpless as newly arrived students refused to move. Dean Early, his perfect helmet of brown hair unbothered by the wind, spoke into his bullhorn.

"Attention students: Those that loiter instead of moving toward their first period class will proceed directly to in-school suspension."

The protest singers broke into "Give Peace a Chance." The crowd joined in. One line of parents formed up close. They watched and whispered, many of them having recently moved to a new condo development. Another group of parents, longtime residents of Riverview standing further back, watched with open disdain. These were probably the same kids bringing drugs into the schools.

"Isn't this cute?" said Polly Harvey's mom to Myra Amos's mom, right near the action.

"It's great that the students are standing up for what they believe in," Myra's mom said.

"What, exactly, do they believe in?" asked Fiona Maggart's mom. "I mean, what are they protesting?"

"Huh? Oh, I'm not sure. Still, isn't it cute?"

"Students. Disperse the area."

Jenny Glass snapped away.

*

Eventually the deans and security guards, with the help of Police Chief Sumner and Deputy Copeland, succeeded in dispersing the crowd. The students that lingered for the fifteen minutes of "Give Peace a Chance," extending beyond the first period bell, were given tardies. Ray Flowers, not wanting any further trouble at home, left with Tibbs and Michael right before the bell.

The protesters—all the students that sang or played instruments—were taken to in-school suspension for the day.

"Oh, brother," Coach John Brown grumbled, looking up from page 684 of whatever voluminous book he was reading at his desk in the suspension room. "What's all this?"

The students piled instruments in the corner.

David Jones of the Wobble Dobbles, the only student already in the room (and still a little stoned from his wake-n-bake), looked up and said, "Far out."

"Quiet," Coach Brown snapped. "Everyone take a seat. No talking."

*

The phone rang in Dean Early's office.

"Good morning. This is Kent Davies, editor at the *Riverview Review*. I'm calling to let you know that we're running a story about the protest at your school. Care to comment?"

"I have no comment at this time," Dean Early said, running a comb through his hair, though it didn't need it.

"Does Principal Merchant have a comment?"

"Principal Merchant is unavailable."

"He hasn't retired yet, has he?"

"Um … No. Yes. Can I call you back?"

"Sure. We hit the presses around four p.m."

An hour later, Ray was dozing his way through Spanish pronouns.

"Repita," said Mr. Santana. The weary class responded half-heartedly.

"Yo."

"Yo."

"Tú."

"Tú."

"Él."

"El."

"No, clase. ¡Venga! ¡Con *acento*!"

"Él."

"Mr. Santana." It was Josephine at the door. The students perked up.

"Sí," Mr. Santana said.

"I need to see Ray Flowers, please."

"Señor Flowers, por favor, sale con Señorita Josephine. OK, clase: él."

"El."

"¡No! ¡Con *acento*!"

Josephine, with her short, shockingly bright red curly hair, and a square face vaguely reminiscent of a piranha, with her protruding jaw and eyes hidden behind tinted red curly-stemmed glasses, turned and without a word led Ray down Q hall, in the opposite direction of the main office. Ray followed her black, generic tennis shoes sliding soundlessly along the tile hallway, where they picked up Tibbs.

"Ray!" Tibbs said as the two high-fived. "Do you know what this is about?"

"Maybe the guitar thing?"

"Sweet."

Josephine escorted them to the in-school suspension room, where the protest singers and the bemused David Jones, on suspension for bringing a lighter to school, sat waiting in front of Coach Brown, the two deans, Chief Sumner, and Deputy Copeland, all standing in a line.

"Far out," David said.

"OK, now listen up, everybody," Dean Early began. He looked tired. A few hairs, like straggly wires, stuck out on the top of his head. "Congregating in front of the school, preventing students from getting to class on time, blocking education—"

"We weren't blocking anybody," Stu said. "This is bullshit."

Both police officers glared at the outspoken lead singer of Gobbler of Lightning.

"That's enough," Dean Early said. "There will be no more outbursts. Unless you want to spend another day here in in-school suspension."

David Jones raised both fists. "Yes," he said.

"That goes for you too, Mr. Jones," Dean Grunderson said. Her clothes and appearance had not changed much since the early '60s.

"Now," Dean Early continued, with a nod at both police officers. "We've spoken about this with Principal Merchant, and he's agreed to listen to your grievances before he goes on retirement."

"I heard he's buying a sailboat," Stu announced with a grin. "That he's sick of this place."

"Quiet," Dean Early commanded, aiming his index finger at Stu. "Principal Merchant has agreed, in effect, to try to understand what you, um, were protesting this morning. You should be grateful." He looked around the room, like he was going to say something else, but he just stood with his mouth open.

"We believe," Dean Grunderson jumped in, "that you may have been protesting the recent Board Policy number 6450, which provides mandatory suspension for drug and alcohol use or possession." Here she glanced at David.

"It was a lighter," he said.

"Not now," Dean Early barked, fixing a wiry wisp of hair.

"Or," Dean Grunderson said, "that you may be protesting the recent restriction on playing guitar in hallways at school, that both Mr. Flowers and Mr. Tibbets here recently experienced."

"Both policies suck," John Bruce, bassist for Pile of Leaves, shouted out.

"This can be over right now," Dean Early threatened. "Are we going to have a discussion or should we leave you in here?"

"We're protesting your unfair restriction on music, art, and self-expression," Stu proclaimed.

"OK." Dean Grunderson nodded. "That's what we thought. Each student involved in the protest will be allowed one sheet of notebook paper to prepare a written statement. We encourage you to focus on solutions. Mr. Flowers and Mr. Tibbets, we thought you would like to prepare statements as well. When you're finished, please return to class. Everyone else, please turn in your statements to Coach Brown."

*

That afternoon, editor Kent Davies of the *Riverview Review* received the following fax from Dean Early:

The RHS administration advocates for and cares deeply about art, music, and self-expression. Look no further than our award-winning orchestra, band, and drama cub. But when that expression precludes the high-quality education that is the right of every Riverview student, it is the administration's responsibility to protect that right. Students playing music in the hallways or the foyer during school hours will face disciplinary actions.

Kent made a copy and walked along, debating between assigning the story to Leslie Bangs, since she was covering the youth music scene, or Jane Mott, the education reporter. He reached the newsroom and frowned. Leslie had not yet arrived, after calling in sick yesterday. He left a copy on her desk and assigned the article to Jane.

*

"Thanks for meeting me here, Rachel," Anne said. "Sorry I'm late."

It was Friday night, and Riverview's newest restaurant was filling up.

"No problem. Where's the rest of Whack-A-Whack?" Rachel asked, opening the Chili's menu. "And what's with the sweatpants?"

"The rest of Whack-A-Whack are still being questioned by the police," Anne said. She had a shaved head dyed blue, and a nose stud. "And I had to go home and change. Let me tell you, tonight got downright ugly. Thanks for meeting me here. I need to *get away* from the music scene. It's out of control."

"Tell me every single thing," Rachel insisted. "And you won't find a more unmusical person to talk to, I can assure you of that. I can sing if you really want to get away from music?"

"How about a little opera?"

Rachel did a mock impersonation of a falsetto opera singer as a redheaded waiter arrived.

"Welcome to Chili's."

Both girls laughed.

"My name is Brad. Wonderful singing. Can I get you anything to drink, to cool off those vocal cords?"

"Yes," Rachel said. "My voice is on fire tonight. Coke?"

"Two Cokes," Anne added.

"Got it. Any food?"

"Should we do the Blossom?" Anne asked Rachel.

"Yes! I'm starving."

"One Awesome Blossom."

"Two Cokes and an Awesome Blossom. Let me know if I can get you anything else."

"Thanks."

"So how did it start?" Rachel asked, adjusting her purple felt hat.

"Well, it started at school yesterday. You know Beth Hazel, the loud-mouth singer for Wawhoo Wang-Wang?"

"Yeah, she's in my world civ class."

"Well, Debbie, our keyboard player, overhears Beth telling Amanda Spruce, their bassist, in the library that she named her band first, and that our band's name was a rip-off."

"Get out."

"Further, she says that we need to change our name because people are confusing Wang-Wang with Whack-A-Whack."

Brad arrived with the Cokes.

"Get out," Rachel exclaimed. "How could people confuse *wang* with *whack*?"

"Right," Anne continued. "Anyway, Debbie told her that our name came first, when our drummer Patrick was playing whack-a-mole at Sluggers, like two years ago."

"I remember—wasn't that back when they were dating?"

Anne nodded.

Rachel said, "The reason I remember is because I was like, Why would anyone take a girl to Sluggers on a date? Batting cages? Video games? Seriously?"

"I know. Maybe that's why they didn't date for very long," Anne reasoned, removing the wrapper from her straw by banging it on the table. "So like, Beth got right in Debbie's face and was saying how the organizer for the Libertyville High School Turnabout Dance booked the Whack-A-Whack by mistake, and that they really wanted to hire Wawhoo Wang-Wang but confused the names."

"I still don't know how people could confuse *whack* with *wang*," Rachel maintained, tearing the end of her straw's wrapper and blowing it up into the air. It floated like a feather before descending rapidly in a current blown by a nearby ceiling fan, coming down at a neighboring table with two older women eating salads.

"Rach," Anne chided.

Rachel lobbed over an apology.

The women returned forced grins. Rachel waved and took a sip.

"They argued in the library about which band needs to change their name," Anne continued. "Turns out the exchange gets around so that I'm sitting in trig and suddenly David Jones passes me a note."

"Isn't he in the Wobble Dobbles?"

"Right," Anne said. "Their guitarist. He passes me a note saying that Whack-A-Whack are Hack-A-Hacks and need to change our name."

"He did not."

"He did."

"Well, it's no secret that David still has a thing for Beth," Anne reported.

"Didn't they used to go out?" Rachel asked, altering the air pressure in her straw by putting her finger over the top to trap some Coke in the bottom, then pulling her straw up and letting it fall.

"They sure did," Anne confirmed. "In fact, David used to be in Wawhoo Wang-Wang. Like a year ago. Before he and Beth broke up and she kicked him out of the band. Then Paul Hewson joined Wang-Wang. No surprise they're dating now."

"She is such a slut," Rachel smirked, letting more Coke fall.

"With a capital S," Anne agreed. "Then David comes up to me after class and starts telling me that he knows the Libertyville organizers really meant to hire the Wobble Dobbles for the Turnabout Dance."

"Shut up."

Brad arrived with the Awesome Blossom. "Do you guys want anything else?" he asked.

"Just the Blossom for now," Anne said.

"Confusing *wang* and *whack* is a stretch. But wobble isn't even close to *wang*. Or *whack* for that matter."

They pulled out some fried onion, dipped, and ate.

"Shit, that's hot," Rachel cried out, sipping her Coke.

Anne chewed with her mouth open to allow as much air as possible to escape the scalding fried onion. She took a drink and continued. "The whole thing kept building, both Wawhoo Wang-Wang and the Wobble Dobbles making false claims against our band."

"So stupid," Rachel deemed, blowing on a chunk of Awesome Blossom.

"Right?" Anne agreed. "Patrick got a note in his locker saying we should change our name to the Whack-Offs because that's the only instrument he knows how to play."

"Ouch," Rachel said. "Not my Patty-Patty Duke-Duke."

"Yep," Anne confirmed. "And he still has the hots for Tiffany Alexander, so no change there."

"Is she still playing tambourine in Glass Eye?"

"Not very well. She's basically a dancer."

"Sheeesh. I should be the tambourine player in your band. I could do better."

"The offer still stands."

Rachel rubbed her chin in mock consideration.

"The whole thing swirled around school all day, all nasty rumors and BS," Anne said, tossing some dipped onion in her mouth. "Well, before sixth period, our whole band was walking through the courtyard, talking about how lame the whole thing is, Patrick and Debbie and our guitarist Floyd, when who should walk out into the courtyard but Wawhoo Wang-Wang, the entire band."

Brad brought two more Cokes.

"And who should come out of the door by the cafeteria?" Anne asked.

"The Wobble Dobbles?"

"The entire band."

"Get out."

"I'm dead serious."

"Sounds like a western. High noon in the courtyard."

"Exactly. We all meet in the middle," Anne continued. "And David, like he's Clint Eastwood or some shit, says the band that plays best tonight at the Water Tower gets to keep their name, and the two other bands have to change their name. There's this big argument, like who's going to be the judge of it all, and Bob the security guard has to break it up. Floyd spit on Amanda Spruce."

"I love it. Love. It. Forget Patrick. I want to date Floyd. I would pay a million dollars to see Amanda Spruce get spat on. Spitted on? Sput on? Whatever. What happened?"

"Somehow in the confusion Beth Hazel gets everyone to agree that Christian Ball, the drummer for the 7 x 10 Splits, would be an impartial judge."

"I loooovvvve Christian. And he *would* be fair."

Anne nodded and ate.

"So what happened tonight?"

"Well, the Wobble Dobbles went first. And they literally died on stage. It was death. Pure death. The crowd was bored to tears."

"Of course they were. They're terrible."

"Well, David starts arguing about how it was all a sham, that we had like *paid* people to come to the Water Tower to not like their band."

"Of course he did."

"Anyway, so then Wawhoo Wang-Wang went next," Anne continued. "And they were OK. Like just OK. I mean they're not a terrible band. I actually like some of their songs. Beth Hazel is not a bad singer, even if she *is* a bitch. They have some catchy tunes, but it was just OK. Nothing earth-shattering."

"Right. They're not bad. But not good either."

"Totally. Then it was our turn. Mr. Pringle Jr., having heard of the dispute, created the order. I think he gave us the last slot because he likes us the most. Just my opinion."

"He's a nice a guy. Even if his son is like the worst singer in the world, just below me, if that's possible."

"Everyone in the world is worse than you, darling," Anne said. "But I don't know what it was, the whole competition or all the Hack-A-Hack and Smack-A-Smack hate we were getting, or the whole like, you know, pride in our name, that we were playing for the name Whack-A- Whack. That it was on the line."

"It was. It totally was."

"We were *on*. Every song. Right from our opener, 'Bang the Mole,' the first song we wrote together. We were totally in the zone."

"I'm sorry I missed it. How did—"

"I'll tell you," Anne said. "We're five songs into our set. Killing it. The audience totally into it. Christian is there in the front row, and it's written all over his face. That's when it happened."

"What, love?"

"Out of nowhere David Jones sneaks onto the stage, creeps up right behind Patrick's drum kit."

"No."

"Yes. Atomic wedgie. Right over the head. Then he grabs a spare drumstick and makes it a twirlie."

"An atomic twirlie? Not on my Patty. Tell me he doesn't wear tighty-whities."

"The tighty part is accurate. But they're not white. Tighty Spiderman undies. His spider powers were no match. Right in the middle of our song 'The Face of the Hammer,' you know, the one with the big drum solo?"

"I love that song," Rachel said. She grabbed her fork and knife and started drumming. She started singing: "So flat. So smooth. Not a place to stammer. It's the face of the hammer."

"Right, well, Patrick starts off into his solo when the wedgie started. He tried valiantly to keep playing, and David has like a stocking cap, the ones with the holes in them, so you can't see who it is, but I know it's David from his red Converse shoes. Patrick kept up the solo during the atomic wedgie, but during the twirl he started to lose it. When David let go, all the twists in the elastic caused the drumstick to spin around and hit him in the back of the head."

"Poor Patty Duke-Duke."

"It threw us off," Anne said. "We never recovered. It was like when the elastic of his undies broke, so did our spirit. I guess it was uncomfortable, like up his crack and all. His drumming was erratic for the last few songs. We had to start 'Get Back in Your Hole' three times. It was terrible."

"I can imagine."

"After the set, Patrick charged David and gave him a fireman's carry wedgie," Anne said.

"A fireman's carry?"

"Right, like a fireman carrying someone from a fire."

"Oh, duh."

"Then all wedgie hell broke loose. The Wobble Dobbles tried to like gang-wedgie Debbie. Floyd gave a frontal dizzy wedgie to their drummer, Jackson Irons, and he—"

"A dizzy wedgie?"

"Right, like spun him around after the wedgie. A frontal wedgie, no less."

"Yikes. Frontal. He grabbed his underpants from the front?"

"Like I said, it was out. Of. Control. Jackson Irons got all dizzy, hit his head on an old water pump that's in the corner, knocked himself out. It became a pile of squirming musicians, this giant writhing thing, all screaming and biting and giving wedgies."

"Holy cow," Rachel said somberly.

"Right, that's why I was late," Anne confessed. "Someone gave me a frozen wedgie."

"A frozen wedgie?"

"They poured a Frosty down my pants."

"Oh my."

"It was madness. Cops everywhere. I ran, Frosty pants and all."

"Darling, you poor thing."

"But it can't be just our name. It felt like something more than that."

Brad arrived and removed the decimated Blossom.

"Anything else I can get you?"

"Just the check."

"Hey, you look familiar. I play guitar in a band called the Laughing Tadpoles. Aren't you in the Wang-A-Wangs?"

Anne buried her face in her hands.

WANING GIBBOUS

"Raaaaaay, Laura, pancakes are ready," Bonnie Flowers called up the stairs.

It was Sunday morning. Ray rolled over. He had a slight hangover. He thought about faking sick. He wasn't up for seeing his dad today. It was getting old. He heard his older sister, Laura, walk down the hallway and go down the stairs.

"Raaaaay," his mom called again moments later. "Get your cakes while they're hot."

Ray sat up in bed. Last night's show was still ringing in his ears. He saw his new harmonica on his nightstand, an early Christmas present from his dad. Well, he should probably go to tell his dad thank you. In the six days since the Flowers family's last Sunday visit to the Joliet prison, Ray had been glued to his newest instrument. With the help of Frets, and a loaner rack so he could play harmonica and guitar at the same time, he quickly became proficient. The sadness he saw in his father's eyes, he blew it all out. Then last night, on their Saturday night set at the Water Tower, Shannon and the Little Brothers closed with a version of the Yardbirds' "Train Kept A-Rollin'." Alex Miller, an accomplished harp player for the Polyps, joined them on stage and traded solos with Ray. The impromptu dual harmonica solo lasted almost ten minutes and had the clapping audience revved up to a frenzy.

It was all coming back to Ray as he stared up at the ceiling. After the set, they had all been sitting outside looking over the lake when a large man wearing a coat and tie approached them. He had his right arm in a sling. "My name's Chester," he said. "I'd shake your hands, but I had an accident." After holding up the sling, he continued. "I own the Elbo Room downtown, on Lincoln Avenue. Maybe you've heard of it."

"Elbow?" Shannon had replied. "Let's see. We've been to the Ankle Room. The Kneecap Room. The Wrist Room is a personal favorite of Tibbs." She made a motion of jerking off.

"We can be in the Elbow Room right now," Tibbs responded, holding up his elbow near Shannon's chin.

"That's good," Chester responded. "I like a group with a little spunk. Anyway, I loved the set. Great mix of tunes. The oldies and goodies. I danced my ass off to your 'Devil in a Blue Dress.' Haven't heard a band nail that one in a while. And your original stuff doesn't make me that nauseous. Not sure about that popsicle song though. What are you singing about anyway? Frozen shit? I guess it's a teenage thing. So whaddaya say? Can you suburban kids get down to the city? I got openings on Friday night, so yous don't even have to stay out late on a school night."

He had given them a card and left with words that echoed in Ray's slightly hungover mind. "Gimme a call; you kids can play."

"Raaaaaaaaaaay," Bonnie yelled. "You are *not* staying home this week. We're leaving in an hour and your pancakes are getting cold!"

*

Later, at White Hen Pantry, Brandon couldn't put his finger on what gave him the feeling. It felt off. Lou seemed tense. The guy in the corner of the store wouldn't leave. Brandon saw Lou look at the guy, like he was indicating something. On this particular Sunday afternoon drive to the convenience store, Brandon and Danny didn't end up buying any pot. They bought chips and two Dr. Peppers and drove back home. It was a good thing, they would realize later.

"Where's Ray?" Brandon asked, stepping into the kitchen.

"It's Sunday," Tibbs mocked. "Duh."

Danny, following behind, let out a prodigious burp as a kind of greeting.

"Oh, right," Brandon recalled with a smack of his forehead. "Visiting his dad. I forgot."

Brandon, Ryan, Tibbs, Danny, and Dave sat around the kitchen table. Ryan was eating Rice Krispies.

"Where's Shannon, Curtis, and Michael?" Brandon inquired.

"Shannon went shopping with Mom," Dave said. "Estimated arrival time sixteen hundred."

"Curtis had a science fair project. Some solar robot contest in Vernonshire," Tibbs reported.

"Michael has a fencing tournament," Dave added.

"What would you say, Ryan? Are those Rice Krispies Snap, Crackle, and Popping in five-eighths time?" Danny asked.

"Beats me," Ryan said.

"Beats me. A pun. Ryan the punster," Danny joked.

"What's a pun?" Ryan asked, scooping sugar onto his cereal.

"Do you seriously not know what a pun is?" Danny marveled.

Ryan shook his head and slurped.

"How can we have a band meeting with only half the band?" Brandon asked. "Who called this meeting?"

"I did. For an important reason," Danny said. "But we have more pressing matters. Ryan doesn't know what a pun is."

"He's messing with you," Tibbs said.

"I don't think so," Danny contested.

"Ryan, do you really not know what a pun is?" Tibbs asked.

Ryan shook his head.

"It's a play on words. Something that makes you groan," Dave clarified. "Like, What's the musical part of a snake?"

"Its tongue?" Ryan offered.

"No. Its scales. What kind of music are balloons afraid of?"

"Rock?"

"No. Pop music."

"Those are all puns. Where did the music teacher leave her keys?"

"The piano."

"You got it," Dave said, smiling. "But it doesn't have to be in a joke format. It can be part of everyday speech."

"Like 'beats me,'" Danny said. "Get it. Beats?"

Ryan nodded while he ate.

"What's up?" Tibbs asked Danny. "You want to be the lead singer?"

"I don't think our audience is quite ready for my falsetto," Danny sang. He sang high in his alien voice, "I'd like to talk about the future."

"What about it?" Tibbs asked. "You mean the offer from the Elbo Room guy? I thought we agreed that Shannon was going to give him a call after we cleared it with our parents."

"Right, that's been decided," Danny conceded, still singing but coming back to his regular mezzo-soprano. "Shannon is graduating at the end of the year. Has she told you guys her plans?"

Brandon, Dave, and Ryan all shook their heads.

"Wow, she doesn't even tell her own brothers," Danny exclaimed, back to his regular nasal speaking voice. "Well, I asked her that very question. During the winter break she's planning on touring some colleges, two in Wisconsin and one in Illinois. Turns out, she hasn't totally abandoned the idea of becoming an Olympic diver."

The crackle of Rice Krispies filled the silence.

"This isn't news, is it?" Danny asked with raised eyebrows. "Shannon is a senior, a state champion diver being pursued by Olympic coaches. What did you expect?"

"I heard her say once that college is for morons," Tibbs shared. "She's always arguing with Mrs. G about it. I thought, I don't know, that she would just stick around."

Ryan's spoon clinked the edges of the bowl.

"And did you guys think your parents would be OK with that? You know that you've got to earn a degree," Danny said. "You have *met* your parents, right? And c'mon, what would you choose, a garage band or the Olympics Games?"

They pondered this choice for a moment, as if no one had ever given it the slightest thought.

"What do we do for a lead singer when she goes?" Tibbs asked. "Is that what this is about?"

"I've got an offer to play in a jazz quintet," Danny replied.

"You're quitting?" Tibbs asked.

Ryan lifted the bowl and slurped. A few drops dribbled on his flannel shirt.

"Not exactly," Danny answered. "The quintet is just forming. At first it would be part-time. I could still play in the Little Brothers this year, even in the summer. But next fall, when Shannon goes off to school, that's when I would start playing full-time. Besides, the rumor is the Water Tower is shut down after the wedgie-rama."

"It's like that?" Tibbs scowled. "Why not just join the fucking quintet now?" He stood up, knocking his chair over. "Way to treat your brothers," he added, walking out.

"What does he expect?" Danny asked. "Without Shannon there is no Shannon and the Little Brothers. It's not like we can stay together forever."

Ryan got up and put his bowl in the sink. Brandon chewed on his fingernails.

"I've got a joke," Dave said. "It's not a pun, though, Ryan."

"Let's hear it," Danny said.

"How do you get a guitar player off your front porch?"

They all shook their heads.

"Pay for the pizza."

*

December 13, 1982

Drug Bust Shuts Down Water Tower

By Leslie Bangs

Over the weekend, Christmas came early for police in both Riverview and Lowland Park. Working in tandem with the FBI and DEA, officers made their first significant drug bust in the face of the ongoing adolescent drug abuse crisis. It occurred at 10:00 p.m. at the Water Tower in Lowland Park, the popular music venue for local youth. Inside, the crowd moshed to the Butter People, a group from Lincolnshire, who closed their set with their teenage anthem, "Melt Me." Outside in the parking lot, a drug deal was going down.

Lowland Park police, working with federal DEA agents,

watched "El Hombre," a Puerto Rican smuggler known for his big straw hat, sell drugs to teenagers in the parking lot of the Water Tower. Agents and police followed him from the parking lot to the new apartment complex on Lexington Avenue in Riverview. With Riverview police providing backup, they found over one hundred pounds of marijuana, cocaine, heroin and methamphetamines in the trunk of El Hombre's car.

In a press conference on Sunday, Riverview Police Chief Gordon Sumner reported that two weeks prior, a sting involving the FBI found several employees of White Hen Pantry to be mules for a massive drug operation known as the Velvet Tunnel.

And now, in what is sure to be a blow to the local music scene — in particular Riverview's struggle to lift the now over-three-decade-old ban on rock music — a sting Sunday night by Chief Sumner has netted a dozen underage arrests.

"We had been following leads for months," Deputy Stewart Copeland said. "We knew it was big."

This comes on the heels of an incident on Friday night, when a violent "wedgie-rama" caused the Water Tower to close early. According to local law enforcement, the music venue has shut its doors to live music indefinitely. Rod P. Pringle Jr., the plant superintendent, declined comment.

*

Monday morning, December 13, Pete Best pulled out of the Riverview Bakery and drove north toward Riverview High School. The sun lingered below the frozen horizon like a head about to peek out. There were only a few cars on the road. He clicked on the radio and, for the first time in his life, driving through the streets of Riverview, he listened to rock music on his FM dial, clear as a bell. Despite the cold, he rolled the windows down and stepped on the gas. The DJ came on at the next red light.

"That was 'Hurt So Good' by John Cougar. Before we get to some Steve Miller, here's .38 Special."

Pete took a sip of his coffee and turned up "Caught Up in You."

He was back. He was still the assistant principal, but now, with Principal Merchant's retirement, there was no one directly above him. He drove along Waukegan Road, tapping his fingers to the beat on his steering wheel, trying to figure out where he stood. For two months he had been on a wild goose chase, exiled, driving all over the county. A silver lining was that Roy appeared to finally be settling into his new school, which made it all worth it, even if Pete's work life was upside down. With Roy doing better, things had calmed on the marriage front, for now, though the distance remained.

The more he thought about it, the more he would get twisted into knots. The only thing that was clear was that Superintendent Jag wanted him as far away from Riverview High School as possible. Until last Friday, that is, when Topper Chimes, one of the established board members that always seemed to blend in, called and informed him that his "learning and observation tour," as they called it, was complete and he should report for work on Monday morning. But Pete didn't want to wait until Monday. He had decided to go in on Saturday. He wanted to get into his office. He wanted to see George. But it was the night custodian, Eddie Severino, working overtime, that he had run into at the front entrance.

"Good morning, Eddie. Good to see you again," Pete said.

"It will be a good morning when I'm paid extra for my overtime," Eddie replied, and closed and locked the door in Pete's face.

So today, Monday morning! He would have to find out the state of things as the day went along. Pete stopped at a red light and considered what his next move should be. He had just finished eating a donut at the Riverview Bakery, reading Leslie Bangs in the *Riverview Review*. The article involved a free concert at a racetrack a week ago Sunday in nearby Arlington Heights. A Riverview student with a severe peanut allergy had been exposed to peanut butter—apparently from, of all things, a wedgie—and hospitalized in serious condition. He passed away. And not just any student. Trevor Gradenko.

Leslie Bangs had been Pete's only source of information about Riverview's growing music scene. And lately that source had been a little erratic. Pete was left to infer and guess. Music had been growing in Lowland Park, but now it had combusted. With the drug bust and now a new tragedy—in another suburb even farther away—the status was even more ambiguous. It was all too much to piece together. And there was one other thing, according to articles by Jane Mott: Both the school board and the town council had experienced some turnover. There were new, younger faces. The light changed.

He needed to talk to George.

He drove along, tapping the groove on his steering wheel, and turned onto Warrior Road. He looked at the van parked in the space next to his. He read the words on the side of the vehicle: GRADENKO HOME GOODS. He turned the radio off and parked.

*

Pete walked toward the entrance. The flags were at half-mast. It felt surreal, like a haunted house—a place haunted by his memories—but peaceful in the low morning light.

He stepped into the foyer and found two women waiting for him. "Mrs. Gradenko, I'm so sorry about your son," Pete said. "Trevor was a wonderful young man." He offered a handshake, which received a tepid and loose acceptance.

"Thank you," Roxanne Gradenko said, and burst into tears. Courtney Harrison pulled Roxanne in for a hug to shield her from Pete's wide eyes.

"It's still so raw," Courtney informed Pete with mouthed words.

Courtney pulled tissues from her purse, smoothing Roxanne's Princess Diana hair. Pete stood and waited at a distance. When it felt right, he invited them into his office and sat down behind his desk, getting his index finger going on the edge in a gentle waltz time, the first beat emphasized ever so gently.

Roxanne swallowed hard and began.

"We are here today so that Trevor's death is not in vain," Roxanne uttered in one breath.

"I understand," Pete said. "How can I help?" He was wearing a button-down shirt and slacks. It was the first time he had been at Riverview High School as an administrator not wearing a tie.

Roxanne faltered. Courtney stepped in. "We believe—Roxanne believes—that the music, particularly the rock and roll scene with its relationship to drugs and alcohol, is responsible for Trevor's death. I mean, look at what happened at that water place."

Pete nodded. "This tragedy never should have happened."

Roxanne stared, removed her glasses, and dabbed her eyes.

"Never," Courtney repeated.

"How can the administration help?" Pete asked. He slowed his waltz to largo.

Roxanne took a deep breath. "We believe that the school is not enforcing—as it should be—the ban on rock music at RHS. First there was that Mudfest in the fall. Then there were those open mic things, right on our campus. And the infestation has spread across our town border to the water place. This corrupting music has crept into the lives of our students like a parasite. An infection. It's rotting their minds."

"Like a virus," Courtney added.

"Yes, a virus," Roxanne agreed, now pointing at the ceiling for emphasis. "Students are hearing it on the weekends, they are getting it on television with this music television, they hear it on the radio, and now they are hearing it in our schools. The Parents Music Resource Center is doing what it can with regards to explicit lyrics—"

"Good morning, Mr. Best," Pam Susan said through his phone speaker. "Welcome back."

"Hi, Pam," Pete said, pausing his index finger waltz to press the button for speaker. "I'm in a meeting."

"Oh—I was wondering when I saw your door closed," Pam said. "Looks like it's going to be a busy day right from the get-go. Jim Plant called. And you have another visitor waiting. Assistant Athletic Director Leneler is here. She would like to discuss something she deems 'super-duper big-time important.'"

Pete smiled at Roxanne and Courtney. "OK. Tell Gayle it will be a few minutes." He returned to a neutral expression, the exact face he used playing poker, but even this had a glint of laughter in his eyes. His finger resumed waltz time.

"We're here this morning," Roxanne resumed, "representing the Riverview Citizens for Drug Awareness, with the support of Nancy Reagan, along with the Parents Music Resource Center—national organizations—to urge you to enforce the ban on rock music and the invasion of an immoral influence on Riverview children."

"Enforce the ban," Courtney emphasized.

Pete nodded. "By all means," he said, after a pause. "Student safety is our number one priority." Courtney and Roxanne both nodded. Roxanne dabbed her eyes.

"That's right," Courtney said.

"If I'm not mistaken," Pete offered, "Nancy Reagan's Just Say No! program is now fully implemented in Riverview schools, K-12, along with Board Policy number 6450, which provides for mandatory suspension. These are steps that have been taken to stem the flow of drugs and alcohol in our schools."

"Yes," Roxanne agreed. "Steps we feel proud to be part of."

"Now is the perfect opportunity for the next step," Courtney added.

"The next step—" Pete began.

"Yes. Enforce the ban," Roxanne said.

"Enforce it," Courtney echoed. "Make a statement. To the students, the town, the board, the newspaper. Show everyone that you are on our side. Especially if you want to be considered for principal. Do it for Trevor."

Pete smiled a tight smile. He heard the sound of acrylic fabric out in the hallway, then a knock on the door. Assistant Athletic Director Leneler burst into the office with a flurry of hugs. Pete's waltzing index finger froze.

"Welcome back, Mr. Best! Mrs. Gradenko, I'm so sorry for your loss! Truly! My heart goes out to you!" Gayle turned to Courtney. "Hi! I don't believe we've met! I'm Gayle Leneler, assistant athletic director here at Riverview High School." She whirled back around to Roxanne, right in her grill. "I watched Trevor develop into quite the baseball and volleyball player. I was just *devastated* by the news."

"It's nice to meet you," Courtney said to her back, letting fall her empty hand.

"Thank you for your kind words," Roxanne replied.

"I don't mean to interrupt! Ms. Susan told me you were here. I just wanted to offer my condolences. I *was* here because I heard through the old grapevine that our recently retired principal was thinking of canceling the annual Holiday Seniors vs. Staff Dodgeball Game."

Roxanne blinked as her smile faded.

"Gayle, if you could just give us —" Pete attempted.

"Yes, last year Mr. Blackburn tore his rotator cuff, Mr. Fair hurt his back, and Mrs. Sheffield tore her ACL. A real rash of injuries … so a lot of the teachers said enough is enough."

"Gayle, this can wait until—"

"But I was thinking about it over the weekend, and I thought, What a loss, what a tragedy it would be if this tradition, this annual rite of passage, an athletic event that really brings the school together, captures our Warrior pride, our school spirit …" Gayle gesticulated, her hands getting higher with each phrase.

Roxanne nodded like she only partially understood a foreign language. Courtney cleared her throat with a glance at Pete, who sighed behind a mixed smile.

"I know from the time they are freshmen, students look forward to whipping a dodgeball at their teacher's head," Gayle said with a guffaw. "Well, not at their head, because that would be against the rules, but you know what I mean." She gave Roxanne a squeeze on the arm. Roxanne glanced at Courtney with a look that said, Did this woman just squeeze my arm?

"*Mr.* Best," Courtney interjected. "If we could return—"

"All day long I was thinking about it. How can we keep the game, but also make it safer for our teachers?"

"Yes, Gayle, please, we were in the middle of a very important—"

"Important is right. These issues demand leadership, sir, and there's currently a vacuum of leadership at this school. That's why I'm here first thing to share my idea with you. When Ms. Susan told me that Mrs. Gradenko was here, well, my idea just seemed to slide into another one, like a hand into a glove." She winked and pretended to put a glove on.

Courtney shrugged her shoulders and crossed her arms.

"Idea?" Roxanne asked. "I'm sorry, you have some kind of idea?"

"Yes," Gayle beamed with a broad smile. "I was thinking that instead of the senior-staff dodgeball game …"

Pete bit down on his lip. All ten of his fingers let fly a burst of fortissimo notes on the edge of his desk. Roxanne looked around like she wasn't sure of her current whereabouts.

Gayle glanced from face to face. "Volleyball." The three faces returned blank stares.

"Volleyball," she said again, nodding vigorously, a wide smile breaking through. "What if we replaced dodgeball with volleyball? It's safer! Everyone loves volleyball! I know you love your V-ball, Mr. Best. It would be like Mudfest without the mud. And this music all the kids are raving about, Mr. Best, I know you—"

"Thank you, Gayle, for your suggestion, now if you could please—"

"And get this. We could name it …" The three faces collectively stared.

"The Trevor Gradenko Memorial Senior-Staff Volleyball Holiday Classic," Gayle said with her hands extended. "We could work out a different name—I only just thought of it—but wouldn't it be cool if we named the senior-staff volleyball game after Trevor?"

Roxanne nodded in a daze. She looked to Courtney to confirm that yes, this was, in fact, happening.

"It's something to think about," Pete conceded, now physically, gently but firmly, escorting Gayle out of the office. "Thank you for stopping by."

"It was nice meeting you," she said to Courtney, who hadn't actually introduced herself. "Again, my condolences, Mrs. Gradenko! Thoughts and prayers. Thank you, Mr. Best! He's *the* best. He's not Mr. Good or Mr. Great. He's Mr. Best, ladies and gentlemen, B-E-S-T!"

"Bye, now," Pete said in the hall. He called over to Pam. "No more interruptions."

"Sorry, Mr. Best. Gayle said she was heading to the bathroom."

Back behind his desk, Pete smiled at Roxanne and Courtney. His index finger resumed the waltz. "You'll have to excuse Gayle," he said. "She's a real asset to our athletic department. As you can see, very enthusiastic and always thinking of the kids. Now, back to the matter at hand."

"Enforce the ban," Courtney demanded.

"Protect our kids," Roxanne said, regaining her bearings.

"If I were to, as you suggest, enforce the ban on rock music," Pete began, as if wading into cold water, "do you think that the students would not listen to it on their own?"

Roxanne and Courtney shared a glance to see if the other would handle the question.

"Mr. Best," Courtney began. "We know we can't control every single minute of our children's lives. We know that. We do. Our kids will someday be around drugs and alcohol and have to make their own minds up. We know that."

"We do," Roxanne added, crossing her legs.

"But sir," Courtney continued. "What message is the school sending our young people by endorsing this music in its own events, its own student union even?"

Roxanne clasped her hands together. "Songs with lewd lyrics, endorsing drugs and sexual promiscuity. Performed at school-sponsored events. We have hard evidence. Trevor probably never would have …" she trailed off.

"We certainly don't endorse the kind of activity that occurred at the race-track," Pete said, jumping to allegretto. "But also, as an administrator I believe the students need an opportunity to express themselves."

"Oh, gosh," Roxanne cried out, a tissue returning to her eyes. "I knew this was a waste of time. We have to go to the board. It's our only recourse."

"Mr. Best," Courtney maintained. "Maybe in your absence, you didn't realize the depth of our school's drug and alcohol problem. The music is part of that problem. Pink Floyd. Prince. Madonna. These artists are sending our kids the wrong message. Being a part of society isn't something that is alienating."

Pete's face stiffened, like he was preparing to take a plunge.

"Would you agree that Trevor's death was an accident?" he questioned, using his wrist to finish the waltz.

Roxanne sniffled into her tissue. Courtney grimaced.

"A horrible accident, but an accident nonetheless. The wedgies, the unknown severity of his peanut allergies, the use of peanut butter in a wedgie itself is… the whole thing …"

Courtney stood. "And won't you be sorry when the next tragedy happens. It'll mean your job. Let's go, Roxanne."

The two women walked out. Pete's hand went to loosen his tie, but he wasn't wearing one.

*

Rick Ocase sat in his mustard-yellow Buick LeSabre at the crossroads of Kenton Road and Dartmouth Avenue. Since being given this new territory to patrol, he had avoided Kenton Road, the one that turned to Sullivan Street. He didn't trust himself. He knew if he pulled onto Kenton, he would turn onto Sullivan Street, and that if he pulled onto Sullivan Street, he would visit Suzie. He sat at the crossroads, looking at the open fields of South Park Elementary. It was the golden hour; the sun was setting behind him, and the field, trees, and red brick building glowed in the fading light. Christmas lights on automatic timers flashed on all around the neighborhood. He sat at the crossroads, his brain squirming, the vehicle he drove so expertly idling. He couldn't drive, so he turned where he always did with his mind: to the past.

Rick was not a retard. That's what they called him, though, during his years at South Park Elementary. He had to go to school with all the other disabled kids, who were also called that. Tommy Peters, who was deaf. Regina Daultrey, who used a wheelchair. Keith Callisto, with his outbursts and tantrums. Joan Oxford, with her therapy dog and the dog whistle that she blew. Like the rest of them, Rick had a disability, but he was not dumb.

He was smart—he just couldn't talk. A reaction to the smallpox vaccine stopped his breathing when he was an infant. Two minutes without oxygen damaged his brain, specifically Broca's area, which is responsible for speech. From then on, the right side of his face was always pulled into sort of a smirk, not quite a grin. And his right eyelid drooped so that his eye was always half closed. He was nonverbal as a child until he was eight. Instead of talking, he bellowed and moaned and yelled. His first words were "ice cream." And from nine years old on, he mumbled more than he spoke. The delay in speech hindered his learning *how* to talk to people. As a teen, though his speech improved, he struggled immensely with communication.

He spoke too fast, then too slow. He missed simple conversation cues, like when to listen and when to speak. His volume was always off—too loud or too soft. Or it would rise and fall erratically. When he finally did get people to listen to what he had to say, he spoke in circles, forgetting in the struggle what it was he wanted to say in the first place. He was easily confused and frustrated, and he would shut down.

He was a lonely kid. His best friend was the radio programming of 1940s America. The other kids teased him. He was bullied or ignored. He had a few fights. His mother was in no place to help him, reeling from the triple blow of losing her husband in the battle of Okinawa, then the vaccine that stopped her baby's breath, and finally her genetics that clicked one day into schizophrenia. Instead of recognizing his intelligence and helping him with his speech, she became overprotective and irrational, believing he was allergic to all food that wasn't McDonald's, potato chips, vanilla ice cream, or Pepsi.

As the decade turned to 1950, Rick entered Riverview High School and had a new cure for loneliness: the television. But at school, he was still lumped in with the other disabled kids at the end of Q hall, known as "the cage," where he didn't belong. His mother bringing him McDonald's every day didn't help. Beneath a calm, quiet surface, he was angry, frustrated, and jealous of his older brother, Perry, the football star, who acted like Rick didn't exist.

There was, however, one person who was nice to him, starting all the way back at South Park. His neighbor, Suzie Quintal. She told the mean kids on the playground to leave him alone. When Kenny Gaspar pushed him into the mud, Suzie told the principal and got Kenny suspended. She walked to Riverview Middle School with him. She taught him how to ride a bike and how to play tennis. They would go on bike rides to play tennis at the park. Suzie knew Rick was smart. She knew he read books and magazines and newspapers and understood them all. She would read him her poetry and show him her drawings, and over those tender, formative years, Rick fell deeper and deeper in love with her. Sometimes she held his hand. She always smelled so nice. He thought she might love him too, but he was afraid of that thought. It scared him, like lightning and loud thunder. It was terrifying.

And so, on the day when Riverview had its first outdoor music festival in June of 1951, Rick and Suzie rode their bikes down to Riverview Park. Standing with Suzie in the outfield, after the high school orchestra finished playing, he heard something he had never heard before, what was at that time called race music. His body moved in time with the rhythm. For the first time in his life, he was dancing, stomping his feet and shaking his hips, right along with Suzie, and it felt good. He was loose, free to move; he could smile and sing and twist and shout and nobody would laugh at him. He watched the singer and did his best to impersonate him, swaying and thrusting his hips. Suzie watched him, wide-eyed. He remembered her speaking to him, her mouth close to his ear, her hair touching his shoulder: "Rick, I've never seen you like this." For the first time in his life, Rick felt free. He had this new crazy sound, and he had Suzie.

Then the storm started. For a while, the music continued, but Rick was getting nervous. His face, the right side, cranked extra tight, closing his right eye while his left eye widened in fright. He started making his nervous sounds, the ones that got stuck in his throat, rattled around, and slipped out the side of his mouth. It started raining, then pouring. The wind was swirling. There was lightning and thunder, and then a nearby branch cracked. The sky opened, a barrage of water and light and sound. But not just from above. There was music, somehow still playing, and shouting and sirens. And then people were running and there were police cars and fire trucks, and he was running too.

He lost Suzie in the melee. He went to the bike rack near the library, but Suzie's bike was gone. He jumped on his green Schwinn and rode as fast as he could, his lungs screaming for air, riding in the pouring rain straight to Suzie's house, but she wasn't there. He cruised over and checked the tennis courts and the secret places they had walked. The places she had held his hand and read him her poetry. She was nowhere to be found.

He went home. The rain was still coming down, but it had lost its vigor, as if the storm, too, was worn out from the day's events. He walked his bike along the puddled, empty streets. He parked his bike in the garage, went inside and upstairs. And that's when he found Suzie, half naked in his brother's room. And so back out, running, into the rain.

He didn't talk to her after that. He ran from her that day, and continued to run from her ever since, avoiding her at every turn. She tried to talk to him. At home. At school. But he stayed away. She wrote him a few letters, but he tore them up. The new reality settled in. He was like a scorned lover, but Rick had a bigger problem, a harder question he now had to wrestle with: Was it ever love?

A year passed, and he got caught spying on her, watching her change in her bedroom. But somehow Suzie smoothed it all out with her dad and the police, and it all went away. Rick knew not to watch anymore. He was smart. Another year passed. Both Suzie and Rick went to college. His mother insisted he attend the University of Illinois, that her son was as smart as anyone. Suzie went off to a liberal college out east, in Maine or Massachusetts. Four years later Rick graduated with a degree in business, but no one would hire him, because he still couldn't talk.

Rick Ocase moved back to Riverview, to his childhood home. He worked at McDonald's in nearby Lowland Park and joined the Riverview Presbyterian Church, where he bought into the teachings that this new music was not a good thing at all. It was part of the evil of this world. It's what drove Suzie into his brother's arms. The evil that lived inside bullies on playgrounds.

Rick became a creature of habit. He worked at McDonald's. He watched University of Illinois football and basketball. He went to church every Sunday. And he joined first the Devil Dashers and next the Cars, patrolling the streets of Riverview, his eyes and ears part of a collective eyes and ears, protecting innocent children from evil. He had been innocent once. And no one had protected him.

He was an excellent employee at McDonald's, and an even better member of the Cars. Matt Welsh had helped Rick buy his LeSabre. Rick was an excellent driver, reliable, steady. And while he couldn't always report the information he had, he could grunt and mumble when the other men asked him questions.

Until a year ago, when Suzie Q moved back to Riverview. Without telling anyone, he skipped out on his patrols of garages and streets and music stores. There were gaps in the time he spent watching for signs of the devil's music. He started watching Suzie again. But he knew not to go on her street. He had learned not to go too close. He never turned down Sullivan Street, and he kept a safe distance as Suzie went about her days working at the library or shopping at the mall or taking her kids to school.

Matt Welsh didn't know this. He didn't know why the last Car he had left, his most reliable all these years, had nothing to report despite signs that the devil's rhythms had infiltrated his town with a renewed vengeance. But Matt suspected something was off, which is why he prayed every night for fresh eyes and ears to protect the vulnerable youth. To provide guidance for the young and innocent, the guidance that Matt's twin brother never received.

*

Pete Best sat in the conference room, dumbfounded. Across from him, Superintendent Jag sat nodding with an arched eyebrow. Around the table cluttered with papers and folders were three other faces, all from the district office. He knew them vaguely. An assessment guru. The director of curriculum. Someone whose role wasn't clear to him. They seemed more like reptiles than people. They spoke human words, made human gestures, had human logic and clothing and accessories, but Pete, sitting through his second hour of this meeting—approaching a third—couldn't concentrate on the proceedings. His mind was elsewhere. He had long since ceased drumming on the table with his fingers. It wouldn't surprise him if a forked lizard tongue flicked out of the mouth droning on about state funding.

It was the last day before winter break. He had been blindsided as he stepped out of his office on his way to find George. Superintendent Jag all but lassoed him into this conference room with these reptiles. Back at work for one week, he had yet to find time alone with George, who had been like a ghost, practically invisible. Pete had spotted him only once, pushing a broom down a crowded hallway, whistling with his eyes closed, somehow not bumping into any students.

It's like some game, he thought. They're screwing with me. Send me on a wild goose chase, keep me from the school, put a hardship on me and my family—in effect punish me for bringing a little rhythm and blues into the lives of these kids—and act like nothing is going on, like it's business as usual and all these papers and initiatives and bullshit are just part of being an administrator, never mind that there's no current principal and the school is like a ship without a captain. The whole thing felt like a tactic, to numb him into submission, show him who's in control.

Roy's behavior that week, after a solid month of improvement, had suddenly taken a turn for the worse. Each night since Pete had returned home, his son had awakened with night terrors, banging his head against the wall, so that they were now considering having the wall padded. The lack of sleep, on the heels of his travels, the strain on his marriage, it was piling up … he was angry, and hungry. When would this Gila monster shut up?

Superintendent Jag stood and turned off the lights. A projector came on, showing graphs. I've got to get out of here, Pete thought, when through the window, out in the hallway, George appeared, pushing a vacuum with a drone that halted. Pete watched as the custodian turned his head, perplexed, leaning over to inspect and ascertain why it had lost suction. After a few moments, he sat down crossed-legged and scrutinized the mouth of the hose for any obstructions to airflow.

The Gila monster turned it over to the horned frog. Out in the hallway, Pam Susan walked around George and muttered to herself. Pete watched her go into his office with a stack of folders and envelopes and come out empty-handed, once again stepping around the custodian as he pulled a tangled hairball from the mouth's rotating brush.

Twenty minutes later, as the Komodo dragon took a turn with the latest slide, Pete sat nodding, almost asleep. George had stretched out the hose to full length and inserted a broom handle to work out all the kinks. The custodian had resumed the cross-legged position, with his eyes closed, and Pete, on the edge of consciousness, could hear faint chanting as George felt for a crack.

"Hey! You can't go in there!" a voice yelled from somewhere in the main office. It was Bob, the security guard. Pete bolted awake.

"Like hell I can't; I'm a taxpayer," a voice responded. "I paid for this room and everything in it."

Pete, instantly alert, knew that voice. Superintendent Jag sat up with a look of concern. The reptiles all looked at each other, uncertain. George continued to chant and probe the vacuum.

Bob, the security guard, got on his walkie-talkie. "Josephine, come in. We have a code blue. Backup requested to the main office. Code blue. Repeat, code blue. Call Winter."

"Call whoever you want," the voice said. "Call Jesus. The pope. The president. The National Guard. This is America. I have rights. And an account balance. And a contract the district has violated. This district owes me five hundred dollars for materials purchased for cafeteria tables. Plus another two fifty for labor, and two fifty in compensation for lost wages."

It was the voice of Jim Plant. He stormed into the conference room. Superintendent Jag rose to meet him. The reptiles all pushed back their chairs with alarm. George kept chanting. Bob tripped over the vacuum, falling outside the door.

"Superintendent Jag," Jim said, surging into the room, smacking on the lights. He dropped an envelope on the table and let loose a torrent of words. "Here is my invoice. One thousand dollars. I expect immediate payment. We had a deal. My own daughter, a freshman, doesn't have a place to eat lunch in the cafeteria. She sits on the floor in the hallway. If you can't provide a quality education, as the whole town knows, the very least you can provide is the fundamental—"

Jim stopped, turned. "Pete."

"Jim."

There was an awkward silence. The reptiles all looked to Superintendent Jag. Bob, back on his feet, staggered into the room. Josephine's voice crackled on the walkie-talkie. "Ten-four. Code blue. Winter in transit."

"You have no right to be in this room," Bob said, his gold badge askew from his fall. "Vacate the premises immediately."

"Don't talk to me about rights," Jim said. "I'm not leaving without my money. The contract is right there. This school agreed to buy tables from Craftwood Lumber. I have it in ink."

Superintendent Jag had recovered. "*Mr.* Plant," she managed. "Mr. *Plant.* This is neither the time nor the place for your grievance. The board has a procedure, which you have repeatedly violated—"

"Yeah, I know all about your procedures," Jim replied.

The two adults talked at each other, their voices rising, until Bob stepped between them.

"Back up, mall cop," Jim snapped. "I have *every* right to be here. It's you, and you, and you," he pointed at everyone in the room except Pete, his arm shaking. "You don't have the right to sit in here and smother kids, drown them in bullshit, without even giving them a place to eat lunch …"

"Jim," Pete heard himself say. It was like a dream. It wasn't real. But it was. George kept chanting out in the hallway. "Jim, listen." Too late. Sergeant Winter, Deputy Copeland, and two more Riverview police barreled into the room. Trailing behind them like a little troll in a blue polyester uniform with a piranha face, waddled high school security guard Josephine. They all had to navigate George, who was lost in a hypnotic trance and still unsure whether the hose was compromised.

They took down Jim Plant. "Get your hands off me!" he screamed.

"Do not resist," Sergeant Winter commanded, looking down at him.

"Arrrrgghh!" Jim wrestled with Sergeant Winter, trying to pin him down, his blond, curly hair thrashing around on the floor. "Not again."

"You don't have to do this," Pete heard himself say, as if from far away, in some other school, in some other suburb.

"Owwww—he bit me!" Winter shouted.

Deputy Copeland pulled out a can of mace and sprayed Jim's face.

"My eyes!" Jim called out, writhing on the floor.

Within moments he was pinned, handcuffed, and dragged away, kicking and screaming in agony.

Ten minutes later, they were back in the dark, the Komodo dragon talking as if nothing had happened. Pete sat frozen, lost in a fog of thoughts when, through the slightly ajar door, came a shout.

"I really want to know you." It was George, crossed-legged with closed eyes. He had the hose wrapped around his shoulders like a snake.

Superintendent Jag stood and closed the door. "Sorry," she said to the Komodo dragon. "We have an eccentric custodian." She sat down and added, more to herself, "But he's quite thorough."

Thirty minutes later the lights came on, papers were shoved in folders and folders into briefcases. Words floated around the room. Hands were shaken. And the reptiles slinked out of the room. Pete sat numb, confused.

Superintendent Jag returned to her seat at the head of the table and regarded him intently. He looked back at her and felt like a fly on a web, facing a hideous spider. Then he looked past her, watching his assistant Pam navigate the hallway. Pete half rose, observing parts of the vacuum strewn across the hallway floor, with George sitting over it all like some mad surgeon trying to bring a monster to life.

Pam walked into the conference room carrying a note. "Yes," Superintendent Jag said, brimming with irritation. She might as well have said, "What now?"

"Superintendent Jag, Mr. Best, I thought you would want to know immediately," Pam said, referring to the note in her hand. "We just received a call from the hospital. Director Francis is in critical but stable condition with mononucleosis. It was his wife. She said he thought it would be best for jazz band to go on a hiatus and for his student teacher James McGuinn to take over concert band in advance of the spring concerts."

Superintendent Jag frowned.

The news hit Pete like a bucket of cold water. "Thank you, Pam," he said, rising and grabbing his papers. "Thank you very much. Now you'll excuse me, Superintendent Jag."

Pete bolted from the conference room, regarded the meditating George, and went the other way down the hall.

*

Christmas day, afternoon. Ray and Tibbs sat in the Golding basement. Ray strummed a ukulele, a gift Tibbs had received that morning, trying to pick out the chords to the song playing: Dylan's "It Takes a Lot to Laugh, It Takes a Train to Cry." Tibbs worked a yo-yo, a Hannukah gift Danny had left behind. Upstairs, they could hear Shannon and her mom arguing over Shannon's decision not to join the diving team, after all.

"It's not too late," Liz said. "Think of how much work you've put in to get to this point."

"This point," Shannon said. "You said it's my decision, so what exactly is the *point* of this conversation?"

Tibbs was using the table to try to walk the dog. The yo-yo wasn't quite coming back to him. Ray fiddled with the tuning knobs trying to get in tune.

"Why would it take a train to cry?" Tibbs asked.

The question hung in the air, unanswered. Upstairs the argument had moved on to the colleges they would visit during the winter break. They heard a scream and the sound of footsteps stomping away.

"Hey, have you written anything for our next practice?" Tibbs asked, walking over to the stereo.

"Nah," Ray said. "I haven't written anything in a while."

"If you're stuck," Tibbs said, "you're welcome to join me on the writer's block. There's safety in numbers." He wound the yo-yo and set it down.

Ray acted like he was considering the offer.

"It's crazy," Tibbs said, putting on the Beatles record *A Hard Day's Night*. "You get an idea, maybe out of thin air, like a bug that lands on you. Then you work out some kind of melody, some chords, then like magic, you've got a song."

"There's a method to the madness," Ray said, searching for matching notes on the uke.

"Right, certainly there is, but it's like the song takes on a life of its own. You play it live. Maybe you record it. If you're lucky, people buy it. Radio stations play it. The song grows and takes on meaning for people. It lives in their head, their memory. Take this song, nothing complicated. Key of G. It's about working all day, then getting with a girl when you should be in bed." He sang with the chorus of the song.

Ray joined him for the next part, not quite hitting the harmony.

"How long will people be singing this song?" Tibbs asked.

Ray shrugged. "Maybe forever."

"Right," Tibbs agreed. "People will always have to work. They will always work long hours and then, instead of going home to sleep ..." He resumed singing.

"That's what it's about, right there," Tibbs said over the solo. "How does a song make you feel? If you can capture that good feeling, that feeling of being all right, somehow put that into a song in a new or interesting way …"

He picked up the yo-yo again and flung it rapidly.

"People will listen to it forever," he concluded, snapping the yo-yo back. "Rock and roll can never die. As long as there are people, they will need songs to help them feel better, more alive, just feel good. That's what it's about."

"I don't think you're going to get that from a song called 'Shannon's Going to Be Pissed,'" Ray noted.

"You may be right," Tibbs agreed. "Maybe we work in a crying train?"

"Guys," Dave called from upstairs. "*Jeopardy!* is starting."

*

A few days later on Tuesday night, Rick Ocase sat on the corner of Sullivan and Kenton in his mustard-yellow Buick LeSabre, listening to the sounds of music coming from every basement and garage on the street. He knew he should turn onto the street, write down every address, call Matt Welsh on his CB, and tell him. Here was the street, the center of it all, the source of the infestation. Greg Bird had told him where to look. All along he knew it was here, but he couldn't bring himself to turn. Not down the street where Suzie Q lived with her family.

But tonight, he pulled in, right past a teenage driver blasting Bud Powell with the windows down. He didn't know why. He felt funny. He couldn't explain why he eased down Sullivan Street with his lights off. He couldn't explain why he pulled into her driveway.

He couldn't explain why he rang her doorbell. Why he stood there when he wanted to bolt as the light turned on and the door opened, and Suzie appeared in the doorway like an angel in a bathrobe.

"Rick? Rick Ocase?" she asked with genuine surprise. "Is that you?"

He told her, right then, how much he cared about her, how much it hurt, all those years ago, how he's been holding the pain inside but that he still cared about her. That he just wanted her to be happy and healthy and to be her friend again.

"Who's at the door, hon?" her husband called.

Then he apologized. He was sorry for watching her undress all those years ago. He shouldn't have done that.

A seven-year-old girl ran up behind Suzie and clung to her leg inside the robe. "Who is it, Mommy?"

"It's an old friend of mine," Suzie said.

He didn't know what to say when she said that. But he started speaking again anyway. Then he looked down at the young girl's face and he knew that he wasn't making any sense, that he hadn't been making any sense this whole time, that he never should have come up to the door. That it was all a mistake.

"Why does he talk like that, Mommy?"

"He has a lot to say," Suzie said, caressing her daughter's hair. "And he's trying to say it all at once."

She smiled at him as he turned away, first walking, then running back to his car. He heard the sound of an acoustic guitar playing low Delta blues coming from the house next door. It was such a lovely sound; it was like a net that his wild feelings fluttered into. He couldn't imagine notifying Matt.

What he did instead was drive. He gunned it down Sullivan Street, his tires squealing as he turned onto Kenton. He didn't know where to go, so he drove to the Riverview Forest Preserve. He drove the long way around the preserve until he came to the quarry.

Rick Ocase was smart. He had read a lot of books. He remembered a book he had read about submarines in World War II, how if they got sunk, the navy still considered the submarines out there, patrolling the ocean. There was a phrase he remembered: eternal patrol. He didn't call Matt that night, even though he knew he should, since he was the last of the Cars. But he knew that Matt would figure it out, would know that Rick Ocase had left Riverview for good, that Rick Ocase had begun his eternal patrol.

*

After the shutdown of the Water Tower, during the nascent weeks of real Chicago winter, when it isn't a drag, when it's magical in its beauty and cold tranquility, a new hangout emerged in Riverview: the Malcolm household. Beverly Malcolm was impossible not to like. At affluent Riverview High School, where image and status were everything, Bev killed it all with the sheer force of abundant kindness. Always smiling, almost annoyingly upbeat and positive, she carried around an endless source of positive energy.

Her house was across town from Sullivan Street, near the Riverview-Lowland Park border, with proximity to Riversprings Park. The Malcolms had a pool, a spacious backyard that included a tennis court, an enclosure of woods ensuring privacy, and tolerant, trusting parents—thus it became the New Place To Be.

Unlike other parties, with selective lists and exclusive gatekeeping at the door, Bev welcomed everyone to her house with open arms. She was like a mom not only to her usually intoxicated class clown boyfriend Cory but also to anyone that hung out in her backyard. It was a garden of acceptance within the withering pressure and intense scrutiny of the image- and group-conscious.

In contrast to the garages and basements where kids moped about the shutdown of the Water Tower, weekend nights at Bev's became celebrations: the end of another week, being young, being free.

On New Year's Eve, with no show at the Water Tower, the Little Brothers finished an afternoon jam minus Shannon, who was away visiting colleges. They left the basement and headed straight to Bev's. The temperature dipped below freezing and snow started to fall.

The Little Brothers—Ray, Tibbs, Curtis, Michael, Danny, and Brandon, without their singer and roadie—arrived at Bev's. A crowd clustered outside for a smoke.

"That will be ninety-nine cents," Cory was saying, cross-eyed from inside the hood of a sweatshirt, doing a spot-on impression of Mary, the Riverview High School lunch lady.

Everyone standing around laughed. Bev did too, despite herself.

"You must have a tray, sir," Cory kept it up. "You cannot make a purchase without a tray."

The laughter rose higher.

"Excuse me, sir. There are two ramekins worth of cheese on that cheddar fry."

Then Cory starting following Brad from the Laughing Tadpoles, getting in his face. "Sir, where is your tray? Your tray, sir. You cannot make a purchase!" Brad was wasted and laughed so hard he couldn't breathe. Everyone was laughing, holding their stomachs, when John Mellor took one sip of schnapps too many and threw up on himself.

The crowd was split between two reactions: one of laughter and one of revulsion. But Bev was on it. She went inside and returned in no time with a bottle of water and a wet towel.

"Are you OK?" she asked.

She took John inside to the bathroom. While he washed up, she went to get a sweatshirt for him to borrow.

The crowd broke into smaller circles. Some drifted off to the woods and started a campfire. Some went down to the basement for music and drinks. A couple disappeared into a bedroom. It was New Year's Eve, and some people were dressed up.

It was like a mini-Gatsby house in the middle of Riverview. The key difference between Bev's house and the house in the novel that they had all been required to read last semester in freshman English was that there was no billboard, no eyes of Dr. T.J. Eckleburg, to watch over it all. No one to see the circles of dark figures, the faces glowing faintly in the flickers of light. No one to see the groups clustered on the patio, around the pool, on the tennis courts, in the backyard, setting off or coming back from River-springs Park—the divisions of adolescence, varied and dependable. No one to notice another couple slip into the woods.

No one was listening either. No one to hear the crisp sound of cans opening, or the hilarity, the deep raucous laughter, the conversations, some hushed and some lacking any semblance of volume control.

Bev's trusting parents were usually upstairs, sleeping, knowing that their daughter would come wake them if there were a problem, but there never was.

"Twenty minutes until New Year's!" Tiffany from Glass Eye called out, carrying a tray of small cups.

"Hello, Jell-O," Stu from Gobbler of Lightning said. "Who else wants a shot?"

"Oh yeeeaaaaah," sang Anne from Whack-A-Whack.

Cory started chasing Brad around the pool. "Sir, you need a tray to make a purchase!"

Twenty minutes later, the house shook with calls of "Happy New Year!"

There was someone, in fact, to hear this youthful, jubilant shout. The figure arrived on his bicycle, having overheard the location in the hallways. He stood out in the street, alone in the darkness, under a streetlight. It was Brian Jones Wyman, shivering. B.J. removed his glasses and wiped the fog off the lenses.

He squinted and perceived a girl alone, along the side of the Malcolm household. She was crying. Then she was running. B.J. hid in the nearby woods as she ran right past him into Riversprings Park. He watched her stop and sit on a park bench.

It was Rose Plant, a girl he sometimes stood near during lunch. What was that object in her hands? He couldn't see; his glasses kept fogging up. It was round and soft. It looked like a softball glove. She put the glove away and took a hit from a pipe. She is like me, B.J. thought. She doesn't belong.

A tall, skinny, redhead burst out the front door of the Malcolm household, laughing like a lunatic.

"Sir, you need a tray to make a purchase!" another kid called after him. B.J. knew the redhead from history. It was Brad, the class clown. And B.J. knew the other one too: Cory, a popular athlete that imitated the cross-eyed cafeteria worker. Cory and Brad always had seats at lunch. B.J. stood still behind a tree, holding his breath to avoid detection.

*

A couple times during winter break, Pete Best arrived at the high school as the volleyball and basketball players arrived for practice, but there no was sign of George. When he stopped in the custodian's office, he encountered Eddie Severino, who told him to get lost. Jim Plant had been charged with trespassing and resisting arrest. Pete tried to find out more information, but the police at the station refused to answer his questions.

For the first week after the break, he searched with every free moment he could find, but it was like George had disappeared. Pete even came in on Saturday, only to be rebuffed once again by Eddie. "Get lost," Eddie said, like it was an official reply. Pete didn't know if George had been coming to work, but he did know one thing: He had a new vacuum. Pete had signed the purchase order. Finally, on Friday of the second week, Pete spied George heading down D hall and into a science lab with the machine on his back.

"Hey, George, how do you like the new vacuum?" Pete called out.

George didn't appear to hear him as he entered the science classroom.

Pete followed him into the room and waited for him to finish vacuuming a row. When he turned, Pete waved. George smiled and turned off the vacuum.

Pete repeated his original question.

"Well enough," George replied, holding up the black coil. "It's nice not having a cord. Freedom from any shackle is a blessing."

"The school board was reluctant to buy it" Pete said, "since we purchased the Floor Buffer 3000 earlier in the year."

"Reluctance is a barrier we all must face, from time to time."

The vacuum beeped, gently.

"Yes, well, our custodians should have the very best. No different from our students."

The two men nodded in the humming fluorescent light. On the chalkboard was a drawing of the transfer of energy from the sun to a pyramid of organisms in a forest food web.

George looked down into the cage of a leopard gecko.

"I look and I see a gecko that's sleeping," George observed. His vacuum beeped again.

Pete looked into the cage with interest. His curious eyes moved from the yellow spotted reptile to the scattered wood chips on the counter.

"The students help Mr. Blackburn take care of the animals," George commented. "But sometimes they make a mess."

Pete nodded, noticing a pile of wood chips on the floor.

"I look at the floor and see that it needs sweeping," George said.

Pete was rubbing his chin, thinking how to frame his next question, when the vacuum beeped. So instead, he asked, "How long does it take to charge that thing?"

"I'm not sure," George replied.

"I don't know why nobody told you," Pete said. "There's supposed to be training for new equipment. Is the charging device on the side?" He examined the pack. "I think this part comes out; it's folded up."

"Nobody tells you how to unfold it."

Pete nodded. "Yes. I suppose that's true." His fingers began drumming his thigh as his mind searched for the right words.

Beep. Beep.

George lifted the coiling tube and held it. "Machines," he said, stretching the tube. "Like people. I don't know how. Someone controls you." His eyes moved to the floor.

"Mmm," Pete said, looking back in the cage. George turned on the vacuum. The debris rattled through the coil. *Beep.*

They moved together along the counter. The next cage contained a hamster running on a wheel.

"I look at the wheel and I see that it's turning," George said.

Beep beep.

Pete looked toward the empty doorway and, with the vacuum's low hum as a sort of cover, decided to go for it. "George, this is crazy, but I feel like you're the only one I can talk to. I know you're busy. I've been trying to find you since I've been back. To ask you how things stand. George. I need your help. I'm trying to bring rock and roll back to Riverview. Maybe it's all one huge mistake."

"With every mistake," George said.

Beeeeeeep.

The hamster jumped off the wheel and burrowed down into its bedding.

Pete's fingers went to work on the counter. "Yes," he began. "Mistakes are integral to learning. I just … um, wondered if you thought that maybe, you know things are changing on the board … there's no principal and I'm sort of like the top administrator … I don't know … What am I trying to say? Director Francis is sick, he has mono … there might be another opportunity to do like an open mic. He canceled jazz band, so I was thinking the room they rehearse in, the smaller one beside the main rehearsal room, since it's soundproofed, it might be available for something… intimate, on the down-low, and it would give the kids a chance to play. I know Jag and Welsh have other ideas, how they think. I just remember what we went through. I hate to see it happening again. After watching Jim Plant get maced … I don't know … I'm not thinking straight … my son is having these night terrors."

Beep beep.

George moved on to a large fish tank. He bent down and watched the fish. *Beep.* "I don't know how," George said. "Fish are diverted." He closed his eyes and breathed deeply.

Pete watched George's reflection in the tank.

Beep beep.

Pete smacked the cabinet above the fish tank like it was a cymbal. George took a magnet off the shelf below the tank to clean some algae off the glass. He replaced the magnet on the shelf, picked up a large metal spoon, and filled it with a water treatment chemical. He carefully opened the tank and mixed it in. He dried the spoon and held it to Pete's face.

Pete looked at a reflection of himself upside down in the concave spoon.

"I don't know how," George said. "You've been inverted." Then he replaced the spoon on the shelf below the tank.

Pete didn't know whether to hug George or strangle him. "What about the district office?" Pete asked, channeling his anxiety into his fingers, drumming on a desk. "Have you talked to Richard Starkey? Have you heard anything specific? Will they try to shut it down?"

George watched the fish swim. "No one alerted you."

Pete sighed and stretched his stiff neck. "George, please, what do you mean? Do you think I should risk it? I feel like I have nothing left to lose."

Beep. Beep.

The last cage had two fire-bellied toads.

"I look and I see, toads that are sleeping," George said.

"Toads? Sleeping? George?" Pete stammered, desperate. George looked from the toads to Pete, from Pete to the toads, and back again. Then he smiled wide.

Beep. Beep. Beep.

"Music is all around us," he said. "If we only learn to listen."

"Right," Pete whispered. He rolled the desk with his knuckles. "Right! We will need to be discreet." Without warning, a laugh escaped. "The toads are sleeping," he said with a guffaw in a voice he hardly recognized. And then he couldn't stop, the mirth erupting like some pent-up lava.

George smiled and marveled at Pete with his dark brown eyes. A series of gentle beeps brought the two men back.

Pete composed himself. "We won't wake the toads," he smiled. "I'll let you get back to work. And I'll see if I can dig up an owner's manual for that thing."

George resumed vacuuming.

*

Bobby Jean Welsh lay in her single bed and flipped through a month-old copy of *Ladies' Home Journal.* On the wall above both hers and her husband's bed was a small wooden cross. There were two pictures in the room: a hanging portrait of Jesus on the wall opposite the beds and a framed portrait of her and Matt on their wedding day, June 9, 1943. Otherwise, the room was tidy and sparsely furnished with a dresser and chair in the corner.

She was glancing through pages of furniture upholsteries when she came to the regular column, "Can This Marriage Be Saved?" She read the first paragraph, about a mother-in-law tearing a couple apart. The wind off the lake whirred against her windows. The temperature outside, with the wind-chill, was near zero.

The phone rang. She looked at the clock on the nightstand. It was 9:45. She shut the magazine and picked up the phone.

"Hello?"

"Hi, Bobby."

"Where are you tonight, Marie?"

"There's a storm in Cleveland, so we didn't make the last connection. I'm in Boston. The glamorous life of a flight attendant."

Bobby Jean let out a little laugh. "Well, it's horrible here," she replied. "It's absolutely freezing outside."

"Is Matt out driving again?" Marie asked.

"Yes. Last night he wasn't home until ten thirty."

"Bobby, I've been thinking about it."

"Uh-oh, I thought you said flight attendants aren't paid to think."

"Haha. No, seriously. I've been thinking. Are you sure he's doing what he says he is?"

"Why wouldn't he be?"

"Well, he might be telling you that it's up to him to patrol the streets of Riverview to keep the children safe from Satan's music, that all the others on this patrol thing have left … but he could be doing something else entirely."

"Like what?" Bobby Jean sat up in bed and tugged at the sheets.

"You know my co-worker Tracy, young gal, started a couple of years ago?"

"Not really, but go ahead."

"Well, she just found out that her husband was cheating on her."

"So? It happens all the time."

"With another man."

Bobby Jean grimaced.

"What's your point, Marie? You think Matt is cheating on me with a man?"

"I'm just saying. You're always telling me about your lack of intimacy, saying you won't leave him. What if he was, you know, not just cheating on you … but … gay?"

"That is absurd, Marie."

"I don't mean anything by it. I know it sounds crazy. But for all you know …"

Bobby Jean heard the garage door open. "Listen. There's the garage. He's home early tonight."

"Bobby Jean, don't be mad at me. I just thought—"

"Don't be silly. Good night, Marie."

She heard Matt walk in from the garage and stop at the hall closet. His footsteps came up the stairs. He walked in the bedroom and kissed her where he always did, smack dab in the middle of the cheek. His lips were like ice. She noticed a slight tremor as he unpuckered his frozen lips.

*

"Let's take five," Ryan said. "I need to use the bathroom."

"Ryan's been eating tacos," Danny announced from the keyboard. "I saw him. He had tacos for lunch. It's going to be more like fifteen."

Ryan ran up the stairs.

"Make it fast," Shannon ordered. "We need to rehearse every song on our list before the gig this Saturday. Every song needs to be tight."

"Don't you think we should drive down and scout out this Elbo Room before we play?" asked Michael, with a fresh platinum blond head of hair.

"Might not be a bad idea," Curtis agreed, changing his reed.

The band discussed the logistics of driving down to the city before Saturday night. Danny had a gig with his jazz quintet in Lincolnshire on Friday, and Michael had fencing. Dave had to work on Friday until five. Curtis and Brandon had a science club meeting on Saturday afternoon.

Ray settled on the couch under the Miles Davis poster. Shannon plopped down next to him.

"I want to hear you sing one," she said.

"What?"

"Not backup vocals. Not a harmony from your cozy little corner. But lead vocals. Step up. To the mic. The spotlight. I want to see it," Shannon insisted. "No. I want to hear it."

"I don't know," Ray muttered.

"I don't think anyone else wants to hear it," Danny chimed in.

"Fuck you, Danny. This is a band. We stick up for each other."

"I was just kidding. Did I mention that I had tacos too?" Danny confessed and darted up the stairs.

"Everyone in this band sings. And everyone has done lead vocals. Everyone except Ray. But that ends today. Pick a song. Anything. Any key. Today. This practice. Or I'll pick it for you." Then she shouted up the stairs, "When you get done pooping, we're doin' one with Ray singing."

Twenty minutes later everyone was back at their instruments. Brandon, Curtis, and Dave had arranged a mission to scope out the Elbo Room on Friday night. Shannon moved the mic stand over to Ray's corner.

"What are we playing, Ray?" she asked.

"I've got a new one," Ray offered, pulling nine chord charts from his backpack, one for each member plus Dave, as was the band requirement when introducing a new song. "It's called 'A Hypothetical Song.'"

"Hypothetical?" Shannon questioned, looking at Ray with laughing eyes. "Are you going to *hypothetically* sing this hypothetical song?"

"There is no try. Only do," Danny said in Yoda's voice.

"Was this the one you were working on over at the Shoppe?" Tibbs asked. "The 'Dead Flowers' D, G, A thing?"

Ray nodded, looking down at his shoes.

"How does the bridge go?" Curtis asked from his stool.

"Just F sharp minor and A," Tibbs replied, playing the chords. "Then it repeats the D-G-A pattern. It's basically 'Dead Flowers.'"

"But we're not dead," Shannon said. "We're alive. I'll even take the first verse for you. Hit it."

Ryan counted off the tempo with his sticks and hammered the intro. Tibbs played the opening riff, Ray started his down-up up-down strumming, and Danny raised his hands for a moment before crashing down on the keys. Curtis came in low with his sax and the band jolted forward on the second measure.

"Oh yeah!" Shannon belted into the mic.

If you should see me in the corner of your eyes

Obviously requiring medical attention

My name might be on the tip of your tongue

But you are afraid to mention

She grabbed a tambourine and danced around the room. Ray closed his eyes and stepped up. He began to sing, a bit nasally.

Keep your eyes off my foaming mouth

Look away from my swollen feet

Keep your eyes on the neon pies

Let the waitress get you a seat.

Shannon came over and danced next to Ray. They harmonized the chorus together.

Go on your way, go have lunch

There's nothing much for us to talk about

I'm on my waaaaay, to the lunar grapefruit

And any other point is moot

Yeah any other point is moot.

The band delved into the bridge. Curtis took off on a solo. Someone came down the stairs. Ray opened his eyes to see who it was. Amber, the youngest Golding, sat down on the bottom step in a bright orange dress. But when Ray saw her, he didn't see a sweet nine-year-old girl clapping. He saw a child convict in bright orange. He blinked, blinked again, and there she was. It was hard to breathe. The basement began to spin. The windows had bars. Dave, in the corner, was a bailiff.

Ray closed his eyes.

Shannon stood right next to him, studying him, thinking it was nerves. "Sing like you mean it, with gusto," she demanded. "Like your very life depends on it. Because it does." Ray stepped up.

This is not supposed to be a sad song

Not even supposed to be that long

More of a hypothetical song

About how things could go wrong

Ray staggered backward. Shannon caught him, her tambourine jangling. Ray looked over and saw Dave dancing with Amber, but to Ray he was restraining her, holding her back. Tibbs shook his head like it was all a joke and took the next verse on the other mic.

Sooooo, when you've paid the check

The medics will have arrived

Don't look back when you step in the sun

To see if my breath they've revived.

Michael, also thinking Shannon and Ray were messing around, joined Tibbs for the last chorus.

Go on your waaaaay

Go for a walk

There's nothing much for us to talk about

I'm on my waaaaay

To the lunar grapefruit

And any other point is moot

Yeah any other point

Is moot.

Tibbs hit a D ninth chord that hung in the air while Danny tinkled some high notes.

"I think we've got something," Curtis announced, adjusting his shades.

"It's a start," Shannon conceded. She observed Ray, her face inches from his. "We'll play it this weekend at the Elbo Room," she said. "Might want to sing it a few times at home, Ray. You're flat."

"Not bad," Danny admitted. "Am I the only one who's hungry? Ryan, are there any more tacos in the fridge?"

*

Saturday, January 23, 1983. They met outside the Golding van parked in the cul-de-sac on Sullivan Street at four thirty in the afternoon as the winter sun began to set. It was a mild, windless, pleasant thirty-five degree day. Dave chauffeured the group down to the city. The deal they struck with their parents was they had to come straight home right after their set ended at nine. They were listening to a tape labeled DAVE'S OPERA TUNES. Luciano Pavarotti was belting it out.

"The Catholic Church prohibited women from singing," Dave said, pulling off the Edens Expressway. "Still, they wanted singers who were able to hit high notes. So do you know what they did?"

"No," Shannon replied. "But I know you're going to tell me."

In the back, Michael was drinking a Dr. Pepper and taking bets on whether he could belch the alphabet.

"Castration," Dave said. "It was a common practice in the sixteenth century, so the voices of prepubescent boys wouldn't change."

"You hear that?" Shannon called, half turning. "If it wasn't for me, someone in the band would have to get castrated."

Michael chugged and started off. "A, B, C ..."

"In fact, opera was banned by the Vatican in the early seventeenth century," Dave added. "They thought it was likely to incite immoral behavior."

"Well, no offense to the Italians, but we need to pick things up," Shannon decided. She hit eject and put in a tape labeled HERE COMES THE NIGHT. Little Richard's "Rip It Up" came on.

Michael made it to X before he ran out of gas, literally.

"That was a good try," Curtis said.

"It's the effort that counts," Michael remarked.

They arrived at the Elbo Room and hauled in their equipment.

Ray peeked out at a bar sparsely populated with living, breathing, adult Chicagoans. He watched a few young adults kick off their Saturday night with some shots. He saw a triumvirate of old hippies in the corner, a group of women on a girls' night, and a few couples and solo, scattered boozers. Ray felt his stomach go hollow. "A Hypothetical Song" was on the set list.

Dave, Brandon, Tibbs, Michael, and an employee of the Elbo Room, a muscular bald dude with a mustache, finished hooking up the amps, tuning the guitars, and setting up the mics. Ray followed them back to the green room. "The stage is set," Dave reported.

"Where's the set list?" Shannon asked.

He patted his pockets. "I've got it right here," he said, pulling out a handful of receipts. From a wad of papers, he handed Shannon what he thought was the night's set list.

"What is this? Irrational numbers? Find the terminating decimals? What the … ?"

Dave smacked his forehead. It was his College Algebra I homework.

"I think it's time I start bringing the set list," Shannon suggested, half laughing.

"No. It's my job," Dave insisted. "I won't lose them anymore."

Shannon looked at him with her wide, smiling eyes. "We're winging it again," she called out.

They stuck to covers, like it was a safer road, less hazardous. Danny led the way and played like he always did, flawless, so that it was easy to imagine he really had been abducted by aliens. Not used to the surroundings, Shannon started out shyly, reserved, singing with her eyes closed. When she opened her eyes, she realized it was just like moving to a higher diving board, but the mindset, the focus, the calm, that was all the same.

Ray noticed the three hippies in the corner seemed to perk up to their opener, Elmore James's "Madison Blues." Shannon changed the chorus to "Elbo Room Blues" and stepped aside for Curtis on the sax. Like always, Curtis played his ass off. He had attached some kind of cork device that gave his notes a deeper, more penetrating sound. That got a few more people's attention, though the girls' night continued chatting like the stage was not full of musicians tearing it up.

Tibbs took over on the second song, Travis Wammack's "Fire Fly," giving the whole band a chance to feel comfortable, get their "stage legs," as Danny would say. Ray noticed the guy in the sling, nodding and smiling in the corner. The group coalesced and took off with the next number, John Lee Hooker's "Dimples." Whatever shyness Shannon had been feeling was gone. Now even the girls' night started to listen. A few more stragglers from Lincoln Avenue came in like hungry people that smelled something cooking.

Shannon held the room in the palm of her hand, just like at the Water Tower. They were jamming, relaxed, like they were playing for fun in the Golding basement. They finished the song "Runaway" by Del Shannon with a few people in the bar singing along. Shannon called out "Please Love Me" by the Rascals, and the band hit their comfortable, cruising altitude, coasting through a set of deep rock, rhythm and blues cuts. The closer was supposed to be "I'm Down" by the Beatles. After Tibbs hit the opening riff, Shannon held up the stop signal and called out "Hypothetical Song."

Ray had been snug in his little corner of the Big City, playing to a roomful of adults in the adult world, where buses and cars and people steadily flowed along Lincoln Avenue, visible outside through the large windows of the Elbo Room. When he looked at the faces in the bar, they were attentive, smiling, nodding with the beat. Bodies were moving, dancing. Lips were singing, drinking. It was all pulsing together in a groove. And he was in the source of that groove, like the heart of an organism. Ray was a small piece of the heart, a valve, doing his part. Hitting notes and chords and rhythms. Occasionally blowing on his harp or lending a bass note to the backup vocals.

But now he stood frozen, like a heart in cardiac arrest. He looked over at the man with the sling, who used his injured arm to point at his watch and make the universal *let's go* gesture.

Shannon came over and kissed Ray on the cheek. "You got this. Just like in the basement. Sing like your life depends on it," she said.

Tibbs patted Ray on the back as he stepped to the mic. "No sweat, man."

Ray looked out into the bar crowd like it was a car wreck that he couldn't help but stare at. Then he saw him: a large man with a shaved head wearing an orange Chicago Bears T-shirt. The man held his hands together and Ray saw handcuffs. The windows grew bars as Ryan counted the tempo. His down-up up-down strum had extra downs and not enough ups. For the first verse Ray wasn't close enough to the mic. Shannon pushed him forward for the chorus, but he was still too quiet. He was looking at the bouncer twirling a giant keychain. Halfway through the second verse he lost his nerve, and Shannon had to swoop in. She and Tibbs did the third verse together.

"Gotta practice that 'Hypothetical Song,'" Shannon said to Ray as they got in the van for the ride home. "Practice is what cures the nerves. Or I might start calling you the Hypothetical Singer. Otherwise, my little brothers, that wasn't half bad."

There wasn't weed to smoke on the ride home. After the White Hen bust, Riverview had dried up. Everyone was tired. When Dave pulled into the driveway an hour later, the whole band was asleep.

*

On Monday, January 31, it was snowing outside the Village Music Shoppe. Down in the lobby, Tibbs and Ray were jamming and experimenting with an alternate D tuning. It sounded a little like the Stones' "Street Fighting Man." Tap worked a tambourine. Upstairs, there were violin and trumpet and saxophone lessons going on down the hallway from B.J.'s lesson with Frets.

"I did practice this week, a few times," B.J. told Frets. "It feels like whenever I learn something, the next time I sit down to play it, I have to learn it all over again. Like music is this liquid, and my head is a bucket with a hole. When I practice, I fill up the bucket. When I come back the next day to play it again, the music has leaked out. It's gone. And I have to start all over again. Does that make any sense?"

Frets frowned. "I've never heard anyone put it like that," he said. "Interesting. I have heard of 'fixing a hole' … Let's see, we've got to plug up that hole then. Maybe with a favorite song?"

B.J. stared at his feet, his tongue plucking his rubber bands. "I don't really have one."

"Maybe a tune from a movie or a show you like?"

B.J. looked up at a Beatles poster. "There is one song that I would like to learn," he said. "Something my mom used to sing."

"Let's have at it."

*

Twenty minutes later, Tibbs knocked on Frets's door.

"You're getting it," Frets told B.J. "That's it. The rhythm needs a little tightening, but you have the chords. Now go practice with the Flower Man downstairs."

Tibbs and B.J. switched places. There was an awkward high five with Tibbs offering knucks and B.J. going in for an open-palm slap.

More a collapse than a sit, Tibbs fell into the student chair. "Frets, I'm desperate. You gotta help me write some lyrics."

"This is ridiculous," Frets responded. "You're too young to have writer's block this bad. For this long."

Tibbs stared at a poster of Ziggy Stardust.

"Have you been feeding your goose?" Frets asked, scratching his beard.

"Yes," Tibbs responded. "I did everything you told me: I listened to the albums you gave me. I've taken walks. I've kept a notebook of thoughts and observations. But I can't put any of it into a song." He looked at Ziggy again.

Frets scratched his beard.

"Shannon keeps saying she's going to kick me out of the band," Tibbs said. "I think she's serious."

Frets stood up. He found a yellow legal pad and a pen. "Here. Write. Don't think about it. Just write what you have to say. I'll be back in ten minutes." Then he walked out and closed the door.

Tibbs roved from Ziggy to the other posters and album covers on the wall. His pen hovered over the pad ...

After ten minutes, Frets came back in the room, sat down, and extended his hand. Tibbs handed him back the blank pad. Frets glanced over at the crumpled sheets in the wastebasket.

"I've never seen it this bad," Frets observed. "Have you ever heard of the expression, 'like pulling teeth?'"

*

Tibbs came down the stairs looking like he had just had a root canal.

Ray and B.J. were playing the Beatles song "Golden Slumbers" with Tap working away on the maracas. B.J. was off-key, but it wasn't awful.

"Did you write a song?" Ray asked.

"I might enter the witness protection program," Tibbs said. "So Shannon doesn't murder me."

Beethoven's Fifth rang out, and two women dressed like fitness instructors walked into the room. They had no instruments. The music students in the lobby regarded them like they had entered the shop by mistake. Their workout jackets said RAINY DAY FITNESS. The first woman was #12 and the second, taller, was #35.

For a moment, it did seem like they were in the wrong place, but then, with a nod at Tap, they went into the office. Outside, a horn honked. It was Aunt Bertha. She had offered to drive the three boys home. B.J., she realized, was on the cusp of making actual friends.

*

Wednesday morning, February 3. The overnight temperatures had dropped below zero. The sunrise brought it up to five degrees, with windchills knocking it right back down.

Leslie drove on Waukegan Road toward the Sara Sweet factory. Her little Pontiac didn't always start during cold snaps, but this morning, after a dubious minute, the engine staggered to life. Her windshield was still frozen except for a small circle she had managed to scrape free before jumping into the car, cursing at her red, frozen hand and missing gloves.

Screw this, Leslie thought. Screw this weather. Screw this traffic. And *screw* these quarterly reports.

The station wagon in front of her was being driven, in Leslie's opinion, overly cautious on the ice. She swung into the next lane, noticing at the last moment a red light. She slammed on the brakes, skidded into an intersection, and almost caused a major pileup. Horns honked. Middle fingers exchanged. She ended up at the next red light, in front of the Historic Village, ignoring the glares from the car next to her.

Leslie had been distracted all morning, her mind working on a nut it couldn't crack: Rik Frets. Rik was a nut, all right. Yesterday, she had driven to the Village Music Shoppe. She wanted to find out where the music had gone since the Water Tower had been shut down. Underground? Garages and basements? Another suburb? It had to be somewhere. Pulling into the parking lot, she had seen the license plate first: Go FRETS. It couldn't be. But then she knew it had to be. He had come back. The only musician to have played electric guitar during the ban in the 60s, when he turned a 1965 Renaissance Fair upside down with a funky set of harmonica-laced blues and folk tunes. It had caused a stir. A brief flare-up in a dormant town. Then he was gone. Vanished. And now he was back. It couldn't be a coincidence.

When Leslie had gotten out of her little car, cursing the cold, there he was. Of all things, it appeared like he was selling shoes to fitness instructors. It was bizarre. She called out to him. The group closed like crabs, trunks and doors slamming. He had refused to talk to her. That was yesterday. It seemed like a movie. Was Frets back? And why was he selling shoes to fitness instructors?

Maybe today would be different? She fought off an impulse to turn, head over to the Shoppe, try again. The light changed. The car behind her gave one more honk and one more middle finger, all for good measure, as it drove around her.

It was another piece in a puzzle that didn't fit. There was Pete Best, who had injected hope and possibility into the town with Mudfest and open mics at the high school. Only to get squashed by the administration, stepped on, and kicked out of town like some bug. He was back now and didn't seem to be doing anything. There was the Water Tower. Another jolt of excitement and hope, like an impenetrable fortress. Only to disappear in the blink of an eye after a bizarre wedgie-rama. There was the bust at White Hen. The death of a student at a racetrack in Arlington Heights due to a severe peanut allergy. Everything was related, but it didn't add up.

Leslie sat in morning traffic at yet another red light, regarding her clouds of frozen breath and her red knuckles with little I-need-a-drink shakes. For Leslie, the breakthrough for rock music was inevitable, bound to happen someday. But no. It would never happen. The town couldn't be beat. All this time, this waiting and hoping. It was too painful.

The light changed. Two cars in front of her, a vehicle stalled, causing a fender bender. Everyone was stuck. Perfect, Leslie thought, just perfect. The things she wanted the most in life never happened. Love. Journalism. Rock and roll. Bust, bust, bust. And then there were the things that did happen. Becoming an alcoholic. Getting pregnant. Trying to go cold turkey, but not being able to quit. The abortion. Her mother never talking to her again.

It was hopeless. She looked out at the stopped traffic, a car pulling up to the stalled car to give it a jump, another car and a truck stuck together, the hitch of the truck tangled with the bumper of the sedan. She closed her eyes and looked inward, down the road that was her life ahead. Now in her mid-forties, what did she have to live for? Her past was one long trail of disappointment. Heartbreak after heartbreak. She was a ludicrous figure. A local journalist writing about dessert factories. Screw it, she thought. She would be late anyway. She reached for the glove compartment, pulled out the flask, and took a long pull. Then another.

When the cars in front of her finally cleared, Leslie's red hand wasn't shaking anymore. She was warmer too. She tossed the flask under her seat just as the police arrived. Then she was driving again, having found another flask she had stashed under the seat that wasn't quite empty. She was shaking out the last few drops into her mouth, relishing the flavor of the warm, soothing liquid, so that she almost didn't see the delivery truck pulling out of the Sara Sweet factory. Almost. She saw it in the nick of time and swerved, slamming hard right into a second delivery truck full of pound cakes. Fortunately, she was wearing her seat belt, but her head slammed into the steering wheel, knocking her out.

*

Kent Davies, the editor-in-chief, sat listening to the debate in the *Riverview Review* conference room. All the editors and reporters were arguing over whether Riverview had become polarized between liberal and conservative views. There had clearly been a demographic shift, with young, urban professionals moving into the new developments, an apartment complex on the edge of town and a subdivision of townhomes. And some of the neighborhoods had experienced significant turnover, with more home sales in the last five years than in the previous fifty combined.

Kent had learned to listen closely and withhold judgment. The room itself seemed polarized. Half the reporters and editors, the older ones, Kent noted, believed that the town's conservative, upper-middle-class identity was intact. Look no further than the factory, they said, which seemed to represent a large ship steadying itself after several years of economic turbulence. Yes, there was an influx of families that worked in the city, but the population overall remained solidly conservative. The town council and school board still had conservative majorities. The top seats of government remained steadfast: the mayor, the city clerk, the school superintendent, the chief of transportation—all churchgoing Republicans.

Still, the other side pointed out, there has been a string of increasingly fraught incidents. The recent debate at the town council over a skate park being added to Riverview Park. The stir at a local middle school when the drama director, a new hire, wanted to cast boys in girl roles and girls in boy roles. The recent drug bust at White Hen Pantry. High school students protesting a guitar ban. The macabre and surreal death of a teen at a rock concert in Arlington Heights from a wedgie with peanut butter given to a kid with an anaphylactic peanut allergy.

The debate started going round and round, and Kent was about to intervene when his secretary knocked on the door. A phone call. An accident at the factory. Leslie. Alcohol was involved. She was at the hospital in stable condition. He went to find Jane Mott, to see if she could head over to the factory and catch the end of the quarterly report. Except she wasn't at her desk. She was at Leslie's desk. The phone message light was blinking near purple gloves, a pair of glasses, and an assortment of pens scattered around. Jane was reading a half-written article about a folk musician named Rik Frets.

*

Saturday afternoon. Cold and gray. Don Golding pulled into the Riverbrook Mall parking lot, turned off public radio jazz, and walked toward a grocery store. He selected a cart, reached into his back pocket, and read the top of his list:

Elbo Room February 5. Set 1 Not Fade Away (Stones)....

*

Danny and Brandon sat at a red light on Lake Cook Road, waiting to turn into Riverbrook Mall.

"Let's just turn around," Danny suggested again. "I mean, why are we trusting anyone that's in a band called Gobbledegook? It could be another setup. Another bust. I don't want to get in trouble."

"It's perfectly safe," Brandon replied. "Don't be nervous. I also received confirmation from the Tadpoles, Wawhoo Wang-Wang, the Polyps, and the Wobble Dobbles. Trust me."

"I might just stay in the car," Danny said. "I got a recital tomorrow."

"It's fine," Brandon maintained, getting a green arrow and turning.

The two teenagers ducked as they drove past Don Golding, who was standing outside the grocery store staring at a slip of paper.

They drove through the parking lot, past the movie theater, down to Rainy Day Fitness. Brandon parked. "C'mon," he said. "Nothing to worry about."

They walked into the fitness center, walked over to the trainer/free weight section, and asked for trainer #12. They bought a three-pound ankle weight with a quarter ounce of sticky, skunky green weed in a plastic bag taped to the bottom. They went back to the car, turned on Coltrane, drove over to the quarry, and got high as kites.

*

Five hours later, forty miles to the south, Dave turned the van onto Lincoln Avenue. He flipped over a tape labeled REGINALD'S CLASSICAL ROOTS. "The term 'classical music' is a misnomer," he said. "The ancients had no way to record or write their music. It wasn't until 1000 AD when an Italian monk named Guido came up with a system of musical notation. No one has a clue what any of the Greeks' or Romans' or Egyptians' or any early civilization's music sounded like. Of course, we know they had music. The ancient pyramids—"

"David, love," Shannon interrupted. "You are simply the smartest person I know. Tell me, why are you living at home and going to a community college?" Dave stopped at a red light and rubbed his chin. Behind them, the Little Brothers were going around asking, Would you rather?

"Ray, would you rather drink vomit or diarrhea?" Danny asked, passing a freshly packed bowl of especially potent Rainy Day Fitness.

"Hmm," Ray pondered. "That's a tough one. Is it my own or someone else's? And if it's someone else's, whose is it?"

"Let's go with your own."

"Definitely vomit."

"For me," Dave said. "Calculus is calculus. It doesn't matter whether you learn it in a community college or an Ivy League. Plus, my instructors know my name. And finally, when you compare the cost per credit hour to the value gained, it's a no-brainer."

"Yes, but don't you want to get away? Didn't mom and dad pressure you?"

Another red light. Dave sprayed the windshield, ran the wipers, and thought.

"Michael, would you rather French kiss a pig or a horse?" Ray asked, blowing a hit out the window.

"Did you see the last girl he made out with?" Danny asked.

"Is it a Charlie horse?" Michael said, jabbing Danny in the thigh.

"I wouldn't call it pressure," Dave said as the light changed. "Mom and dad encouraged me to go to a four-year college. And I still plan on transferring. It was just ..."

"What?" Shannon asked. They were stuck in traffic. Two cab drivers honked at each other.

"I'd go pig," Tibbs said, smoke pouring from his nostrils. "Horses are beautiful animals, but you might lose your tongue."

"Don't pigs have more diseases?" Curtis asked, trying to squeeze one last hit from the cashed bowl.

"The band," Dave said. "I didn't want to leave the band. I know I only play sax on one song, but I just feel it's where I belong."

The traffic opened up. Dave pulled the van forward and into the alley behind the Elbo Room.

"I'm actually going to go pig," Michael said. "I believe it's a misconception that pigs are filthy animals. I think they're pretty clean."

"You're right about that," Dave announced to the back of the van. "Pigs are unable to sweat. They wallow in the mud to cool down, which gives them a bad reputation. Also, pigs only excrete—"

"David, I love you," Shannon said. "Now shut up and let me see the set list."

Dave pulled a folded paper out of his back pocket.

"Here are tonight's songs," Shannon called out. "Milk, granola, wheat bread, waffles, Amber's yogurt, fruit, spinach, chicken breasts, ground beef, sloppy joe mix, buns, BBQ sauce, vanilla ice cream, and, for an encore, syrup."

She turned to her older brother. "You've got to be shitting me."

*

Shannon sang the last verse of Danny's new song, "Little Green Love."

Now it's done

Now I can see

We are one

The green men and me

They set me free

The band drove through the chords hard until Ryan set everyone up with a drum roll on the snare. Shannon raised her arm. Ray, Tibbs, and Michael all jumped up. Danny and Brandon both stood at their keyboards. Everyone and everything crashed down. Ryan smoothed it over, working the edges of his cymbals.

"That set actually wasn't bad," Shannon announced in the green room after the show. All the band members were spread out on the dirty couches. She was standing in front like a head coach, as was customary after a show. "Dave, add 'Little Green Love' to the set list for next Saturday." She glanced at Danny with those wide, smiling, dark eyes. "But sorry, it's not a closer." She turned to Dave. "And if you lose the set list again I might use whatever it is you bring instead to slice my wrists. Papercut suicide … hmm, Tibbs, maybe that's your next song?"

Everyone smiled and laughed as Tibbs winced. "Got it," Dave said from the doorway. He was still sweating a little from returning gear to the van.

"Oh, and I've decided to go to college in the fall," Shannon announced. She glanced around the room. "I just figured that, um, it was the right thing to do." She studied her black nail polish. "Liberal arts. It's called St. Norbert, near Green Bay. They offered me a full scholarship for diving. I met the coach, the team. They seem like good people. It's right next to a prison." She looked at Ray. "I don't mean anything by that."

She made her way to the door. "This spring will be our farewell tour," she said, turning back to talk to the band. "I signed up for like a summer orientation thinger-ma-jigger." And with that, she went out and disappeared in the crowd as Gobbledegook, the latest Riverview band to make an appearance at the Elbo Room, shredded their version of heavy death metal.

*

In M132, a room formerly dedicated to rehearsal space for the symphonic jazz band, the Windows were in a frenzy. Denny pounded the drums with a vengeance. Craig's fingers flew up and down the neck in a soaring electric solo. Even Manny's keyboard lurched to life, a departure from its usual droning chords. Morris had a gray turtleneck pulled up over his face and danced around the small wooden stage that George had assembled, with wood from Craftwood Lumber, in the cramped rehearsal space. He picked up and smelled one of the sunflowers that lined the stage, a gift from Henry Martin of Riverview's Martin Floral.

The audience, a small group of Riverview musicians (including Shannon Golding) invited personally by Pam Susan for a lunch club dedicated to "art exploration," sat stone still, as if watching something mildly unpleasant.

Morris tossed the sunflower into the audience, where it landed on a bare portion of the tile floor, and ripped his turtleneck off. He held it behind him like a glider, circling what space he had like a bird of prey. He climbed on an amplifier and hovered over the edge. The music began a crescendo and ascended even higher, approaching a height that even the musicians themselves seemed astonished to reach. Morris balanced himself precariously with his turtleneck pulled taut for extended wingspan. With small, careful steps he edged farther out on the lofty branch in his mind. With a flap of his turtleneck, he steadied himself and leaned out over the brink, keenly studying his surroundings. He peered down like he was scanning the floor of a vast canyon. The song reached a feverish pitch and, just as students started to cover their faces and ears, the Windows climaxed and exploded. Morris, like a bird shot down out of midair, screamed and fell to the ground. He rolled around with the turtleneck wrapped around his face. The row of students responded with a mixture of surprise and bewilderment. Morris dragged himself on his stomach to the microphone. With wounded effort, he reached up and pulled down the mic. The three musicians behind him each found their own musical parachute to lazily drift and float on. From the ground, under his turtleneck, came sucking sounds. Then Morris began to speak.

Genital fortress

faces and warts

The rear is vulnerable

As pillow forts

The thieves have stolen the Trinity

Not even Christ wears

The stain of divinity.

Morris put the turtleneck over his waist and pulled the microphone out from underneath, like he was giving birth. He threw it on the ground as Denny, Manny, and Craig each drifted softly, delicately, into silence.

"Thank you," Mr. Best said. "That was, um … really something …" He clapped and encouraged the appalled students to do the same, yet no one complied. "The Windows, everyone. Chosen, at random I might add, once again for our new arts exploration club. You guys should buy a lotto ticket with your luck." The Windows filed off the stage. "Somehow, they manage to keep winning these drawings. If you are interested in playing in our new lunch club, any type of performance art, all you have to do is submit your name and the type of art you will be performing to Ms. Susan in the office.

I want to emphasize that this is not just a music venue. Now, let's welcome Victor Burdon and his juggling act." Pete surveyed the still shell-shocked row of students. Morris came back and picked up the turtleneck he had left behind.

Near the main entrance, Pam Susan winked at board member Roberta Anderson as she steered the school board, like a flock of tourists, into the computer lab, far away from M hall.

*

While B.J. took his turn upstairs with Frets, Ray and Tibbs sat on the couch in the lobby of the Village Music Shoppe. Outside, a blizzard raged.

"Hey, what happened with you and that girl, what was her name? Jung-Woo?" Tibbs asked Ray. "At the Elbo Room. I saw you guys fighting. During the Tadpoles set."

They both had acoustic guitars on their laps.

"We're done."

"What happened?"

"She said Johnny Cash was a redneck. That he played hillbilly music and should only play in prisons."

"Ouch. Does she know your dad is in prison?"

Ray half nodded, half shrugged. "So, you're up for rehearsal this week?" he asked.

"Yep," Tibbs acknowledged, taking a gulp.

"Got anything?"

"Nope. I'm totally hopeless."

"Do you think Shannon will really try to make you drink her pee?"

"I'll throw it in her face."

"She sounded really serious." Ray imitated her voice: "You can write a song about drinking urine."

"Yeah, well," Tibbs muttered, looking away. "I don't know. It's brutal. I try to write something stupid … something about anything. My shoes. Sloppy joes. Which belt do I wear today? I just rip it up."

Tap walked by, carrying a shoebox from Rainy Day Fitness, his yellow and orange tie-dye shirt especially bright with the snow swirling in all the windows behind him.

Tibbs strummed the open strings. "I've been listening to a lot of music. I try not to force it. Then I force it. I've been bored and waiting. I've been looking at small things, thinking about big things, but I'm just stuck. An epic case of writer's block. Not a word."

Beethoven's Fifth sounded. A trombone player walked in, the snow and wind hissing from outside like an angry beast.

"Sometimes, when I get stuck, what I do is I borrow," Ray said. "All the greats borrow. It's what you do when you're stuck."

Tibbs sighed and muted his strings. Ray put down his guitar and got out a notebook and pen from his backpack.

"I was thinking of a song the other day," Ray said. "We could write it right now, and you could use it so you don't have to drink pee."

"You mean so I don't have to throw Shannon's pee back in her face?"

"Exactly."

"All right, what you got?"

"Well, I thought of it the last time Mrs. G brought us down some veggies to eat. We were listening to the album *Born to Run*. The song 'Jungleland' was playing."

The trombone player had finished hanging up his coat. He stomped his feet free of snow and went up the stairs.

"I started with a line from Springsteen, changing it a little," Ray said, writing.

The kids out here don't write nothin at all

They just stand back and let it all be

"Here," Tibbs said, reaching for the notebook. "You better let me write. Shannon knows your handwriting." Ray passed it over. Tibbs turned the page and rewrote the line.

"See," Ray said, "I was thinking about being green, you know, being a beginner, eating a cucumber, so I came up with this line for the next part." He picked up the guitar and started strumming an F chord, into a C. Tibbs wrote as Ray sang.

Yeah they're so green,

the greenest things you've seen

Like green cucumbers

Trading words for numbers

He hit a G chord.

These kid cucumbers

Yeah they're just like me

they can't be free

without poetry.

"That's not bad," Tibbs admitted, looking at the words.

"Yeah, thanks," Ray said. "I don't have a title. I guess you could call it 'Green Cucumbers.' With all our songs about fencing and zebra mussels and aliens, I figured pretty much anything goes."

"Hey, it's Ray-Ray," B.J. called from the stairway. Since the carpool and guitar lessons and one visit to the Golding basement, he had started an annoying habit of calling everyone by nicknames they didn't really go by. "And it's Sir Tibbet!"

"Hey," Tibbs called back, with a look at Ray. "Well, I guess I'm up. Thanks, Ray-Ray."

Ray shot him a look.

"Ray-Ray the Raven," B.J. said, plopping down on the couch. "Want to play 'Golden Slumbers'? I've just about got it."

*

Bobby Jean Welsh looked out at the cloudy night, the street blanketed with snow, watching the flurries twirl in the streetlight. She moved away from the window, slid into her single bed, and picked up a romance novel entitled *The Flame and the Flower*. In addition to the two crosses and the portrait of Jesus, something new adorned their bedroom wall: a large map of Riverview.

The phone rang. She looked at the clock. It was 9:45.

"Hello?"

"Hi, Bobby Jean."

"Where are you tonight, Marie?"

"I'm in Denver. Tomorrow I have a morning flight to Houston and then back to Chicago in the afternoon. Although I hear it's raining down in Texas."

"I saw the floods on the news."

"Wonderful. I might not be back tomorrow. The life of a flight attendant. Is he out driving?"

"Not tonight. At least I don't think so. He's at a board meeting. I thought he'd be home by now."

"Maybe you should ask to go with him?"

"What on earth for?"

"Just to, you know, be sure."

"You and your theories. What's next? That he's a spy?"

"I just want you to be happy."

"I am."

"Happily married?"

"I've been praying about it, and the Lord has helped me to see that I have a good husband doing the Lord's work."

"Bobby Jean. I'm telling you this as your friend. Matt driving the streets at night is crazy. Crazy. It's not against the law to listen to rock music. And what if people are? What's he going to do about it? I don't care for the music myself, but I've always thought that ban in Riverview is—"

"Marie, I'm not getting into it again with you." The garage door opened. "Besides, I hear the garage. I've got to go. Good luck with the floods."

She hung up and dashed over to the dresser where she tucked the novel into her drawer, burying it beneath her underwear. She slid back into bed and heard the familiar sounds: the garage door closing, the hall closet hinges that creaked, the steady footsteps ascending the stairs.

Matt walked in. He went straight to the map. With a red felt-tip pen, he circled four more houses. "Sullivan Street," he said. He had difficulty putting the pen's cap back on. The map looked like it had chicken pox.

"How did the school board meeting go?"

"Huh? What?"

"The meeting?"

"Oh, that," he said. He reached under the bed, pulled out a phone book, and started circling names.

"Honey? Is everything all right?"

He kneeled over the book and continued his search, his finger moving with little vibrations up and down the pages. "Guh-guh-Golding. Guh-guh-Got you," he said. He pulled out his notepad and wrote down the name, the pen shaking. "Just buh-buh-blaring Satan's horn, ruh-ruh-right out into the sss-street," he said, mostly to himself, as he walked to the closet to change clothes.

He returned wearing pajamas.

"What about your proposal to get Pete Best fired? Did anyone get behind it?"

"Huh? Oh, th-th-that. Puh-puh-president Can't, I mmm-mean Brandt, as always, lacks a spuh-spuh-spine." Matt's stutter was becoming more frequent, and he struggled to get words out. "Never muh-muh-mind that duh-duh-drugs are on the ruh-ruh-rise again. They had another buh-buh-bust at the high school this muh-morning. He'll have to sssss-screw up royally for them to ruh-ruh-realize one of sss-sss-Satan's puh-puppets works in their school. Puh-puh-plus, half the sssss-school buh-board is muh-muh-made up of these new liberals. With their … their …"

Bobby Jean stared at her husband. His whole body was shaking. "Today, when you left," she said, "all you could talk about was Pete Best this and Pete Best that. You sounded angry. I think it's influencing your health."

"The anger of muh-muh-man pales compared to the righteousness of guh-guh-God," he said, fighting against his stutter. "We must prepare our hearts for the cuh-coming of the Lord. Sooner or later the di-di-district will ruh-realize the duh-duh-devil himself is playing a flute, the guh-Great Piper at the guh-guh-Gates of Hell. Pray with me."

*

It was a warm, sunny day, with temperatures in the fifties; the basement sub pumps were working overtime with the melting snow. Everyone had a cold or a cough. Dave had the flu. Shannon had had her license taken away by her parents again, this time for coming home with alcohol on her breath, even though she wasn't driving. For the show at the Elbo Room on Saturday, February 26, Brandon, the only licensed member of the band, drove the van. As the driver, it was also his job to carry the set list, which he managed to doctor up a little.

Forty-five minutes after their arrival, in the middle of their set, Brandon powered through his sore throat to sing lead vocals for the first time on a song that sounded a bit like a Talking Heads tune.

The zebra mussels are getting in the pipes

You know, the ones with the stripes

You might think they're your type

But not when they're getting into your pipe

Zebra mussels

Out of control

Zebra mussels

In our water and our soul

Ray looked out from his pocket next to Curtis and to the right of Ryan. Shannon pranced around him with a tambourine. He watched her shake, then looked past her and noticed the audience had grown to capacity, with a line out the door.

Michael thumped a bass solo, and they hit the bridge.

Not lions

Or giraffes

Not hippos

Taking a bath

I'm talkin bout wild, wild

zeeeeeeebrraaaaaaaaaaaaaa

mussels.

Ray gazed toward the back of the room and saw the RHS in crowd, the cool kids, upper classmen: the preppies, jocks and cheerleaders. They had come down to the city from the suburbs, like a migration of animals that shifts when a resource becomes unavailable. In the middle, like a buffer, stood the adults.

The song ended. Ray watched the people in the back of the crammed space. There was a hardness to their faces. They didn't clap or even move much. They glared, like the songs were in some way offensive. His eyes moved to the front, the clapping and sweating throng. Their fans, who showed up every week. Ryan counted off four and they were off on "Confabulations," a Danny song about a tour of an alien ship.

The set was over. A Riverview High School group called Cool Pressure followed them. The number of suburban bands playing the Elbo Room since the Water Tower shut down kept growing. Ray meandered out into the audience and stood in the back with the very people that had been up front during their set. The teenagers that migrated to the back for Cool Pressure were the punks, freaks, geeks, burnouts, M-hallers, and misfits of Riverview. Ray watched the jocks in front trying without success to start a mosh pit. "There's a divide," he said to himself, as Michael pulled him outside with the universal *time to smoke* signal.

They stepped out into the empty city street at night. The temperature was plunging again, turning piles of dirty snow into hard chunks on the street corners. A taxi cruised by. Ray thought about bringing up the divide, but Brandon burst out the door.

"That mussels song killed!" he boasted.

*

The following Monday, Shannon and the Little Brothers agreed to wear sunglasses to school.

"We do things as a band," Shannon said.

It happened in Q hall, between first and second period.

"Take off those stupid sunglasses. And wipe that grin off your face."

Tibbs ignored the comment, not knowing it was directed at him. It surprised him when a hand reached over and knocked his glasses off. Another set of hands pushed him up against a locker.

"Listen, punk," said Clare Danko, a sophomore and the bassist of Cool Pressure. "You guys think you're hot shit at the Elbo Room. But here you're just lowly freshmen. Don't think any different. Got it?"

"Whatever."

Clare emphasized her point with a shove into the lockers. Eric Horg, the drummer of Cool Pressure, added, "And tell that to rest of your band, the Little Assholes."

So officially began the feud between Shannon and the Little Brothers and Cool Pressure.

Ray learned of the animosity when singer Dave "Diamond" Roth knocked down his new binder with the Stones logo. Shannon and the Little Brothers addressed the confrontation the next weekend at the Elbo Room, playing a new punk tune, "The Little Assholes Take a Big Shit on You."

The song ended with a coda that featured Shannon wailing with both middle fingers extended:

Here's a little gesture

For uncool pressure

Leave my little brothers

the FUCK ALONE!

The song brought into the open the division between the migrating suburban adolescents. The Little Brothers watched from backstage as the crowd's reaction intensified during the next band, a new experimental progressive rock group called Gallimaufry.

When their last song ended, a group of football players led the in crowd—along with the upper-middle high school social class that *wanted* to be elite—in a chorus of boos and heckles.

Everyone else, the outsiders and misfits and eccentrics, joined with Shannon and the Little Brothers and cheered on a song about eating boogers. The battle line was drawn. Bands and audience members had to choose a side. The Elbo Room became a battleground.

There was some pushing and shoving. Stevland Morris, the linebacker and new front man for the recently formed Spinning Wheels, stepped in front of his defensive line that was making a rush at Shannon and the Little Brothers. "Find some higher ground," he told the football players.

"Thanks," Shannon said over her shoulder.

"That's what friends are for," Stevland called after her.

The bouncers working the Elbo Room got between the two frenzied mobs. They defused the situation just long enough for the Butter People to take the stage. Fortunately, the band opened with a ballad entitled "Spread It Goopy."

*

"Next up," Mr. Best announced in the jammed, invitation-only rehearsal room, "we have a solo act. Let's all give a warm welcome to Brian Jones Wyman, a.k.a. B.J."

George the custodian, standing in the corner by the side door that served as a staging area for the musicians, amidst a clutter of music stands, stacked chairs, and covered percussion instruments, signaled to B.J. that it was time. As he had done for all students that performed at open mic, George patted him on the shoulder and wished him luck. B.J. walked through the narrow aisle kept clear for performers to enter.

Mr. Best pulled up a stool to the microphone and adjusted the mic stand to the proper height. Red roses lined the small stage. B.J. sat down, pulled out his guitar, and strummed a few E chords to make sure it was in tune, discovering it wasn't. Mr. Best, without the microphone, said to the row of watching students, "C'mon everyone, give B.J. a big hand. Let's make him feel welcome." The students clapped loudly, with scattered whistles and shouts expressing how glad they were to be cheering for an act besides the Windows.

This sound attracted a group of jocks out in the hallway who had congregated for an unclear purpose, now arriving on the scene like a pack of jackals.

With shaky hands, B.J. lifted his thick glasses and wiped his forehead. "My aunt is making me do this," he said and tried to smile. When he smiled, one of the luminous green rubber bands on his braces snapped free and shot into the crowd, landing on Dee Snider's hair. Her friend John Giovi pulled it out with a look of repulsion.

B.J.'s face turned bright red. He looked at Mr. Best with a face full of fear, who returned a thumbs-up and mouthed "you're fine," as if speaking to a beginner in a lip-reading class.

The jock jackals, smelling fresh prey, made a call down the hall. Students began arriving from the main hall, crowding into the little space while B.J. fumbled with the tuning knobs, twisting the strings further out of tune.

"Anytime you're ready, B.J.," Mr. Best encouraged, with fingers drumming underneath crossed arms. More and more students arrived from the main hall.

The crowd started chanting, "BEEEEEEEEEE JAAAAAAAAAAAYY, BEEEEEEE JAAAAAAY, BEEEEEEE JAAAAAAAAAY."

Mr. Best returned to the small stage. George appeared by B.J.'s side to help him tune the instrument. "Students, please, those of you who have just arrived, this is an invitation-only performing arts club. I will permit you to stay only if you show respect to the performers." This quieted them down, a temporary restraint; the still-growing crowd smiled and elbowed each other. B.J. saw it in their eyes, shining and ready for him to fail.

"There's a Beatles song …" he began. His voice cracked on the "-tles." The laughter came swiftly and crashed on B.J., a wave of adolescent mirth. The jeers and laughs drowned out his next sentence.

"I do it a little different."

B.J.'s face was bright red, matching the row of roses. He looked over at Mr. Best, who was frowning at the jackals. B.J. wanted to run. He wanted to hide. But there was nowhere to go. The aisle had closed off. He was trapped.

George emerged again, as if by magic, from a cluster of xylophones. "Isn't it a pity?" he said, without the mic. The students all exchanged *whatever that means* glances. For many, it was the first time they had heard the custodian say something that wasn't a chant. George turned to B.J. in the lull he had created and mouthed, "NOW PLAY."

So B.J. did. He closed his eyes and started strumming a C chord, quietly. Then he changed from a C to an A minor seventh, lifting his third finger and letting the A string ring out. For a moment he was with Frets again and he could hear the music. "That's it," he could hear Frets say. "Not too fast."

But he was playing too fast. He strummed the low E string on accident. Then he lost the rhythm. "Concentrate," Frets said. "Feel the music. Let it come from the inside, a place no one else can get to but you. That's where music comes from."

B.J. began singing. It was quiet, and a little off-key, but both Mr. Best and George breathed sighs of relief.

Golden slumbers kiss your eyes

Smiles awake you when you rise

Sleep, pretty wantons, do not cry

And I will sing a lullaby.

The rhythm suffered a little, and he botched the change to a D minor seventh chord, but still, he hit a clean G7 and moved into the next verse.

Rock them, rock them, lullaby.

Care is heavy, therefore sleep you

You are care, and care must keep you;

Sleep pretty wantons, do not cry

And I will sing a lullaby

Rock them, rock them, lullaby.

The chords didn't quite match up with the next part, and he was still off-key, but he made up for it with an openness that quelled the jeering students into a begrudging acceptance. One of the jackals stifled laughter, and Mr. Best escorted him to the door.

Sleep pretty wantons, do not cry

And I will sing a lullaby

Maybe it was the abrupt change in volume when B.J. hit the next chord. Or the dissonance between his singing and his guitar. Or the way his glasses jarred loose and clung crookedly to his nose. Either way, when he shifted to the Beatles classic and belted out the "Gooooolden" of the chorus, the crowd lost it. He tried to continue, but his left hand failed to form the F chord. His guitar made an unmusical sound. Then his voice cracked again on "eyes." He stumbled through the next line, playing haltingly. The E minor and A minor arrived way behind the lyrics. Then it all became a moot point. The audience, led by the jock jackals along the window, began chanting, "BEEEEEEEEEE JAAAAAAAAAAY BEEEEEEEEEEE JAAAAAAAAAAAAY."

No one knew who changed it first. A lot of people thought it was Diamond Roth of Cool Pressure, though he vehemently denied it later, in vain, as Mr. Best banned Cool Pressure from performing at the new arts club. Others said it was bass player Clare Danko. A few people claim it was Scott Kline. Either way, the chant changed from "BEEEEEEE JAAAAAAAAY" to "BLOOOOOOOOOOOOOW JOOOOOOOOOB BLOOOOOOOOOOOOOOOW JOOOOOOOOOOOOOB."

B.J. steered the song back to the original lullaby, practically whimpering with his eyes closed behind his thick crooked glasses, though the chanting drowned out most of what had become a whisper.

Sleep pretty wantons do not cry

And I will sing a lullaby

Then he shoved the guitar in its case, slammed it shut, and ran out. Some of the jeering students who were seated near the door had to dodge his case as he flew by.

The bell rang. Mr. Best leaped to the microphone, futile in his efforts to both calm down the riled-up students and tell them that applications to play in the performing arts club would be available directly from Ms. Susan in the main office.

The students filed out boisterously but steadily. Mr. Best looked for George over by the cluster of xylophones, seeking some sign of reassurance that this was a good thing, that they could somehow manage it and keep it from spreading to the people that would harm it or shut it down, but George was gone.

*

That afternoon, Ray received a hand-delivered envelope from Ms. Susan in his first period world civilizations class, informing him that he had been selected to play at the new performing arts club. At the end of the school day, he found out that Shannon had applied on his behalf.

"You need to get up there on your own," she said in E hall. "You never know what you got until you give it a shot."

"Is that from a song?" Ray asked. She smiled with her eyes and walked away.

All week, he dreamed he was performing at his dad's prison. All the inmates crossed their arms in disapproval as he played. He would try different songs: rock, blues, country, gospel, Johnny Cash. Nothing worked. They would crowd around and get closer and closer until he woke up.

He didn't hear a word his teachers said on Wednesday morning before his performance. There was a note in his locker. Meet in the smoking area before you play.

Shannon and Danny were waiting.

"I don't have a smoking pass," Ray said. "I'm not supposed to be here."

"Here, borrow mine," Shannon said. She reached inside her pocket and offered Ray her middle finger.

"Take a hit. It's alien pot," Danny said. "It will calm your nerves. Side effects include cotton mouth, and it turns your balls into cones."

Ray took two big hits off the Rainy Day Fitness joint, coughed his head off, and turned toward M hall like he was heading to his execution.

"You got this, Ray," Shannon said, squeezing his arm. He was numb, he realized, and very, very high. Like it was all a dream—but it wasn't, because he clearly felt Danny punch him in the shoulder.

He had decided to play the Buddy Holly tune "Crying, Waiting, Hoping." He hit every drinking fountain on his way to M hall. He walked through the instrument storage room, per the invitation's instructions, and found George, who patted him on the shoulder with an expression that suggested a funny smell. Ray stepped into M132 to find it packed with students. Mr. Best did his best at crowd control, but it was chaos. Many students had shown up without an invitation. He had tried to get some to leave, but they protested, and in the end the room was packed, standing room only, and it was time to introduce the first artist.

"Let's give a warm performing arts welcome to Ray Flowers," Mr. Best announced.

"Have fun," George whispered to Ray as the room filled with a smattering of applause and a few jeers coming from the pack of jackal jocks.

Ray walked along the narrow path between cross-legged students. He stepped over the bright turquoise orchids and onto the stage. He took a deep breath and plugged in his Strat. "Hi, everybody." He clipped on a capo and made sure it was in tune. The spotlight was blinding. He closed his eyes, tapped his foot, and ripped into the intro. Then he realized his capo was on the wrong fret. He would have to sing in a different key, one he hadn't rehearsed. He had to find the first note.

"Crying," he sang, but it was too high. He did the intro again.

"Crying…" This time it was a little too low. But he went ahead anyway. "Waiting, hoping …"

He homed in on the key and opened his eyes. In the audience, through the glare of the spotlight, he glimpsed a bright orange shirt. He closed his eyes, but he still saw bright orange. His mind went blank as the chords reached the second verse. No words came, so he made some up.

Rolling (do, do, do) doubles in the dice

Waiting (do, do, do) to make it right

I keep trying, so you'll come back

My eyes will set you free

He opened his eyes. Beyond the blinding spotlight in the packed rehearsal room, orange shirts started popping up. They were all looking at him like he was telling them something private and disturbing. The room started to spin. He closed his eyes and hit the pedal. With the loop set, he tapped the pedal again, squeezed his eyes tight, and dove into the solo: first low pentatonic, then leaping up an octave. Something was off with the lights. It was too bright.

He ducked out of the spotlight and fired out triplets. To his dismay he saw more and more orange, not just shirts but jumpsuits. The room was spinning faster. He looked over at George, who was twirling an insane number of keys. Ray started playing faster, trying to compensate, but he was getting ahead of the chords. The loop came around a second time. He played faster. Faster. He looked out at all his peers, his friends, the Little Brothers, Mr. Best, George. Everyone was in orange jumpsuits, spinning around like a carousel out of control. He threw more and more notes out. Wrong notes. Right notes. It didn't matter. He moved unsteadily back to the mic and grabbed the stand like a life preserver. He was getting light-headed. It was so bright. He let the looper play the chords and went to the verse like it was a tunnel that he was almost out of.

Crying (do, do, do) my tears keep falling and I can't see

Waiting (do, do, do) so useless can't get out of jail free

The room spun too fast. An orange blur. He trailed off. "I know it's wrong …"

He was on the floor. Mr. Best was tapping him on the shoulder. "Mr. Flowers, are you OK?"

*

Lunchtime. It was a mild, sunny, raw day in early March. Spring was close, yet the cold wind off the lake blew it away. B.J. walked down Q hall and slipped out the side door, walking along the student-driving course. He moved past the sophomore parking lot, plucking his rubber bands, like everything was normal as can be. He passed the wooden stumps that kept cars from driving onto Summit Drive, no looking back, off campus and onto Overland Trail. He saw the idling brown van with Gradenko Home Goods on the side.

"Thank you for meeting me, B.J.," Roxanne Gradenko said, rolling down the window. "You have no idea how much this helps our cause. Having someone from the school telling the truth."

He told her everything. It gushed out of him. About the bullying that goes on, the pot being smoked in the bathrooms, the teachers and administrators that don't do anything, about not having a seat at lunch. About how there are lots of kids like him that don't have anywhere to sit and eat standing up.

Roxanne wrote it all down, whispering things like "I knew it" or "This is unacceptable" or "You're so brave, B.J. You're doing the right thing."

He stopped, on the verge of tears. He looked away, down the empty suburban street, and took a deep breath. Then he told her about open mic. How it was back, crammed into a rehearsal space. How it was being run by Mr. Best. How kids did drugs or drank alcohol before they played. He started to cry. He told her how he wanted to perform a lullaby his mom used to sing, but how he didn't feel safe. How they bullied him, yelled at him.

"Here, honey," Roxanne soothed, passing him a tissue, fixing her fresh Princess Diana 'do. "They bullied my son," she said. "He's not here anymore because they bullied him relentlessly, these kids on drugs, until their carelessness killed him. But it's going to stop. Because of you. You are being so brave."

He wiped his eyes and found he couldn't stop. He told her about the Windows performance yesterday, how he snuck into it because he knew she would want to know. He told her everything about the Windows.

"The singer, this Morris, he actually said and did all of this?"

"Yes."

"He actually said, 'Adolf Hitler is alive and well in Riverview'?"

"Yes. That's how he started the song."

"He ranted about the students being effing slaves?" Roxanne asked. "Did he really use the F word?"

"Yes."

B.J. pulled a folded stack of papers from his jeans and passed it to her. "Here, I wrote down the lyrics so I wouldn't forget them."

"Down here at the bottom, it's a little hard to read," Roxanne said. "Could you read it for me?"

B.J. took the paper back and read slowly as Roxanne wrote it down.

"'I'd like to see a little nakedness around here. Take your clothes off and love each other.'"

Roxanne gasped. "The PMRC is going to have a field day with this."

B.J. turned the page. A car drove by and he squinted to see who was inside. It wasn't anybody. He kept reading.

"'I know why you're here. I know why you're at the open mic. To see my cock.'"

Roxanne inhaled sharply as she wrote it down. "C-o-c-k," she mouthed as she wrote. "He actually used that word. You've outdone yourself this time, B.J."

He gave the papers back to her. She read them over once more. "What's this word? At the bottom."

"Allegedly. He allegedly whipped it out."

"You're not sure? Weren't you sitting in the front row?"

"It got a little crazy. All these jocks rushed the stage. There was a big fight. Plus, I wasn't wearing my glasses."

"Well," Roxanne said, "whether he exposed himself or not is beside the point. We have more than enough to go on here. Good work."

"Thank you."

"Next time we talk, I may have another task for you. Have you used a tape recorder before?"

B.J. shook his head.

"This will look very good on a college application, your support of D.A.R.E. and the PMRC," Roxanne said, setting down her notepad and B.J.'s papers. "I will see about having Nancy Reagan herself sign a letter of recommendation."

"Thank you," B.J. said. "I don't like it here."

"Understandably," Roxanne said. "The school district has let you down. They've failed to keep you safe and create a nurturing environment. But that's going to change. Starting today. Because of you."

B.J. nodded, sniffled, and wiped his nose with the crumpled tissue.

"By the way, why do you go by B.J. now?"

"That's what my mom used to call me. My initials. Brian Jones."

"Oh, that's nice."

"My mom ran away. Because of me."

"You poor thing."

*

Jane Mott thanked the Riverview High School parent (who wished to remain anonymous) for the tip about the parent protest and hung up. She grabbed her keys, a notepad, a pencil, her camera, and her purse. In contrast to her friend and fellow journalist Leslie Bangs, Jane was fastidiously organized. She glanced over at the desk that had been empty the past four weeks, the pair of glasses and the random scattered items that no one had bothered to clean up—and the blinking light on the phone. She walked out of the *Riverview Review* office and drove over to the high school, wondering what she would find there, thinking it was as much Leslie's story as hers. At the red light on Warrior Way, she saw the crowd and something that surprised her: news vans from Chicago TV stations. The light changed. Jane pulled in, thinking of Leslie, worrying about her, wishing she was in the passenger seat.

It was overcast, with a forecast of rain, but so far the rain had held off. The air was chilly though, as winter clung stubbornly to the shores of Lake Michigan. A crowd of parents marched around the entrance to the high school carrying signs. Jane pulled out her camera and snapped some photos. The signs read: PROTECT OUR KIDS, KEEP DRUGS OUT OF RHS, and STUDENTS ARE NOT SAFE. Jane focused her camera on Courtney Harrison, who was carrying a sign that said: EXPLICIT LYRICS AND ILLEGAL DRUGS ARE POISONING OUR KIDS. Another few signs had SEX DRUGS AND ROCK AND ROLL with the words crossed out.

They were all wearing Just Say No! T-shirts pulled tight over coats and jackets, and they were bundled with scarfs and hats and gloves to fight off the chill. Jane observed Superintendent Jag, Dean Early, and Deputy Copeland standing alongside the protest. She watched as Roxanne Gradenko did an interview with a news reporter she recognized from ABC 7, WLS Chicago. Jane stood off by herself and watched the parents march and chant, thinking it was a little silly to protest at 9:05 in the morning, with classes in session and nobody except herself and a worker delivering milk to hear the chants of "Just Say No!" She looked more closely and noticed something else: All the protesters were her age—mid-forties—or older. Some of them she recognized from her own graduating class or as the parents of children that had graduated with her daughter, who was now about to graduate college. It was as if their leader, Roxanne Gradenko, after the tragic loss of her son, had rallied them, pulled them out of the woodwork, and dragged them to the high school on this bleak morning to stand up against teen drug abuse. And the numbers were impressive. It's like some fairy tale, Jane thought to herself; a sleeping giant has been awakened.

They were loud, even if it was in front of a parking lot full of empty cars. Jane knew that since the drug bust at White Hen, drugs—mostly pot—had found another way in. She had seen the arrest reports. She knew some students had been caught at school and suspended. What she didn't know was how music fit into all this. The Water Tower in Lowland Park had been shut down. So where did that leave the surge in teenage rock bands? Had it gone underground? Leslie would know.

That's when Jane noticed another curious sight: In the first row of the parking lot, Vincent Furnier, the factory union boss she had been covering since Leslie had been put on leave, was passing out Danishes and coffee to the protesters taking a break.

"This is so silly," she said, blowing out a cloud of breath. "Leslie, where are you?"

*

Two hours later, the protest had departed, and Pam Susan welcomed the school board for its monthly visit. She led them to Assistant Athletic

Director Gayle Leneler's office, who took them—despite the drizzle and cool temperatures—on an unexpected tour of the track, pointing out its many cracks, and then to the back forty, to show them how uneven the softball fields had become and the dangerous holes in the outfield.

They were about as far as they could possibly be, as the crow flies, from the rehearsal room in M hall, where roughly twenty invited kids listened as a hoarse and visibly sick Assistant Principal Pete Best introduced Shannon and the Little Brothers as the next act in the open art forum. Everyone had a seat.

The only one standing was George in his corner.

"Let's give them a hand," Mr. Best announced, and coughed. "Shannon and the Little Brothers. Take it away." The audience, like a loyal Little Brothers fan club, screamed and cheered.

"I'm allergic to cats," Shannon hinted to the crowd with a wry smile.

Danny hit the keys at the exact moment that Ryan kicked in the drums, and they were off.

Shannon stepped up and belted out the first line.

Duuuuuh Deedle Dee Duh Dum

The Little Brothers surged in behind her.

Little kitty where did you come from?

Come on kitty!

Ryan beat away at the skins with metronome precision. Danny flew up and down the keyboard. Tibbs, Ray, and Michael stood in a line and danced and played. In the background Brandon bobbed his head with his hands gliding along the organ while Curtis wailed with his saxophone. The band rocketed forward, then stopped on a dime for Shannon to deliver the next lines. The audience clapped and moved. A few couples stood up and danced.

Kitty you know you drive me crazy

All day laying around so lazy

Got my senses reelin

Baby what a feeling

Come on Kitty let me pet you

Say meow

Say meeoow

Say meeeooooooooow

Say meow meowmeowmeow

C'mon kitty

I wanna pet you!

The band jumped and grooved. Everyone in the room was moving and shaking.

C'mon kitty let me pet you!

Say meow

Say meeeoooooooow

Say meowmeowmeow meeoow me-OW

C'mon kitty

I wanna pet you!

The living and nonliving elements in the cramped rehearsal room seemed to meld together: Along with the people, the covered furniture and the very walls shook to the music. Shannon danced off and Curtis stepped forward to launch into a funky solo. He came back to the melody, and the band led him into the next verse. Shannon stepped up just in time.

Tuna fish craving

Dead mouse saving

You see what I need

But you just wanna feed

C'mon baby don't treat me like this

C'mon kitty

I wanna pet you

Say meow meow meow

MEEEEEOOOOOOOOOOOOW!

Oh how I wanna pet you!

The Little Brothers as a unit hit one last "duh-dunna duh." Ryan hit a drum roll, and to the surprise of the twenty or so onlookers, the band took a left turn that made George reach for a nearby broom. Tibbs and Ray stepped forward and ripped right into the AC/DC tune "Girls Got Rhythm." After a healthy dose of the riff, Shannon started singing, an octave higher, with all the Little Brothers filling in background vocals.

The cat's got rhythm (cat's got rhythm)

The cat's got rhythm (meow meow rhythm)

She's got the purrrrr-fect rhythm (cat's got rhythm)

The cat's got rhythm (and how rhythm)

You know kitty's really got rhythm (cat's got rhythm)

She's got mouse killing rhythm (meow meow rhythm)

Rock n' roll rhythm (cat's got rhythm)

Purrrfect rhythm

Just as Tibbs stepped up for his solo, the bell rang. The remaining students were dancing and jumping around in a frenzy. Tibbs wailed away. Mr. Best made his way to the microphone and called through his congested throat, "That's all for today. Students! Students!"

The song trailed off. Tibbs kept going, his eyes shut tight.

"Andrew. That's enough. Stop. Very impressive, but please."

There was an awkward silence. Feedback hung in the air. Tibbs opened his eyes. No one wanted to leave. The sound of thunder filled the sky above the high school, and for a moment it seemed like the boom had come from the musicians. George was dusting his broom.

Outside, Matt Welsh and the rest of the school board, led by Assistant Athletic Director Leneler, in their haste to get inside from the sudden, freezing downpour, ran from the outfield right into a large patch of mud. They had to tiptoe carefully in their dress shoes across the oozing ground.

*

Bobby Jean finished making the bed. She came downstairs carrying a load of laundry, and that's when she heard him. The sound she noticed was a soft but perceptible jingle-jangle of his keychain, with the pitter-patter of rain on the roof as a backdrop.

"Matty," she cried out, opening the door, "you're soaking wet."

He had been standing in the rain, drenched and shivering, unable to steady his key to insert it in the lock.

"Buh-buh-buh-Best, for the last time, Best," he managed. His stutter was exacerbated by his chattering teeth.

"You're freezing!" she said, pulling him inside. "What on earth? Let's get you dry and warm."

She guided him upstairs like a child, step by step. She helped him out of his wet clothes and wrapped his shivering body in two towels, one around the waist and another around his shoulders. "I'll draw a bath and fix you some tea," she said, rubbing his back, shoulders, and arms. "Are you okay, honey? Your lips are purple. Dear heaven."

"Best," Matt stuttered, "for the la-la-last time."

She left the room, started the bath, and went downstairs for tea.

When she came back up, Matt had moved from the chair, on hairless, wobbly legs, to the phone near the bed. The little green book of phone numbers was open on the bed. His trembling fingers fumbled with the rotary dial.

"Matthew," Bobby Jean scolded. "What on earth has gotten into you?"

He ignored her, focusing all his attention on dialing numbers.

She took the phone away and held his arm. "Matthew, talk to me. What's happening?"

Matt turned to his wife with his wide, dark eyes, his nose flaring, and saw her, perhaps, for the first time in years. The look of concern from his loving wife steadied him. He stopped shaking.

"It's the assistant principal," he said. "Pete Best. He's running the high school like a zoo. He's mad. Out of control. And the board is being led around like a …"

Bobby Jean saw the anger flash in her husband's eyes. The shaking seized him in a frenzy.

"A … buh-buh-bunch of ki-ki-kindergartners on a fuh-fuh-field trip," he finished, his stutter creeping back in as his temper flared. He broke free from her arms, his towels falling to the floor. "Let go, woman," he said. "Chief Suh-Su-Sumner must be notified. Laws are buh-bu-being broken."

Bobby Jean stood back and watched her husband of over thirty-five years, his naked body quivering, his fingers unable to dial a rotary phone. Then she remembered the bath, like a voice whispering a reminder to be a dutiful wife, and went into the bathroom to check on the running water.

*

Monday afternoon. The first legitimately warm day of spring had finally arrived. The students walked out into the bright sun, their senses buzzing, trying to adjust to the light and warmth.

Aunt Bertha, her trunk full of guitars, with B.J. in the passenger seat and Tibbs and Ray in the back seat, exclaimed, "What is all this?" and swerved around a line of parent protesters outside Riverview High School. The parent at the end of the line seemed to flash his sign at her: No Explicit Lyrics! No Drugs! Kids First!

"How was school today?" Aunt Bertha asked.

The teenagers responded to the universal parent question with the universal teenage response, in unison: "Fine."

The car lapsed into silence as Aunt Bertha navigated the after-school traffic and made her way to the Village Music Shoppe. Tibbs and Ray flicked their cheeks and popped their lips like fish, trying to make the best water-drop sound. Tibbs had the far superior drop, deep and resonant, but Ray's steadily improved.

The sound irked Aunt Bertha, but she didn't say anything.

Ten minutes later, she turned off Waukegan Road, drove past the post office, and pulled up to the Village Music Shoppe to find three police squad cars in the parking lot.

"Oh, dear," Aunt Bertha exclaimed. And then, like an automatic response, "What is all this?"

Beethoven's Fifth sounded as an expressionless Sergeant Winter led Tap, in his tie-dye shirt and sandals, to the back of a squad car in handcuffs.

"This does not look good," Aunt Bertha said. "What is happening?"

Again, Beethoven's famous opening notes sounded, and Deputy Copeland accompanied a bound Rik Frets to a squad car. Tibbs and Ray jumped out of Aunt Bertha's car and ran over.

Frets turned and saw them. Despite being strong-armed into the back seat of Deputy Copeland's patrol car, he called out, "Remember, freedom lives in your heart and mind, no matter where you are, be it factory or prison or school."

"Let's go," Copeland said with a shove, and slammed the door closed.

Frets smiled at the two young musicians and mouthed a phrase: "It's OK."

*

On a warm, spring Friday night, they sat around the campfire near the woods behind Bev Malcolm's house. Tibbs reached into a case of harmonicas and tossed Ray the harp. Ray snapped the harmonica into the rack around his neck. He counted four beats and strummed the progression on guitar. Ryan tapped on a bongo. Tibbs did fills on a second acoustic. Brandon passed Danny a xylophone and received a maraca in exchange. Everyone else tapped along on thighs. Ray closed his eyes and started singing.

Lalala la la la

The circle repeated his "la's" while he sucked in on low harp notes. Then he was on to the verse:

The best way to learn from your mistakes

Is to put your hands in roller skates

And climb up to the top of the stairs

And pile up a couple of chairs

Rise, rise with the moon in your eyes

Rise, rise with the moon

Rise, rise keep the moon in your eyes

Rise rise rise with the moon.

The circle repeated the chorus as Ray strummed and blew. They did another round of "la's," and Ray came to the second verse with eyes still closed.

You will need to get higher still

So reach for the edge of the windowsill

But since your fingers have become wheels

Wrap your toes in banana peels

The circle sang the chorus together. "Rise, rise with the moon." Tibbs did a solo over the verse chord progression. Ray opened his eyes to a circle of smiling faces, glowing orange in the light of the fire. He shut his eyes, but it was too late. He kept his eyes closed, but he knew what was happening, so he opened them, just to confirm. He watched the soft orange flickering glow spread from his friends' faces to their clothes. Orange jumpsuits again.

He missed the arrival of the third verse and played the progression again—but not in the correct order. Shannon's bracelets became handcuffs. He stared directly into the fire and sang the third verse a half measure too early.

Open the window and get on the roof

Still that's not quite high enough

Crawl out on the limbs of the trees

Use your elbows and your knees

Another round of the chorus. Danny took a solo on the xylophone. The fire turned into his dad's face, contorted in pain and sadness. Like breaking from a magnetic force, Ray steered his gaze to the moon for the last verse, found something deep inside that he didn't know was there.

Get up, get out to the branch's tip

As the limb bends bite down your lip

Prepare yourself for an amazing leap

No matter what happens

Just remember to keeeeeeeeeeeeeeeeeeep

The moon in your eyes

Keep the moon in your eyes.

Keep the moon in your eyes.

He blew out one last chord on the harp over a final progression. The song ended. He opened his eyes. His dad was gone.

"So you *can* sing," Shannon said. "I knew you were holding out on us."

*

From the woods nearby, they heard the snap of a branch, and an inebriated B.J. stumbled out of the woods. Carrying an empty bottle and reeking of gin, he staggered toward the fire. He lost his balance and his cookies, the spray of vomit landing just outside the circle.

"I lost my glasses," he said. "In the woods."

Ray, Shannon, and Danny went to look for his glasses. Michael and Tibbs lifted B.J. and helped him back through the woods and toward Bev's house.

"I'm OK (*hiccup*) guys," he said. "Listen, I gotta tell you something …"

"We'll get you some water, find a place you can lie down," Tibbs said.

"Seriously," B.J. maintained. "I just blacked out (*hiccup*) for a moment. I'm better. Listen. You guys need to know this."

"It's cool, man," Michael assured him. "We've all been there."

"It's about the parents' group. The parents' music thing (*hiccup*)," B.J. said. "Music. Muuuuuuuuuu-sick. Mu-siiiiiiiiiiiiick. (*hiccup*) It cures what ails you."

"It sure does," Tibbs agreed, holding his breath to avoid B.J.'s puke stench.

"I haven't really told anyone this (*hiccup*)," B.J. confessed. "But my dream, (*hiccup*) my deepest wish and desire, is to become a musician. (*hiccup*) My mom is a musician. It's what I want (*hiccup*) more than anything in the world. Just to play music (*hiccup*)." A loud, staccato fart escaped from his other cheeks.

"And you do," Michael said with a laugh. They were out of the woods and making their way up the hill toward Bev's house.

"No. (*hiccup*) Not like you guys. You guys play on stage and people listen and dance and sing. (*hiccup*) I played on a stage once, at open mic. (*hiccup*) And look what happened. Everyone yelled Blow (*hiccup*) Job. Because I suck. I suck. I suck. But listen … the parents …"

"Nonsense," Tibbs said. "Everyone yelled that because Riverview is full of asshole jocks and preps. A couple of assholes started yelling it, and then everyone else joined in. To fit in."

"Everyone sucks at the beginning," Michael said. "Bruce Springsteen sucked."

"I know (*hiccup*)," B.J. lamented. "The whole world sucks. When you don't have any talent. (*hiccup*) I'm tone deaf."

They crossed the fence around the tennis courts and made their way toward the pool, which had recently been filled for the spring. B.J. was getting there through a combination of walking and being dragged.

"You never know what you got until you put on wings," Tibbs offered. "Take a test flight."

"You know when you crash (*hiccup*)," B.J. said. "Listen … I'm trying to you … to say … The parents' group is planning … (*belch*) at open mic …"

"That's when you learn, from crashing," Michael instructed.

"I fucking love you guys (*hiccup*)," B.J. gushed. "Do you guys need a manager? (*hiccup*) Could I come to your practices? I'm sure I could help in some way. (*hiccup*) Some small way. I could help. (*hiccup*) I'm very good at numbers, math, information (*hiccup*). I'm just sort of screwed up at the moment. (*buuuuurrrp*)"

"Yeah," Tibbs said. "You mentioned that."

They walked around the pool. Tibbs and Michael allowed B.J. to loosely steer the triumvirate. If there had been snow on the ground, their footprints would have been zigzags.

"My sister got all the musical talent (*hiccup*)," B.J. complained. "It's not fair."

"I remember," Tibbs recalled. "Your sister plays the flute, right? I think she played at open mic."

"She sure did (*hiccup*)," B.J. said. "And no one yelled 'Blow Job' when she finished. I can tell you that (*hiccup*)."

"Learn to forget," Michael quoted.

"Hey, let me take a quick dip (*hiccup*)," B.J. said. "It will clear my head. I need to essplain sumthin'."

"No," Michael said. "I don't think that's such a good idea."

"Yeah," Tibbs agreed. "You need to lie down."

B.J. squirmed free and jumped into the pool.

"Shit," Tibbs said. "I hope he can swim."

"Shit is right," Michael responded. "Look."

"Oh man. Not in the pool."

Michael threw a large inflatable swan into the pool. "Grab the swan!" he shouted. Then to Tibbs he said, "Make sure he doesn't drown. I'll go tell Bev."

*

That was Friday. Tibbs and Michael were back at Bev's the next night, late, after their gig at the Elbo Room.

"Welcome," Bev said with a smile, doling out hugs. "We have a keg going on the deck and Jell-O shots in the fridge."

"Hey, Bevs," Tibbs said.

"Whaaaaasup?" Michael added.

"I heard you guys really rocked the Elbo Room tonight," Bev said. "I wish I could have been there. Some people are already back. Shannon and Brandon and Ray are out in the woods."

"It's all good."

Cory and Michael struck up a conversation in the hallway.

"Tellin' you, Mikey," Cory slurred. "If you ever need a stand in on bass, jusss lemme know."

"Will do."

"My 'Smoke on the Water' bass line has made grown men weep," Cory joked.

"I heard you guys are trying to plan a concert, like before Shannon goes away this summer," Bev said to Tibbs. "Here in Riverview."

"That's the idea," Tibbs replied. "Except with the Water Tower shut down, we can't find a venue."

"Will it really be the last show for Shannon and the Little Brothers?" Bev asked. "You guys are so good."

"Time will tell," Tibbs said.

"It makes me sad," Bev said with a pout.

"There'll be other shows," Tibbs said. "I've got a feeling it won't be the last you hear of the Little Brothers." Then he sang, "But it maaaaay beeeee the last time, I don't know." Then he executed a drum roll on the wall.

"Seriously," Cory said, playing an air guitar. "Grown men. Sobbin' like babes."

They walked down the hall toward the kitchen.

"Don't forget," Bev called after them, "the pool has been drained. You know the reason."

Tibbs and Michael turned.

"Oh, right," Michael recalled.

"Sorry again," Tibbs said. "I didn't know he was going to shit."

Cory squatted down and belted out a loud, squirting fart noise. "Poooooop in the water!" he sang to the familiar melody.

*

Shannon danced in the dim moonlight, singing "So You Wanna Be a Rock and Roll Star". Brandon put out the joint on his shoe, blew on it, and put the roach into a baggie in his pocket. "Speaking of Dave," he said, "I think the others should be here about now and may want a little smokey smokey. I'll go find them."

Brandon walked back toward the house. Shannon danced over to Ray, took his hands, and sang slower.

La la la la la

la la la la la

la la la la la la

"Listen, Ray," Shannon said, moving his hands to her waist and holding his shoulders. "Listen."

They heard the faint sound of voices coming from the house. Shannon looked at him. Ray heard someone singing "Smoke on the Water."

"Are you listening?"

"Yes."

"I believe in you."

"I know."

"No. I don't think you do," Shannon said. "I believe in you."

"OK."

"No."

"Shannon."

"I believe in you. You hear me? I fucking believe in you."

"All right."

"So don't let me down."

She kissed him on the lips.

They walked back to the party and went over by the pool. Shannon sat down on a pool chair. Ray bumped into Cory and Derrick, the drummer of Glass Eye.

"Serr-eee-uuss-leee, if you ever need someone to stand in," Cory bellowed.

Shannon started singing. Ray heard her, vaguely aware that she had moved. He recognized the tune from the Stones album "Exile on Main Street."

Got a sweet little angel

A diving board girl

Got a sweet little angel

On a diving board

David from the Wobble Dobbles joined them and handed Ray a red cup full of beer. They were all laughing at Cory's imitation of Coach Fogerty leading a PE class in burpees. Shannon sang again. Ray was half listening.

Well she ain't no swimmer

And she can't swim far

But she can sure jump good

She's a diving star

Corey was hamming it up as Coach Fogerty. "Down-up-down-up-gooooooooood." Shannon kept singing. Ray was quarter listening. He turned and saw Shannon on the diving board, her back to the pool.

Yeah air is freedom

You can close your eyes

When the water embraces

Don't you feel surprise?

Ray didn't hear Shannon singing anymore. He heard the vibration of an empty diving board. And he heard a low, hollow sound that caused him to turn: Shannon hitting the bottom of the pool, headfirst.

*

Monday morning. The temperatures dropped back into the forties, but the sun was shining. Outside, the parent protest continued. Courtney Harrison led the chorus with bull horns. "Let the kids know. Just Say No!" Over and over. Jane Mott snapped pictures in the parking lot, noting the protest line was getting longer every day. She interviewed Courtney and learned the parents weren't going anywhere until their demands, which Courtney wouldn't commit to, were met. Jane also learned that Roxanne had a major order with her home goods company that would keep her away from the front lines of the protest. Courtney added, somewhat ominously, that this order was related to the protest, would support the cause, and would make the town very proud.

Inside, in the office, Pam Susan rummaged through an open slotted shoebox until she found the note with a small swirl of blue highlighter in the corner. She unfolded it and announced to Donna Henley, "The Windows." Five marked slips of paper later, the list was complete and Donna went to inform the students. Pam picked up the phone and dialed. "Your kid's band is set for next week. I'll see you tonight."

The halls and classrooms of the school were a tornado of gossip. Teachers battled the whispers. *Did you hear what happened to Shannon Golding, the singer from the Little Brothers?*

The rumor spread that she was dead. But the truth was she was in the Lowland Hospital trauma center on a morphine drip, with ten broken thoracic vertebrae. The Little Brothers weren't saying anything except she dove into the pool thinking it had water, she was alive and hurt.

Ray walked around in a daze until, in Q hall, on his way to Spanish, he received a hand-delivered envelope from Mrs. Henley with Friday's performing arts playlist. His lips parted in surprise.

Friday: 1. Gobbledegook 2. The Windows 3. Danny Preston jazz piano 4. Brandon Golding organ / Ryan Golding drums 5. Andrew Tibbets guitar / Michael Blazary bass 6. Ray Flowers guitar

On Tuesday, they went to visit Shannon in the hospital. On Wednesday, Ray wrote the first draft of a new song titled "Crazy Eyes." On Thursday, the Little Brothers were sitting at lunch.

"What are you going to play?" a spikey-haired Michael, pulling a strand of string cheese, asked Danny.

"A song I've been working on," Danny responded, slurping applesauce. "To finish my Alien Abduction album. It's called 'Aftermath.'"

"How about you, Brandon?"

"Ryan and I were thinking of doing a Booker T and the M.G.'s song," Brandon answered while peeling a banana. "Shannon loved to dance to those. What about you guys?"

"I was thinking of doing a new song I wrote,"Tibbs said. Everyone turned.

"What? So I had a little writer's block," Tibbs said with a shrug. "It's called 'Put a Sock in the Block.' Michael and I practiced it last night."

"It's a good song," Michael said. "The lyrics need a little work, but it's almost there." He whipped Tibbs in the arm with what was left of his string cheese. Tibbs rubbed his bicep with mock soreness and a *was that really necessary?* face.

"What about you, Ray?"

"I was thinking of a Pink Floyd song that Shannon taught us," Ray said. "'Fearless.' Either that or a new song I'm working on."

"Do you need an alien coda?" Danny asked.

"I'll let you know," Ray said.

*

Boos from a back row of jocks rained down on the Windows as they took the small stage. The student audience was right on top of them. They did get cheers from a few M-hallers, though. No one was neutral. Everyone was curious when Morris Jameson put on a gleaming silver helmet, which looked to have once belonged to an ancient Spanish explorer. Morris, in his usual plain turtleneck, stared at his feet, his long hair billowing out of the helmet. He kneeled, as if in prayer, as students shouted. Mr. Best, squeezed in between amps, struggled in vain to control the heckling.

Morris rose and grabbed the mic. "The Chemist," he said. Then he turned his back on the audience and began, speaking soft and slow.

A student turns in his chemistry report

The teacher calls it plagiarism

A copy of Nature

He takes it to the movies

Where the science is rated X

Manny began soft chords in his usual droning pattern. Craig plucked his classical nylon string guitar. Denny pattered the cymbals with mallets that looked like fuzzy marshmallows. Morris faced the audience, his voice rising.

The Chemist portrays

The sex of minerals

The pressure and heat of lithification

The copulation of matter

Denny started working the mallets on the bass drum. Manny droned on with Craig accenting the pocket. Morris didn't move a muscle beyond his throat, which barked an angry shout.

A drizzle of rain is lubrication.

His voice surged in volume for the next verse.

Clouds are sensual

Storms suggest fertility

Morris dropped his helmet and danced a tight circle around it. The drums picked up, the rhythm changing to something primal, like natives at an ancient ceremony. Craig was playing faster and faster. Manny went up an octave. The audience tensed collectively. Morris screamed.

The Explorer usurps the armor and sets sail

Stars provide romance and navigation

Mariners imagine island orgies

The lapping waves spurt white foam along the hull

The music climaxed. The students shuddered. Morris spun from his circle and kneeled in front of Craig as the guitarist ripped into a solo. Several jocks stormed the stage and fought over the helmet. Mr. Best tried to intervene. Morris fell away from Craig, rolling on the ground and sucking his thumb. Somehow the Windows found a groove like when a flying object crashes, bounces, and begins to roll down a hill. More students surged onto the stage and pushed together. Bob the security guard appeared, fighting his way through the throng of students in the doorway. Morris pulled out his thumb and reached for the microphone. He groaned. Legs moved all around him.

Sharpened spears, ancient erect stone,

Heated with fire

Cannibals waiting to feast.

The band shifted and found a new direction where none had been apparent, and the groove took off again. The scrum over the helmet turned into a real fight between jocks and the redhead Scott Kline and his friends, a new band called the Pilots. Others surged onto the stage. Bob called for backup. In the corner, George stroked his beard. On the small stage, students, locked in struggle, rolled like a sea. A pile fell on Morris. He continued, angry and loud, from the bottom.

The Explorer is asleep in his cabin

The lament of a seagull

Reaches the whorl of his ear

Wild dogs roam the beach

Mr. Best managed to apprehend the helmet. The security guards had separated the jocks from the Pilots. They pulled bodies off the pile. The struggle drowned out Morris's voice.

The clatter of metal and stone ...

(Get off me!)

juxtaposed with

(That's my foot! Get your elbow out of my chest! Hey!)

The labia of foliage

reaching for dawn's light

(OOOOwww!)

Morris crawled off the stage. A jock yelled a homophobic slur and kicked him. A melee erupted.

But only for a moment. Piercing whistles filled the air as adults stormed the room. Security guards. Dean Early and Dean Grunderson. Cops. Board members. Courtney Harrison. Superintendent Jag entered last, surveying the scene with a regal air. Everyone was rounded up and led to in-school suspension. Everyone involved in the club had their lockers, pockets, backpacks, and cars searched.

The Little Brothers never got to perform what was to be their Shannon tribute show. Brandon was taken into custody when they found pot in his locker.

Jane Mott was there to watch as over fifty students were led into police vans and taken away. She took photos of the parent protest line chanting while the vans filled up and drove away. She took statements from the police, Superintendent Jag, a vindicated Courtney Harrison, and board members. When everything died down, she headed back to the office and began typing her article with the following headline: DRUG BUST ROILS HIGH SCHOOL.

*

For Pete Best, it all felt like a drain. Something opening at the very nadir of his hope and desire and future. He stood helpless, watching it all swirl down, around and around like a vortex, a bad dream, déjà vu, musicians being handcuffed and taken away like criminals. Then a horrible emptiness, a pervasive silence in both his heart and the room that had been filled with (mostly) happy sounds.

He wandered in a daze. Bells rang, the hallway filled up, emptied, filled up, emptied. For Pete, it was no longer Friday, March 25, 1983. He had slipped into a timeless space, a muddle of the past, the present, and a vague feeling of falling endlessly. He staggered on, seeing bodies but no faces, hearing voices but no words, seeing clocks but no times. The day must have ended, because the bells stopped.

He slipped and almost fell, then became aware of a machine whirring. It was the Floor Buffer 3000.

"What are you, sleepwalking, Best?" a voice called. It was Eddie Severino. "Nice. Now I have to do E hall all over again," he complained.

"Sorry," Pete stammered. He looked up at the hallway clock, and suddenly he was back in the present. It was 5:15. Sandy would be worried about him. He usually called if he was going to be home later than five o'clock. He turned and headed back toward his office, leaving another set of tracks on the freshly waxed hallway floor. "Sorry again," he called to the night custodian.

"Whatever."

*

The main office was empty except for Pam Susan, who was typing away. Pete saw that his door was closed. And he never closed his door. Suddenly his stomach dropped and he was filled with dread. He swallowed hard and opened the door, expecting to see Matt Welsh, Superintendent Jag, Chief Sumner, Dean Early. Maybe Albert Francis had finally recovered from mono.

"Pam, you're not usually here this late," he said.

"I know," she said with a smile. "This isn't a usual day. And someone has to do this paperwork. Also, you have a visitor I wanted to be sure you met with."

He opened the door to his office and saw a pair of blue suede high heels perched on top of one of his giant and omnipresent stacks of paper. Behind the stacks he saw the smiling face of Roberta Anderson, her dark, curly hair freshly permed, wearing a lime-green blazer and violet pants.

"Hi, Peter," she said. "Where have you been?"

"Oh, hello, Mrs. Anderson," Pete responded. "I've been … um … you know? For such a long time."

"Call me Roberta," she insisted. "How would you like to be the new principal of Riverview High School?"

"The what?"

"You heard me. The board has changed. Welsh and Brandt, they're the minority now. The other new members and I, well, we want you."

"You want me?"

Roberta giggled, her hair jiggling like gelatin. "Yes. We want you."

Pete stood with his mouth open, lost for words.

"And you know something else?" Roberta asked.

"No. I mean, sorry, there's something else?"

"Oh yeah."

"What?"

"Rock and roll is not a crime."

*

Ten minutes later, Roberta Anderson, who never walked anywhere, strutted out of his office.

Her message, in a nutshell, was: Clean up the drugs, raise the test scores, and you can play "Jailhouse Rock" down the hallways as far as the new board majority is concerned.

Pete stood behind his desk, trying to absorb the news. His phone message light blinked. He knew he should call Sandy, but a strange feeling overtook him. The bottom, the drain that everything had swirled down only five hours ago, was a false bottom; there was a reservoir below that he hadn't anticipated, and everything, all his hopes for the future gushed back and went right to his head. He was giddy, tingling, smiling to himself, and he couldn't resist.

He shoved over the stacks on his desk with glee. The papers swirled like a flock of pigeons in a town square, fluttering down to the floor. He danced around in the midst of them like a madman, singing "Twist and Shout." He felt a looseness he had never really let go before. Principal Best. It had a nice ring to it.

The phone rang. It was Sandy. She was worried. The news of the bust had spread around town. He assured her everything would be fine. "Trust me," he repeated. He knew Sandy hated surprises, so he blurted it out. "You're speaking to the new principal of Riverview High School."

Sandy was incredulous. "This isn't a time for jokes," she said.

"The board has changed," Pete assured her. "I just spoke with Roberta Anderson. They are going to nominate me at the next board meeting, and they have the votes."

He heard the joy in her voice, reminding him of how much he loved his wife despite everything, all the difficulties. "I'm coming home," he told her. That's when he noticed something odd.

On his desk was a postcard with three hula dancers. He flipped it over. It was from Henry Martin, postmarked from Honolulu. There were three sentences. I FOUND HIM. THE KING IS ALIVE. BE IN TOUCH.

Pete held the postcard in his hand, a feeling of euphoria coursing through his veins. He was about to shout, to let out more of everything he had been holding inside for so many years, but then another piece of paper on the floor caught his eye. It had the presidential seal. He lifted the paper to his eyes and read that Ronald Reagan would be in Riverview this spring, to visit the Sara Sweet factory. The president's team wanted to know if a stop at the high school would be possible.

The gears in Pete's mind began spinning. I am the principal of Riverview High School. Levi King is alive. The president of the United States is coming. Spring break is coming up. It all clicked into place. A Hawaiian vacation for his family. Then a concert, headlined by Levi King, at Riverview High School, with President Reagan and the eyes of the nation watching. Rock and roll, baby.

"Pam?" he called out.

"Yes?"

"Is Jim Plant still in jail?"

"I believe he posted bail a few weeks ago."

"Get him on the horn," he said. "We're gonna need a helluva big stage!"

THIRD QUARTER

Pete Best kissed his sleeping wife on the cheek. She roused.

"Leaving already?" she said with a yawn.

"Yes. I should be back this afternoon. Have a good morning at the beach." He kissed her again, this time on the forehead. He opened the door to the adjoining room a crack and peered in. Roy was snoring. He started to mutter in his sleep. "No one will ever know … at sunset … the house … it has no windows …"

Pete tiptoed into the room and felt Roy's forehead, which was warm from a fever that had come on the night before. Pete frowned. He waited for more words, but after hearing only snores, he turned and left the room. He picked up his hotel key, his sunglasses, and a map, then he went down the hall and took the elevator to the lobby. At the front desk he grabbed a newspaper and went out to the hotel restaurant. He sat out on the patio and ordered coffee, toast, and a side of mixed fruit. There were a few other vacationers up this early. He pulled out the sports section and read with interest about a beach volleyball pro-am the previous day. The sun was just rising, and it was already warm.

A server arrived with coffee and toast, along with a dish of pineapple, banana, papaya, mango, and a round, scarlet-colored fruit, small and soft with hair-like spikes, that Pete had never tried before.

"What's this fruit?" he asked the server.

"It's rambutan. Peel off the spines."

He pulled the spines off to reveal a squishy, white, oval-shaped fruit.

The server smiled. "It's sweet, like a grape."

"This is my first time on Oahu."

"Enjoy your stay."

Over his second cup of coffee, Pete removed his map and, with a hotel pen, drew a line on the streets from his hotel to Ward Avenue. Then he calculated the distance, using his finger to roughly gauge the scale, figuring it was almost two miles. The server brought over a second helping of fruit. He bit down into a piece of fruit shaped like a star and looked up at the cloudless sky. Should be a nice walk, he thought. And I will get to see the city.

*

Forty-five minutes later, Pete pressed a bell on the gate outside a large estate.

"Hello," a voice said. "May I help you?"

"Hi. My name is Peter Best. and I'm here to see the musician Levi King."

After a pause, the voice said, "Mr. King does not accept visitors."

"I'm the principal of a high school in Riverview, Illinois," Pete said. "And Mr. King is invited to perform in front of Ronald Reagan, the president of the United States."

Another pause. "One moment."

Pete stood waiting, looking at the neighboring gates, expansive lawns, and large homes on the hillside street. Beyond, a blue ribbon of ocean spread along the horizon.

"Mr. King is not available now. But the Captain will see you."

The gate opened and Pete walked up a winding drive leading past a fountain to an elaborate double-door entryway. The door opened and a tall man with bushy, unkempt eyebrows, wearing white gloves and a coat and tie, greeted him. "Good morning," the man said. "Right this way."

Pete followed the man into a large marble foyer with a giant chandelier, past a winding staircase, through a hallway, past several elegantly furnished rooms, into a kitchen, and then out onto a patio, where a man in white linen sat smoking a cigar.

"Good morning," Pete said, approaching. "My name is Peter Best, and I'm the principal of a high school in Riverview, Illinois."

The Captain nodded and blew a perfect ring. A cane leaned against his straw chair.

Time had not been kind to the Captain. He was a large man, with a red, blotchy, bloated face perched on a turkey neck above a prodigious stomach. He had a short, wispy, white beard and gleaming white dentures. His eyes were still sharp though. He wore a western string tie, a large cowboy hat, no socks, and leather shoes— the laces tied with roughly seven knots.

"Have a seat." The Captain motioned Pete to a seat beside the wide swimming pool, overlooking well-manicured gardens and the ocean.

The Captain puffed another smoke ring and put away a magazine. Pete noticed that it was a periodical for off-track betting.

"What can I do ya for?"

"I'm here to see Levi King. I believe he's in a unique position to change something in Riverview that needs to be changed. A poetic justice, if you will, long overdue. Thirty years ago—"

"Thirty years ago nothin'. What do you *want?*"

"To see him. Talk to him. The president of the United States is coming to our high school. I need a musical act, and it can't be just anybody. You see, there's this peculiar bias in our town, sort of a misguided … misunderstanding. Toward music. Rock and roll, specifically—which has enjoyed a resurgence of late. And I thought, well, what it would mean to this new generation of musicians, the people of the town …" Pete's voice trailed off, his mind hovering on the edge of doubt.

The Captain stared at Pete and sensed an advantage. His left eye squinted permanently so it looked like he was always winking, except the rest of his face rarely so much as smirked.

"The president of the United States," the Captain practically spat the words. "Now you listen. Levi is alive. That part is true. But the Levi you remember, the musician, he's gone. Dead. Ya hear me? Your king is dead. Now git outta here."

The Captain waved, and the tall man with the suit came out.

"Git, now," the Captain said again, pulling out his racing paper.

The tall man raised his bushy eyebrows expectantly. Pete stood and followed. In the distance, he heard what sounded like a man shouting and kicking a wooden board.

They went back into the house, through the kitchen and the other rooms and the marble foyer; Pete's eyes cataloged all the furniture, the paintings, and the ornate decoration. The man escorted Pete down the winding drive past the fountain. Near the gate, the tall man turned and looked back toward the house. Then he removed his glove and, with two long fingers, reached into his coat pocket and handed Pete a note.

"Read this around the corner," he said. Then he turned, pulled his glove back on, and walked back up the long driveway. On his return to the house, he was surprised to see the Captain in the kitchen.

"Go find my black book and get me Matt Welsh on the phone," he directed.

Outside, Pete walked down the street. Then he unfolded the paper and read: MEET ME AT THE STARLIGHT LOUNGE TONIGHT AT 11. OFF NUUANU STREET. — D.J. MONTANA

*

Once again Pete kissed his wife goodbye and checked on his son sleeping in the adjoining room. Roy was whispering, "Blue … so blue … the avenue … the bayou …" Pete replaced the washcloth on Roy's forehead, left the room, and then left the hotel.

It was ten thirty on a warm, breezy Hawaiian night. The sky was full of stars. He took a cab to a run-down neighborhood with formerly glitzy storefronts that now stood vacant. The windows all had protective bars, and trash littered the streets. The cab eased past a liquor store with two ragged men shouting at each other out front. On the corner stood the Starlight Lounge, a one-story brick structure surrounded by battered fences and overgrown bushes. It had an electric sign with a star that blinked on and off erratically. The G had gone dark, and the H was fading. The sign had a tilted martini glass next to the neon words with more missing letters, so the blinking message read: _IVE _USIC EI_HT N_GH_S A WEE_.

"I'll see you in hell," said one of the tattered men to the other, limping off.

Pete paid the cab driver and crossed the street. By the door was a large, tattooed Hawaiian man with his arms crossed. "Five bucks," he said.

Pete paid and went in. It was a strip club. There was a long runway down the middle of the main room with near-naked women in high heels strutting for dollar bills. Each side of the room had a bar. Women swung from poles on islands on each side of the runway. In one corner was a curtain, guarded by two more large Hawaiians, with women walking in and out, sometimes with company. The room was thick with smoke and mostly empty. A half dozen men sat along the runway, and a few scattered patrons lounged at the islands. There were no windows.

In the corner opposite the curtain was a stage with a band. As Pete reached the bar, they started "Brown Eyed Girl." The balding, middle-aged singer wore a cheap tuxedo, a red-checkered jacket, and an untied bow tie. Pete sat down and listened as the first verse started, the words slurred and slightly off-key.

Hey did you know

That day that I came?

Now I can follow

Playing the same game

Laughing and humming, hey, hey

Jump skip thumping

On a misty morning jog

With you, my bright-eyed girl

You, my bright-eyed girl

Pete watched with fascination. Playing behind the singer—a man he had never met—was D.J. Montana on drums, Bill Gray on bass, Glen Harding on keys, and Scotty Less on guitar. Levi's band, the Kingsmen. They sounded great. The singer was shit, but the band still had it. They grooved into the second verse.

Whatever happened

To Tuesday and oh no?

Go down the grapevine with

My sister's radio

Standing in the alley laughing

Hide behind the rainbow's fall

Slip sliding

With a little butter ball

And you

My bright-eyed girl

Do you remember when ...

The bartender came over, and Pete ordered a Budweiser. A tired, busty, platinum-blond woman came over and put her hands on his shoulder.

"Want a dance, sweetie?"

"No thanks," Pete said and smiled at her. The singer mumbled through the chorus, staggering and almost falling off the edge of the stage. Then Bill stood out for the bass interlude. The band let him take it for a walk. Pete closed his eyes and listened to the low notes vibrate a variation on the melody. He was a little sad when the singer came back in for the third verse, the lyrics of which he continued to butcher.

Now ... I am on the way

To find out all on my own

Whuzzzalala ... the other day

My my how much I was shown

Cast the girl back here

All the time overcome drinking

The stadium

With you

My bright-eyed girl

A patron along the runway yelled, "Hey, jackass, it's supposed to be 'Brown Eyed Girl.'"

"You think I don't know that? My first wife had brown eyes. And I'll be damned if I'm going to sing a love song about some brown-eyed bitch. You want to get up here, cowboy?"

They shouted at each other. Bill Gray barred the singer with his bass. Scotty stepped up to the mic and rescued the song. He carried the chorus mercifully to the end. No one clapped or even noticed that the song had ended. The girls kept dancing and strutting. Pete sat, tapping four-four time with his hands on the bar as if the song was still going.

The singer staggered back to the mic and belched. "Any requests out there? Except that lunatic over there. We play what you say. Unless we don't know it. Nothing? Not a lot of music fans tonight. Well, screw it. 'Jack and Leanne' it is."

The band broke into "Jack and Diane" just as a skirmish broke out near one of the islands to Pete's right.

Little ditty

About Jack and Leanne

"Hey, man, don't do that," the singer said, cutting off the song.

"C'mon baby, just a little sweetness." A thin man with a beard was holding a dancer by the wrist. She kicked at his face with her stilettos. He fended her off with his other hand.

"Bobby!" the woman called.

"Bobby," the singer repeated. "Need a little help out here."

"Don't fight it, honey. Just a little sweetness, just a little ..." the bearded man said.

"Bobby! Get over here," the woman called again, straining without success.

"You're trembling like a sparrow, baby." The bearded man pulled her close so she couldn't kick, only squirm. "I should know—I've personally felt many a tremble from many a sparrow."

"Bobby! What the fuck!" she screamed. One of the big Hawaiian guys poked his head out through the curtains that sealed off the hallway and came over, walking fast.

"Am I going to have to be the singer *and* the bouncer in this shithole?" the singer asked no one.

The bearded man leaned down and looked into her eyes. "You're as mighty as a flower, girl. And I've known some mighty flowers in my day." The girl bit the man's shoulder and squirmed free, only to be caught by his other arm.

In one motion she rolled and kicked him between the eyes with her five-inch heel. He fell backward but managed to grab her other foot.

The large bouncer arrived and put the man in a headlock.

"Jesus. About time," the woman griped, getting down from the island and rubbing her wrist.

The bouncer carried the man out.

"I had a lot of dreams once," the bearded man said. "And none of them came true." The large man's grip tightened around his neck as the door shut behind him.

"Shit, people, control yourselves," the singer ordered, downing a glass of brown liquid. "What should we play to keep you lowlifes from acting like animals?" The singer belched again into the mic.

"How about 'Old Shep'?" Pete called out. The singer used his hands to shade his eyes from the stage lights so he could peer in Pete's direction. The band members did likewise.

"What the hell? We don't play church music."

"How about 'Till I Waltz Again with You'?" Pete said, tipping his beer.

"Who is this asshole?" the singer asked, running his hands through his thinning hair. "Look around. You're not at the Prince Waikiki, you know." Then he threw his glass behind the stage. "Screw it. Time for intermission anyway." He dropped the mic and the room was hit with piercing feedback.

Scotty Less shut down the amps, and the band followed the singer back-stage. A tall brunette woman strutted over to Pete.

"How about a lap dance?"

"No thank you." Pete drank his beer and drummed his fingertips.

A minute later D.J. came out. "Pig, two more longnecks, please." He sat down next to Pete. "You look familiar. Do I know you, friend?" The two drummers shook hands.

"We met once, at a music festival," Pete said, "a long time ago, another lifetime, in Riverview, Illinois. Pete Best. They used to call me Pete the Beat."

The Kingsmen drummer's face was like a spinning wheel as he scanned his memory.

"Pete the Beat … Riverview, Illinois … oh sure, I remember. Well, that was a helluva day. What on earth brings you to the Starshit Lounge?"

"I heard from a friend that Levi King was still alive. I had to find out if it was true. So I brought the family on vacation to see for myself."

D.J. nodded and glanced back toward the stage. He wore a pressed white shirt, dark tie, and suspenders. He had a thick head of black hair combed back high and straight, with a little salt sprinkled on the sides. A big nose bulged in the center of his face. Dark circles rimmed eyes that smiled out at the world, a joy that paradoxically made him seem sad. The beers arrived.

"I assume the butler with the eyebrows gave you my note?" D.J. asked.

"Indeed."

D.J. nodded. "That's luck for you," he said with a grin. "A few years back I slipped him some money and told him if anyone ever asks for Levi King to send them my way. I was hoping someday someone might come along, like a prince in a fairy tale."

Pete took up his bottle. "Here's to good fortune."

"To good fortune."

They clinked bottles and drank.

"Do you still shred the skins?" D.J. asked.

"My playing days are behind me," Pete answered. "But I'm very fortunate. I married a wonderful woman. We have a son, Roy. He's in middle school."

"Does he play the drums?"

"Well, sort of … he's a special guy, and he *does* like to bang things, but mostly with his head." Pete laughed. "At his current school, his teachers seem to think that the drums are, well … bad. That's part of why I'm here. You see, after that festival in '51, it wasn't just Levi King that went away. It was like all traces of rock and roll departed. And it's never returned. The town put in a ban that somehow kept it out. Until now. There's a new generation of rockers that want to break through."

D.J. sipped his beer and absorbed the news.

"So, I'm thinking that if there's anyone on this planet that can bring rhythm and blues back to Riverview, it's Levi King. And I have a once-in-a-lifetime chance. I'm the principal of a high school that soon will have Ronald Reagan paying a visit."

"Why don't you have the kids play?"

"Yeah … about that. A lot of the kids ran into some trouble recently. Teenage stuff, drugs. Plus, if Levi still has the gospel and soul, along with the rhythm and blues, being of the same age as most of the conservative residents … religion is very important in the community … it just feels like a golden chance to make things right."

D.J. stared at his beer and didn't say anything. Through the speakers Frank Sinatra started singing "Luck Be a Lady." Halfway through the song, with Pete's fingers drumming the bar double time to the tune, D.J. finally asked, "Did you get to see Levi?"

"Well, when I went inside the mansion, instead of Levi, I found the Captain."

"'The Captain,'" D.J. said with air quotes. "He wasn't ever really a captain, you know. He got that title because he was part of the Illinois State Militia. The governor gave it to him as an honorary title, for some work he did on his campaign."

"I thought the title seemed strange."

"And what did 'the Captain' tell you?"

"He told me Levi the person was alive but Levi the musician was dead. Then he told me to 'git out,' in so many words."

"That sounds about right," D.J. said with a grin.

Pete centered his bottle on its coaster, which he adjusted so that it lined up with D.J.'s. He examined the alignment for another moment, then leaned close to D.J. and asked in a low voice, "D.J., what happened to Levi?"

"I've been asking myself that very question for over twenty years," D.J. mused.

Pete nodded and was about to say something but didn't.

"Well, I guess I should start where you left off," D.J. said. "After the state militia cracked down on the Riverview music scene."

Pete glanced around at the women dancing topless on the tables, as if to confirm that he was here, in a strip club, listening to D.J. Montana.

"Luck Be a Lady" ended and "Strangers in the Night" started. D.J. lit a cigarette and put his pack and lighter back inside his jacket after Pete declined his offer of a smoke.

"Smart man. These things will kill you. So the Captain showed up on the scene, when it's all about to go down. He's a very connected man, all the way up to the Illinois governor, who at that time was a die-hard country music lover. I guess the Captain had some connections through him and was trying to make it in the music business. So, in 1951, when he saw our act, as the militia closed in around us and the screaming girls, he saw right in front of his face that he had something. The Captain is many things, but he's no fool."

Pig brought over an ashtray.

"Oh, I almost forgot. The other guys will be out in a minute. Our singer's a real pain in the ass. Some band shit to work out. They'll be out soon."

Pete nodded and absently took up the beat with his fingers on the bar.

"The Captain came up to us, right on the side of the stage, with all hell breaking loose around us. He said, 'Boys, I believe you all got something people want. And I aim to help you give it to 'em.' He and Levi worked out a deal in that trailer. We sat outside, so we didn't know the specifics, but we learned that day that the Captain was our manager."

D.J. started to peel the label from his bottle of Bud. "We were all just kids; what did we know? We figured with our single 'That's Alright' being a hit, playing on the radio, and having some success playing small-town shows like Riverview, that we were set to take off. An album, a tour—we thought the sky was the limit."

He crumpled the pieces of label as he peeled. "But the Captain was interested in one thing and one thing only: money. So where did he take us?"

"Vegas?"

"Bingo. Las Vegas. Playing six nights a week at the Tropicana Casino Lounge. A place as lonely and sad as this, just without the naked girls. Mostly middle-aged alcoholic gamblers. And we weren't playing the music we wanted. We were a casino lounge act, just like the Starlight Wranglers you heard a minute ago. It was brutal."

Over the speakers, "Fly Me to the Moon" started.

"We weren't in Vegas long before Levi met Gloria. They were married in a Vegas chapel. We'd only been there a few months." He used his thumbnail on the remaining wrapper. "Things went from bad to worse. Levi and Gloria and the Captain were all living the high life, up in suites on the top floor of the Tropicana. Meanwhile Scotty and Bill and Glen and I were shacked up in some dumpy motel off the strip. We had one meal a day, at an all-you-can eat buffet at the Tropicana, and were basically broke."

D.J.'s bottle was now label-free. He took a sip. Pete's drumming shifted to his knuckles to hit the low notes.

"The only thing that kept us going was the music. Even though the songs were not what we wanted to play, it was still the Kingsmen, and Levi was still the King. Even though it wasn't our brand of music, he still put all his heart into it. I always thought, you know, this is just what musicians do. Paying those dues."

He took another sip. Pig brought over two shots. "On the house," he said.

"Paying those dues," D.J. repeated. They raised the glasses and downed the shots.

"We lasted almost a year, until it all blew up. Levi never drank, but he started taking some prescription drugs, and they had an effect on him. He started becoming sort of paranoid, like he wasn't always there all the time, if you know what I mean. Gloria ran off with Levi's karate instructor, and that was the final straw for us in Vegas. We hit rock bottom one night when Levi collapsed on stage."

D.J. paused and looked away.

"I'll never forget that last performance in Vegas," he recollected. "Out of nowhere Levi said, 'Screw it guys, let's play our song.' We played 'That's Alright.' All the drunks looked up from their beers like a spaceship had just landed. We rocked the hell out of that song, and Levi sang his heart out. We had these ridiculous costumes from the casino. You know how Levi has always been into karate. We had white suits like in karate, with these diamond-studded eagles on our backs. Big huge collars. Bell bottoms. Sunglasses. *In 1952*. People didn't know what to make of us."

Pete laughed.

"We finished 'That's Alright' and just as I hit the big cymbal crash, Levi extended his arms, the studded eagle on his back ascending as if in flight, one last time before crashing to Earth. And crash he did."

D.J. looked down at the floor.

"I knew you guys went off to Vegas," Pete said. "But I never heard what happened from there. Nothing until the news of his death."

"Well, the Captain, again he's a sharp cookie, and he could read the writing on the wall. Plus, I think he owed those casinos considerable money. Still does, if you ask me. Which is why he's out here, in hiding. I think they're still after him."

D.J. looked around the club, like there might have been a casino hit man amongst the scattered crowd.

"He got us out of town in the dead of night in a van. We took all our instruments and our suitcases and drove across the desert. Drove straight through the night, only stopping for gas."

D.J. scratched his glass bottle as if the label was still there. Pete took a sip and leaned in as "Come Fly with Me" started.

"What happened next?"

"We ended up in Hollywood. The Captain started us on B movies. Levi starred in them; we played the soundtracks."

"Movies? No kidding—how come I've never heard of this?"

"Because they were terrible. Absolute shit. Formulas. They were all the same. Beaches and girls and all that. *Trouble with Gals. Gal Happy. Gals! Gals! Gals!*" D.J. indicated the stripper dancing behind them. "But they sold well, mostly in India because people thought they were accurate portrayals of American life."

"Levi in movies. I can picture it," Pete said.

"They were bad. A few of them weren't horrible, but for the most part just crap. And the music." D.J. leaned back and laughed. "'Room to Rumba in a Station Wagon.' 'Rock-a-hula Sweetie.' 'He's Your Dad, Not Your Uncle.' 'The Walls Have Earlobes.'" He shook his head, laughed, and coughed a wheezy smoker's cough. "That one was particularly awful." He put out his cigarette and lit another. "Once again, who do you think made all the money?"

"The Captain."

"Ding ding ding! Give this man a hundred dollars. You got it. The Captain made all these shady deals with these studios and got rich. Once again, he was living the high life, up in the hills in some mansion, putting Levi in the guest house, while the band slummed it out in East Hollywood."

Pig brought over two more beers. D.J. glugged down what remained of his first beer and slid Pig the peeled, empty bottle. Pete took another sip of his first beer, still more than half full.

"Scotty and Glen and Bill, we all talked about getting out, heading back home. Both Glen and Bill were thinking of going to school. Scotty and I didn't know what to do, other than we wanted to keep playing music."

"The Way You Look Tonight" rang out from the speakers.

"We had one semi-hit. It's probably the only movie you can find out there, if you dig hard enough. It was called *Blue Honolulu*. It wasn't completely terrible. Your basic Hollywood crap. But it made us some money, enough for the Captain to keep us around. He moved us into a nicer place. Gave us a little more money. Besides, we were still making a living as musicians. The work was steady if nothing else. Southern California. Girls. Sun. We had a good time."

D.J. looked back toward the curtain as if looking for the band. Pete followed his eyes.

"Levi slept around. Young and attractive and always paired up with these aspiring actresses. And he got more and more hooked on pills. Narcotics. Sedatives. Amphetamines. He was always popping 'em. It was a slow and steady decline. That last year in Hollywood he was a shell of himself."

D.J. drank and started in on the label. "It couldn't last."

"Nothing does," Pete said, knocking his knuckles in a little drum lick.

The label came off in one piece. D.J. crumpled it and tossed it behind the bar, missing the garbage. Pig shot him a look. D.J. shrugged and drank.

"Levi overdosed. I'll never forget it. Right in the middle of recording this corny tune, 'Scratch My Back, I'll Tickle Yours.' They took him to the hospital.

"Then I don't know … It gets a little blurry. I don't know if it was the casino guys or what, but again the Captain came to us in the middle of the night. He owed somebody money, that much was obvious. He said to be ready in the morning for a flight to Honolulu. Just the band. No girlfriends. Some big show. Finally, he promised, we could play the music we wanted to. A big rock and roll show with a bunch of big acts, being broadcast all over the world."

Pete raised his eyebrows.

"It was all a lie. The whole thing. We were his last poker chip, and he wanted to bet on us one more time."

"That's Life" came on.

"Levi never came with us. The Captain told us he was dead. From the overdose. He got us a gig at the Prince with some other singer. We played there for about six months before it ran its course and the Captain dropped us like a bad habit." D.J. drank his beer and stared straight ahead.

"But he isn't dead? He's alive, right? Levi is alive?"

"Sure he is," D.J. confirmed. "He's alive. He does karate all day in the Captain's garden."

The band came out from behind the curtain.

D.J. introduced Pete, and they all shook hands.

"It's good to meet you guys again," Pete said.

Pig brought over a fresh round.

"What on earth brought you to us?" Bill asked.

"Well, I heard through the grapevine that Levi was still alive, and I had to come see for myself."

The men nodded.

"What are you doing with yourself these days?" Scotty asked. "Still pound the skins?"

"Unfortunately, no. Believe it or not, I'm now the principal at Riverview High School."

"Get out."

"Pete the Beat, a principal in the town that shut down rock and roll. Far out."

"Yes indeed. And, well, that's why I'm here. To at long last bring rock music back to Riverview. I thought, Who better than Levi King to help pull it off?"

The men nodded and sipped. They all wore dark suits and looked like identical middle-aged men dressed up as a band from the '50s.

"Sort of like a revival," Pete added.

There was an awkward silence as "I've Got the World on a String" floated out into the air.

"But I never expected to find the Kingsmen," Pete said. "D.J. got me all caught up,"

"All the way?" Scotty questioned.

"Well, not quite all the way," D.J. conceded.

Pete looked from face to face as the men exchanged glances.

"Scotty and Bill have a plan to, eh … rescue Levi," D.J. announced, looking around. "And that might mean killing the Captain."

Pete dropped his beer. Pig shook his head.

*

The next morning Pete followed the same routine: He kissed his wife and glanced in at Roy sleeping. Roy's fever had abated somewhat, but it still stubbornly clung at one hundred degrees. He tossed and turned, talking in his sleep. "Shah … da … ro … ba … sha … da … ro … ba …"

Pete dropped down to the lobby for breakfast. After a quick bite, he went out to the street. Except this time, it was an hour earlier. The taxis weren't lined up yet, so he had the doorman call him one. The sky was still dark and full of stars. Pete looked off toward the west, and a crescent moon lingered low in the sky. A taxi pulled up and Pete gave the driver the address D.J. had given him. Makiki Heights Drive. Pete liked Hawaiian words.

He didn't want to be a part of this. He didn't want anything to do with a kidnapping heist. But he couldn't pass up the tantalizing prospect of seeing Levi again, alive. And possibly helping bring him back to a life of music. To have Levi himself lift Riverview's archaic ban on rock music. It would be an act of redemption. All those lost years.

Besides, his only role was to serve as lookout. And really, what crime were the Kingsmen committing compared to the crimes the Captain had committed against them? Also, they insisted that violence would only be a last resort.

Pete rode along the city streets in the predawn morning. The cab followed the route from the previous day's trip: past the university, exit into suburbia, then winding its way up the mountain into a forest. As he rode along, Pete heard D.J.'s voice from the Starlight Lounge telling him the plan: Drive to an estate behind the Captain's and use a ladder to scale the wall. This wall was in close proximity to the garden where Levi started his karate every morning at dawn. The Kingsmen would climb over and talk to Levi, convince him to come with them. Pete would serve as the lookout with a walkie-talkie, in case any trouble appeared.

"And what about the Captain?" Pete had asked.

"Don't worry about him," Scotty had said. "That's the Rooster Man's job."

"The Rooster Man?"

Bill had laughed first. "We had to outsource the muscle. The Rooster Man is a friend of mine from Philadelphia. He owes me a favor."

The taxi pulled up to the address. Pete paid and got out. The taxi drove away.

"And don't forget to wear dark clothing," Scotty had added. Pete stood in the street wondering if his dark dress pants and black Mudfest T-shirt would be acceptable. Down the street, a parked van's lights came on and the van glided over to him. The door opened. "Get in," Bill said.

The Kingsmen had new uniforms: they looked like gardeners. Pete made his way to the back row and sat next to D.J. Scotty was next to Bill in the middle row. Glen drove. In the passenger seat was a large Italian-looking man with a mustache and a face with rough, blemished skin.

The tires squealed as they pulled away. Pete held on for dear life, managing to get his seat belt clicked as the van skidded around a corner. Glen hit the tape deck and Jimi Hendrix's version of "All Along the Watchtower" came on. The van raced through hairpin turns shrouded with trees. Pete had the alarming sensation that not all four tires were contacting the road. They cruised off-road, the bumps lifting Pete physically off his seat, then crashed through some bushes as the song ended and the Rooster Man turned off the stereo. They were in the Captain's hillside neighborhood, and the sky had just started to lighten. Pete glimpsed the ocean on the horizon.

The van screamed to a halt. The Rooster Man and Bill got out. Bill nodded and slammed the door, and the van pulled away.

Glen eased the van forward and they crept along. He flashed the headlights at a large gate with stone lions standing guard. The gate opened. The van pulled in. The four men rolled up to a garage and got out. Scotty had a backpack. A ladder lay along the side of the garage. D.J. and Scotty picked it up. Glen handed Pete a walkie-talkie.

"If you see something, say something," Glen said. "It's on channel two and ready to go." Then he went back to the van and drove off.

Pete followed D.J. and Scotty around the garage and past a tennis court. They walked quickly, Pete trailing the other two with the ladder across a wide, dew-soaked lawn and through a well-manicured garden. This is crazy, Pete kept thinking. Crazy. Crazy. I'm really doing this. They entered a small orchard of fruit trees. The sky was brighter behind them and Pete realized they were walking west, toward the Captain's estate. They weaved through the rows of trees, and all around them were small, brightly colored birds. Pete did not know any of the species. Chirps filled the air. As Pete ran, his fists did little drum rolls on his stomach.

They came to a stone wall eight feet tall and turned to the south. There was a gravel path, and their wet shoes scrunched as they trotted along, D.J. and Scotty ahead. Pete saw the headline in the *Riverview Review*: New Principal of Riverview High School Arrested in Hawaiian Kidnapping Heist. This is insane, he thought. They ran along for several minutes before they reached a corner.

Scotty leaned the ladder against the wall. D.J. climbed up and pulled a pair of binoculars out from his jacket. He gave a thumbs-up signal, set the binoculars down on top of the wall, then climbed over and jumped down. Then Scotty went over. Pete climbed up and grabbed the binoculars. The sun had risen over the horizon behind him. Peering through an opening in the trees, he could see a small garden with marble statues. There in the middle was Levi, wearing a white karate robe and standing across from an instructor in a dark robe. They were doing stretches. Pete could hear faint eastern music accentuated by the instructor's loud directions. Beyond them: the city, the ocean, and the setting moon.

Pete watched in fascination. He was alive. The man that electrified Riverview all those years ago. He would always be the original King of Rock and Roll, to Pete anyway. A king without a kingdom. He played a potent mix of gospel and the blues, sounds from across color lines, something no one else was doing. His performances set audiences on fire. Yes, they were sexually provocative, which is why first the school district, then the local law, and finally the state militia had to be brought in. But to Pete it was something else, an intensity of emotion. The word that always hit Pete was *vulnerable*. When Levi sang, he didn't hold anything back. He was a human being that needed one thing above everything else: to be loved. And yet all that, the *feeling*, was lost in the hysteria over sexuality. Before anyone with any sense could confront it, the Captain intervened and swept Levi and the Kingsmen away, off to Vegas, then Hollywood, and now here. To make a buck. Greed. Leaving Riverview and its inhabitants behind in a town that, instead of being the birthplace of rock and roll, no one has ever heard of.

Pete watched Levi do a series of stride punches in response to his instructor's shouts. He could see that Levi was still in good shape, still had his boyish, youthful look with his thick blond hair and sideburns.

All of it, the whole thing, because of swinging hips. Pete laughed to himself. Gyrations. Pelvic thrusts. How times have changed.

Pete watched Levi do squats then begin a series of snap kicks, both forward and reverse. Through the binoculars he saw Scotty and D.J. creep onto the scene from behind a row of hedges. Levi froze. A conversation started, with Scotty and D.J. doing all the talking. Pete heard their voices but couldn't make out what they were saying. Levi finally spoke. He said it again, louder, and Pete heard him clearly.

"I ain't goin'."

Levi backed away. Scotty reached out, but Levi did a karate move to block his hand. D.J. tried to intervene, but the instructor stepped in. The instructor reeled off kicks that D.J. had to dodge. Scotty set his backpack down and pulled out a ukulele and a small bongo drum. He tossed the drum to D.J. With Levi crouched in a karate stance, Scotty started to play a Hawaiian rhythm. The instructor held his threatening position near D.J. The two musicians sang to him in harmony. The song filtered through the trees.

Dreams can come true

We can still set people free

With the magic inside you

In Blue Hawaii

Then Pete heard, coming from the direction of the estate, the Captain's howling voice.

"What in tarnation? Over my dead body!"

From the same direction, a single gunshot rang out in the morning air. Pete watched through the binoculars as everyone scattered. The calm morning air exploded with a clatter of shooting. A bullet pinged somewhere off to Pete's left. He rolled and almost fell off the wall. Like a worm, he inched his way to the ladder and hustled down, his heart pounding. A voice, maybe D.J.'s, called out, "It's now or never."

"Pete, we got a problem," came Glen's voice over the walkie-talkie. "Gotta pull out. Make your way off the property. Stay outta sight. Get back to the main road and we'll pick you up. Keep your walkie off."

Pete's mind whirled. The ladder. I touched it. Fingerprints. He hooked his forearm around two rungs and took off in the direction of their earlier footprints. More bullets whizzed beyond the wall. The ladder was light and only six feet long, but combined with the crouch he was maintaining, it was enough to make his fleeing cumbersome and awkward. Crazy. This is crazy. He worked his way through the rows of trees, veered away from the lawn and the tennis courts, cut behind a swimming pool, and ran past a quizzical gardener. He reached the edge of the property, looked around, leaned the ladder up against a wall, and, using his wrists and forearms, climbed up. He straddled the wall and looked back. There was no one. What do I do about the ladder? Oh well. Jump!

A station wagon appeared around the bend. I'm a dead man, he thought. Roy, Sandy, I love you with all my heart. The vehicle slowed and a soccer mom–looking driver cast a curious glance as she rolled by. For some reason, he smiled his assistant-principal *good morning* smile and waved.

The station wagon drove on. He turned the walkie-talkie back on, but no one responded. Whistling, tapping sixteenth notes on his thigh, Pete waited for the car to be out of sight. The road was clear. He ran in the direction from which they'd come. He lingered for a time, then made his way out of the neighborhood. At the main road, he hailed a taxi and went back to the hotel.

Up in his room, Roy was dozing on the bed, and Sandy was out. He put the walkie-talkie in his desk drawer and took a shower. Ten minutes later he was toweling off when his wife came in.

"Roy's fever broke. He's back to ninety-eight," Sandy said.

"That's a relief."

"Did you see Levi?" she asked.

"Yes."

"And?"

"And … I don't know."

Three days later, at the hotel's front desk for their morning checkout, the concierge handed Pete an envelope. "This came for you last night, sir. Quite late, so we thought to hold it until morning."

After checking out, with Roy and Sandy in the gift shop, he opened the envelope and read: WE'VE GOT HIM. THE PLAN IS ON. WILL BE IN TOUCH. — D.J.

WANING CRESCENT

Five thousand miles to the east, the moon rose over Nancy Reagan pulling a knot on her violet silk bathrobe in her spacious walk-in closet. She saw her Ronnie, standing in front of the bathroom mirror, combing his lustrous black hair. Ronnie glanced down at a note card on the sink and spoke into the comb.

"People who think a tax boost will cure inflation are the same ones who believe another drink will cure a hangover," he said.

She kissed him on the cheek, walked down the hall to her office in the East Wing, and removed a pen and a small spiral notebook from the bottom of a drawer.

Staring at the phone, she chewed the end of the pen for another moment, then began to dial.

"Hello?"

"Hi, Joan."

"Hi, Nancy. It's nice to hear from you."

"How's Egypt?"

"Wonderful. It's amazing to be where astrology was conceived, in the cradle of civilization."

"I can imagine."

"From antiquity to the Middle Ages, through the Renaissance and the seventeenth century, every court had an astrologer. Kings, queens, popes, the great generals and wealthy princes—they all consulted us."

"Just as I consult you now. Have you had a chance to look at our charts lately? For some reason Ronnie is determined to take this trip to this Riverview place. Do you have a date?"

"I studied my charts as we crossed over to the Valley of the Kings."

"What did you see?"

"Your charts are excellent. I'm seeing many favorable aspects of the moon."

"Wonderful."

"You know, you are Ronnie's moon—the woman who means the most to him in life. And he is your sun."

Nancy was speechless.

"The moon moves through every sign in the zodiac in twenty-seven-and-a-half days. It is the fastest moving heavenly body and acts as a catalyst in astrology. It makes things happen. And so do you, my dear Nancy, for your beloved Ronnie."

Nancy looked out at the moon and smiled.

"It's looking like the date of the journey will be April twentieth," Joan continued. "The major planets Jupiter and Saturn make a conjunction, an ideal time for your journey to begin."

"Thank you so much." Nancy wrote down 4/20 in her notebook.

"But I should tell you of the zero-year phenomenon."

"Oh?"

"It is a matter of record that every president elected in a year ending in zero since William Henry Harrison has died in office."

"Oh, dear." She wrote ZERO YEAR and underlined it three times.

"But all the other conjunctions have fallen in either water or earth signs. This one falls in an air sign. While dangerous, it is not fatalistic. And there's a little problem with Neptune, the planet of deception. Protecting his safety will not be easy, but it is possible, in my opinion."

"Oh, Joan. What would I do without you?"

"The only problem now is what time to leave. I'll give you a detailed account once I'm back in San Francisco."

Nancy thanked Joan and hung up. Then she wrote, I AM RONNIE'S MOON.

She replaced the notebook and walked back down the hall.

She could hear her Ronnie, still practicing in front of the mirror.

"Room bugged? Every time I sneezed the chandelier said, 'Gesundheit!'"

*

"Busy, busy, busy," Nancy said. "Very busy."

"I can imagine," Betsy Bloomingdale said, sitting by the fireplace as the morning light streamed into the China Room on the ground floor of the White House. Betsy could just make out the inscription on the large portrait to her right of a woman in a red gown with a white collie. 1924. First Lady Grace Coolidge (with Rob Roy). She inhaled sharply. "Since you're the First Lady, do you think I could be the First Friend?"

"I'll have something drafted by evening," Nancy said, smiling. "With any luck, Congress will vote on it and Ronnie can sign it into law before the weekend."

Betsy laughed, sipping her tea. "Tell me, what have you been up to?"

Nancy crossed her legs. "Our drug awareness campaign is flourishing."

Betsy bit into a small biscuit and nodded. "When did you first get the idea for the program?"

"During the first campaign," Nancy replied. "Ronnie and I made a stop at the Daytop Village in New York, a drug treatment organization, and the visit has been on my mind ever since."

Betsy rubbed a small chip on the bottom of her cup with her thumbnail. "And where did you come up with that name?"

"I was in Oakland, and a girl asked me what to say if she's offered drugs," Nancy replied. "I told her, 'Just Say No.'"

Betsy laughed, flicking a small piece of china off the cup.

Nancy examined her own saucer and noticed a hairline fracture.

"Can you imagine if Patti or Ron or Michael or Maureen were addicted to drugs?" Betsy asked.

"I simply can't imagine it," Nancy replied.

A head poked through a door.

"Madam First Lady, Deputy Chief of Staff Michael Deaver is here to see you," the head said.

"Please, send him in after five minutes," Nancy directed. "I'm finishing tea with my dear friend."

"Well, I'll say, being First Lady is keeping you busy," Betsy observed, noticing another chip on her plate.

"Of course, that's not all," Nancy said. "There are a thousand little odds and ends. As you can see, the White House desperately needs new china. It hasn't been updated since the Truman administration in the '40s."

"Would you like me to have my father make some inquiries?"

"I was speaking with Joan, and the way the press has been behaving lately, I'm not sure about the optics of that. Ronnie is planning a trip to a town in Illinois called Riverview, and there happens to be a lovely home goods shop there run by a mom in my organization. It's best if I support a small business."

"Delightful."

A door opened. "Madam First Lady, this just came for you."

Nancy opened the folded note:

SINCE WE CANNOT CHANGE THE DEPARTURE DATE, I'VE FOUND A SOLUTION TO OUR NEPTUNE PROBLEM. THE CEREMONIES AT BOTH THE FACTORY AND THE HIGH SCHOOL MUST TAKE PLACE ON THE WEST SIDE. THE PROXIMITY TO JUPITER SHOULD NEGATE THE RISE OF NEPTUNE. — JOAN

On Fifteenth Street nearby, a van crept along. Nobody at the White House paid it any attention. It was from A Taste of Yu Chinese Food, a van that circled the White House regularly and never made any deliveries.

*

President Ronald Reagan looked across his desk at his troika: Chief of Staff James Baker, Counselor to the President Ed Meese, and Deputy Chief of Staff Michael Deaver. He looked each man in the eye.

"This Sandinista Group, the revolutionary government in Nicaragua, has got to go," he said. "I believe this group of rebels, these Contras in Honduras, are just the people to pull it off."

Three heads nodded in unison.

"I'm thinking we honor the deal we made during the campaign. I'm referring to the deal with the Iranian government of Ayatollah Ruhollah Khomeini."

Three chins tilted up.

"This Iran–Iraq war isn't ending anytime soon," the president continued. "Iran is going to get weapons anyway. Why not sell them through Israel? That way we can keep the Iranians away from the Soviet sphere of influence and funnel the profits to these Contras in Honduras. Everybody wins."

The chins went back down.

President Reagan looked each man in the eye. "Make it happen."

Nancy Reagan entered the Oval Office. "Sorry, Ronnie. I didn't know you had a meeting."

The president smiled at his wife. "This one wasn't on the schedule. It's all right, Mommy. Do you need anything?"

"I wanted to talk about new china. But it can wait."

In the distance, the tires of A Taste of Yu squealed.

*

Nancy looked up at the crescent moon, pulled out her notebook, and dialed.

"Hi, Joan."

"Hi, Nancy. My latest report has all the times of departures and press conferences to ensure Ronnie's success and safety. All to the exact minute as always."

"OK, I have my notebook ready."

"I also have Gorbachev's horoscope finished. I think you'll find it of great interest. But before we get to any of it, I thought we should discuss your daughter, Patti."

"Yes, please. I'm all ears. I'm at my wit's end. At least she's finally left that guitarist from that band. Eagles. A disgrace to our national symbol if you ask me."

"Yes, she's deliberately flouting you. And I know why."

"Tell me."

"It's the remote, slower-moving planets again. They have much to do with modern life. Thank you, by the way, for the new computer. As you know, I base all my astrological analysis on data provided by astronomers and charts. The computers make the calculations much easier."

"My pleasure. Whatever helps you with your work."

"I base my conclusions in the same way a doctor supports a diagnosis with lab reports. You know, I don't gaze into crystal balls."

"I know," Nancy said with a laugh. "Of course. Now, please. Tell me what you've seen regarding Patti." She doodled her daughter's name.

"It's Neptune again, so prominent in her chart. It's why she likes to masquerade and pretend to be other than she is. Neptunians never want things to be the way they are, which is why they resort to drugs and alcohol. Usually, things represented by Neptune are romanticized unrealistically. Take for instance her interest in rock music. And fiction." Joan snorted.

"It makes so much sense." Nancy wrote NEPTUNE and drew a line to Patti's name.

"But it's not just Neptune with its valleys. Acting together are Uranus and her desire for overnight success. Compounding it all is Pluto, with its control over the media."

"Oh, dear."

*

In the next room, President Reagan looked out at his troika.

"Clearly," Chief of Staff James Baker said, "the Boland Amendment outlaws assistance to the Contras."

"It's a ban," Counselor Ed Meese said.

"A ban using the CIA," said Deputy Chief of Staff Michael Deaver. "And any other agency involved in intelligence activities."

"However, we were discussing that the ban wouldn't necessarily include the National Security Council," Baker said.

"Intelligence activities certainly don't apply to them," President Reagan said with a twinkle in his eye.

Three faces laughed.

"No. But seriously. Can we do this?" the president asked.

Six eyes blinked.

"The broader constitutional question at stake is, Who has more power, Congress or the president?" Baker asked.

"Overthrowing the Sandinistas in Nicaragua is a presidential prerogative," Deaver said.

A door opened and Nancy's voice could be heard from the next room. "Go in and ask him which one he likes; I have to take this call." An aide wheeled in a cart with an assortment of different fine china samples. "Mr. President. The First Lady would like to know which of these three different china sets you might prefer."

They heard Nancy again. "I'll wait for the alignment."

"I don't care about china!" the president shouted with a fist to his desk. "This china thing is Nancy's deal. Let her figure it out. I don't want to hear another word. Get new china. I don't care what it costs or if she has to use the military!"

The aide wheeled the cart back out of the Oval Office. In the distance tires squealed. The men heard Nancy again.

"Can you say that again, Joan?"

The president blew out a long breath as the door closed. He shook his head and smiled at his troika.

"Who's on top at the NSC?" President Reagan asked.

"Admiral Poindexter, sir."

"Get him on the phone. We've got to keep the Contras together, body and soul. I don't care what Congress voted and I sure as hell don't care about this ban."

*

The waning crescent moon was on the rise over Washington, DC. President Reagan looked each member of his troika in the eye.

"The operation is codenamed Staunch," Chief of Staff James Baker said. "It's a diplomatic effort to persuade other nations not to sell arms to Iran."

"And Israel?"

"The sales will continue," Counselor Ed Meese said. "The Contras will continue to receive support."

"It appears that Congress will add on to the Boland Amendment. Possibly this year. They are seeking to prohibit all covert assistance," Deputy Chief of Staff Michael Deaver said. He leaned in. "From the CIA."

The president raised his eyebrows. "But nothing about the National Security Council?"

"Nothing."

"We've found a way around the ban?"

"We've found a way around the ban."

"Good."

"Maybe I can help Nancy with new china after all," the president said.

The troika laughed. They didn't hear the crash from a van rear-ending a vehicle a block away.

*

Nancy Reagan took out her notebook and dialed.

"Hello?"

"Hi, Joan."

"Hi, Nancy. Are you ready?"

"I'm ready."

"I have an update for Ronnie's trip. It's the stop at the high school. There's a similarity to his last trip to the demilitarized zone in Korea. I've been up all night scrutinizing my charts."

"Oh, thank you, Joan. I know this trip has been a lot of extra work for you."

"It is my duty. As you know, I study both your and Ronnie's horoscopes hourly."

"I do so appreciate it. What would I do without you?"

"My dear Nancy. It pains me, but I will always be honest with you. There's something I can't quite see. An obstruction. Regarding this trip to the high school."

"Oh?"

"The issue is Venus. It will be quite close to Jupiter. Whatever is hiding behind these planets could have drastic ramifications. And the thing is …"

"The thing is? What's thing? Oh, Joan, tell me."

"If I can guide you through this high school stop, the results of next year's election look quite good."

"Really?"

"Like every chart for beginning a venture, my chart shows not only the events but how they will end. The chart for his second term is as perfect as

I've seen in all my years. It's superb. It will be like sitting down to a poker table with a royal flush. He's a cinch to win. But there's something about the morning of the high school visit. A great darkness that I can't seem to see around. But I will keep watching."

"Oh, Joan. What would I do without you?"

A NEW MOON

"Yelllllllo, Edward Severino here."

"Eddie? This is Jim Plant. How are you?"

"Dandy. Peachy. Dandy and peachy. A little more dandy than peachy."

"All right, well, that's good," Jim said. "Listen, I'm over at Craftwood. Can you talk?"

"Sure," Eddie replied. "What's on your mind? And you don't need to tell me you're at Craftwood. I can hear the buzz saws."

"Yeah, well, I wanted a little privacy for the call, so I went back to the warehouse."

"What's up?"

"Well," Jim began, "you remember how I gave you a discount on the wood you bought for the fence around your home?"

"Was that a discount? I can't remember."

"Yes. Thirty percent if I recall. Because I respect what you do, being the night custodian over at Riverview High."

"What, you want more money now?"

"No, no. Nothing like that," Jim said. "You know, the last time I saw you, over at Half Day Inn, you mentioned that the district hasn't given custodians a raise in over fifteen years."

"Yeah. So what? Where's this going? Can you speak up? Those saws are loud as hell."

"Sure." Jim turned his head away from the phone and hollered toward his shop: "Al, can you keep it down?" Then he said to Eddie, "I've got a way for both of us to get even. Settle a score. In a couple of weeks. On the twentieth. Ronald and Nancy Reagan are visiting Riverview."

"The president?"

"What are you drinking, bleach? Yes. The First Lady and the fucking president. Jesus."

"Hey, keep your shirt on," Eddie said. "What are you, like, planning to assassinate the president?"

"Assassinate the president? What are you talking about? I may be crazy but I'm no murderer. I'm talking about settling a grievance, that you and I both share, with the school district, and specifically school board president Nancy Brandt."

"I'm listening …"

*

"Good morning, sir."

"Good morning, Agent Padovani."

Agent Padovani passed a report across the desk to Bob Henry, his supervisor with the Secret Service. Bob opened the file and began skimming.

"It's the advanced scouting for the Riverview visit on April 20."

"Thanks. I can read. Let's hear it."

"Of course. As you can see, sir, Marine One will be landing at a local high school," Agent Padovani said. "The school is next to a large, wooded area so I'm recommending, in addition to the standard twelve agents, six more be assigned to the perimeter."

"Request noted." Bob scribbled on the report.

"Six agents can remain behind for the First Lady as she tours the school."

"Yes, continue."

"The motorcade will travel three fourths of a mile to the Sara Sweet factory for the president's address. The factory itself poses some unique issues that I've detailed in the report."

"OK. What about inquiries with local law? Anyone on our radar?"

"Riverview is an affluent area with a low crime profile. We found the typical three to four lowlifes that have made threats against local government. One nutjob thinks the governor is a communist. Routine stuff, nothing serious. But then we talked to the school district. We may have a credible threat."

"Oh yeah?"

"Yes, sir. Page thirteen."

Bob Henry flipped through the pages.

"Yes, the owner of a local lumberyard. He's got some beef with the school district because they won't buy his tables. I guess his proposal has some weird design like a semi-circle or something. He's had some altercations at board meetings that resulted in a restraining order, which he violated and then resisted arrest. Right now, he's out on parole awaiting trial."

"I see his name here is listed as Jim Plant."

"In following our policy of leaving no stone unturned, we had the FBI drop a bug on Mr. Plant's phones over at Craftwood Lumber."

"Yeah?"

"Yes, sir. The transcript is on page fifteen."

Henry flipped the page and kept skimming.

"The conversation was between him and one Edward Louis Severino III, the night custodian at the high school."

"Mmm."

"This Severino fellow has a bit of rap sheet. Small-time stuff. Mostly just drugs and alcohol, but he did assault a police officer and had to undergo some counseling. Almost cost him his job."

"This transcript has a lot of missing phrases."

"Yes, sir. It is believed that Mr. Plant intentionally used power saws to drown out his conversation."

"All this over semi-circle tables? I like a good semi-circle. Gives a lot of flexibility. Increased seating. Facilitates conversation. Why didn't the district go for it?"

"It's not clear, sir."

"Much better than a rectangle. All the leaning."

"Yes, sir."

"All right. Keep an eye on both. Print this transcript out and show it to Director Webster. Consider this Plant a threat to both the president and the First Lady."

*

Director Webster opened the envelope and began skimming.

Classified

Top Secret

To: Director Webster

Re: Riverview Visit to Sara Sweet, transcript of recent conversation between potential assassins

ES: Yelllllllo.

JP: Eddie? This is Jim Plant. How are you?

ES: Just dandy. Peachy. Dandy and peachy. A little more dandy than peachy.

JP: All right, well, that's good. Listen, I'm over at Craftwood. Can you talk?"

Webster's eyes skimmed down.

JP: ... (Inaudible) ... On the twentieth. Ronald and Nancy Reagan are visiting Riverview.

ES: The president?

JP: (inaudible) the First Lady and the fucking president. Jesus.

ES: All right all right, keep your shirt on. If this is a plot to assassinate (inaudible) ...

JP: Assassinate the president ... (inaudible) I'm talking about settling a grievance, that you and I both share, with the school district, and specifically the president Nancy (inaudible).

Webster's well-trained eyes scanned for the necessary information.

JP: Yeah, well, they haven't announced it yet. I heard about it from a friend on the board.

ES: Interesting. The cafeteria will be empty. What do you have in mind?

JP: (Inaudible) ... When the school clears out for the president's chopper, then you and I (inaudible) Craftwood Lumber (inaudible).

ES: I know a few (inaudible).

JP: Well, we slip in (inaudible) ... tables ... then we slip out with all the frenzy about the president and the First Lady. We'll take the truck out to a little hiding spot. Then when everyone goes back (inaudible) ... body will have to eat standing up.

ES: Exactly.

JP: Brilliant.

(Inaudible)

JP: Look. It's the perfect opportunity (inaudible) ... grievances. With Reagan's taxes you guys are barely making a living wage. And just when the eyes of the nation are on our little high school (inaudible) ...

ES: You might be onto something, Jim.

Webster put down the document and picked up the phone. "Upgrade the Severino/Plant threat. And contact the codebreakers. Something about cafeteria tables we need to get to the bottom of."

*

"Ok, D.J.," Pete said, fingers drumming sixteenth notes on his desk. "I'll head right over."

"Thanks Pete," D.J. replied. "We never should have come down to the city for these guitars and amps. This traffic is insane. We'll be there when we can. Remember, Levi said no doctors, no police."

Pete hung up the phone and looked out the window. A school bus pulled away, revealing George trimming some hedges as only George trimmed, with eyes closed, chanting.

He grabbed his briefcase and keys. Everything had fallen into place. It was all set up. A visit from the president of the United States, with a performance by Levi King and the Kingsmen. A chance to shatter the ban once and for all. One week to go. Now this call from D.J. and the whole plan was in jeopardy. Pete had to see for himself.

He left Riverview High School, gunned it through a yellow light, raced south five blocks, and turned right. He parked at the Riverbrook Suites, a hotel on the edge of town, and went up to room 1009. He was about to knock when he saw the door was already ajar.

"Hello?"

He stepped into the narrow entrance. The hallway was littered with empty donut boxes.

"Levi? Are you here?"

He waded through the boxes that covered the floor.

"It's Pete the Beat, checking in on you." He walked into the hotel room. The only light was from the curtained windows. He turned on a lamp. The coffee table had a jar of peanut butter with a knife, blackened banana peels, and a clutter of orange prescription pill bottles.

Pete inspected the bottles. Codeine. Valium. Morphine. Demerol. There were some with the labels peeled off. A half-eaten peanut butter, banana, and bacon sandwich sat on a napkin.

"D.J. called and asked me to stop over."

"Ooooooooooooohhhh."

Pete rushed toward the sound in the bathroom.

"Ooooooooooooohhhhh."

He tripped over donut boxes, turned on the light, and saw him. Levi King, sitting on the toilet with his pants around his ankles.

"I would give my right hand to pinch a loaf."

"Levi, are you all right?"

"I haven't taken a proper shit in two weeks. Two weeks. Ohhhhhhhhh-hhhh. It's now or never."

"Let's get you to the hospital," Pete said.

"No. No doctors. It's over. I died long ago."

"Levi, you're alive."

"No. I'm not. This isn't living. They killed me. When they killed my music. And the Captain took me away."

"Levi, you're not dead and neither is your music."

"I tried to come back. Didn't I? Hawaii. Hollywood. And now I'm back at the scene of the original crime. Riverview. They killed me. They wouldn't let me play. Like I was some criminal … oooooohhhhhhhhhh."

"That's nonsense. Levi …"

The King fell off his throne.

"Levi!"

*

During second period on the following Monday, security guard Josephine, with fresh, bright orange hair and new generic black shoes that might also serve as bowling shoes, escorted Michael (with bright blue, shaggy, Cookie Monster hair), Brandon, Tibbs, Ray, and Ryan to the office.

"Principal Best will be with you in a moment," Ms. Susan said.

They sat down and waited, looking at each other with raised eyebrows. There was a man in overalls in Principal Best's office. They could hear the heated conversation through the closed door. The man's long hair was in a ponytail. He shouted, "Hey, what can I do?" and then something that sounded like "Bron-Yr-Aur."

"Jimmy … listen … calm down," Principal Best was saying, standing across from him.

They heard something muffled that sounded like "D'yer Maker," then the man in overalls stormed out of the office without so much as a glance at the Little Brothers.

Principal Best's door opened.

"Please come in."

They filed into his office. He pulled another chair over to his desk and they all sat down.

Principal Best smiled, tapping his fingers. "You're probably wondering why I called you into my office today," he said.

They nodded and let out little gusts of nervous laughter.

"Do you still play music?"

They looked at each other.

"Don't answer that," Principal Best said quickly, holding his hands up.

"I would like to offer you an opportunity to play music, right here, at Riverview High School."

"What kind of music?" Michael asked.

Principal Best looked at each student in turn, tapping notes.

"Well, you know how President and First Lady Reagan are scheduled to visit Riverview?"

"Yes."

"Uh-huh."

"Sure."

"You bet."

"Of course," Michael said.

"Well, you probably know that the marching band is scheduled to play," Principal Best said, executing a galloping combo with his thumb and ring finger. "'The Star-Spangled Banner' and 'Hail to the Chief.' Since we're having music, I thought it would be appropriate if a band performed as well."

"Um ... ?" Ray said.

"I was thinking, you know, if you could write something in support of Mrs. Reagan's Just Say No! program," Principal Best said, hitting a short, punchy fill with his knuckles. "It could be a real win-win for our community." He closed his mouth, resting his chin on his fist. "Just think about it," he said. "Let me know what you decide. You would perform right after the marching band. Guitars. Amps. The whole thing. Let me know." He stood and led them out. In the hall, George was vacuuming.

Beep beep.

*

"Here is the completed speech, Mr. President," Jim Baker said, handing the laminated folder across the president's desk in the Oval Office.

"You know, Jim, I'm not sure we're going," President Reagan said.

"Sir? I didn't—um … may I ask why?"

The president's eyes darted away. "I'm not sure it's the best use of our time."

"Sir, the CEO of Sara Sweet, Mark Stein, has personally extended this invitation. A major supporter. We've planned visits to two large area high schools. Riverview High near the factory and Gordon Technical Institute in Chicago. Thousands of young people that will all be of voting age in 1984. Harold Washington, the mayor of Chicago, called to inquire about flight times so he can meet us at the airport along with Illinois congressmen … Sir, the tax plan. Your speech."

President Reagan looked down at the folder in his hands and leafed through the papers.

"Sir, the title is yours."

"A bigger pie for Americans," he said as if speaking to himself. "It's clever, isn't it? Sara Sweet. Pies. The Tax Relief Plan."

"Very clever, sir," Baker agreed. He sat up. "May I speak candidly?"

"That's what I expect from my chief of staff."

"Did Nancy have anything to do with this decision?" Baker asked. He leaned forward. "Specifically, that woman she talks to?"

"Nancy is opposed to going. But the decision is mine."

Baker leaned back. "Then my decision will be to resign from my position if the Sara Sweet trip is canceled, as I presume the reasoning is based on the whimsical advice of an astrologer."

The president stared at Baker.

A light on his phone came on. "Mr. President? I have Lieutenant Colonel North on line three. He says it's urgent. And the Secretary of Defense is here waiting for you." The stare-off resumed. A door opened. "Mr. President?"

"Not now," both men said.

President Reagan blinked. "Great minds think alike. Let's go to Sara Sweet." He stood up.

"Where are you going?" Baker asked.

"To the East Wing. To tell Mommy the trip is back on. It's better if I tell her to her face."

*

Nancy stared out her window, daydreaming. The phone rang.

"Joan?"

"Hello, Madam First Lady. This is Roxanne, from Gradenko Home Goods in Riverview. I'm calling to let you know that the new china has arrived. We can deliver it to you while you are here in Riverview."

There was silence.

"Mrs. Reagan? Hello? Are you there?"

The door opened. "Mommy, we need to talk," President Reagan said.

*

They had been at it for over an hour in the Golding basement. Tibbs had a Stratocaster and was playing the opening riff to the Stones' "The Last Time." Ryan was eating a bowl of cereal at the table. Michael was restringing his bass. Brandon was working on a Rubik's Cube. Ray reclined in a La-Z-Boy.

The sound of Shannon's motorized wheelchair went past the door at the top of the stairs.

Then Dave's voice: "What is *Of Mice and Men*?" He was watching *Jeopardy!* again.

"I say we do it," Michael said, fed up with the discussion going round and round. "What have we got to lose? We could write our own 'Just Say No' song, and the 'No' could mean whatever *we* want it to."

Tibbs worked the whammy bar on the last note. "What?" he asked. "What are you even talking about?"

"You heard Mr. Best," Michael said, twisting a tuning post. "It's our song. The way we want to play it. This is an opportunity of a lifetime. The eyes of the nation."

Ryan lifted the bowl to his lips and slurped.

"What is *Ulysses*?" Dave hollered.

They heard Mrs. Golding in the kitchen. "Shannon, honey, please let me get the straws for you when you need one."

"I'm perfectly capable," she said. The sound of her wheelchair went by again.

"It's a big deal," Ryan said, wiping his mouth with his sleeve. "The president of the United States."

"Yeah, no duh," Michael mocked.

Brandon turned a side of the cube green and kept twisting.

"What is *The Color Purple*?" Dave shouted.

"Shannon, honey, I only want to be helpful."

"When I need your help, I'll ask."

Tibbs switched the pickup and played the riff an octave higher. Brandon twisted a side red but lost the green side. Ray was staring at nothing.

"You guys heard Mr. Best," Michael continued. "We could lift this stupid local ban. Maybe we could get back to playing live again. Instead of sitting around and jamming at Joe's Garage." His bass was strung and in tune. He experimented with harmonics using his fencing sabre.

"Can I fix you a snack?"

"Mother! Please stop pestering me!"

"Shannon."

"What is the *Tropic of Cancer*?"

Brandon twisted two rows yellow. He had another yellow row, but he couldn't get it over. The green and red sides were gone.

"We could get Curtis to play some horn parts," Michael speculated. "Maybe Danny? C'mon, what do you guys say?"

"I don't even know what we're talking about," Tibbs said. "Shannon and the Little Brothers are done. Who would even sing? What, are you going to ask a Gobbledegook or a Wang-Wang? It's too short notice. We'll fall on our face in front of the entire country." He put his guitar down and pushed play on the stereo. A live version of Hendrix's "The Wind Cries Mary" floated out into the room.

They sat and listened. No one said anything. The Rubik's Cube was a complete jumble. Brandon set it down.

Hendrix abruptly shifted from "The Wind Cries Mary" to "The Sunshine of Your Love."

"Leave me alone," Shannon shouted.

"I'm your mother." They could hear Mrs. Golding crying. "It's my job to take care of you."

"Tell Mr. Best that we'll do it," Ray said, standing, the La-Z-Boy snapping upright. "I have the song. I wrote it the other night."

"What is *the Awakening*?" Dave exclaimed.

*

Liz and Dave Golding sat at the kitchen table. They could hear the Little Brothers rehearsing downstairs.

"All of the sound engineering classes are available in the summer, so they won't interfere with the electrical classes," Dave said. "Oh, and I almost forgot." He got up and ran out the door. A minute later he came back with a bag.

"Here, this is for you," he said. "I have one for dad too."

Liz reached in the bag and pulled out a DeVry Technical Institute sweatshirt. "I love it," she said and pulled it on. "Give me a hug."

Dave stood and they embraced. Downstairs, the music stopped.

"I'm so proud of you," Liz said with a tremble in her voice.

"Thanks, Mom." He started to let go, but she held on tighter and started to cry. "You've chosen your own path … your father and I couldn't be prouder."

She wiped her tears on his shoulder. Footsteps sounded on the stairs.

Liz gave her son one last squeeze and kissed him on the cheek. She grabbed some tissue, opened the fridge, and blew her nose inside the door.

Michael, Ryan, Ray, Brandon, and Tibbs filed into the kitchen. They all gave Dave fist bumps and high fives.

"How about some chips and salsa?" Liz asked.

"Sounds great, Mrs. G," Michael said.

They joined Dave at the kitchen table. Liz pulled out a jar of homemade salsa and began chopping green onions on a cutting board.

"What are we celebrating?" Michael asked.

"Did Ryan tell you that I'm going to take sound engineering classes?" Dave inquired. "I start in June. That way I can help you guys make your first album."

"First album." Michael laughed. "Instrumental elevator music?"

Liz put a large bowl of chips on the table. She poured the salsa into a smaller bowl, scraping the onions off the cutting board. She set out glasses and a pitcher of lemonade.

"Ryan tells me that you guys are playing for Ronald Reagan next week," Dave said.

"Is the president going to be there?" Tibbs asked with a smile, pouring himself a glass. "I can't remember. I thought we were playing for the queen of England."

"No," Michael replied, crunching a chip. "I believe it's the German chancellor."

"You're both wrong," Ray said. "It's the premier of Canada."

Amber came in from soccer practice and gave Dave a big hug. Don Golding appeared, smiling. Dave brought out another bag and gave his father a DeVry sweatshirt and Amber a game involving circuits.

"It's so nice having all of you home," Liz said.

"Mom, are you crying?" Ryan asked.

"No, honey, it's just the onions."

Amber went upstairs. Don went to put on a record.

"What day is the show?" Dave asked.

"Wednesday."

"You know, I'd be honored to drive you that day, in the van, for old time's sake," Dave said.

"As long as we hold the set list," Brandon said.

*

Bobby Jean Welsh dozed in her bed. It was 9:40 p.m. and the house was quiet. She didn't hear the usual sounds.

Matt walked in and tapped her on the shoulder. "Forgive muh-muh-me," he said. He was shaking uncontrollably.

"What are you talking about?"

"Forgive me," he said. "Just as I ask for the Lord's fuh-fuh-forgiveness, so I ask it of my f-f-f-faithful wife. Forgive me for what I am about to do."

She sat up, rubbed her eyes, and turned on the lamp.

"What on earth are you talking about?"

"I have certain … information … a … group of students will be … playing the duh-duh-devil's music. I have to stop them."

"I don't understand."

"I've puh-puh-prayed, Bobby Jean. I've prayed and prayed. There's no other way. I've protected the innocent lambs of this … tuh-tuh-town for over thirty years. The Lord is calling his good … shepherd home." The phone rang. It was 9:45. On the fourth ring Bobby Jean picked it up.

"Where are you tonight, sweet Marie?" Bobby Jean said.

"Put on your best dress. I'll be there in fifteen minutes. We're going out tonight."

Bobby Jean looked at her trembling husband, his rigid body knelt over, his tight lips curled around his teeth, his dark eyes.

"I'll be ready," she said and hung up.

*

The morning of April 20, 1983, dawned cold and foggy on the shores of Lake Michigan. At six thirty, Pete Best walked across the parking lot from his minivan. A light drizzle began to fall. The marching band rehearsed in the distance.

Two Secret Service vehicles were already parked. Four large figures and one small one came around the corner in the mist. At first, Pete thought the shadows were agents. Then he saw who it was. *Swish, swish, swish.*

The figures turned. Pete approached.

"Good morning," Gayle said. "The players were just leaving."

Pete nodded.

"The players tried to take the field, but the marching band refused to yield," Gayle explained.

"Let's go, guys," Walter Payton said.

The players moved on.

George poked his head out the front doors. "The bleachers are in position," he reported. "Now, just need to be sure the amps stay dry."

Four hours later the parking lot was full. A caravan with a limo waiting to take the president to the nearby Sara Sweet factory sat in front of the school. News vans lined the newly named Principal Merchant Way. The marching band was in position. The sound of an approaching helicopter grew louder. The chopper appeared above the trees. The entire student body and faculty stood by in raincoats and umbrellas. The students were chanting "USA! USA!" Everyone watched Marine One land in the center of a large field.

A parade of people stepped off: first Secret Service agents, then Chicago Mayor Harold Washington, Illinois Governor James Thompson, and a bunch of guys in suits—Chicago aldermen and Illinois Congressmen. Then finally, to a chorus of cheers and chants of "Reagan! Reagan! Reagan!" the First Lady and the president came down. The procession moved to a stage with folding chairs, an American flag, an Illinois flag, and a podium. In the corner of the stage, under a tarp, were a drum kit, a keyboard, and three large amps. All the dignitaries stood.

Pete walked to the podium. "Riverview High School, let's give a warm Warrior welcome to the President of the United States, Ronald Reagan!"

Everyone cheered. The marching band rose and played "The Star-Spangled Banner" and then "Hail to the Chief." President Reagan saluted, shook Pete's hand, accepted a Riverview High School jacket, and approached the podium. All the dignitaries sat down.

"I'm supposed to be neutral on issues like this," the president said, now wearing the red-and-gray jacket, "but I want to wish the Riverview baseball, volleyball, softball, and soccer teams good luck in their games this week. Tell the coach the Gipper is ready to go in."

The crowd went crazy. The Secret Service men standing nearby put their hands over their earpieces. The Little Brothers stood offstage with guitars in hand. Curtis held onto his sax. Michael's mohawk was spray-painted red, white, and blue. Brandon heard from an earpiece, "The van is from Gradenko Home Goods. The driver says that she has permission from Rainbow." One of the agents nearby said, "Inspect the vehicle."

Each Little Brother, in turn, felt a punch on the arm.

"Knock 'em dead."

It was Danny, giving his Vulcan salute.

"Except not the president," he said. "That would be bad."

President Reagan finished his remarks and shook hands with Pete Best, Superintendent Jag, and Board President Nancy Brandt. The president moved down the line, shaking hands with the rest of the board. At the end of the line, he reached for the trembling hand of Matt Welsh. Pete returned to the podium.

Ray could hear voices on the agents' earpieces. "Truck has cleared inspection. It checks out. New china ordered by Rainbow confirmed. Sending the truck through."

"Before we hear from First Lady Nancy Reagan about her important Just Say No! message," Mr. Best announced in the same voice he used at open mic, "let's welcome to the stage Riverview's own the Little Brothers Band, here to play a surprise song for the First Lady." A murmur went through the crowd.

Board President Brandt exchanged a curious glance with Superintendent Jag and mouthed, "What's this?" Superintendent Jag frowned.

Mr. Best continued. "These five students are part of our musical community ..."

Matt stood and inconspicuously strolled behind the row of chairs toward the Little Brothers.

The field was quiet. Two things approached the Little Brothers at vastly different speeds. First, Matt's plodding gait, with his uneven, rigid movements. Second, at the speed of sound, voices on walkie-talkies. "Sir, we have a district vehicle moving away from the cafeteria area."

"Keep eyes on it."

A different voice came through: "We have another vehicle in motion. Far student parking lot. Van. A Taste of Yu. Yu as in Yankee Uniform. Moving to intercept. Driving south behind school."

The sun poked through the clouds and shined down on the field.

Matt was almost there. He reached inside his suit coat.

"Riverview's own … the Little Brothers!" Mr. Best announced.

The Little Brothers walked onto the stage. Ray strapped on his guitar and looked out at the sea of people. The orange tide rolled in, fast. It drowned the audience and crashed against the stage, spraying an orange mist. Ray looked out at a pulsing sea of orange prisoners. Ryan counted off four beats and the Little Brothers filled the air with music. Curtis belted out a sax solo to kick off the jam.

Mr. Best looked on. The sunlight streamed down on a rock band, playing rock music, at Riverview High School. In front of everyone, including the president of the United States. And the cameras, the eyes of the world. Pete tapped along with his fingers. He had done it. He had finally done it. He looked out, found Sandy and Roy in the audience. They were smiling. He waved and patted his palm over his heart, keeping the beat.

Matt was still moving, trying to get through the throng lining the stage.

The opening lines swirled in Ray's mind. The first verse was three measures away. Two measures. In the final measure, he heard Shannon's voice: "I fucking believe in you." He stepped up to the mic, shut his eyes, took a breath, and hurled the first verse out into the orange sea like a life preserver.

Some say it's a shame

How we have to the play the game

When your yeses and nos have become the same

Maybe it's time you unbecame

After the verse, Tibbs stepped forward for a guitar fill that lasted a few measures. Ray, Michael, and Tibbs leaned into the mics for the chorus.

Just say no

And go away

Tell 'em no

And say yes to today

Matt worked his way out onto the stage. He reached the center, and that's when all the shaking he worked so hard to restrain and control broke free. His body shook head to toe. Ryan, watching the wobbling board member, lost the beat for a moment and the tune hit a lull. Everyone watched Matt shaking, then President Brandt and the rest of the school board followed his lead. They left their seats and joined him centerstage. The song roared back. Everyone was a-movin' and a-shakin'.

Another verse, another chorus. Ryan rolled the snare, signaling the Little Brothers into an improv jam. Brandon took the first solo on the organ. The security guards stopped the first few students but quickly realized the futility of preventing the rush. The stage filled up with students and politicians alike. Pete twirled Roberta Anderson out into the fray. The president and the First Lady, inside a circle of Secret Service agents, clapped along. Matt was in the middle of all of it, shaking like a wildwood tree. If there was a roof, the sound pouring from those amps would have ripped it clean off.

The Little Brothers stepped to the mic and sang one last "No!" Tibbs bent a sharp note like a giant brake. Feedback hung in the air. The president and First Lady held rigid smiles. Nancy's hands froze, framing her face. Ray changed keys and ripped into a savage punk rock riff. Michael climbed on top of an amp. He took to the air as Ryan exploded like a jet engine. Tibbs tore into power chords, and the energy from the Little Brothers flowed straight to the rollicking audience, who were dancing on the stage and out in the field.

Ray played the riff one last time. With his eyes closed he reached out, found the mic, and sang.

Don't lock me up

Don't lock me up again

I'm free now

I'm free now to sing

I don't need your permission

Here is my submission

Stuff your ban in a sock

Because I'm free now

Free now ...

TO ROCK!

Ray stepped back and strummed his way into a tight pocket of sound. He opened his eyes to see the orange tide receding. He saw the Little Brothers, Principal Best, the president of the United States, George the custodian, all in color. In the cheering crowd he saw Danny, surrounded by the musicians from the Water Tower: the Wobble Dobbles, Wawhoo Wang-Wang, Whack-A-Whack, the Laughing Tadpoles, Gobbler of Lightning, Glass Eye, the Polyps, Gobbledegook, and more.

They were all in color.

Tibbs took off on a solo. Ray walked over to the side of the stage and snapped a picture with his Polaroid camera. He watched the Little Brothers tearing it up; he tried to catch every little detail to remember. He heard the sound of a nearby walkie-talkie.

"All units. All units. A van has penetrated the safe zone. All units. Protect Rawhide."

Big arms took Ray down. The photo he had just taken fell from his hand on impact. He reached and grabbed it. "Stay down," the man said. Ray looked at the photo as it developed. He saw that curious board member, the one that had started all the shaking, going down, holding a knife poised over Tibbs's back, with Michael swinging his bass like the leading edge of a fencing sword to block it.

*

Night custodian Edward Louis Severino III stepped on the gas. He eased the district van loaded with cafeteria tables around a turn near the driver's education course. Out of the corner of his eye he saw two unmarked vehicles accelerating down Merchant Way.

"They're onto us," he said. "We'll have to go out a different way." He jammed the accelerator as he spun into a U-turn and leaped a curb. The tables rattled in the back of the van.

"What are you doing?" Jim Plant asked from the passenger seat.

"Improvising."

He accelerated through the student driving course and flew over another curb.

"This is insane. Stop the car," Jim cried out.

"Relax, I know a way out."

Eddie drove the van tight along one side of the school. He stayed close to the building and nearly ran over a Secret Service agent as he swung around a corner.

"Stop!" Jim yelled. "Let me out!"

Eddie didn't stop. He kept to the side of the school like a racecar driver with the inside track. He came around the side and went full speed ahead across a softball field. The sound of bullets whizzed past them. He took a gravel path along a creek around to the back forty.

Pebbles and bullets flew as they sped toward an intersection of the gravel path and the main paved path. He cruised into the intersection and swerved wildly to avoid a truck. Out of nowhere another van came hurtling from another direction. All three vehicles swerved at the crossroads. Eddie saw A TASTE OF YU while Jim saw GRADENKO HOME GOODS. The two vans collided violently and crashed into the truck, making a metal sandwich and releasing a cacophony of busted steel and glass. Three unmarked Secret Service vehicles rammed into the pileup. The sound of china shattering filled the air like a crash of cymbals.

Jim looked up through the cracked windshield to see Marine One lift off. An agent was on him, a pistol inches from his face.

"Cafeteria seating is a fundamental right," he said.

Marine One disappeared in the clouds, flying off toward the horizon.

*

Standing back behind the curious onlookers packed around the yellow POLICE LINE DO NOT CROSS tape, Leslie Bangs rifled through her purse for a piece of gum and finally found one. The last siren had died down. The students were back inside. It seemed like everything was over, but the people hung on, hoping to catch a glimpse of more action in their quiet little town. The police waved a car through. Leslie watched Pam Susan pull out in her little white tooth of a car with Morris Jameson in the passenger seat. "That's odd," Leslie thought. "Where are they going?"

She felt a tap on her shoulder. She turned, but no one was there. She turned the other way. She knew before she saw him. Neil.

They gazed a long moment at each other and smiled. He looked the same as when she had last seen him years back. A visit when he was here for work that didn't go particularly well.

"I knew it was you," she said. "I thought you might be here."

"How are you?"

Leslie looked away, at the crowd, the sky, her shoes. "Never better," she said with a laugh.

"Yeah, Jane told me about the job," Neil said. "I'm sorry."

"It's OK."

"I didn't come here for the president," Neil said.

Leslie felt it rising and managed to keep it down.

"I came for you."

It rose up and Leslie was powerless to stop it. Neil took her in his arms, and he stood holding her in a crowd of gossiping Riverview High School parents.

"I accepted a transfer to the *Trib*," Neil whispered. "I'm coming home."

Leslie surrendered to the embrace. Her body was loose, and she wrapped her arms around him.

"You know, the Metro section has an opening. They need someone to cover the music scene," Neil said, looking down at her.

"I was thinking of writing a book," Leslie told him. "The story of a town that banned rock and roll."

Neil hugged her laughed. "I don't know, babe. It seems like people aren't reading as many books today. Come work with me. You know people will always read newspapers."

A siren filled the air and one more squad car drove out, Deputy Copeland taking away Eddie Severino and Jim Plant, both handcuffed in the back. Eddie had a bandage wrapped around his head.

*

Saturday afternoon. Dave sat in his usual spot on the sofa; Brandon had the armchair. In the kitchen Liz Golding was talking to Bonnie Flowers on the phone. Shannon's motorized wheelchair reached the top of the stairs. She descended on a platform attached to a rail on the wall. The faint sound of Amber playing the violin in her room drifted down the stairs. Ryan filled up a bowl of ice cream and sat down next to Dave.

"And the category for today's *Final Jeopardy* is ..." Alex Trebek paused. "Greek Mythology. We'll be right back." Dave pressed mute as the TV went to commercial. Shannon reached the first floor and whirred into the living room.

"The new guitar teacher's name is Keef," Liz said, twirling the cord in her finger. "I met him. He's British and has the loveliest accent."

"Did you get the message on the machine?" Dave said to Ryan.

"No."

"The FBI called. They want to search your drums," Dave said. "They think the Little Brothers are part of the conspiracy to kill the president."

"Really?"

"No. The FBI does not call people. They just show up. Bro, you *are* gullible."

"Brandon can take them from school if you can get to the Shoppe after their lesson," Liz said.

"Give me a break," Ryan said, licking his spoon. Dave twirled the remote and Ryan ate ice cream. The commercial break ended.

"Today's *Final Jeopardy* answer is ..." Alex Trebek paused. "This pair who accompanied their father into battle were called Timor and Formido, 'fear' and 'terror,' by the Romans."

"Who are Phobos and Deimos?" Dave said.

"Obviously," Shannon said.

"Deimos and Phobos were the gods of fear," Dave explained. "Deimos was terror and Phobos was flight. They were the sons of the war god Ares, who spread fear in the wake of his chariot."

Brandon gave the peach fuzz on his chin a scratch. Shannon pretended to snore. Ryan kept eating his ice cream.

"And as the sons of Aphrodite, the goddess of love, the twins also represented fear of loss."

Shannon snored louder. A car honked from outside.

The first contestant answered, "Bert and Ernie."

"No," Alex Trebek said. "We can't accept that. But you waged zero dollars, so you don't lose anything."

"And," Dave continued, "they also happen to be the names of the two moons orbiting Mars. Though they're shaped more like potatoes than moons."

There was a knock at the door. Tibbs walked in.

"Hi, Mrs. G.," he called out. "Let's go, guys."

"Hello, Andrew," Liz said, holding her hand over the phone.

Tibbs looked at Ryan. "You ready? I wrote another one last night."

"You're on a roll," Ryan said. He went and put his bowl and spoon in the dishwasher. "Is Little Roy Best going to be there?"

"I believe so."

"Cool, I think this two drummer experiment is working out," Ryan said and turned toward the kitchen. "We'll be down at Joe's Garage."

"I'll go grab Ray," Brandon said, and left.

Liz waved. Ryan and Tibbs followed Brandon out the front door.

"One of the moons is slowly getting closer, and one is slowly escaping," Dave pointed out. "In a hundred million years Mars will finally be on its own."

"And I should care why?" Shannon asked.

MUDFEST 1984: AN ACKNOWLEDGMENT

(Riverview Park is filled to capacity with mud-drenched adolescents on a warm late summer afternoon. The crowd buzzes with anticipation. The stage is set: amps piled high, guitars, drums, keyboards, a sax, and microphones await the musicians. The magic moment is at hand. A flash of light appears on the horizon. A UFO zooms over the field, hovers, and shines a spotlight on the stage. The crowd goes berserk. Twelve-year-old Amber Golding walks out onto the stage.)

AMBER

(She starts speaking, but the microphone is too high. A stagehand rushes over and lowers it to the correct height. The crowd eats it up. She smiles, blushing, and looks to the side of the stage for encouragement. Once the crowd quiets down, she starts again.)

The writer wishes to thank his family for their support. First, his father, Jack. Without him, this book never would have been written and would've wasted away in the author's imagination. Megan, Mazey, Mia, and Delaney, for their love, encouragement, and keeping the volume down on the TV when Daddy was writing. Leanne, for always being there, even on the other side of the USA. The writer would like to give a shout-out to all his writer allies who directly contributed to these pages, including the San Marcos Writers Group—Wanda, Gary, Richard, Woody (RIP), Marsha, Jack, Devon, and Debbie. Rich and the good people at San Diego Writer's Ink. Michael Wolfe of Cover to Cover Co. for his developmental edit that made this novel a novel and not just a bunch of published pages Tim's friends feel obligated to buy. Nimmy Dumm at Aspen Root Editing for her faithful copy edit. Jessica Bell for her wonderful cover art. Amie McCracken for her skillful typesetting. Nate Wilkerson for giving Tim's lyrics a home in the indie rock band Meteor Truth. Jay Rosen for pushing Tim to learn how to surf. All the other friends and musicians and writers that helped inspire this story. And finally, the reader. Thank you. Now, who is ready to hear some music?

(The crowd goes bananas.)

ABOUT THE AUTHOR

Tim Miller is a writer and musician from Deerfield, Illinois. This is his sixth book and first novel. He writes lyrics and plays bass for the indie rock band "Meteor Truth." He is considering starting a blog called Postcards from the Right Lane of Traffic. But then again, he might not. Sometimes he's indecisive. He is on Instagram at timmillerwriter. Sign up for his monthly newsletter at timmillerauthor.com.

VISIT

WWW.TIMMILLERAUTHOR.COM

FOR NEWS AND UPDATES.